SODA SPRINGS

CAROLYN STEELE

BONNEVILLE BOOKS ™

An Imprint of Cedar Fort, Inc.
Springville, Utah

ALSO BY CAROLYN STEELE

Willow Springs

© 2015 Carolyn Steele

ISBN 13: 978-1-4621-1700-0

Published by Bonneville Books, an imprint of Cedar Fort, Inc.
2373 W. 700 S., Springville, UT 84663
Distributed by Cedar Fort, Inc., www.cedarfort.com

LIBRARY OF CONGRESS CATALOGING-IN-PUBLICATION DATA

Names: Steele, Carolyn, 1958-
Title: Soda Springs / Carolyn Steele.
Description: Springville, Utah : Bonneville Books, an Imprint of Cedar Fort, Inc., [2015]
Identifiers: LCCN 2015039152 | ISBN 9781462117000 (softcover : acid-free paper)
Subjects: LCSH: Young women--Fiction. | Fathers and daughters--Fiction. | Family secrets--Fiction. | Mormons--United States--History--19th century--Fiction. | GSAFD: Romantic suspense fiction. | Historical fiction.
Classification: LCC PS3619.T4334 S66 2015 | DDC 813/.6--dc23
LC record available at http://lccn.loc.gov/2015039152

Cover design by Michelle May
Cover design © 2015 by Lyle Mortimer
Edited and typeset by Melissa J. Caldwell

Printed in the United States of America

10 9 8 7 6 5 4 3 2 1

Printed on acid-free paper

To my parents,
who taught me to keep going even when life is hard,
and who gave me Grays Lake every summer.

To my family and friends from Grays Lake.
You live in a magical land that is eternally in my heart.

And especially to my husband,
who holds our home together and keeps me fed while I write,
and who provides the male point of view
for the characters jumbled in m'noggin.
I love you most.

Praise for
Soda Springs

"Reading *Soda Springs*, I bonded with the residents of the Idaho frontier settlement, as though I'd made my home with them for a spell. Beautiful storytelling unites reader and true-to-life characters, nestled within a compelling slice of history."

— KRISTIN HOLT, author of *The Bride Lottery*, #1 bestselling title in five Amazon categories

"Full of twists and turns, *Soda Springs* takes the reader for a wild ride across the American continent from North Carolina in the last days of the Civil War to Soda Springs, Idaho, where Tessa Darrow and her father find themselves stranded due to tragedy and disease. The characters grow in unexpected directions in this second historical romance novel by Carolyn Steele, which leads to an ending I didn't see coming. Good job, Ms. Steele!"

— MARSHA WARD, author of *Gone for a Soldier* and other historical novels

"In *Soda Springs*, Carolyn Steele takes us on a journey back in time and shows us the struggles and triumphs of a family from a bygone era in a way that makes us feel we are really there. A very enjoyable read."

— TRISTI PINKSTON, author of the Secret Sisters mysteries

CHAPTER I

"Father!" Tessa jumped off the porch, skipping the four steps, her bare feet landing upon the dusty cobbles with a soft thud. She raced toward the man silhouetted by flames. "Father, what are you doing?" She whispered her shout as loudly as she dared, fearful of waking the rest of her family. "Stop!"

"Go back inside," he hissed at her, scarcely turning his head in her direction as he tossed a jacket into the fire.

She gasped in horror. "Your uniform . . ." Flames consumed the gray woolen coat and trousers. "Why?"

"Go back inside, Tessa. Now." He turned her toward the house and nudged her away from him.

"But—"

"Now!"

Stumbling across the fifty yards to the house, Tessa couldn't help snatching glances over her shoulder as her father continued to heap various items of uniform garb in the fire. Reaching the top step on the porch, she turned around one last time and saw him remove something from the brim of his kepi and then toss the hat in the flames.

Careful to not let the screen slam behind her, she bounded up the stairs to her room. Safely inside, leaning with her back against the bedroom door, she gasped in great gulps, trying to calm her pounding heart, squelch her tears, and stifle the sobs that caught in her throat with each exhaled breath.

Why would he burn his uniform? He's only been home a few hours. What if the army wants him back? She knew the Confederate Army had paid for his uniform because he was an officer. But if he had to rejoin the fighting, they might make him pay for a new one. She also knew that their family would be hard pressed to pay for the several pieces of clothing that made up an officer's uniform.

That was a perfectly good coat. Even if he doesn't get called up again, it would have been a nice layer in the winter. It made no sense why her father would be so wasteful when he knew the desperate situation his absence during the war had placed them. *Something must have happened,* she reasoned. There was no other explanation. *But what?*

DURING BREAKFAST THE next morning, Tessa Darrow looked across the table at her dad. Her questions about last night roiled about in her head, but her father's dark scowl warned her against asking them. At thirteen years old, Tessa knew better than to speak out of turn—especially when her father was in a foul mood.

Tessa's mother, grandmother, and little sister, Bethany, were also gathered around the table; that's when her father, Henry Darrow, broke the news. "Your mother and I have an announcement," he said. "We've decided the time has come to move west to Oregon."

"Oregon?" Tessa blurted. She stared at her father, aghast.

"Oregon!" Bethany squealed, delighted.

"What?" Grandmother paled, stunned at the announcement. "What are you talking about?"

"Oregon," Henry stated as a matter of fact.

"When?" Tessa demanded, momentarily forgetting her place.

"Yes, Henry, when?" Grandmother's gentle Southern voice took on a steely edge. She carefully folded the napkin in her lap, never dropping the icy stare she locked on her son. "I'd be curious to know when you're planning to uproot this household. I'd also like to know when you came to this decision without even asking my thoughts on the matter."

"When, Father?" Bethany's young voice grew with excitement.

"Bethany!"

Tessa recognized the warning tone in her mother's voice and grabbed Bethany's hand, dragging her from her seat. "Be quiet," she ordered. "Let's go upstairs."

"Girls," Henry called after them. "Start thinking about what you want to pack. You may each take three dresses, five books, and one or two playthings. We're leaving at the end of the week."

Bethany started to protest, but Tessa dragged her out of earshot before their father heard her whining about leaving the rest of her toys.

With Bethany busily arranging dolls by order of favor and repair, Tessa escaped to the refuge of her room. She had so lovingly tended everything in here for as long as she could remember. The housekeeper, Eula, had only one task in this room: change the bedclothes. Tessa had insisted on doing her own dusting and polishing for as long as she could remember. She looked at the shelves of carved horses and porcelain dolls that she had collected. She couldn't even remember when she received her first ones. She had received a new horse, lovingly carved by her late grandfather, on each birthday. As his health began to fail, he carved several extras with instructions that Tessa receive one each year for as long as the supply lasted. She had twelve horses and six porcelain dolls. How could she possibly narrow her collection down to two or three?

"Tessa?" her mother called softly, knocking on the bedroom door before opening it.

Tessa stood before the tower of shelves, holding a horse painted to look like a palomino.

"Oh, Tessa." Her mother's eyes filled with tears at the sight of the treasured carvings.

"I can't leave these," Tessa said, choking back the tears. "I just can't."

Mother wrapped Tessa in her arms. "No. You can't. We'll find a place. We'll just tuck them in here or there and not speak of it."

With her head on her mother's shoulder, Tessa's gaze rested on the dollhouse her father had built. It was about four feet tall and just as wide—a replica of one of the grand plantations in Charlotte. She hadn't played with it in years, but she still kept it close. Tessa stooped down to straighten the paper shade on one of the miniature lamps in the parlor. "I suppose Father will make me leave this behind."

Mother nodded, a resigned smile tightening her lips.

Tessa moved the tiny rocking chairs and table from the porch to inside the main foyer. She remembered the Christmas she received it, when she was six. She remembered watching in fascination as her father crafted the little furniture, hung dainty curtains, even fashioned a chandelier out of beads salvaged from one of Grandmother's discarded handbags. Her father was not a demonstrative man, but his love for Tessa was evident in the weeks after Christmas that he spent trying to make his creation a perfect replica. She straightened the tiny plaque nailed above the door—"1851 Tessa Lane"—commemorating the year she was born.

Tessa remembered the many fights with Bethany whenever the little girl was caught playing with the house. "This is an heirloom," Tessa had chided her sister. "I shall give it to my daughter, and she shall give it to hers." Sadly, Tessa realized that this was never to be. Whoever moved into the family home next would inherit the dollhouse as well. With a sigh, she closed the plantation-shutter doors and swung the little hook over the little doorknob to hold the little doors closed.

"Sweetheart," Mother said softly, stroking Tessa's hair, "Eula's going to need your help today organizing the linens. We'll use as many as we can to wrap around the breakables. And gather all the quilts to protect the furniture."

"Yes, ma'am," Tessa said. "I'll go help her. Is Eula coming with us?"

"Of course not," Mother answered. "She has her own family to take care of here."

Her parents were among the few farmers in the South that didn't believe in slavery. They purchased Eula and her husband from a neighboring plantation, and then they immediately gave the couple emancipation. They paid her a wage as a housekeeper, and her husband worked alongside the other hired hands in the fields. Both were free to come and go as they pleased, but they didn't dare travel too far from the plantation. Her parents had bought a few other slaves and then set them free during the last few years, but Eula and Buck were the only ones who stayed in the area. Tessa knew that her parents' stand against slavery had put them in ill favor with many of the plantation owners in Charlotte, but this made her admire them all the more.

"I'm going to miss Eula."

"Yes," Mother said, "we all will." A long moment passed before Tessa's mother reminded her of the huge task at hand and shooed her out to find Eula.

FATHER'S LAWYER MADE several visits over the following few days, and the two men would hole up in the study for hours on end while the women wrapped china, rolled carpets, and arranged boxes that would make the westward trek with them. Her mother's brother, David, agreed to buy the farm in a few months' time, when he could get the financing together. Grandmother arranged to move in with her sister, Arla, until the family was settled in Oregon.

On Friday morning, the farm hands came in to help load the wagons that would transport the family's belongings to the train the next morning. Tessa and her family would travel as far as St. Joseph, Missouri, by train and then join a wagon train for the rest of the journey. What couldn't fit in the wagons, including a piano that Tessa's great-great-grandparents had brought from Scotland, would remain in the house for David. "At least it will stay in the family," Mother said.

Three generations of Darrows had lived in this house, clearing the land for it shortly after the Revolutionary War, adding to the home and land as resources permitted. Tessa's mother was a Price, another long-time Charlotte family. Tessa knew her uncle David Price would take good care of the house, but it was still strange to think it would no longer belong to the Darrow family.

Tessa watched from the library window as a few of Grandmother's belongings were put in a carriage for the trip to her sister's house. The rest were crated up and stored in the attic. The crates would be shipped west when the family was settled in Oregon and could bring Grandmother to their new home. Tessa looked around the library, at the sheets tacked to the fronts of the shelves lining the room, covering the books. *So many books.* She remembered her grandfather, sitting in one of the leather wing chairs that flanked the tall window. He always sat in the chair on the right when he read, with the sun streaming in from behind his shoulder, flickering off the cut facets of his scotch glass, casting rainbow prisms about the room. How many times had she lain in the middle of the room on the thick Oriental rug, trying to count all of the books, only to fall asleep before she finished? *Oh, Grandfather, you'll watch over the books till we come back for them, won't you?* A suffocating darkness twisted in her chest. *We will come back to collect them. Father promised.*

Reaching up to draw the curtains closed, she saw her mother and grandmother standing toe-to-toe on the curved drive. *What's wrong?* She unlatched the window and eased it open just enough to hear the exchange below.

"Don't be dramatic," her mother said.

"Don't be naïve," Grandmother responded. "Where will she be presented? In some Wild West bar? What kind of match will she make if she misses her season?"

"She's not even fourteen yet. We have two years before we need to think about her coming out."

They're talking about me! Tessa pushed the window open further, leaning out to hear more clearly.

"We'll summer in San Francisco for her season."

"San Fran—with the gamblers and whores?" Grandmother's voice rose with her indignation.

"Clarice. Don't be crude." Her mother's shocked whisper carried almost as clearly as her grandmother's shout had. "Will you let it be if I tell you we'll bring her back here for her coming out?"

"I'll let it be when I see that day."

"Well, Henry is your son. He'll listen to you. If you have your heart set on it, I suggest you take it up with him."

"Hmmph," Grandmother snorted, waving her hand in front of her. "If he cared a fig about me, we wouldn't be crating our belongings like a bunch of vagabonds. Or giving our estate to that Price boy."

Tessa gasped and clapped her hands over her mouth.

"That Price boy is my brother!" her mother exclaimed.

Tessa pulled the window closed, forgetting to flip the latch tight. She nearly knocked the table lamp over in her haste to warn her father. *There's a tussle a brewing for certain.*

IT WAS NEARLY nine o'clock before Tessa, her mother, Bethany, and Grandmother climbed into the covered portion of the carriage and pulled their lap robes tightly around them. The January weather had been unusually fine, but at this time of year, the slightest breeze cut to the bone. Father checked the load secured in back one last time before climbing up to the driver's seat. Arla's house in Yorkville, just south of the North Carolina border, was just over twenty miles away, but the journey there and back would take most of the day.

"Bethany, your doll's digging in my side," Tessa hissed, shoving the little girl's doll away from her ribs. Taking her cue from her mother's lifted eyebrow, Tessa scooted closer to the edge of the carriage where she wouldn't be so cramped next to her little sister. *If we start bickering now, Father will make us stay home.* Without knowing when she'd see her grandmother again, a fight with Bethany wasn't worth the risk. *Forty miles to Auntie Arla's and back.* Maybe it would be better to stay at home. No, all of the family's belongings were packed and either stowed in the attic or filling two buggies in the yard, waiting to begin the journey to Missouri in the morning. *May as well be bored in the carriage as twiddling my thumbs all day waiting for Mother and Father to get back from Yorkville.*

"Henry," Grandmother called through the carriage window, "take a turn around the grounds before we go."

"We're late enough as it is," Henry responded. "I don't want it to be dark when we get back."

Before anyone could stop her, Grandmother threw the carriage door open and marched up to Henry on the perch. "Who knows when I'll see this place again," she insisted. "I said I would like to see my plantation one last time."

Though mere moments, it seemed like hours while those still inside the carriage waited—silently holding their breath—waiting for mother or son to acquiesce. Tessa watched the back of Grandmother's dress, unmoving, rigid. There was no doubt from whence her father got his stubborn streak.

At last her father gave in. "Fine, Mother," he said. "Get in the carriage."

Grandmother gave just one curt nod in acknowledgment before climbing back in the buggy.

It took Henry about thirty precious minutes to navigate the circumference of the plantation. While Grandmother muttered about the upkeep of the fields, Tessa watched how the winter sun danced around the house's gables. The buds on the magnolia outside her bedroom window were beginning to swell already, even though spring was still several weeks away. She and Bethany wouldn't be here this year to craft fairy gowns with the snowy blooms.

Tessa craned her neck out the window as her father steered the rig into the lane. Riders coming their way from the north kicked up clouds of dust. *Soldiers?* Tessa's mother and grandmother stared straight ahead, unable to see the riders approaching in the distance behind them, but before Tessa could say anything, her father whipped the two horses pulling the carriage into a gallop southward. The jolt was so sudden, the occupants inside nearly tumbled from their seats.

"Mercy!" Grandmother grabbed onto the leather strap next to the door.

Tessa's father urged the horses faster and faster, and Tessa watched as the riders turned onto the lane leading to their home. In moments, the plantation disappeared from view as they rounded a bend in the road, rocking precariously. Grandmother banged on the side of the door, trying to get her son's attention, but to no avail. Helpless, the four passengers clung to whatever they could to hold themselves steady.

After several minutes at breakneck speed, Tessa's father finally slowed the horses to a trot. Despite protests from the ladies, he refused to stop, even when Bethany begged for a moment to relieve herself. It wasn't until they were well past Mint Hill that he finally slowed the horses to a stop and let his passengers out to stretch their legs.

"That was inexcusable behavior, Henry Darrow," Grandmother scolded. "What would possess you—?"

"You're right, Mother," Henry cut her off but offered no explanation. "Please, take care of your needs and let's keep moving."

"There's no need to be crude," she rejoined before moving off the path and behind some bushes.

Tessa's mother took her husband by the arm and steered him in the opposite direction. Tessa strained to hear what was being said, but all she could make out was her father's urgent voice. "Just hurry. We've got to keep moving." When they came back into view, her mother's eyebrows were drawn together, as if she were frightened, but she only urged the girls to get back in the carriage without giving any clue as to what worried them.

"Are you ready?" Tessa's father called softly to Grandmother, careful to keep turned away from the direction she had gone, and frequently glancing northward along the road from which they had just come. After a few moments, Grandmother picked her way back onto the path. Icily, she refused her son's help as she clambered back into the carriage.

WITH WINTER'S SNOW melting down to a sloppy ooze, the Darrow family prepared their team and wagon to start the long journey westward from St. Joseph, Missouri, to Oregon. During the three-day train ride from Charlotte to St. Joe's, Tessa's father spent much of his time fidgeting on the edge of his seat, staring out the window while Tessa's mother prepared lists of supplies they'd need for the wagon journey from Missouri to Oregon. And with each day of their seven-week stay in St. Joseph, Henry grew more and more restless to get on the trail. At last, the snows receded enough for the first wagon trains to begin the trek west.

Sitting on a stump, with her back against a tree, Tessa carefully opened her new journal and set her graphite pencil to the first page.

> *March 5, 1865*
>
> *Today I leave the last remnants of the life I have known and begin a new existence. On January 14, my family and I delivered Grandmother Darrow to Aunt Arla in Yorkville and returned to find our home in Charlotte burnt to the ground.*

Tessa looked down the short embankment to where her father loaded bags of corn, flour, and other supplies into the wagon as her mother checked the list in her notebook. The twist of emptiness, guilt, and fear curled in Tessa's chest as she viewed the sum total of their earthly possessions. *If I'd warned father when I saw the soldiers coming, he would have stopped them from setting fire to our home.* Even now, she could taste the acrid air as they returned from Yorkville to the skeleton of their home, still smoldering. Even now, she could hear her mother's agonizing wails as they wandered among the charred rubble Buck and Eula had carried out of the ruins. All of their belongings, so carefully packed and covered, destroyed. Even the two wagons of furniture and keepsakes, bundled and ready for the family's journey west, had been reduced to cinders.

The same question echoed in her thoughts. *Why us? Why would the Yankee soldiers target our home?* She knew they'd burned other homes in the South—even in Charlotte—but none of the other plantations in their vicinity were burned. *Why us?*

She watched her mother pushing against a large sack while her father cinched down the rope securing the canvas covering the hoops spanning the wagon. *And why won't they talk to me about it? I'm not a child. They can't just pretend nothing happened.*

"Tessa," Bethany said, pulling her from her reverie, "I can't get my shoe on." The little girl hobbled beside her, trying to push her foot into her heavy leather shoe.

"Wait," Tessa said, setting her journal and pencil on the ground. "Quit pushing a minute." She pulled the shoe off her sister, then loosened the laces and held the tongue of the shoe out while Bethany forced her foot back into it. Feeling her sister's toes curl against the end of the shoe, Tessa pressed her lips together and shook her head. *She'll be crying with blisters before we've gone a mile.* She kept the laces as loose as she could as she tied them just above Bethany's ankle. "You let me know if your shoes hurt too much. Maybe you can ride in the wagon some."

Bethany leaned over and dusted the dirt off her shoes. "I'll be all right. Mama said she'll buy me new shoes when we get to Oregon." Without waiting for an answer, Bethany bounded down the embankment, startling a ground squirrel foraging in the weeds.

I think it'll be awhile before we can afford new shoes. Tessa had lain awake many nights listening to her parents whisper about how low their money was getting, and what they might trade for supplies. Losing their belongings in the fire had left them in a sorry state when they tried to buy a wagon and team and food adequate to make the trek westward. And her father hadn't realized they'd be stranded in Missouri for seven weeks waiting for a wagon company they could join up with.

Tessa drew in a deep breath and then blew it out through pursed lips, trying to ease the familiar squeeze of panic. She picked up her journal and pencil again, rereading where she had left off writing about the fire, before continuing her account.

> *We departed for St. Joseph, Missouri, the morning after the fire. The tremendous sadness I felt at abandoning our home in North Caro-lina now gives way to dread of the road ahead. Father has set his sights on Oregon, and Mother has agreed to uproot our family that he might realize his dream. Never mind my dreams. Never mind that we must leave Grandmother behind. I bear witness that I will return*

for her—somehow—and establish her in a home as proud and strong as she is. She will join us in Oregon, though she denies it, and we will all be a family again.

Mother made a present of this journal to me this morning for my fourteenth birthday. The flowers decorating the pages are Mother's handiwork—gathered and pressed from our home in Charlotte. I dearly love the journal, but I have taken a solemn oath not to express any kindness toward my parents. They were wrong to uproot our family without even talking to me about it. Mother says I have inherited my father's stubborn streak, and his mother's. Father says I have inherited my mother's sense of melodrama. Well, if that is all I have to show of my inheritance, at least I have that much.

The wagons are nearly ready, so I must make an end of my writings for now.

FOLLOWING THE WAGON master's bellow, Tessa climbed into the back of the wagon to sit beside Bethany. Bawls from oxen and mules mingled with the shouts of anxious men and cracks from whips to start the procession of wagons and herds that would eventually lead to Oregon.

"I'm not scairt," Bethany whispered.

Tessa felt a lurch as the wagon fell into line. "No reason you should be," Tessa said, but she pulled her sister closer. Watching the town grow smaller against the pinking dawn on the horizon, she felt the embrace of anxiety tightening around her heart.

"Are you scairt?" Bethany asked, clutching Tessa's arm between her tiny hands.

"Naw," Tessa lied.

Another shout from the wagon master rang above the commotion of wagons and animals. Tessa caught her breath at the sound of her father cracking his whip and shouting at their mules. A flutter of nerves washed over her and she could feel her pulse hammering in her chest and ears as their wagon joined the other wagons and herds on the rutted trail.

CHAPTER 2

Tessa wiped her eyes with her hanky and then blew her nose as quietly as she could so she wouldn't disturb her father, lying curled on his bedroll under the wagon even though it wouldn't be dark for at least another hour. The weight of the day settled on her heart and she rested her face in her hands, pressing on her tear ducts with her index fingers. *Feeling sorry for yourself will not get the job done.*

Tessa looked toward the mounded stones under the trees a few yards from the campsite. Her mother's voice rang in her mind—her beautiful, cheerful mother, who was stronger than any disappointment. Tessa clutched her balled-up hanky to her quivering lips, trying to keep her sobs from becoming audible and disturbing her father.

She'd dreaded recording the day's events, instead keeping busy making broth for dinner, straightening the wagon, and stepping away from camp when her grief overwhelmed her. In the back of her mind, committing the day to paper made it real; as long as she could put that off, there was still hope that she would open her eyes and her mother would be calling her to breakfast. And now there were two deaths to record. She opened her journal, gripping her pencil tightly to steady her script.

May 6, 1865

We buried Mother and Bethany today. Mother took ill three days ago. Fever came upon her so sudden, we were unawares till she was burning to the touch. The jostling of the wagon caused her pain too great to bear. Father decided to camp until she could recover. Company moved on without us.

Early this morning, before daybreak, Mother sat straight up in her bed and called for us to join her. I thought surely her fever had broken and was joyful. She spoke more calmly than she had since the fever

11

struck, but her heat rash still burned brightly. She held Bethany and I each by the hand and instructed us to be good girls and to mind Father. Then she instructed Father to take good care of us. After leaving her instructions, she lay back down and departed this life.

Bethany was underfoot much of the morning while we prepared the gravesite. When ready to bury Mother, we found Bethany huddled on the back of the wagon. She looked so tired, I wondered if she had also taken the fever. I know I should have kept a better watch over her, but she said she was just going to take a rest. We buried Mother, covering the shallow grave as best we could, then piled rocks on top to shelter her from wild animals or Indians.

Bethany lay next to the fire whilst I prepared a small supper. When supper was ready, I could not awaken her. Father found that she was dead. While our thoughts were consumed with Mother, the little darling never once complained. I don't even know how long she was ill. I should have watched her better. Mother's one dying request, and I did not think to pay it heed. We buried Bethany next to Mother before nightfall. Bethany would have celebrated her fifth birthday next week.

Father says it is a blessing that Mother went before Bethany. Surely the heartbreak would have killed her. My heart is heavy with these events, but Father is determined to continue with our journey to Oregon. I'll plant a tree in their memory when we arrive.

We've been on the trail for two months now; the last few days have been without companionship of the other wagons. I'm embarrassed to admit that until this evening I had never cooked anything other than gingersnaps and pound cake. We always had our Eula to see to meals. Mother said she would make a proper job of teaching me to cook and keep house when we got settled. Father wouldn't know a griddle from a stockpot. It's up to me to take care of him now. God willing, we won't both starve.

Hearing her father stir, Tessa snapped her journal shut and shoved it into her tin treasure box. She swiped at her tears with her apron before standing and turning toward him. "Father? Would you like some broth?"

"FATHER," TESSA WHISPERED. "Father, please. Wake up," she begged. Stretching her arm behind the backrest of the wagon seat, Tessa shook her father's shoulder. "More Indians are coming, Father, and we have nothing left to trade."

A shrill whoop rent the air, and Tessa grabbed for the rifle strapped to the side of the seat. Fumbling with the thong holding the rifle secure,

Tessa could hear the growing thunder of the approaching riders. Behind the Indians, a gray cloud of dust ascended to meet the purple Rocky Mountains. Thunderheads towered overhead in smoky-rose pillars completing the oppressive wall.

Henry Darrow struggled to hold his head high enough to see over the shallow wagon bed. "They're not Shoshoni, Tessa. Can't tell if they're friendly. Tie the mules off on the handbrake. We don't want 'em bolting if they get spooked." Tessa's father groaned, heaving himself to a near sitting position. "Lay the rifle in your lap and pull the hammer back. Let your hand rest easy, but be ready to fire."

With the mules tied, Tessa laid the rifle on her lap, letting her left hand rest lightly on the barrel. Raising her right arm, she opened her palm and shouted the traditional greeting, "How, Kola!" The dozen advancing riders showed no sign of slowing down, and she called more urgently, "How, Kola!"

Decorated with stripes of red and black paint on their faces and chests, the band of marauders stopped about five yards from the wagon and then fanned out into a quarter-circle. The center man, more heavily decorated than the rest, urged his horse closer to the wagon. Holding his spear upright, he thrust it toward Tessa and her father in short jabs. He grinned fiercely, shouting guttural words that Tessa didn't understand.

Circling toward Henry, the Indian curled his lips back from his teeth. He kicked his horse to a gallop and raised his spear high. He was about to let loose his spear when his eyes bulged in terror. He reined his horse up short and reeled it about. Shouting something to the others, he dashed away, followed by the other riders, leaving Tessa and her father to the quiet prairie.

Tessa's arm, still raised to the square, fell to her lap, and she gasped for several shaky breaths.

"The sickness," Henry struggled to whisper. "He must have seen the rash."

Tessa turned to examine her father and felt her breath catch in her throat. The rash, which looked like a slight sunburn just hours ago, had advanced to clusters of bright red pimples. "Father!" The terror that the Indian had displayed clutched at Tessa's chest. She knelt on the seat to crawl into the wagon to help him.

"No! Don't!" he ordered. "There's nothing you can do for me out here, and you'll just contaminate yourself more." He paused long enough to drag a breath of air into his lungs. "It will be night before long, Tessa-bear. Find a place to camp and take care of the animals. We'll be to Soda Springs by nightfall tomorrow."

"But what if there isn't a doctor in Soda Springs?" Tessa cried.

"There's a fort there and a settlement. There will be a doctor. The wagon company is likely there too. I'm surprised we haven't caught up to them already." Henry struggled to raise himself again. "Tessa, if something should happen to me, I want you to go on with Mr. and Mrs. Clark. They're good people. I know they'd welcome you."

Tessa stared at her father, pulling her eyebrows together and shaking her head. *Why would you say such things?* It had been two months since her mother and sister died out here. And only six months since they said good-bye to her grandmother in North Carolina, knowing full well they would probably never meet again. *If Father dies* . . . A stab of grief ripped its way from her stomach to her throat. *He won't—but if—he can't—* She fervently pushed thoughts of "what if Father dies" from her mind.

Swallowing hard, Tessa fought to hold her voice steady and firm. "We don't need to talk about the Clarks, Father. Nothing is going to happen to you. I'll get you to Soda Springs, and we'll stay there until you're well again. Mother would be so disappointed to hear you talk such nonsense. You just lie back now and plan the farm we're going to have when we get to Oregon."

Tessa waited for her father to slip back down on his bedroll before clicking her tongue at the mules to resume the journey. The tired mules ignored Tessa's signal and placidly munched on grass. She bellowed at them several times, flicked the reins, and hollered some more.

"If you'd give 'em a crack right off," her father rasped, "they'd know you was boss without you having to waste all that good yelling on 'em."

"Well, I'm not the boss," Tessa snapped.

Henry sighed but kept quiet.

Tessa grabbed her whip and gave each mule a smart lash on the rump. Startled, they jerked forward, nearly pitching Tessa from her seat.

Feeling badly for taking out her frustration on her ailing father, Tessa tried to keep up a light, one-sided conversation while they traveled. She talked of the soil she'd heard rumors of—black as pitch and fertile as horse dung—of the trees that harbored beehives full to busting, and of the Willamette Valley itself with weather so kind a body could farm year 'round.

"We'll have the finest piece of land in the western territories," Tessa assured him. "Just you wait and see." From the bed of the wagon, Tessa heard only an occasional pained groan when the wheels hit a stone or a rut in the road while she threaded the team around the few stands of aspen dotting the trail.

As twilight turned to dusk, Tessa kept the wagon moving. If they were as close to Soda Springs as her father said, she wanted to travel until she could no longer see the road ahead.

As the last of the sun's reflections faded, the jagged sandstone canyons turned to ghostly outlines with shadows following the wagon like ghouls in the faint moonlight. Tessa lit the oil lantern and hung it on a hook beside the seat, but the lantern gave little relief from the seemingly flat road before her. After misjudging several dips and ruts, sending the wagon tipping precariously or causing the mules to stumble, Tessa led the team to a sparse clump of cedar. She hobbled them as best she could beside a shallow stream before setting camp.

It didn't take long to gather enough tinder and buffalo dung to light a small fire, and she made quick work of putting a pot of coffee onto the heat. Dinner that evening, as it had been for the last week, consisted of jerky and hard biscuits. How she yearned for the taste of chicken, eggs, or a fresh, juicy peach.

Sitting on the side of the wagon, she watched the shadows from its hickory bows flickering in the firelight. *Like ribs of a giant whale*, Tessa thought. And there, in the belly of the decrepit beast lay her father—eating only what Tessa could guide into his mouth. With each swallow, Tessa would pray the food would stay down long enough to nourish him.

Tessa checked on the mules and stowed all the gear but the coffeepot. She dragged the tattered canvas tarpaulin over the bows of the wagon, securing the corners, and hoping it would hold together for just one more day. Her family was forced to make do with a used wagon when they began their journey in St. Joseph. They had waited for two months in Missouri for the snow to melt and had used up much more of their funds than they had planned. Though the wagon was sturdy and solid, small moth holes riddled the canvas. As soon as the trek began, so did the spring rains, and with each storm, the breaches in the canvas ripped wider.

She wiped her father's face once again with a cool, damp cloth and then helped him sip some water. Tessa bid him good night, then slid under the wagon, and wrapped herself in the cotton quilt that had been her bed since they left their home in Charlotte. Nearly two months had passed since her mother and sister died. Two months in which she had unflinchingly ridden beside her father in the wagon or trudged across the hot, rocky plains. Two months in which she unsuccessfully struggled to stretch the last of their supplies into small meals that would temporarily soothe their hunger.

Pulling her ribbon-tied journal from her treasure box, she briefly recorded the day's journey.

July 3, 1865

    Father has grown much weaker. He has red patches on his skin
that Mother never had. I don't think his fever is as high as Mother's

was, but he is in much pain. I grieve silently for my mother and sister because I don't want to add to Father's burdens. How can I go on if my father dies too? Surely, God will be merciful.

She watched for a long time as the half-moon made its way across the inky sky. The thunderheads had dissipated with the approach of the cool evening, and now the stars winked to keep Tessa company. She fell asleep with memories of her grandparents' orchards—of peaches, pears, apricots, and plums as big as her fist. Dreams of her elegant mother filled her slumber: sitting regally on a quilt under the dogwoods, standing in front of the mirror weaving Bethany's hair into glistening black braids, perched on the edge of the chair in the study, worrying over the chessboard while gnawing the inside of her cheek. How beautiful her mother had been—small and delicate like porcelain, black hair left to float about her shoulders, dark blue eyes rimmed by thick, dark lashes, ruby lips poised always in a smile. How painfully different from Tessa.

With the first rays of dawn, Tessa awoke to the cheerful warble of chickadees high in the treetops. Edging her way from under the wagon bed, she peered through the branches to discover the birds' hiding place, but as soon as she stood up, the chickadees flew away in a great cluster.

"Good morning, Father." Tessa shook her quilt and began folding it up for the day. "Father?" Untying the corner of the canvas, Tessa checked on her father. His lips were swollen and parched with dehydration, and beads of sweat had dried where they had formed, leaving salty rivulets streaking his face.

Tessa tore at the canvas, pulling it from the protective bows, and leaped into the wagon. "Father!" His eyes, swollen and crusty, opened a mere slit. For a moment he followed her movements and then closed his eyes again. He breathed shallowly from his cracked mouth.

Tears swam in her eyes as she burst into motion. "You'll be all right now," she chattered, trying to find something comforting to say. She grabbed a pail from under the wagon and thrust it into the stream. "We'll be to Soda Springs in no time." She dipped a cloth in the cool water and then squeezed a few drops into his mouth, stroking his throat to coax him to swallow. "That's right . . . there you go now . . . nice, cold water." At last her father began gulping the water without Tessa having to force his reflex. "See there," she murmured, wiping his face gently, "you're coming around now."

Racing around camp, Tessa packed away the coffeepot and the pail, then stuffed a handful of jerky in her pocket for breakfast. She plunged her hand into the grease bucket, filling her fist with muck, and smeared the grease around the wheel axles, shoving it between each groove and joint. Hastily untying the mules' hobbles, she hitched the animals to the wagon, making sure she cinched them securely.

Balancing on the rim of the wagon bed, she dragged the canvas over the bowed frame, folded a front corner back, and tied it midway up. "I'll leave as much open as I can, Father," she assured him. "You'll be wanting the fresh air, but leaving you out to get sun baked won't do you any good a'tall."

Without waiting for her father's usual go-ahead, Tessa snapped the reins, shouting a hearty "hyaugh!" to urge the mules into motion. "Getup, there!" Tessa commanded again, cracking her whip on their backsides. As they ambled along, Tessa guided them clear of the cedars and back onto the hard-packed trail. "Hyaugh! Hyaugh!" With each crack of the whip she shuddered at treating the animals so harshly, yet each time the mules slowed, she cracked the whip again. At last the beasts began picking up speed, carrying Tessa and her dying father in a race against time to Soda Springs.

THROUGHOUT THE MORNING, Tessa occasionally felt as if she was being watched. She kept her back rigid, a tight grip on the reins, and the rifle lying ready at her feet. *It's just your nerves*, she tried convincing herself. *There's nothing to worry about.* Perhaps yesterday's Indian visitors had been only a small band of renegades—perhaps not.

Emerging now and again into a grassy valley, she gave the mules full rein at their insistence. Did the mules sense her father's danger? Or were they exhilarated at being free of the scraping sage lining the twisting trail? Beyond each meadow lay another rise into the mountains through which the team must struggle.

Tessa peered at the mountains surrounding her. The volcanoes had been quiet long enough for scrub to climb the pockets of lava rubble. The hillsides were streaked with zigzags of bleached white rock. The further northwest they traveled, the more white rock littered the path. Quite often Tessa was forced to guide the mules around large black or white boulders recently dislodged from the hillside.

Shortly past noontime, Tessa and her father descended once more into a valley, stretching away to the north and west. This one was filled with dense stands of aspen and clumps of reeds. Looking like an oasis in the desert, a large pool shimmered before them.

"Father," Tessa cried. "We're almost there! The springs! I can see the soda springs ahead!" Tessa raced her team through the valley to where several hearty springs bubbled and frothed in the small lake.

Clambering down from the wagon, she tied the mules to a fallen log. She gingerly stepped from one mound of thatch to another, carefully adjusting her balance whenever a spongy mat compressed under her weight and the marsh water oozed up. She knelt beside the spring to fill her bucket just as the breeze shifted to blow the hair from her face. She stumbled back, nearly losing her footing among the thatch and reeds.

"What's that smell, Father? It's coming from the spring." Tessa wrinkled her nose at the foul stench. She cupped her hand over her nose and mouth. "Smells like rotten eggs, doesn't it?"

"Sulfur," her father choked out.

"The ground around it is yellow and crusty, and it looks muddy where the spring bubbles."

"Mineral deposits . . . don't drink."

"I don't think I could stand to try," Tessa confessed. "Makes me feel sick to just kneel beside it. I think we'd best be moving on. The guidebook says there are better springs further on. Sweet as soda water."

Climbing back onto the seat, Tessa urged the mules forward and chatted with her father to keep him conscious. "Remember the lime sodas Mrs. Rampton used to serve? So bubbly you'd get fizz on your mustache? I used to wish Eula would make them so I could drink all I wanted with no one watching, and not have to worry about spilling on my party dress. . . . I read that in Soda Springs you can just walk right up to any ol' spring and dip yourself a soda water any time you please."

A few miles farther into the valley, the trail turned from the hard packed, dusty plain to a path lined with odd patches of sweet, tender grass. The mules nuzzled in the tender tufts, despite Tessa's prodding to keep going. When the pair settled on a particular spot, their noses buried, Tessa climbed from the driver's seat to see what had enraptured her team.

"Father!" she cried. "More springs! Must be a dozen here within a stone's throw!"

"Fresh?" He was barely able to rasp the question. "Are they fresh?"

"Oh, yes, Father," Tessa declared. "Just as clear and cold as you please." As if to verify her statement, a white-tailed deer slipped from the cover of the aspens downstream to sip from the ribbon of shimmering water. Tessa grabbed the bucket from the wagon and dunked it in the frothy pool. At the same time, the water bubbled up, sprinkling her face and dress with cool drops. Laughing, she held a ladle of icy cold water to her father's lips.

With a scrap of canvas tied over the top of the bucket to keep the water from splashing out, and her own waterskin filled from the spring, Tessa again set her whip to the mules. "If I can keep these mules out of the springs," she reassured her father, "we'll be in town in no time at all." Passing the spot where the deer had appeared, Tessa raised her hand and waved toward the protective aspens, wondering if the deer were watching.

The sun had descended halfway in the afternoon sky by the time Tessa's ragged team made its way around one more hill. A military fort stood sentry a half mile off. "A fort, Father." Tessa was so tired, she could barely get the words out. "There's a fort just ahead." The mules were slick with sweat, heads hanging low against their yokes, and Tessa, exhausted from a grueling nine-hour drive, could barely keep hold of the reins. With no strength left, she guided the mules over the last leg of the journey and pulled them to a stop outside the spike-poled gate.

A wooden sign above the gate swung gently in the breeze, creating its own rhythmic knocking. Knock, knock, pause, knock, knock, pause. "Fort Connor," Tessa read the sign aloud and then bowed her head. "Thank you, Lord. Thank you for delivering us."

Tessa eased herself down from her perch on the wagon and approached the towering walls. "Hello?" *Where is the guard?* "Can you help me?" Receiving no answer, she pushed in the center of the double gate, sending them swinging wide. Stumbling into the void, her fatigue gave way to despair as she realized the fort was deserted. Tears seized her throat. "Hello?" she called in vain. "Please. Someone." She covered her face with her hands and sobbed. "Please, God. Help me."

With her father still outside in the wagon, Tessa scanned the different buildings in the compound and spotted a building marked Officers Quarters. *That will have to do,* she determined. *Maybe they've left some food behind.* She quickly pushed the thought out of her mind that they both might starve before they made it as far as Soda Springs. "First things first," she said aloud. She would get her father situated in the Officers' Quarters, then figure out how to feed him.

She returned to her father and gathered her skirts to climb up into the driver's seat. "We're at Fort Connor, Father. We're just going to rest here a while before we go on to Soda Springs." Faintly, she heard a dog barking. She let go of her skirt and walked a few steps forward, straining to hear it again. There. Coming from the southwest. So faint she wasn't convinced she had heard anything. Shading her eyes from the glare of the late-afternoon sun, she peered westward. "Cabins!" She leapt into the driver's seat. "Father, I see it! I see Soda Springs!"

The settlement was a half mile to the west of the fort, in a valley rimmed with pines and aspen on the south, and cedar and sagebrush on the north. A smattering of small log buildings, some of them nothing more than crude lean-tos, dotted the main street.

This is the "Oasis of Soda Springs"? Tessa's heart sank at the realization that the town the guidebook had described as a bountiful layover stop to rest and restock for the trek to Oregon was no more than a bedraggled collection of shacks. The little log homes were roughly aligned along the widened trail to form the main street. More homesteads were sprinkled widely throughout the valley. Some of the land had been worked, but any crops growing were sparse and dry.

Not a soul was in sight. In fact, the street was completely deserted. *They're not here!* The realization was too painful to verbalize, and panic knotted in Tessa's chest. *The rest of the wagon company has gone on without us.*

Tessa continued down the street before drawing up in front of a slightly larger building with a painted sign nailed above the door: "Trading Post." No one was about. Not on the street, not in the store . . . *Why would the entire town be deserted?*

"Tessa?"

"I'm here, Father." Tessa climbed into the wagon bed with her father and adjusted the canvas to shade him better. "We're here. We're in Soda Springs."

Too weak to lift his head, Henry gingerly turned his head from side to side, frowning. "I don't hear . . . is our company . . . ?"

Tessa shook her head. "No." Her eyes glistened with tears. "I was too slow. They're already gone."

A deep sigh escaped Henry and he sank deeper into his pillow.

"I'm sorry," Tessa sobbed. "If only we hadn't stopped at the springs. If only I were better with the mules. As soon as someone comes back to the trading post, I can find out when the company left. Maybe we can still meet up with them."

"No, Tessa," her father whispered. "It's finished. No farther."

"But we can't just stay here," Tessa protested.

"'Til I get better." He struggled to make his voice light. "Maybe . . . a company . . . next year."

Next year? Our money is gone. What will we live on for an entire year? Tessa wondered. *And what if you don't get better?* "Yes, of course." She smiled at him, wiping the perspiration from his brow. "Everything will be just fine."

CHAPTER 3

A soft, steady beat woke Tessa. The sun hung low enough in the sky now to merge the shade of her wagon with the storefront. *Horses?* She strained to make out the sound in the distance. Hoisting herself from her resting place against the wagon wheel, Tessa stretched her stiff muscles. She listened to the distinct throb of horses trotting, coming from the north, punctuated here and there by the giddy laughter of children or the baritone guffaws of men. Peering toward the approaching sounds, she could make out faint snatches of music and voices singing.

"Father!" Tessa said. "Someone's coming! Listen! It's a whole group of them!" Tessa stood on the axle of the wheel to peer in at her father. He lay with his eyes closed, the slight rise and fall of his chest all but indiscernible. But perspiration still beaded on his forehead and above his lip before gently slipping from the hollow contours of his face.

Tessa plunged her handkerchief in the water barrel and wrung it out. She blotted the fevered moisture from her father and murmured, "We're here now, Father. Someone will be here shortly to help us. You'll be fine now. Just a few minutes longer." She held the back of her hand next to his lips and scarcely felt the wisp of breath.

As the music got louder, Tessa fumed at the inconsiderate group. Her father needed help, and all the townsfolk were out gallivanting. At last she saw them—several wagons filled with hay and teeming with men, women, and children, coming from the north. Young men astride tall horses mingled with the wagons. A man with a mouth organ sat on one of the seats, next to the driver, keeping the whole lot entertained with his jaunty tunes.

Tessa ran out into the street to enlist their aid. A large man, whose belly hung fully over his belt, rode ahead to meet her.

"Evenin', miss," he called, lowering himself from his saddle. The acrid smell of fresh sweat and old liniment washed over Tessa as the man lumbered toward her. He was bald except for the swath of gray hair encircling the sides of his head. His hat hung down his back, held on by the string around his neck. He fumbled to remove the hat and held it to his chest, tipping his head in a bow. "Dale Pixton," he proclaimed, introducing himself.

Tessa watched the folds of skin connecting his head to his torso quiver as he spoke. "I'm—I'm Tessa Darrow," she stammered. "My father . . ." She looked toward the wagon where the canvas shielded her father. "He's sick. He needs help."

"Sick, is he?" Pixton trudged to the front of the wagon to get a better look. "Gaw-awmighty!" he yelled, staring at the unconscious man covered with red splotches.

Pixton stumbled backward, holding his hands up as if to ward off the illness. "Get 'im out of here!" Curling his hand into a huge paw, he pointed one stubby finger at Tessa and snapped it back and forth directing her back the way she had come. "You take your father and your filthy belongings, and you get outta here now! Go back to where you come from! We don't need the likes'a him comin' in here to infect our folk! Go on with ya!"

Tessa stood with her mouth agape, unsure what to do. Infect the town? She hadn't considered that possibility. But she couldn't take him back out on the trail—he'd surely die. "Please," she begged, "you must help him."

"I said get 'im outta here!" Pixton roared, his face so flushed he was beginning to resemble Tessa's father.

"Brother Pixton! What kind of Christian are you?" A middle-aged woman climbed down from one of the hay wagons, holding her full skirts halfway to her knees to keep them from tangling her descent. "Fellow here needs help. You cannae just send him off on his own!" Unlashing one of the corners of canvas, she pulled the awning back to get a better look at him. "Lord, have mercy!" she cried. "How long's this man been sick?"

"He's my father, ma'am," Tessa replied, trying to sort one blurred day from the rest in her memory. "He took sick three, maybe four days ago. He didn't start getting the rash until yesterday."

"My land, it's a wonder he made it this far." The woman got to work untying the canvas. She yelled toward the wagons, standing immobile a few yards off, "A coupl'a you boys come help me carry this man inside!"

No one in the wagons moved.

"Maureen," Pixton said, "you take him inside, you'll contaminate the whole store. None of us'll be able to do business there."

"If you're the kind of people who'd druther leave a man out here to die," the woman countered, "I wouldn't want your business! And," she snapped, "you'll do well to refrain from using my familiar name, Brother Pixton."

"Sister Holt, be reasonable."

The woman stood fast, her hands on her hips, sparkling green eyes flaming nearly as brightly as her coppery hair. "If you're not going to assist, then I'll thank you to make way." Stepping in front of the man, she entreated the passengers of the wagons. "I need some help here. Surely one of you men is a good Christian."

Tessa saw the hands of several of the women clutch the arms of the men they were near, to restrain any thoughts of aid. *Christians*, Tessa fumed. *Prob'ly don't know the meaning of the word.* "I'll help you, ma'am," she declared. "I've gotten him this far. Reckon I can carry my father inside."

"That's the spirit, girl." Mrs. Holt pursed her lips and furrowed her brow for an instant. "Tell you what we'll do. There's a shed out back. I've got an old cot he can use. Give me a minute to get a bed made up, then you can help me get him settled." With a swoosh of her skirts and a dark look at Mr. Pixton, Mrs. Holt strode around the side of the trading post, dodging a few odd barrels, and disappeared behind the small cabin.

In Mrs. Holt's absence, Tessa busied herself tucking the quilt her father lay on securely around him. She pulled the corners together, twisted them, then folded them back under the smooth edges. Tessa tidied the wagon, bathed her father's face, fussed with the quilt—anything to ignore these people who were content to stare and not help. When Mrs. Holt returned, Tessa had her father wrapped tighter than a caterpillar in a cocoon.

"Done a fine job of wrapping him, honey," Mrs. Holt softly said, "but I'm afraid we'd best leave the quilt out here."

"But why?" Tessa dropped her hand protectively to the precious quilt.

"It's infected with the smallpox. It's gonna have t'be burned."

"Smallpox!" *I should have known that's what the rash was*, Tessa chastised herself. Tears sprang to her eyes with the confirmation of how sick her father was. There were some folks back home who had survived smallpox, but she knew many had not.

Tessa clutched the quilt—her mother's wedding quilt—that had traveled with them all the way from North Carolina. She traced the outlines of the lovingly pieced double rings that she so vividly remembered draping her parents' bed.

Maureen laid her hand on Tessa's shoulder. "Your ma's quilt?"

Tessa nodded. "She died on the trail. My sister too."

"I'm sorry, love. But you wouldnae want anyone else to get the pox, now would you?"

"No," Tessa agreed and then slowly untucked the quilt.

"Did your mom and sis have the smallpox as well?"

"I don't think so. My father called it 'mountain fever.'" Tessa recalled how their rashes looked more like a spotted sunburn. "Their rashes didn't look like blisters like this."

"Darn shame, it is," Maureen murmured. She pulled a handkerchief over her nose and mouth like a mask before slipping her arms under the dying man's arms and then clasped her wrists. Tessa took hold of his legs and the two of them carefully navigated the limp body to the shed out back into the waiting bed.

Tessa struggled to completely strip her father of his contaminated clothing and undergarments, and then dressed him in the nightshirt Mrs. Holt had provided, all while trying to keep her eyes averted. It took a bit of fancy talking to convince the kind woman that Tessa could manage the task by herself. It was awkward enough to have your daughter undress you, Tessa imagined, let alone a complete stranger.

Tessa then replaced her fitted dress with the too-large dress Mrs. Holt had given her. "Anything that could hold onto the smallpox germs must be burned," Mrs. Holt had said. So Tessa placed the last articles of clothing she or her father owned in a pile outside the door, ready for the fire pit.

With her father sleeping fitfully, Tessa nestled in the mounded hay at the back of the shed and pulled out her beloved diary. Lying sideways in the hay so she could watch her father, she roughly sketched the memorable points of the day's travels: the view of Mt. Sherman rising in the far distance at the break of day, the meandering trail leading past yellow mounded formations encrusted around several of the springs, Sulfur Spring protected by reeds and aspen, the deer drinking from the meadow springs. Tessa even drew likenesses of Mr. Pixton and Mrs. Holt. She tried to draw an image of her father, but the contrast between her strong, muscular father and the weak, withered man she now cared for was too painful to be put to paper.

She lay pondering their journey—how far they had come and how far they had yet to go—when she heard voices just outside the door.

"I told you, Tildy"—Tessa recognized Mrs. Holt's strong voice with her hint of a foreign accent—"nobody's going in there, save for me. No sense everyone being exposed to it."

Who's there? Tessa wondered. *Why would anyone want to come in here with the smallpox?*

"... matter with you ... selfish ... glory ... bossy ..." Tessa couldn't quite make out all of the other woman's words, but the anger and suspicion in her voice were unmistakable.

"That's not what I meant at all." Mrs. Holt's voice sounded very terse. "But I just don't think they're up to visitors yet. It's very kind of you to bring dinner by. I'm sure you understand—"

"What I understand, Maureen Holt," the other woman huffed, "is the reason you're known as the most stubborn woman in these parts. You be sure to tell the girl who brought these fixings."

"You know I will."

Tessa leaned closer to the small window above her. *Not really eavesdropping*, she reasoned. *Getting stuffy back here is all.*

The unfamiliar woman was leaving. "Don't forget about the gathering at the fort at sunset."

"I'll have to see what evening brings, Tildy. My heart will be there if my body isn't."

A few moments passed before the door opened and Mrs. Holt entered the shed carrying a basket on one arm, a blanket and pillow balanced on the other. Tessa shoved the journal under the hay and jumped to her feet, brushing the hay from her skirt.

"Making yourself ta'home, I see," Mrs. Holt greeted her. She again wore a triangle of white cotton over her mouth, tied in back of her head, rather like a bandit's kerchief.

"I hope you don't mind," Tessa said, motioning to her shoes placed neatly near the door.

"No, of course not, dear. You're welcome to make yourself comfortable."

Tessa held her hand over her mouth unconsciously imitating the shape of the kerchief. "Why are you wearing—"

"Oh, the mask!" Mrs. Holt laughed. "I think we should be protecting ourselves from the pox if we can." After setting the basket and bedding down, she pulled a cloth from her pocket and held it out to Tessa. "Let me help you with this."

"But haven't I already been exposed?" Tessa asked.

"Most likely, but on the chance you haven't—"

Tessa held her hair tightly to her head so it wouldn't catch in the knot Mrs. Holt tied. "When my mother took ill," Tessa said, "Father made sure we boiled our water and washed our hands before cooking. We washed everything after she and Bethany died. When we got to Fort

Bridger, Father tied the mules outside the fort and left me there with the wagon. He scrubbed up real good just to make sure he wasn't carrying the fever inside the fort." The familiar swelling of fear and disappointment choked off her words as she looked at her father.

"That must be where he picked up the smallpox," Mrs. Holt whispered. "It's a darn shame." She watched while Tessa dunked a cloth in a basin of water, folded it, and replaced it on her father's head. "You're a good nurse to your da, Tessa. Your mother would be well pleased."

Mrs. Holt set about pulling a nail keg out from the corner and laid a white cloth over it. "Tildy Pixton sent some supper over for you." She arranged fried chicken, beet greens, some apricot preserves, and a hot, charcoal-covered baked potato onto a tin plate. Scooping a chunk of butter with a knife, she plunged it into the center of a fist-sized roll. The warm, yeasty fragrance filled the room as the butter melted.

"That smells like heaven." Tessa rose from her father's side and sat at the makeshift table on an overturned milk pail.

"Tildy cooks it all in a big pit dug in the ground. Simmers it all day long." Eyeing Tessa's gaunt frame, she circled the girl's wrist with her thumb and forefinger. "Reckon it's been a while since you had a good home-cooked meal."

"Not much more than mush or stew after we left North Carolina six months ago." North Carolina. Seemed so far away, now. Like a whole different lifetime.

"Now, try a bit of this." Mrs. Holt held out a glass, a sly twinkle in her eye. "Tell me what you think."

Tessa pulled the kerchief down under her chin and hesitantly took a sip of the cold liquid that fizzed a bit on her tongue. "It's delicious! Like lemonade—only sparkly!"

"Made it myself," Mrs. Holt boasted. "Finest soda water on earth comes from Hooper Springs just up the road. Splash of lemon syrup and a sprinkle of sugar, and there you are! Folks come from all over to get a taste of our spring water."

"Will you join me?" Tessa asked. As there was only the one stool in the room, Tessa stood up, politely offering her seat to Mrs. Holt.

"Heavens, no!" Holding her arms across her stomach, Mrs. Holt waddled about as though her stomach hurt. "I ate enough to feed Gideon's minions not more'n an hour ago. Couldn't eat another bite. You sit down now and have your fill."

"But there's enough here to feed—"

"There's no more there than what Brother Pixton would call a snack.

Poor Tildy spends her life just cooking for him and defending his actions to the neighbors." Stopping herself, Mrs. Holt looked about, seeming rather embarrassed. "Now see, there I go. I need to learn to keep my opinions to myself." She bowed her head. "My apologies."

Tessa laughed. "Please, at least stay and chat while I eat."

"No, dear, there will be plenty of time for that later." She shook her head and started for the door. "First, I must see to your wagon. I'll save what I can—what's not been contaminated, but I'll have to burn the rest. And I'll look to boarding your mules."

Tessa nodded, not certain how Mrs. Holt would determine what had been infected. "There's a small wooden box under the seat," Tessa said. "It's my treasure box. Please, may I keep it?"

"Well, if it's been under the seat, I don't suppose it carries the pox. I'll see what I can do about it."

Mrs. Holt left and Tessa finished her dinner in solitude, accompanied only by the occasional moan or raspy snore from her father across the room.

After sponging her father again and coaxing a few drops of water into his mouth, Tessa returned to the pile of hay to arrange her bedding. *Mrs. Holt knows what she's doing. Father will be fine now*, she tried to convince herself. She used a stick to wedge open the canvas flap covering the window, and then lay down on top of her blanket. Though the sun was low enough to leave the shed in the shadow, it was still light outside and mercilessly hot. *But, what if— No. No what if. He will be fine.*

BOOM! Tessa leapt to her feet, cracking her head on the rafters overhead. Dropping to her knees, she covered her head with her arms trying to squeeze away the throbbing. She bit her lips to keep from crying with the pain.

BOOM! The blast echoed again. Creeping to the window, she peeked out trying to discern the source of the noise. A thin column of smoke rose from the direction of the abandoned fort, but it was too far away to make out its cause.

BOOM!

"Incoming! Take cover!" Tessa's father shouted, thrashing on the cot.

With her hand on his chest, Tessa felt the sharp hammering beat. "It's all right, Father," she cooed. "I'm here. Nothing to worry about."

BOOM! He went rigid, his eyes opened wide, staring with fright. She grabbed the cloth from the basin and sponged his face, his neck, and his arms. He relaxed with her ministrations, and Tessa urged him to swallow a few drops of water.

BOOM! Henry stiffened again but kept his eyes closed. "I'll make them stop, Father," Tessa cried. "I'll make them stop!" Jumping to her feet, she ran from the shed out into the street. A couple of chickens scattered at her appearance.

"Stop it!" she screamed. "Do you hear me? Stop!"

No one replied, and no one came. The town seemed ghostly quiet again. Tessa bent over, dragging deep gulps of air into her lungs to calm her pounding heart. A ways down the street, a spectral, whining tune wafted on the sunset. A bugle, she realized. Playing taps. Tears welled in her eyes, spilling down her cheeks. How often that tune had wailed from the cemetery back home. For the duration of the war, it seemed a weekly duty to accompany her mother to yet another soldier's funeral. Outwardly grieving, Tessa and her mother shared a secret rejoicing that her own father's name was not on the list. When she and her father heard at Fort Bridger that the war had ended, she hoped that would be the end of the killing—and of the mournful bugles. She thought of her father, lying just on the other side of the door now, so near death himself. Leaning against the side of the shed, she cried.

"Tessa?" Mrs. Holt stood beside her, a worried hand on Tessa's shoulder. "Your da? Has he . . . ?"

"Father? Oh!" She swiped away the tears on her cheeks. "No, he's—I mean he hasn't . . . The bugle." She waved vaguely toward the edge of town. "I heard the shots, then the bugle."

"I forgot to tell you, didn't I, child?" Mrs. Holt offered Tessa a hankie from her pocket. "For the president."

The president? she wondered. She had seen him once before. In a carriage, on his way somewhere. "President Lincoln is here?"

"No. Of course not. His memorial service."

"Memorial?"

"President Lincoln was assassinated. In April. Surely you knew."

April. No, Mother died in May. Tessa relived that horrid morning on the trail, burying her mother and then finding Bethany. Tessa couldn't recollect anything of the past April, between her birthday in March—when they'd left Missouri—and the day her mother and sister died, all the days in between blurred together. Tessa shook her head. "No, I didn't know."

We lost our land in Lincoln's war. We lost everything but each other, she thought. *And now he's dead. President Lincoln is dead.* Though Tessa associated the war with Lincoln, the thought that the president of the United States was dead saddened her. Tears again filled Tessa's eyes. "How?" she whispered.

Mrs. Holt shook her head sadly. "He was at the theater with his wife. Someone just up and shot him."

Why would anyone want to kill him? Even when Tessa's home in North Carolina was burned to the ground, her mother cursed the soldiers who'd burned it, not the president. If for no other reason, than the fact that he was the president of the United States made him a man to respect.

"What will happen now?" Tessa asked Mrs. Holt. "Will there be another war?"

"No, dear," the woman assured her. "We have a new president. Andrew Johnson, the vice-president, took office. The war is over, and there won't ever be another one to worry about."

It's just not possible, Tessa told herself. Standing there, wrapped in shadows, calmly discussing the death of the man whom her father respected so much. *I can't tell Father. It will break his heart.* "If President Lincoln died in April, why are you holding a service tonight?"

"The Indians. We've had a few problems, now and again, and we worried that they might take advantage of our sorrow back then. Thought it would be fitting to save our farewells for Independence Day. A detail of soldiers came in from Fort Hall for the evening—that was the cannon you heard. They'll be gone in the morning, I imagine. Now"—Mrs. Holt's tone was clearly meant to change the subject—"I've brought you a bit of bread and cheese to see you through till morning. Let's go inside and have a look at your da."

Henry Darrow now slept soundly. His head felt not quite as hot as Tessa remembered, and she set to sponging him off again with the cool water. A large barrel kept fresh spring water at hand just outside the door, and Tessa frequently replenished her basin. "Folks come from far away as Great Salt Lake City to bathe in the soda springs," Mrs. Holt boasted. "Claim it will cure anything from rheumatism to sour stomach."

Before she left for the evening, Mrs. Holt placed her hands on Tessa's cheeks. "My room is just right there." She pointed to the window across from Tessa's window. "You just holler if you need anything."

Tessa lay awake for what seemed like hours, listening to the leaves rustle outside her window. After lying on the hard ground for months, burrowing her face in her quilt to shield it from the cold, Tessa now felt stifled in a building surrounded by hay. Occasionally a horseman would ride by. Once a brawl broke out somewhere south of town, and Tessa cringed from the coarse language being yelled. She heard a horse gallop by the shed, more yelling, and then all was quiet. But for Tessa, fear, relief, and silent prayers for healing and of gratitude precluded sleep.

CHAPTER 4

Jerking awake, Tessa sat up in her bed of hay, keeping her head lowered to just below the rafters that waited to crack her skull. The rapping on the door sounded again. Not the vicious pounding she had dreamt, but a soft, rhythmic tap. She scooted off the mounded hay and straightened her baggy shift. Though still early in the morning, the shed felt stifling compared to the cool, sweet air drafting in between the stacked log walls.

Tappity-tap. "Tessa? Are you awake?"

Recognizing the welcome sound of her hostess's voice, Tessa fumbled to pull open the stiff door. "Good morning, Mrs. Holt. Please come in."

"How is the patient today?" Squinting to adjust to the dim light, Mrs. Holt carried a basin of fresh water in front of her with a stack of clean towels draped over her arm. "Tessa! Where is your kerchief?"

Tessa's hand instinctively flew to her head as she remembered the face mask Mrs. Holt had fashioned the day before. "I must have left it—" She could see it already, hanging on the nail on the rafter, where she had hooked it during the night.

"Fetch it at once," Mrs. Holt ordered. "You need to wear it whenever you're in here."

Crawling across the hay, Tessa remembered sleeping with the mask on until the suffocating heat had prompted her to take it off. "Mrs. Holt," Tessa said, retying the cloth behind her head, "surely I shall suffocate if I'm forced to wear this in my sleep."

"Surely you shall not!" Mrs. Holt countered. She tugged Tessa's mask up to the bridge of her nose. "I suppose it won't do no harm to take the kerchief off when you're sleeping. But you must be certain to carry it with you, and tie it on when you come anywhere near your da. And you need to be certain to scrub up real good whenever you leave the hay shed.

Folks are real skittish about smallpox. It'll make 'em feel safer if they see the both of us scrubbing."

Kneeling beside Tessa's father, Mrs. Holt lifted the neck of his night-shirt enough to inspect his chest. Tessa peered over the woman's shoulder. The pustules had taken on a tinge of gray. Tessa turned away, bile rising in her stomach.

"Now don't you go soft on me," Mrs. Holt chided. "If we're going to pull your da through this, it's going to take a keg o'work from the both of us."

Tessa nodded her submission.

Pulling a small bottle from her apron pocket, Mrs. Holt pried the man's mouth open just wide enough to accept a capful of the golden syrup. "A bit of laudanum," Mrs. Holt explained, "he'll be in a sight of pain before long . . . if he's not already. The infection's beginning to deaden the skin around the pox. We've got to do what we can to draw the pus out before it does much more damage." She stood up, dropping the bottle back into her pocket. "I'll fix up a plaster for him. While I'm gone, I need you to strip him down to his birthday suit."

Tessa shuddered at the memory of undressing him yesterday—of the fear of tearing his skin as she dragged clothing over his tender sores. "Oh, I . . . I . . . I simply—"

"Buck up and do as I say. Better for you to do it than me, a complete stranger. I won't be but a minute." Mrs. Holt rushed from the shed, letting the door slam behind her.

Tessa watched Mrs. Holt hang her apron and kerchief on the clothesline and then scrub her arms and hands at the water bucket before dashing inside the trading post.

"Oh, Father," Tessa whispered, her hands fumbling under the thin sheet. "I'm sorry. I'll be as careful as I can." Trembling, she unbuttoned the damp nightshirt, and gingerly rolled it down his shoulders. She fought down the urge to gag every time the nightshirt stuck to one of his sores. Turning her head and trying to keep her eyes averted, she slipped the garment past his torso, and pulled the sweaty garment off his feet. She made sure the sheet covered his naked, festering form, then bolted outside to vomit.

"It's a terrible way to have to see your da." Mrs. Holt rested a comforting hand on Tessa's shoulder. "Let's go to work so that's not the last memory you have of him."

Tessa splashed her face from the rain barrel one more time before following Mrs. Holt back inside the shed.

Mrs. Holt placed a basin beside the bed and then dumped a mound of brownish yellow powder in it. Pouring a small amount of clean water into the basin at a time, she stirred the mixture into a thick batter. With the back of a wooden spoon, she spread the paste on the man's chest and abdomen, then she covered it with a flour sack towel. Within seconds, steam began rising from the towel, filling the air with its putrid odor. "Ah, there we go now." Mrs. Holt winked at Tessa and began applying the paste to one of his arms.

"What is that?" Tessa pressed her kerchief to her nose with the back of her hand. "Smells like—no, smells *worse* than mule droppings."

Mrs. Holt chuckled but went on with her ministrations. "Bit of this'n that. Smell's the iron oxide from the springs. Gather the rocks up and then crush 'em into a powder. Stinks to high heaven, but beats the devil out of an infection." With her father's arms plastered and covered, Mrs. Holt placed a dish towel to conceal his private parts before removing the sheet.

"Come over here and see how it's done, Tessa. S'pect we'll be at it all day."

Tessa approached her father, fighting the nausea the smell prompted. "What shall I be doing?"

"Let me finish slickering him up, then you can take over. When the towels stop steaming, take them off and rinse them in the water. Rub some more plaster on and lay the towel back down. Think you can handle that?"

"I guess so." Each time Tessa felt her stomach settling, Mrs. Holt would thrust her spoon in the plaster, renewing its stench.

"Well then," Mrs. Holt said, handing the spoon to Tessa, "there you are. I've got chores to tend to, but you just holler if you need anything." Once outside, the woman repeated the ritual of hanging up her apron and kerchief and scrubbing herself at the basin before entering the store.

Tessa turned back to her father. The cloth on his chest barely steamed now, so Tessa gently peeled it away. Pieces of ashen skin came off with the plaster, as well as smears of yellowish pus. Her stomach lurching, Tessa struggled not to vomit where she sat. *Concentrate on a cool breeze,* she ordered herself to ward off the nausea. Hiking in the Appalachians, breeze humming in the tops of the pines, sweet scent of honeysuckle . . . Tessa rinsed the cloth in the water basin, watching it spritz just a bit at the pus. *Spring water,* she mused. *Cures what ails you.*

She carefully laid a dollop of plaster on her father's chest, smoothing it just as Mrs. Holt had done and then draped the cloth over it. Again the cloth began to steam. *Go on, steam,* Tessa thought. *The more the better.* As she worked, she recalled a time a few days after Bethany was born. Her mother lay in bed, breasts swollen to the size of muskmelons. Eula hovered nearby, laying cloths soaked in cold water over her mother's breasts to take down the swelling. The cloths steamed from the fever that had infected her mother, and Bethany would fuss and cry when laid to a hot nipple to suckle. In the end, her mother had resorted to squirting breast milk into a cup to relieve her engorgement enough to nurse her baby.

Limb by limb, Tessa replastered her father's sores. "Don't you worry, Father. I'll not leave your side until you're well." Though her father's eyes remained closed, she thought she felt his hand tighten slightly around hers.

Diligently cleansing the cloths and replenishing the plaster, Tessa's arms ached from wringing the water and from the weight of the plaster on the spoon. Yet, her father's skin was not peeling off as readily, and he had managed to open his eyes and look at her once.

Time and again her gaze wandered to the window. The smell of the plaster no longer bothered her, and Tessa wondered how long she had been tending to her father. Time and again she debated going in search of Mrs. Holt before replacing the plasters once more.

At last Mrs. Holt returned, this time laden with an aromatic basket. "Breakfast," she announced gaily. "This'll make you feel better."

Tessa stood up, rubbing her aching arms, amazed at how hungry she felt. "I think I could nibble on a horse!"

"Didn't have a horse handy, but I did fry up a pork chop."

Tessa inhaled deeply. "And biscuits."

"Cinnamon rolls," Mrs. Holt corrected. "Mixed 'em up first thing this morning. Took awhile raising, I'm afraid. How's your da?"

"I think he looks a little better. His skin quit coming off with the plasters, and he opened his eyes once."

"That's a good sign. Look it here. His cheeks are pinking up with the fever."

"Oh no," Tessa gasped.

"No, no, that's good!" Mrs. Holt put a calming hand on the girl's shoulder. "Means his body is starting to fight back. Sure didn't expect it this soon."

"Do you think he'll be all right then?"

Mrs. Holt shook her head. "Too soon to tell. He's a stubborn one, though. Figure there's still plenty of fire in him. Now," she said, turning Tessa toward the basket, "you sit down and eat a mite."

"I'll just get washed." Tessa walked to the door.

"Not dressed like that, you won't. You'll have every young rowdy in the territory hankering after you!"

Tessa blushed, realizing she was still dressed only in the shift that Mrs. Holt had provided the day before.

"Here," Mrs. Holt offered. "I brought you a wrap."

Tessa slipped her arms into the calico robe and tied it around her waist. "Thank you."

"How old are you, anyway?"

"I'll be fifteen in ten months."

Mrs. Holt smiled. "'Round here that's marrying age."

Blushing, Tessa didn't know quite how to respond.

"Soon as we're sure you're not infected too, I'll make you a pretty new frock."

"Oh, but you needn't go to the trouble," Tessa said. "I have another dress in the wagon."

Mrs. Holt shook her head again. "I had to take the one you were wearing, and the clothes from the wagon, and burn them with the quilt."

Tears filled Tessa's eyes. *My mother's clothes—destroyed. They were all I had left of her.* She remembered the frilly white gown Bethany wore on her christening day. Tessa had hoped to preserve it for her own daughter. Though her father lay only a few feet away, Tessa felt utterly alone.

Throughout the day, Tessa dressed her father's rash, pausing only long enough to eat or stretch her aching muscles. Mrs. Holt stopped in every couple of hours, but with the trading post being closed for the picnic yesterday, she stayed busy tending to a steady string of customers. After dinner, Tessa helped Mrs. Holt dig a pit beside the shed to dump the buckets of plaster and rinse water in.

"Only sure way to keep the pox from spreading," Mrs. Holt explained, "is to burn it or bury it. After we're sure the pox has run its course, we'll burn these buckets, the plaster cloths, and the wooden spoon."

Though Mrs. Holt did run a thriving mercantile, Tessa felt sure she couldn't afford to burn so much good equipment. "We ran out of money quite a while ago, Mrs. Holt, but perhaps you'll let me work the cost off by helping in the store?"

"Work the cost off? Heavens sake, dear, that's like putting a price on your da's life." Standing right in front of Tessa, Mrs. Holt took the girl by the shoulders and spoke earnestly. "We were all put on this earth to take care of each other. I'm just thankful I could help."

A knot welled in Tessa's throat, but she remained in Mrs. Holt's grip. When tears trickled down her cheeks, Mrs. Holt pulled her into an embrace.

With a fresh kettle of warm water in the bucket, Tessa helped Mrs. Holt sponge the remaining plaster off her father, bathed his hair and combed it, and laid a fresh sheet over him. Mrs. Holt had already brought in a new union suit to dress him in when his sores stopped festering.

He opened his eyes once and tried to raise his head before sinking deeper into the pillow.

"Father?" Tessa knelt beside him. "I'm here for you."

He worked his mouth but was too weak to voice his words.

"Mr. Darrow, I'm Maureen Holt. You're in Morristown."

He managed a slight nod.

"Morristown," Tessa gasped. "No! I was supposed to get us to Soda Springs!"

"You have, dear," Mrs. Holt interrupted with a laugh. "Travelers call it 'Soda Springs,' but we call it 'Morristown.'"

Tessa placed her hand on her chest, feeling her heart pounding through the shift and dress. "Oh." She felt silly for so easily flying into a panic, but she also felt so, so relieved.

Mrs. Holt returned her attention to Henry Darrow. "You've been through a spell of smallpox," she continued. "Your daughter worked like a Trojan, though, to pull you through."

Henry squeezed Tessa's hand weakly. When his hand rested on the sheet covering his naked thigh, his eyes opened wide. Tessa's face turned red.

"Now don't worry yourself—your modesty's intact. We didn'a see anything more'n necessary."

Smiling at Mrs. Holt's frankness, Tessa relaxed and lifted her father's hand to her cheek. She thought the woman's accent might be British, but she wasn't quite certain.

Pulling the union suit from the shelf, Mrs. Holt shook it in the air and held it up to show. "I e'en brought you new underthings when you feel up to dressing."

Tessa politely averted her eyes from the underwear when she saw the color rising in her father's cheeks. "Mrs. Holt," she said softly, "is there nothing that needs to be done in the store?"

"Laws, child," the woman said, replacing the garment on the shelf, "there's always something that needs doing. I'll take my leave then." Mrs. Holt patted Tessa's shoulder. "I'll stop back in a while to check on things."

With Mrs. Holt gone, Tessa primly straightened the sheet covering her father's feet, then under his arms. Fluffing the pillow around his head, she cooed the reassuring words she had so often heard her mother coo over Bethany. It wasn't too long before her father slipped into a gentle slumber, and Tessa was left with nothing to do but watch him and wait.

CHAPTER 5

As shades of purple filtered through the windows of the little shed, Tessa carried her wooden chair outside to watch the fading sunset. She heard several voices to the southwest but, dressed as she was in only a robe, she didn't dare go investigate. She had scarcely settled herself when Mrs. Holt joined her and rested on a nail keg beside her.

"Won't be long now."

"What won't be?" Tessa asked.

"The fireworks. Didn't I tell you?"

"Real fireworks? Out here?" Tessa had only seen a fireworks display once, before the war when the daughter of one of their wealthy neighbors had her coming out. Tessa's father had said that the town would have a celebration with fireworks when the war ended, but they had begun their westward trek before that time.

"One of the soldiers from the fort brought in some fireworks from Sacramento awhile back. We felt it would be disrespectful to shoot them off after President Lincoln's memorial on Independence Day, so the troops stayed over so we could have a show tonight."

A soft boom interrupted their conversation, and Mrs. Holt pointed a finger toward the southwestern sky. "There we go, now!"

Tessa clapped as a brilliant white streak exploded into an orb of glittering lights. Burst after colorful burst filled the sky with hues of yellow, orange, red, and even green. After several minutes, the dramatic display faded away to the sounds of laughter and chatter as spectators made their way back home.

"Well, how about that?" Mrs. Holt said after a long, comfortable silence.

Tessa sat quietly, enjoying the magical cloak the fireworks had cast on the night.

"Guess we should sponge your da again before we get you settled for the night."

"Mmm," Tessa murmured, "s'pose so." She followed Mrs. Holt into the shed, with globes of sparkling color dancing in her head.

Mrs. Holt struck a match to light the lantern hanging beside the door. "Mr. Darrow?" she called. "Time to wake up a mite." She shot an alarmed look at Tessa before bounding the short distance to the man's bedside. "Mr. Darrow?" Setting the lantern on the table, she shoved her hands under his armpits and dragged him to a sitting position. "Mr. Darrow, wake up! Mr. Darrow! You gotta work with me now."

She blew a puff of air onto face, and he gasped for a shallow breath. His head flopped back, and he let his eyes fall closed. "Oh, no you don't," she scolded, shaking him back to consciousness. "We've worked too hard."

His eyes fluttered, and he drew another breath.

Holding her breath, Tessa felt powerless to go inside. *He's dying,* Tessa thought. Time seemed to move so slowly. She wanted to run to him, but she was terrified to watch him die.

"Gotta do better'n that," Mrs. Holt scolded again. "Draw it in deep, and blow it out hard. Like this." She sucked a deep breath and then blew it out right in Henry's face. "You came all this way, dragged this lass away from her home, buried her mum and sister, and you're not giving up now! I'll be hanged if I'll let ya!"

"Mrs. Holt! Stop!" At last, Tessa flew from the door to the woman berating her father. "What are you doing?"

"Here." Mrs. Holt propped the man in his daughter's arms and climbed around in back of him. "Do you hear that rattle when he breathes? He's got the pneumonia. Fluid in his lungs." She smacked him between the shoulder blades with the heel of her hand. "If we can't get it out of there, he'll suffocate and die."

"Father!" Now Tessa shook him. "Do you hear that? You've got to blow it out, or you're going to die!"

"... can't ...," her father struggled to say.

"Oh, yes, you can, Father. You've got to!"

Together, father and daughter drew a breath—his shallow, hers deep—and blew it out. As he blew, Mrs. Holt thumped him on the back again. Breathe, blow, thump, breathe, blow, thump. For several minutes, what seemed like hours, the three worked together. Breathe, blow, thump, breathe, blow, thump. At last, with his breath coming easier, Tessa slumped in exhaustion, and Mrs. Holt scooted the man back on the bed so he sat propped against the side of the shed. She fluffed his pillow and tucked it behind his head.

"This'll help the fluid drain away from his lungs," Mrs. Holt explained, swiping a stray tendril from her brow.

"How did you know to do that?" Tessa gasped, willing her racing heart and trembling hands to be calm.

Mrs. Holt smiled sheepishly. "To be honest, that's all I could think to do." Sitting on the edge of the bed, she took Tessa's hand in her own. "When I was a girl about your age, a neighbor in Scotland got pneumonia. You could just hear the phlegm rattling in her lungs every time she took a breath. The doctor would come by and make her blow hard breaths out while he thumped on her back." Tears filled her eyes, and she hastily swiped them away with the heel of her hand. "Gracious. That was a long time ago."

Tessa looked at her father, propped up with his head slightly askew on the pillow. Pale and gaunt, he seemed much older than his thirty-eight years. She turned her gaze to Mrs. Holt, with her bright green eyes and coppery blonde hair, and realized that this energetic woman was probably close to his same age. "Is my father going to be all right?" she asked.

Mrs. Holt put her arm around Tessa's shoulder and pulled her in close. "I think so," she answered. "His breathing didn't sound labored earlier today. I think the pneumonia just started up. We'll keep him propped up and work with him to blow his breath out hard and pray with all our might." She studied Tessa for a moment. "Think you can sleep light enough to hear him breathe?"

Tessa listened to his quiet sighing and nodded.

"If he stops breathing, or if his chest starts rattling, you bellow out that window and I'll come running."

Tessa squared her shoulders and tried to look alert. "I'll do it. You can count on me."

"I know I can," Mrs. Holt replied. Before leaving, she turned and faced Tessa again. "Tess? We can only do what we can do. The rest is in God's hands."

Swallowing past the lump aching in her throat, Tessa braved a smile and nodded. Then she turned away to hide her welling tears.

IN HER SLEEP, Tessa marveled at the images of brilliant fireworks casting a flickering glow over the surrounding buildings. As the glow intensified, she found herself inside the shed, helpless as flames engulfed her father's cot like a funeral pyre. With pulse racing, she leaped from her chair and found herself midway across the room before awakening from the horrifying dream.

"Whoa there," Mrs. Holt said, steadying Tessa's flight. "Were you dreaming?"

Disoriented, Tessa stared at the cot where her father slept peacefully. The startling glow that had invaded her slumber was magenta shards of dawn slipping through the crevices of the shed's eastern wall. Her relief was quickly replaced with mortification. "I fell asleep!" She bounded to her father's bedside and dropped to her knees. "How is he?"

"Doing very well, I'd say." Mrs. Holt reached for a small crockery bowl on the shelf. "I mixed up a remedy for his pneumonia, and the phlegm's been coming up right nice."

Tessa stood, sniffed at the bowl, and nearly gagged at the pungent concoction. "Another plaster?"

"No." Mrs. Holt smiled. "This one he takes by the spoonful."

"Ugh, you can't be serious." Tessa grimaced at the thought of placing the bitter taste in her mouth.

"Oh, I'm serious right enough. Horseradish brings up the phlegm that's been blocking your da's lungs. Don't know anything that'll get him on his feet quicker."

As if on cue, Tessa's father started coughing so hard he curled up on the edge of the bed. Mrs. Holt held a crock for him to spit in and then helped him sit up.

Tessa dropped to her knees beside her father. She patted his back as firmly as she dared until his coughing abated, and he caught her hand in his.

"I'm better, Tessabear," he rasped. "I'm better." With Tessa's help, he sat up, swinging his feet off the side of the cot.

Tears choked off her attempts to speak, and she knelt with her head on his knee and closed her eyes while he stroked her hair. Sometime during the night he had dressed in a fresh tick cloth nightshirt that smelled of lye and rosewater. At length, when Tessa lifted her head, she found his eyes filled with mist too. Even Mrs. Holt dabbed at her eyes with a hanky and sagged onto a nearby crate. For several minutes the three rested in the cocoon of the shed while the sun rose and filled the air with dancing dust fairies.

TWO WEEKS PASSED with Tessa tending to her father, strolling the countryside, and meeting the few townspeople who dared approach the shy girl and her frail father. Worried about the summer slipping away before they continued their trek toward the Willamette valley, Tessa tried to brooch the subject with her father.

"Not yet, Tessabear," was always his reply before sauntering away.

Not yet. Not yet. Of course not yet. But she couldn't help but worry. The warm summer months were half over. If they didn't leave soon, snow in the mountains that stood between them and the Willamette Valley might trap them. Before coming down sick, Oregon was all her father could talk about. But since her mother and sister died, it seemed his passion for a new life had seeped away with his strength. Always a man who attracted admiring glances from women, her father now seemed very old. Stooped. Drained.

"He's had a long haul of it," Mrs. Holt said, trying to comfort Tessa. "Lost a wife and child along the way . . ."

"I lost them too," Tessa gulped. "My dear mother and Bethany. I feel as if I've lost him also."

"Give him a while to put his grief in its place. Then he'll snap out of it."

"Is there nothing else I can do?"

"Just don't give up on him. Help him find his happiness."

Though Tessa tried to find activities to interest him, he remained close to the shed they now called home, forlorn and distant.

Late one afternoon, Mrs. Holt called Tessa into the kitchen that adjoined her bedroom in the back of the trading post. "We're gathering at Hooper Springs tomorrow for a picnic. Would you and your father like to join us?"

"Who is?" Tessa asked.

"Those of us left in Morristown."

"Why?" Tessa wondered again.

"For the Twenty-Fourth."

"The twenty-fourth what?" This town's traditions were becoming more and more strange to Tessa.

Mrs. Holt chuckled. "The Twenty-Fourth of July. To celebrate the day the Mormons first set eyes on the Great Salt Lake Valley."

At last Tessa recognized one of the places Mrs. Holt mentioned. But Great Salt Lake City must be nearly a week's travel south of Morristown. "Why would you celebrate what the Mormons did in Salt Lake?"

"We used to be Mormons," the woman explained, scrubbing the dirt off a potato. "And most of us made the trek to Great Salt Lake City with them. Celebrating the Twenty-Fourth is as important to us as celebrating the Fourth of July."

"I thought all the Mormons were in Great Salt Lake City?"

"Well . . ." Mrs. Holt was thoughtful for a moment. "Most of the Mormons are in Salt Lake, but many of them have started new settlements in different parts of the West."

"You said you used to be Mormons," Tessa pressed. "Aren't you any more?"

"You're not one to give up, are you?" Mrs. Holt stopped peeling the potato she held, leaving the knife resting under the slender strip of peel, forgotten. She chose her words carefully before continuing.

"Isak—Mr. Holt—and I emigrated to America in '55. We had joined the Church—he in Denmark and me in Scotland—and we were coming to dwell with the Saints." She paused and shook her head softly. "He was traveling alone, and I was a widow. We met onboard ship and were married before we docked in Boston Harbor."

Tessa smiled, thinking of how romantic it must have been to meet, court, and marry at sea.

"We came across the plains with the Mormons in '56," Mrs. Holt continued. "Over time, Isak became friends with a man named Joseph Morris. Brother Morris said he had a vision from God—that he had received revelation of when the Second Coming would occur. Now Brother Morris was a mighty good talker, don't ya know, and before long, he had a good following believing anything he said—including my Isak. They called us the Morrisites. When the First Presidency got wind of Brother Morris's preaching, they threw him out of the Church. He gathered as many as were willing and we all moved up north a piece."

"Goodness," Tessa murmured. She had heard a little about this new religion, but knew nothing about the Mormons except that the man who started the church had claimed he'd seen God. He'd been killed by a mob somewhere in Illinois, and the rest of the Mormons moved west to Utah. "So that's how you came to Morristown?"

"Well, not directly," Mrs. Holt said. "We lived north of Salt Lake City for a while at an army outpost—Kingston Fort—but we ran into some trouble." She paused for a long while, worrying the strip of potato peel with the edge of her knife. "One thing led to another, and when General Connor was assigned to build a fort up here near the soda springs, several of us decided to come along with him. That was more'n two years ago. Things didn't turn out much like we had planned."

"How many of you came up here?"

"There were fifty-three families to begin with. Well over two hundred people, all told."

"Two hundred!" There were no more than twenty cabins clustered in the center of the valley, and Tessa had seen perhaps another ten dotting the outlying areas. She couldn't imagine two hundred people in Morristown. "Where are they all living?"

"Well," Mrs. Holt continued, "two hundred came up to begin with, but we've had two very harsh winters and this is the third summer with too little rain. That first year, we didn't have enough homes built or enough food. We buried nearly seventy souls that first year alone—and many more the next year. Those that survived got discouraged and left from time to time. The farming's just no good up here. Too many folks are feared of starving."

Tessa knew about being afraid of starving. She and her father had come awfully close to it already. She began to understand why her father didn't seem to be in a hurry to resume their journey to Oregon—they had no food and no supplies to carry with them.

"So!" Mrs. Holt began scooping flour into a big bowl. "Tomorrow, we'll all gather at Hooper." She made a hollow in the center of the flour and filled it with water, a chunk of butter, and a generous pinch of salt. "In between eating, there'll be games for the children, quilting for the women, and pitching shoes for the menfolk. Really does make for a lovely day." She wielded two knives and showed Tessa how to cut through the mixture until the dough resembled a bowlful of pea-sized nuggets, which she then turned out to knead. "Will you come?"

Tessa smiled at the thought of spending a day outdoors away from the shed. She might even meet some girls her own age. "Sounds like fun," Tessa conceded. "We'd love to come."

"Speak for yourself," her father growled from the doorway.

Both women jumped at his voice and whirled to face him.

"Father! How long have you been standing there?"

"Long enough."

Tessa recognized the tone of voice that signaled one of his black moods, but she couldn't stop herself from pressing. "Please, Father," she begged. "It will be nice to go on a picnic."

"I said no."

Mrs. Holt's eyes narrowed, and she gripped a hand towel in two fists. "Standing there long enough," she huffed. "Were you standing there long enough to hear the excitement in your daughter's voice at the prospect of meeting some young people?"

Her father's glare could have melted the butter in the pie dough, and Tessa braced herself for his inevitable angry outburst, but Mrs. Holt didn't back down.

"Long enough to see the color rise in her cheeks just to think about a day away from that shed?"

"You're out of line, Mrs. Holt." Anger tinged his deep voice, but still Mrs. Holt stood her ground.

"Mr. Darrow, you leave me to wonder if you've been there long enough to feel the worry this girl's been under, watching you pine away for something you cannae have. It has been long enough. Long enough for you to leave yesterday behind." Mrs. Holt placed her towel on the hook and turned slowly to face the man. Her voice was calmer, but the tension percolated just under the surface. "Tessa's all you have left now. She's here, today. Have you been there long enough see how she needs her da?" With an earnest look, Mrs. Holt stepped past Tessa's father and into her bedroom, sliding the curtain closed behind her.

Tessa's shocked stare returned to her father. She had never heard anyone speak to him that way and was at a loss as to what to do now.

Without even looking at his daughter, Mr. Darrow turned and shuffled down the steps of the trading post and back to the shed, where he disappeared inside without a backward glance.

CHAPTER 6

"Take cover!"

Tessa bolted from her sleep at the sound of her father's yell, instinctively crouching in the hay and covering her head. *What's happened?* Becoming aware of her surroundings, she lifted her head, searching for her father in the dark. She saw his silhouette lying on his cot on the other side of the room. As she scooted to the edge of the hay, preparing to check on him, he leaped from his bed.

He dashed toward the door. "Cinch down that bleeding! You two! Get him to the infirmary!"

Terrified, Tessa huddled in the corner. Her father stopped and looked around, raking his fingers through his hair.

"Father?" she ventured from her corner.

He looked at her briefly and then grumbled, "Go back to sleep," before lying back down on his cot and turning away from her on his side.

Another nightmare? She wrapped her woolen blanket tightly around herself and lay back in the hay, reliving for what seemed like hours the many nights her father had cried out in his sleep. *Is he going mad?* She'd heard of soldiers coming back from war, half out of their minds. "Soldier's heart," neighbors whispered. Was it happening to her father?

When she awoke again a short while later, Tessa knelt on her bed of piled hay to stare out her window, watching as the morning rose shrouded by gray clouds. The slight humid breeze weaving its way through the chinks in the shed encased her in its bone-chilling pall. The creak of the cot signaled her father waking as well. Through the gloom, she watched him hunch on the edge of his cot, clutching his blanket around his shoulders.

"Father?" Tessa asked, still curled up against the morning chill. "Are you all right?"

He didn't raise his head to look at her as he mumbled, "I'm fine."

She sat up, wiggling her bare feet deeper in the hay. "If you're not feeling well—"

"I said I'm fine. Looks like a great day for a picnic."

Tessa recognized the tone in his voice—the tone signaling one of his dark, volatile moods. She knew that he would take exception to whatever she said. If she offered to stay home, he'd bark at her. If she tried to cajole him into a better mood, he'd bark at her. One way or another, Tessa would pick up a scolding. Her mother had learned to steer clear of him when he was like this, but it seemed like Tessa always ended up in the crosshairs. Bethany would hide under the bed when he got in a huff, but Tessa was too big to hide. So, again, Tessa bore the brunt of his anger. He never raised a hand to her, but in her mind, a tongue-lashing cut just as deep.

She kept quiet and still, hoping that wouldn't irritate him further. After a moment, he lay down on the cot again, curled on his side away from her. *Well, so much for the picnic.* If this is how he wanted to spend his day, this is how she would spend her day too. She didn't dare lie down, so she just sat there, trying to not make a sound.

Many minutes passed—perhaps half an hour—before her dad sighed deeply and stood up. "Let's get some breakfast." He wedged his feet into his shoes and headed for the door without waiting for an answer.

Hurriedly jamming on her own shoes, Tessa followed him outside and across the yard to the trading post.

The shed wasn't big enough to put a cookstove in, nor did they have any of their own food yet, so they relied on Mrs. Holt's generosity for every meal. She didn't seem to mind. She always prepared enough for all of them, but Tessa knew it bothered her dad to accept charity. He tried to help out by sweeping the store or fixing a loose leg on a chair, but in his weakened condition, he wasn't strong enough to move big stacks of fur pelts or grain sacks yet.

"Morning, Mrs. Holt," he mumbled without looking up as he shuffled through the door.

"Yep," Mrs. Holt replied without turning from the wooden crate she was packing.

Tessa looked from her dad to Mrs. Holt and back again before realizing that Mrs. Holt was still upset from their exchange the night before. Tessa froze where she was, fully aware that this woman could turn them out of her home just as sure as not.

Instead of the usual bacon and eggs, or sausage and hotcakes, there was a cold pot of oatmeal resting on the back of the stove. Henry scooped up a mound of the congealed mush and plopped it into his bowl and then sat down at the table to eat. Following his lead, Tessa also flicked a ladleful into her bowl. The cold, sticky paste clung to the roof of her mouth, but she didn't dare ask for milk to thin it or honey to sweeten it.

By the time the two had nearly finished their oatmeal, Mrs. Holt had packed a wicker basket in addition to the crate. "Mr. Darrow," she said, "if it's not to much ask—" She corrected herself. "Kindly help me load these in the wagon."

His jaw tightened, but he rose from the table without saying a word. Mrs. Holt was already out the door with the crate, so Henry followed after her carrying the basket.

"Mr. Darrow, I have been more than Christian by taking you in," Mrs. Holt spoke quietly, though tersely, from outside the door, and Tessa had to strain to hear.

"I'll not trouble you much longer," Henry returned.

"Don't try my patience. I'm happy to help you and Tessa, but I'll not cotton to your moods if you're going to stay here.

"I said we'll be moving on."

"Henry, just listen to yourself. You can barely walk from here to the outhouse without leaning on a stick. You know you're not strong enough to travel. And what would you do for supplies? You'll naw be goin' anywhere just yet." Mrs. Holt's voice rose in pitch and volume, and her Scottish accent got thicker with each level of exasperation.

"We've worn out our welcome."

"Not yet, you haven't, but you're gettin' there quick."

"What's your point, Mrs. Holt?"

"My point—the point is—you're a proud man, Henry Darrow. Plain to see accepting charity rubs you the wrong way. Well, I could use some help around here and it's cheaper to offer you room'n board than to hire someone."

"Help?" Tessa's father scoffed. "You just said I'm too weak to be much use to anyone. What kind of help do you think you'd get from me?"

"I know you're still recovering, but you could do some odd jobs while you get stronger. Fall's coming on and we'll be getting more trappers coming through to trade pelts and buy supplies. You could help out in the store and help me get the place buttoned up for winter."

Tessa couldn't quite make out the next few snatches of conversation, but she did hear Mrs. Holt say, "Good. We have an understanding then." The two of them came back inside and Tessa busied herself stirring the last of her porridge.

Mrs. Holt picked up a calico quilt from the counter in the store. "Henry," she said quietly, "I meant what I said. I've had enough unpleasantness to last me two lifetimes. I'll not have you bringing it in with you."

Several seconds passed. Tessa held her breath and her spoon tightly.

"No, ma'am," her father finally said. "Pleasant as you please."

"Tessa," Mrs. Holt ordered, "finish up. The wagon's all loaded."

"Yes, ma'am!" Tessa shoved the last spoonful in her mouth and jumped up from the table.

"Not so fast, miss." Her father put his hand on her shoulder. "First, you'll help me clean up these dishes."

Mrs. Holt smiled and tipped her head in the man's direction.

SITTING BETWEEN MRS. Holt and her father on the wagon, Tessa kept plenty warm under the quilt draped over their legs. She watched the clouds racing overhead, producing barely a breeze at the valley floor, and hoped the sunshine on the horizon would overtake them before they got to the picnic site.

Hooper Springs was only about an hour north of town, and there were already several families gathered there by the time Mrs. Holt's wagon pulled up. Twenty-five or so children raced around playing tag, jumping ropes, and kicking tin cans back and forth between them. A dozen women were scrambling to keep their picnic quilts anchored to the ground with baskets, crates, or rocks. And the men were busy pounding stakes and raking pits for horseshoes. Well away from the crowd, Mr. Pixton and a few other men were setting up the framework for a roasting spit.

The clear spring, an oblong pool of about ten by fourteen feet, was encircled by a rock wall around three-quarters of its circumference and stacked about two feet tall. The spring bubbled and churned like a simmering caldron, but the water splashing from it was cool. Tessa stood at the edge and bent over to peer straight down into its depth. It was very clear and looked as if she could pick up the stones lying at the bottom.

"Watch out," her father teased, bumping into Tessa but holding her arms securely so she wouldn't fall.

"Mr. Darrow," Mrs. Holt scolded, "this i'na the place for tomfoolery."

Tessa laughed. "Oh, don't worry. It's not very deep."

"I beg to differ." Mrs. Holt picked up a flat stone and held it over the roiling spring. "Lookit here." She dropped the stone into the water and the three watched as it slowly sank lower and lower. "See there? It's terribly deep. And cold. We lost six souls to the springs our first year here."

Tessa felt her father's grip tighten on her arm, and he pulled her back from the edge. "Darn shame," he said. "I'm sorry for your loss."

"Darrow!"

Tessa and her father turned toward a group of men gathered at the edge of the meadow. One of the men strode toward them, resting a rifle against each shoulder. "Ed Forsgren," he introduced himself. "We're going to take down some game for dinner. I've got an extra Henry here that could use some breaking in." He held the rifle out, waiting for Tessa's father to take it. "Bet you've never shot a buffalo!"

Her father took a step back, putting up the palm of his hand as if warding off the rifle. "No, sir," he said, "can't say as I have."

"Well, this might be your lucky day, then—more likely we'll just take deer today, though." The man pointed westward to where the hillside sloped up into the trees. "There's a valley on t'other side of the rise. There's usually some pretty good hunting."

Tessa's father eyed the hillside for a moment before slowly shaking his head. "I'm afraid I'd just slow you fellas down. You're best to go on without me this time."

"I don't mind taking my time. We'll go around to the north where it's not so steep." The other man held the rifle out to her father again. "We can guard the flank in case the deer get spooked and run."

Her father shook his head again and opened his mouth to speak when Mrs. Holt nudged him forward.

"It'll be good for ya, Mr. Darrow," she said softly. "Stretch your legs and meet some of the menfolk."

Her father's eyes narrowed as he fixed a dark glare on Mrs. Holt, but the glare she returned was even darker. She folded her arms across her chest and tilted her head toward the other men.

Without moving his head, Mr. Forsgren met Tessa's shocked gaze and raised an eyebrow.

Just that quick, her father shrugged, picked up his walking stick, and took the rifle. He walked past Mr. Forsgren toward the group of men watching from a distance. "Guess I'll be joining you."

As they walked away, the two men's voices carried back to the women. "Not a woman to cross," Mr. Forsgren murmured.

"No, sir," Tessa's father agreed. "That she is not."

⁓✵⁓

FOR A COUPLE of hours, Tessa tried to find things to keep her busy. The few girls that were about her age stayed to themselves mostly, and Tessa couldn't quite summon the courage to break into their little circle.

Instead, she helped Mrs. Pixton peel potatoes for her Dutch ovens and braided several little girls' hair into fanciful shapes. She sat next to Mary Anderson, a pretty woman who wore a handkerchief over the lower portion of her face, and helped stitch even rows on a pieced quilt that Mrs. Anderson had stretched on a wooden frame. Every now and then a gunshot echoed across the valley, causing everyone to glance at the hillside, waiting for the men to come back with their kill.

The sun wasn't yet midway in the sky when a lone rider leading a pack mule ambled his way around the side of Chester Hill into view. One by one, heads began to turn in his direction. Mrs. Holt sat at the quilting frame with her back turned to him, intent on the row she was stitching.

"Maureen," one of the women said, peering southward with her hand shading her eyes. She nudged Mrs. Holt with her elbow. "I say, Maureen, isn't that . . . ?"

Maureen Holt glanced casually over her shoulder, then sprang to her feet with a gasp, tripping over the log she had been sitting on. Scrambling for her footing, she clutched at her skirts with one hand while struggling to an upright position to run to the rider. "William?" she whispered. Tears streamed down her cheeks as she bolted toward him. "William!"

"Mother!" Leaping off his horse, he caught her in both arms and held her tightly.

The other women dropped whatever they were working on and swarmed around the sobbing mother and son. The children in the group stood watching, wide-eyed, and a few of the youngest began to cry with the commotion.

Tessa stepped closer but didn't want to intrude on the reunion. The young man wasn't much older than she was, maybe eighteen or nineteen, and his sun-bleached hair fringed at the collar, looking as if he had cut it himself.

At last, the crowd parted a bit and ushered them to the picnic tables. Tessa stood apart from the rest, trying to hear over the gaggle of women, trying to understand who this young man was. He had arrived in the Great Salt Lake Valley four days ago and learned of the group's exodus to Soda Springs. He had followed the muddy wagon tracks from town north to find the group at Hooper Springs. But who was he? He called Mrs. Holt "mother," but she had never mentioned having a child.

Finally, with the mass of women dispersing and going back to the activities they had abandoned, Mrs. Holt pulled the young man to where Tessa stood.

"Tessa," she said, "this is my son, William." She put her arm around his shoulder and pulled him close. "William, this is Tessa Darrow. She and her da are staying with me while they get set to go to Oregon."

Suddenly feeling self-conscious at being introduced to the young man, Tessa's cheeks begin to burn. "Nice to meet you," Tessa said quietly. There was a weariness—a sadness about him. Tessa pulled her gaze away from his crystal-blue eyes, afraid she was intruding on his private pain . . . afraid he might see hers.

Before he could return the greeting, a great tumult erupted from the edge of the meadow and fifteen boisterous men charged across the clearing carrying what looked like fifty or sixty dead chickens. "Stoke up that fire pit! We've got dinner to cook!"

"What in heaven's name?" one of the women exclaimed.

"It's not venison, but it'll do well enough!"

Mr. Forsgren dragged Henry Darrow to the front of the group. "While we were all out chasing deer, Darrow here sat in the trees and got swarmed by sage hens. Scooped them up, snapped their necks, and tossed 'em in a pile!"

Tessa's father, looking pleased as could be, swiped his hand in the air. "Shoot, I just didn't want to slow you fellas down."

Another man shouted, "Why, we'd be having taters and beans if it weren't for him!"

With the clamor dying down, the men finally noticed William sitting next to Mrs. Holt, and the whooping, cheers, and tears started up again.

Tessa marveled at the change in her father from even just a couple of hours earlier. He had lost the stoop in his posture and no longer shuffled when he walked. And he hadn't brought the familiar walking stick back with him from the woods. For the first time in weeks, he had color in his cheeks. He resembled once more the man who had climbed the peach trees with her back home and played hide and seek with her and Bethany in Grandmother's attic.

Once the hubbub died down, the adults in the group carried the sage hens out to a table near the fire pit to pluck and thread on the spits. Mrs. Holt motioned for Tessa and her father to stay behind with her and William.

"Henry Darrow, I'd like you to meet William Bates, my son."

Bates? Tessa wondered why he would have a different last name than his mother.

"Bates?" Her father voiced Tessa's question.

Mrs. Holt put her arm around William's waist and pulled him closer.

"My sister's son. He's been gone from us for—let's see, more than three years now—fightin' in the war."

With furrowed brow, Henry regarded William for a long moment. He tilted his head down a bit so the brim of his hat cast a shadow over most of his face, but he extended his right hand to shake the hand William offered. "William."

"Mr. Darrow." William was peering just as intently at Tessa's father, as if he were trying to place his name or face, and neither man released his grip for several moments. After a pause, William asked, "Have we met before?"

"No," Tessa's father muttered. "Not likely."

At last, William turned to Mrs. Holt. "Folks in Great Salt Lake City told me some about trouble at Kingston Fort, and that Ma had died. Not much more'n that." He looked off in the distance, a frown pulling at the corners of his mouth. He massaged his forehead just above the bridge of his nose where a furrow of worry lines was beginning to be etched. "I need to hear it from you, Mother. What happened to my ma?"

There it was again. He called Mrs. Holt "mother," but inquired after his "ma." *Does he have two mothers?* Tessa wondered.

"Tessa," her father whispered and motioned with his head that they should step away from this private moment.

Mrs. Holt chewed on her bottom lip, looking at William. "Ah, lad, it's a tale I'd hoped I'd never have to tell."

"I'm sorry. I didn't mean to upset you," he said, taking Mrs. Holt by the elbow and steering her to an empty table. "Have you told Mr. Darrow and Tessa how we arrived in Great Salt Lake City?" Mrs. Holt shook her head. "Maybe you could start there? Work into the trouble when you're ready."

"We shouldn't intrude," Tessa's father said.

"Please—" Mrs. Holt interrupted their retreat. "You're like to hear about it eventually," she said to them. "I'd like you to stay, that is if William doesn't mind."

William helped her climb over the bench. "Don't mind a bit. You take your time." He walked around to the other side of the table and sat down opposite her.

Reluctantly Tessa and Henry sat across from her as well, next to William.

Blowing out a deep breath, she pulled a hanky from where it was tucked in her sleeve at her wrist and then focused her attention on Tessa and her father. "William's ma and pa were in our handcart company in '56 when we—my husband Isak and I— crossed the plains with the Saints to the Great Salt Lake Valley. William was just ten at the time, but strong as they come and cheerful as you please. He got to be good friends with my little boy, Hyrum, who was seven. Both families kept each other company on the trip."

"I didn't know you had a son," Tessa said and then remembered that Mrs. Holt had mentioned she was a widow when she sailed for America.

Mrs. Holt nodded once and hurried on. "We got a real late start to make the crossing, then ran into one sort of trouble after t'other. The Cheyenne attacked several companies ahead of us, so that slowed us down even more. We just got pushed further and further behind schedule. We made it to Wyoming in late October, but the snow came early that year and we were poorly prepared to deal with it.

"We were mighty low on food, and many of the company, including my little Hyrum and William's pa, were suffering with illness. Shortly before we reached Devil's Gate, that's in the Eastern part of Wyoming, William's father passed in his sleep. Three other members of our company passed that very night. Well, that delayed us even longer, but we knew we should all perish if we didn't push on. A week later, we were near out of food, our clothes were ragged, and the snows were midway to our knees. Isak had to help wrangle what stock we had left, so 'twas only William's ma—Elsa—and me to pull the handcarts."

Tessa reflected on the trek she and her family had just made, traversing much of the same route. They had the luxury of traveling in a covered wagon during the spring and early summer, and still two of her family had died. Pulling a handcart through ice and snow—just the thought brought tears to her eyes.

"Hyrum was so weak that he just couldn't walk anymore," Mrs. Holt continued, "but even his little body in the cart made the cart too heavy for me to pull. But William was always there to help me out. He'd run along behind our two carts, pushing on one then the other. I don't know how we would have made any distance without him."

William sat with his hands cupping his head, fingers laced through his hair, his elbows propped on the table. His eyes were shut, but the lines etched in his forehead reflected the painful memories as they were recalled.

"We had to cross the Sweetwater several times over the course of a few days. The river was iced over, but not enough to support people and carts crossing. The ice shattered under our weight and we were forced to drag our carts through water that was sometimes as deep as my waist. All of our belongings were soaked through, and the water was seeping into our carts, making them that much heavier. Isak was busy trying to get everyone across, and then he'd ride ahead looking for the next crossing, so it was up to Elsa and me to manage our own carts. Every time we had to cross the river, William would carry Hyrum like a sack of potatoes slung around his neck. I don't know how the river didn't carry them both away."

Mrs. Holt paused for several moments, carefully smoothing her hanky on the table and then folding it neatly. At last she continued. "After the fourth crossing, when William put Hyrum back in the cart, my boy was dead."

Tessa listened to William softly dragging jagged breaths, and a lump welled in her throat.

"We buried Hyrum on the hillside. Two weeks later, we entered the Great Salt Lake Valley."

Mrs. Holt let out a long sigh and dabbed the corners of her eyes with the hanky.

Before she could continue, one of the other ladies came and stood behind her. "Sister Holt, I'm sorry to interrupt. The chickens are on the spit and Brother Pixton thought you might have brought some seasonings. If you can tell me where to look, I'm happy to fetch 'em."

Mrs. Holt looked toward the crate and basket sitting underneath another table, and shook her head. "I couldn't tell you where to start looking. I'll get up." She looked apologetically at the others, and then she reached over and squeezed William's arms. "Be right back."

William, Tessa, and her father sat in awkward silence while Mrs. Holt rummaged through her stash and carried a few tins out to the fire pit.

William cleared his throat and took up the tale. "Like she said, my pa died on the trail. When we all got to Great Salt Lake City, we rested a few days, and then the men in the company got busy looking for work and finding or building homes for their families. My ma and I stayed in different homes for a few days at a time, but we're not the sort of folk to take advantage. I looked for work too, but with so many men coming into the valley, the jobs went to them instead of a ten-year-old boy." William stopped and shifted on the bench. He softly tapped his fingertips on the table before continuing. "After Brother and Sister Holt got moved into a house, President Young dropped by and called Brother Holt to take my ma to wife."

Tessa gasped. "But he already had a wife!"

"So you were polygamists," Henry stated flatly.

"Yes, Mr. Darrow," William said. "We were polygamists."

Mrs. Holt, who had walked up behind them, came around and sat down on her side of the table. "Please don't say it with so much disdain, Mr. Darrow. Polygamy started out as a noble principle. So many of our men had been killed by the Gentiles in Nauvoo and Ohio and Missouri and anywhere else the Saints have gathered, that the surviving men had to take multiple wives to save the families. Without polygamy, Mr. Darrow, all of those widows and children would have been destitute."

Henry looked her squarely in the eye and planted his index finger firmly on the table between them. "That was twenty, thirty years ago. You're not being persecuted anymore, yet you still practice polygamy. It's a wicked practice and a perversion before God."

Mrs. Holt's slap across Henry's face knocked him sideways into Tessa, and Tessa grabbed the table to avoid toppling into William. Shocked, she waited for the familiar boom of her dad's angry voice. Before he could respond, however, Mrs. Holt attacked.

"The perversion, Mr. Darrow, is that you and people like you presume to stand in judgment of us when you have no idea at all of what we've been through. Good families took suffering widows into their homes, then and now. Look around you! The suffering never stops! Would you turn children out into the wilderness because their father died?" She grabbed the hanky from her sleeve and blew her nose. "Don't you dare talk to me about perversion or offending God, Mr. Darrow. You have no idea—and no right."

With arms folded across his chest, Henry stared at the wood plank table for nearly a full minute before speaking again. He worked his lips, pursing then clamping, then pursing again as though he were chewing on his response. At last he lifted his head briefly, just long enough to acknowledge Mrs. Holt's glare, and then dropped his gaze. "I apologize for causing affront, Mrs. Holt. There's much I don't know about this religion of yours and I had no right to criticize. I hope you'll forgive my rush to judgment."

In her fourteen and a quarter years, Tessa couldn't remember her mother ever standing up to her father as Mrs. Holt just had. And in all those years, she had never, ever heard her father apologize for his cruel words.

"Mother," William broke in softly, "what happened at Kingston Fort?"

Tears brimmed in Mrs. Holt's eyes as she studied her adopted son. "Ahh, William," she sighed. "So much has happened since you've been gone." She turned her sad gaze back to Tessa and her dad. "I've told you about Joseph Morris's vision, and my husband's determination to follow him. When my husband moved our family out of Great Salt Lake City to

Kingston Fort to be with the rest of the believers, William here decided to follow President Lincoln's call for troops to fight in the war."

"You're a Yankee," Tessa gasped. The disdain for northern soldiers rose like bile in her throat. Though her parents had never spoken ill of them, even after they burned the plantation, her neighbors spoke with such vehemence that Tessa was naturally swayed.

William looked at her, then her father, then back at Tessa again. His face appeared calm, but Tessa recognized the sadness in his gaze. "I'm an American, Miss Darrow. I served at the will of our president."

"Indeed," her father said, not lifting his gaze from the table.

Tessa wondered how her father could sit so calmly next to a Yankee, but she didn't dare voice her opinion. Nevertheless, she scooted a bit farther away from William.

Mrs. Holt resumed. "We moved to the fort, and William's squad went back East."

"Tennessee," William said.

"Tennessee!" Tessa exclaimed. "That's where—"

Henry gripped her leg sharply under the table and shot her a warning glance. Tessa fell silent, and he removed his hand.

"You never wrote," Mrs. Holt whispered. "So much has happened, but I didn't know how to find you."

William reached across the table and covered her hands with his. "I couldn't. You know how things were between Brother Holt and me. I hope you'll forgive me, but I just couldn't."

Mrs. Holt swiped a tear from her cheek. "I know." She twisted her hanky so tightly that it curled into a knot. "Sarah didn't go to Kingston Fort with us either. She moved back home with her parents."

William just looked down at the table and nodded.

Who is Sarah? Tessa wondered, but this seemed like such a personal conversation she didn't want to intrude. From the cock of his eyebrow, she knew her father was wondering the same thing, but neither gave voice to the question.

"Your mother—" Mrs. Holt began but then stopped. She let out a big sigh and looked off in the distance. "After Brother Morris announced the date of the Second Coming several times, and those dates all came and went, many of the followers became disillusioned. They began taking what they had contributed from the storehouse and leaving the fort. Do you remember Louis Gurtson?"

William nodded.

"He and a couple of others tried to take their share one day. Let's see . . . it would have been May of '62 . . . but when they tried to leave, Morris wouldn't give them as much as they had brought in. So when Brother Gurtson and the others left, they made off with a wagonload of wheat headed for milling. Morris sent his thugs after them, and all three were brought back and locked in a cabin."

"Locked up?" William blurted.

"I'm not condoning anyone's actions," Mrs. Holt said. "But without that wheat, we would have been in a sorry state for the winter."

' "So what happened?"

"Brother Gurtson managed to escape, but his friends weren't so lucky. He made it to the valley and brought Marshall Stoddard back to the fort. They brought some of the Mormon militia with them."

Tessa's father and William's heads snapped up. Startled, Tessa caught her breath.

Mrs. Holt paused a moment, drawing in a deep breath before continuing. "Morris gathered us together in the bowery. He was recalling a revelation he said he'd just had when, suddenly, a cannonball ripped through the wall."

Tessa had secretly watched from a distant hillside in North Carolina one of the many battles near her home. With sickening clarity, she recalled the sight of bodies propelled in the air when a cannonball struck in the middle of a group of soldiers on the field. She squeezed her eyes shut, willing the memory to fade. In the silence that engulfed them now, Tessa heard a fly buzzing nearby and then William's strangled whisper.

"My mother?"

"We were huddled together, terrified of what might happen if Morris didn't back down. The cannonball"—Mrs. Holt choked back her tears— "exploded right behind us. A shard of wood caught your mother in the back." She buried her face in her hands, trying to speak between her sobs. "I tried to stop the bleeding, William. I promise I did. She was just gone . . . so quickly."

William moved around to Mrs. Holt's side of the table and wrapped his arms around her, cradling her head against his shoulder. As sobs racked through his stepmother, William stared off in the distance, silent tears sliding down his cheeks.

Several minutes passed before Mrs. Holt's anguish quieted. Tessa stared uncomfortably at her hands folded in her lap, uncertain whether she should offer some words of comfort or make a polite retreat. At last, Mrs. Holt brushed the tears from her and then William's cheeks.

"I'm so sorry, William. I hope one day you'll forgive me."

William held her away from him and looked intently in her eyes, a puzzled expression in his. He wiped a tear from her chin with the back of his palm. "There's nothing to forgive."

"It's my fault she was there," Mrs. Holt whispered. "She didn't want to go to Kingston Fort anymore than Sarah did. Anymore than I did. But when Sarah left, I begged your ma to come with us. I didn't want to be alone with Isak again. I couldn't bear to think of her leaving us. If I had let her stay in the valley—" She bit her lower lip and her chin quivered. "If I hadn't been so selfish . . . she'd still be alive."

"Nonsense," William said. "If anyone needs forgiving, it's me. If I hadn't left, the three of us could have stayed in Great Salt Lake City and Isak could have moved on by himself."

Mrs. Holt huffed a humorless laugh. "You know he wouldn't have let us stay behind. If you hadn't left, he would have forced you to go to the fort with us and you'd just as likely be lying next to your ma in the grave."

As if suddenly remembering they were not alone, Mrs. Holt looked across to Tessa and her father.

"Oh, heavens. I'm sorry. I shouldn't have gone on like that."

"No," Henry said. "My apologies. We shouldn't have stayed." He swung one leg over the wooden bench and started to stand up, pulling Tessa with him.

William reached across the table and put a restraining hand on the man's arm. "No need to leave," he said. He nodded across the meadow to where the sage hens were browning over the spit. "It smells like supper's just about ready. Stay and eat with us."

Tessa stared up at her father, willing him to sit back down.

Her father looked awkwardly at Mrs. Holt, who nodded for him to take his seat. "No family secrets here, Mr. Darrow. Tragedy strikes us all, I s'pose."

William motioned for him to sit back down before asking Mrs. Holt to return to the story. "What happened to the rest of the followers?"

"You know Morris wouldn't back down after that," Mrs. Holt said. "There was a gunfight that lasted two days. Brother Morris died in the attack. In all, eleven souls were lost. Mary Christofferson's jaw was shot clean off, but she survived. In fact, that's her right over there." Mrs. Holt nodded to the woman sitting at the quilting stand wearing the handkerchief over her face. "She and Neils Anderson were married not long after we came up here. They have a beautiful baby boy now—"

"Mother," William interrupted, bring her back to topic. "What happened after the attack?"

"Yes, well, after that, the militia left us to bury our dead."

"And Brother Holt?"

Tessa realized that neither she nor her father had ever asked about Mrs. Holt's husband.

"Was he killed at the fort too?" William's voice sounded almost . . . hopeful.

Mrs. Holt's brow wrinkled and she looked rather startled for just a moment. "No. He was in the bowery with us. His ankle was crushed under a log, but he wasn't killed."

William looked around as if he expected Isak Holt to come forth from one of the shadows.

"General Connors was dispatched to build a fort up here," Mrs. Holt continued. "After the siege, we didn't dare stay so close to Great Salt Lake City, so Connors suggested that the soda springs might be a good place for Morris's followers to settle. Our numbers had dwindled to about two hundred by then. Isak said this was our only chance to start fresh, so we packed up again. Connors's troops escorted us up here early in '63. We carried Isak the whole way on a wagon bed."

William's eyes hooded over. The sweep of his jaw hardened, but Tessa couldn't tell if it was disgust or anger she saw reflected there.

"If his leg was crushed so bad," William asked through tight lips, "how did he expect to earn a living up here? Live on others' charity?"

Mrs. Holt shook her head. "I had experience running a bakery in Edinburgh, so when Isak saw how many trappers were coming through the area, he was determined to open a trading post. His ankle never did set proper, so he spent what little money we had and traded most of our furnishings for men to build the shop for us."

William tensed and began scanning the area again. He asked through clenched teeth, "Is he here?"

Tessa and her father also looked around, half expecting Mrs. Holt's husband to appear.

"Isak died that first spring." She looked pointedly at Tessa's father. "Smallpox."

Tessa covered her gasp with her hand, and her father flinched. Both softly offered their condolences, but William said nothing.

CHAPTER 7

After lunching on crispy sage hens, Tessa, her father, Mrs. Holt, and William strolled along the banks of Soda Creek that wound past the spring.

"Mrs. Holt, was it your spices that made the grouse so delicious?" Henry Darrow asked.

"Mmmm," Tessa agreed. "They tasted like Thanksgiving turkey."

Smiling, Mrs. Holt nodded. "The right flavorings can make good eating out of just about anything." She carried a basket into which they placed watercress picked from the water's edge. Where aspen grew in thick clumps, the foursome hunted in the shadows for wild mushrooms nestled among the moss and scrub.

"This'll make a lovely supper," Mrs. Holt declared, holding up the basket of greens and mushrooms. "Tessa, have you ever made biscuits?"

Tessa recalled the mixture of flour and water that she had baked on hot rocks rimming a buffalo-dung fire during their journey across the plains. With a shudder, she nodded her head. "They were more like hardened lumps of clay than biscuits, though. And they always tasted like the fire they were cooked in." She grimaced. "Like buffalo droppings."

"Mercy! No wonder you were such a skinny thing when you first came in. Well then, I'll be teachin' ya to make proper biscuits to go along with the salad and mushroom soup."

"Mother is the best cook west of the—well, west of anywhere, I reckon," William bragged.

"Don't you let Tildy Pixton hear you say that," Mrs. Holt scolded.

Tessa's father smiled. "I believe William here speaks the truth."

"I should be pleased to have you teach me." Tessa laughed, giving a short curtsy.

"Done." Mrs. Holt handed the basket of greens to Henry, and then she hooked her arms through Tessa and William's, leading them toward Hooper Springs.

Back at the picnic area, with Mrs. Holt and William immersed in conversation, and her father snoozing in the grass under a cedar, Tessa wandered to the horseshoes pit. She looked around to be sure no one was watching, then picked up a horseshoe and awkwardly tossed it toward the stake about forty feet away. As she released her grip, the shoe caught on the tip of her thumb, breaking her nail, and landed about eight feet away. Undeterred she tried again and again, each time tossing it farther, but never in a straight line.

"Hold it closer to your fingertips," William said from close behind her, while she was in mid-swing.

Startled, she held her grip for too long and pitched the shoe nearly straight up in the air, ducking as it landed two feet in front of her.

William gasped but didn't laugh.

"How long have you been standing there?" Tessa demanded.

"Not long." A grin pulled at the corners of his mouth and then he shrugged. "Long enough." His grin broke free and dimpled creases streaked down his cheeks.

Despite her embarrassment, Tessa burst out laughing as well. "I'm pretty bad at this."

"No—well—yes, you are," he agreed. "Have you ever played horseshoes before?" He bent down and picked up the errant shoe, along with the other three she had been practicing with.

She shook her head. "Never."

"Well, then, let's have another go." He led her forward to halfway between the stakes and placed the horseshoe in her hand. "Hold it like this." He turned the shoe ninety degrees, rested it midway between her middle knuckles and fingertips, and then curved her hand around so her thumb could maintain the balance. Standing next to her, he showed her how to raise the horseshoe, keeping her arm straight to "site in" the stake, and how to then bend her knees, let her arm swing down and back up, and take a step forward as she released her grip.

With steadfast concentration, Tessa mimicked his technique. Her shoe came closer to the stake each time she pitched it, and William had her stand farther away with each throw. Growing up without brothers, Tessa had always been uncomfortable around boys. And she had no desire to giggle and flirt the way girls her age did back home. But with

William, her awkwardness was quickly forgotten. Tessa tried her best to throw the horseshoes correctly—not because she wanted to impress him, but because she wanted to be a worthwhile opponent. He was extremely patient with her initial clumsy attempts and seemed genuinely keen to teach her. With a mighty swing, she released another shoe and watched it sail the full distance to the opposite stake. It landed with a resounding clang as its heel came to rest against the metal goal, its toes buried deep in the soft earth.

"Very nice, lass," Mrs. Holt called.

Tessa looked up to see Mrs. Holt and her father approaching.

"William taught me how to pitch horseshoes," Tessa said.

"Care to give it a go?" William held two of the shoes out to his mother.

"Och, no," Mrs. Holt said. "Mr. Darrow, you play with them. I'll sit here and watch."

After a moment's hesitation, he accepted the challenge and took the horseshoes from William. Tessa showed him how to hold and pitch the shoe, just as William had taught her, and after a few practice tosses, they were ready to begin.

"That doesn't look like a fair matchup," a young man called. A little girl rode on his shoulders, and he held her steady with one hand. A young woman walked beside him, carrying a baby wrapped in a blanket.

"Jens?" William held his hand poised in front of his forehead to shield his eyes from the sun. "Jens Larsen?"

The man lifted the little girl off his shoulders before rushing forward to embrace the soldier returned. "It's so good to see you, William. So good to see you." He pulled the woman in close, circling his free arm about her waist. "You remember Anna Christensen—Larsen now."

"Your wife? You're married?" William shook the woman's hand. "Congratulations. Really. And two children! Well, that's just grand."

"Thank you, William," Anna said.

William leaned over and opened the blanket to peek at the baby. "A boy?"

"Yes," Jens replied. "Christian. And this," he said, swooping the little blonde girl into the air, "is Gracie."

"Christian and Gracie," William repeated. "That's just great."

"So, horseshoes." Jens took the two shoes William held. "Do you need a fourth?"

"You bet." Henry stepped forward, holding out his hand. "Henry and Tessa Darrow. But Tessa here might give you a run for your money."

"How do you do?" Tessa murmured.

"Oh! You're the folks that came in on the Fourth," Anna exclaimed. "I'm sorry I haven't been over to meet you before now. This is my first day out after confinement."

Mrs. Holt joined the group and explained to Tessa, "Sister Larsen just had a baby a month ago."

Tessa smiled. "Yes, I know what confinement means. Women have babies in North Carolina too."

"Och! What was I thinking? Of course they do!" Mrs. Holt laughed and took the little girl, Gracie, from her father. "Jens, you go play with them. Anna, you come sit over here with me."

"Tessa has me a little worried about losing to her," Jens teased. "Why don't she and I be on one team, and William and Henry, you be on the other?"

"As you say," William agreed. And so, for the next hour, they pitched horseshoes with one person from each team standing on either end of the makeshift court. Jens and Henry on one side, William and Tessa on the other.

Dark clouds once again rolled in from the south and the wind picked up with great gusts. The townspeople set about gathering their belongings, hoping to make it home before the rains began. Tessa and her father stood apart from the rest of the townsfolk, carefully stacking horseshoes in a crate. "Tessa, I need you to make me a promise." Henry Darrow put a horseshoe down and turned to look at his daughter.

"Of course, Father. What is it?"

"I don't want you talking to these folks about me serving in the war."

"All right," she answered. "But why?" She knew he had only served because the neighboring plantation owners had pressured him into it, but her mother had taken such pride in his advancement that discussion of his service was commonplace among neighbor gatherings.

Henry let out a tired sigh. "For once, could you please just do as I ask?"

"Of course, Father." She looked at him squatting next to the crate. His back was rounded, and for the first time, Tessa saw a few strands of silver threaded through his light brown hair. It startled her to think of her father aging. Until recently, she had never considered her father's age—but since taking ill, he seemed so much older, and tired. She knew only too well the danger of pursuing answers when he was tired, but the questions racing through her mind won out over common sense. "Is it because he's a Yank?"

"Who?"

"William Bates," she said, "Mrs. Holt's son or stepson—or whatever he is."

"No, of course not."

Henry Darrow picked up another horseshoe but then stopped and looked intently at his daughter. She braced herself for a tongue-lashing, but he just continued gazing at her. It unnerved her a bit, having him stare at her that way—as if this was the first time in a long while that he had really seen her. At length, he took her hand in his and they sat down side by side, facing away from the others.

"Tessa, you're growing up. You're becoming a fine young woman, and I'm very proud of you."

A twist of trepidation snaked its way through her gut at his show of tenderness.

A long moment passed before he continued. "There are things that happen in wartime that are hard to make sense of, even to us in the middle of it."

"Did something happen to you?" She remembered the evening he came home unexpectedly from the fighting. He slipped quietly in the kitchen door, not triumphantly through the front portico. He seemed so upset—worried—but not injured. And then discovering him in the middle of the night, burning his uniform . . . "Father, tell me what happened."

He withdrew his hand from hers and studied the callous forming on his finger where it had gripped the horseshoe. He looked off in the distance, avoiding her gaze.

"Father."

He took a deep breath and blew it out slowly. "It wasn't the Union army that burned our house—it was the Confederates."

"What?" *It can't be.* "Why would they . . . ?"

"We had a disagreement."

In an instant, Tessa recalled the evening they returned from taking Grandmother to Yorkville, the acrid smell as they approached their drive, the terror of seeing the smoldering ruins of their home. And Tessa remembered her mother's anguish as she picked through what was left of their belongings scattered about the yard.

"A disagreement!" Aghast at his oversimplification, she felt the tone of her voice rising but was powerless to contain it. "What kind of disagreement? They burnt our home!"

"Tess," he interjected. "Keep your voice down."

"I most certainly will not!" Tessa was startled to hear her grandmother's voice leap out of her mouth and would have laughed in any other situation. "They burnt our home!"

Her father's voice was uncharacteristically calm—patient. "War makes men do horrible things, no matter which side they're fighting on."

"What did you do?" she accused. She felt tears of frustration threatening. Lowering her voice, she gritted her teeth to keep it under control. "Is that why you made us leave in such a hurry? Tell me what happened."

"I've told you. We had a disagreement."

She folded her arms and glared at him. "They burnt our home over a disagreement."

"All you need to know is that the Rebels committed just as many terrible acts as the Yanks did. Hating either side will not change that."

"But they—"

"You know what you need to know," he said, not bothering to look at her. "Now we'll speak of it no more."

Dumbfounded, Tessa watched her father return to the horseshoe pit, grab hold of the stake pounded firmly in the ground, and start wiggling it from side to side to loosen it. So many questions swirled in her mind, but she knew from past experience that this wasn't the time to ask them.

Watching him, she silently fumed. *He did something to make the whole army mad enough to burn our home. And now he doesn't want to talk about it? Well, he won't have to worry about that.* For the umpteenth time since her father came home from his service in the war, Tessa determined she would never speak to him again.

With the horseshoes stowed, Tessa begrudgingly helped her father lug the horseshoe crate back to a waiting wagon. With one hand holding up her side of the crate, Tessa clutched the ties of her borrowed bonnet to keep the rushing wind from snatching it from her head. Errant strands of hair whipped about her eyes and mouth, but she didn't have another hand free to hold her wild hair in place.

Grateful that the wind precluded any conversation between them, she silently fumed at how his "disagreement" had destroyed their family. She grunted as they swung the heavy crate up into one of the wagons, and then Tessa turned and stalked off without a backward glance.

"Tessa!" Henry shouted. "Don't wander off. Help us get loaded up."

She ignored him and flounced to a wagon where several girls about her age were helping to arrange crates of picnic supplies. The girls looked at her and then at one another. "Are you lost?" one of the girls scoffed. The rest of the girls snickered while pretending to adjust baskets.

Forget it. Tessa turned without speaking and strode to another wagon.

She found Anna Larsen trying to sooth her baby while little Gracie screamed and clawed at her mother, trying to climb on her lap where the baby fussed. Tessa didn't have much experience with children other than Bethany, but she had to look busy—to save face with the other girls and to avoid helping her father pack up.

"Hey, there," she cooed, tickling the little girl under her chin. "This is some pretty silly wind, isn't it?" She waved her arms over her head as though the wind were pitching her to and fro. Gracie stared at her for a moment, nestling closer to her mother, but stopped crying. "I'm Tessa. Would you like to play?"

"I would be ever so grateful," the child's mother said. "Gracie, would you like to play with Tessa?" She motioned to Tessa to join them on the seat of the wagon. She pointed several yards away where her husband was just finishing loading another wagon. "Jens will not leave until the last wagon is loaded." She pulled the blanket up tighter around the baby. "All this wind will give Christian colic."

Tessa held Gracie on her lap, hugging her closer as the wind grew even more fierce and thunder rumbled in the distance. For the next fifteen or twenty minutes, Tessa and Anna sang children's songs and chanted rhymes to keep the little girl entertained, almost shouting to be heard above the wind. All the while, the sky grew dark with thickening clouds and the fury of the storm closed in around them.

Lightning jumped between the clouds, setting the veiled sky aglow, as the party raced to get wagons loaded. Wind whipped tarps from their moorings, but rain had not yet begun to fall. The women had spent much of the afternoon gathering discarded sage hen feathers and rolling them up inside of quilts to transport home. But now, those fattened quilts took up valuable space in the wagons, making it difficult to find room for crates, picnic baskets, and children. As each wagon was secured, the driver made a mad dash for the safety of home.

At last, there were only two wagons left—the Larsens' and Mrs. Holt's—and William with his horse and pack mule. Tessa now sat in the back of the Larsens' wagon trying to keep Gracie happy while the baby slept in Mrs. Larsen's arms. Tessa showed Gracie how to sit sideways in the wagon. She turned her face into the wind with her mouth open until the whipping vortex made it difficult to breathe and then quickly turned the other way. They made a contest of seeing who could withstand the current the longest. Tessa could face the wind longer, and Gracie would erupt with laughter when Tessa turned her head away and the wind whipped her long hair in every direction.

Henry, Mrs. Holt, William, and Jens Larsen struggled with Mrs. Holt's wagon about thirty feet away. Without a tarp, they had been trying to tie her patchwork quilt in place to protect the contents of the wagon. But every time they got one corner secured, the wind would whip underneath and the rope ripped through a different section of the quilt.

"Brother Larsen!" Tessa heard Mrs. Holt called over the wind. "We can finish this. Get your family out of this weather."

As she spoke, the first fat raindrops began to splash.

"No," Jens called back, "we're nearly finished. We will leave together."

"Jens! Please," his wife called.

"You go," William directed. "We'll be right behind you."

"All right, then. You hurry—and drive safe!" Jens shouted, breaking into a run.

Seeing Mr. Larsen dashing toward them, Tessa settled Gracie in the wagon bed and raced for Mrs. Holt's wagon. As she passed Jens, the hairs on her arms and back of her neck prickled just as a brilliant light and explosive clap flung her in the air.

IN THE DISTANCE, Tessa heard a young girl's voice singing, "Tessa. Tessa. Tessa." Plumes of red and yellow fireworks billowed in the blackness around her as she listened to Bethany's little voice singing her name. "Tessa, Tessa." It was too dark to see her sister. "Tessa." But Bethany was dead. Tessa realized she must be dreaming. "Tessa." The sing-song voice grew in pitch, changing to a wail. She became aware of many more voices, calling, screaming, crying. She told herself to wake up, but her mind fought back to stay in this cocoon.

"Tessa!" Her dad's voice was yelling at her now. "Open your eyes!" Obediently, she struggled to pry them open. She first became aware of the sound of the rain pounding around her, and then the sting as it slapped against her face and bare thigh—then the pain throbbing down her knee and ankle, searing through her foot. "Tessabear, please." She heard the anguish in her father's voice. "Please wake up."

Finally her eyelids fluttered open and her dad's crushing embrace nearly knocked the wind out of her. Like a limp doll, she lay with her head pressed to her dad's chest, listening to his heart pounding in her ear. Her arms and legs felt too heavy to move.

"Thank you, thank you," he whispered over and over, rocking while he cradled her.

Tessa's tongue felt too thick in her throat to respond, and she realized he was offering thanks to God rather than to her. She had never heard her father pray aloud before, and she found comfort in hearing his gratitude expressed for her salvation.

"Henry, let me take a look at her leg."

Tessa heard Mrs. Holt's voice but didn't have the strength to turn and look at her, let alone speak.

"Scorched clear up to her knee. Doesn't look like it's broken, though."

Tessa wanted to cry out with the pain Mrs. Holt's prodding evoked, but no sound passed her lips, and she was powerless to pull away.

"William!" Mrs. Holt shouted. "Bring some water this way."

"That fellow, Larsen?" Tessa heard her father ask. "How bad . . ."

In her peripheral vision, Tessa saw Mrs. Holt shake her head back and forth.

Tessa squeezed her eyes shut, unsure if it was a tear or a raindrop that slipped down her cheek.

IN TWO DAYS' time, a solemn procession followed the wagon carrying Jens Larsen's body to the cemetery just north of town. The people of Morristown gathered together on a knoll to lay him to rest. The cemetery was dotted with various headstones marking the resting places of residents and travelers who had passed beyond the veil.

With her leg bandaged with gauze, Tessa eased herself out of the wagon that had carried her up the hill. While the group was assembling and setting up the gravesite, she limped among the headstones reading names, birth and death dates, and sometimes a sentence about their lives or deaths. She rested her weight on a crutch that her father had fashioned from two branches laced together at the bottom, with smaller pieces of a branch wedged across the midpoint and top to force the wood into somewhat of a "Y" shape. He had wrapped several layers of fabric around the handgrip and the portion tucked under her underarm to cushion the crude device.

Reading the names and dates on the markers, she noticed how many babies and children were buried here. Once in a while she saw several headstones clustered in a family group. Henry Darrow walked alongside his daughter. Touched at how attentive he was being, she still keenly felt a barrier between them. The knowledge that he had done something to cause the army to burn their family home to the ground was more than she could easily forgive. Memories of the many times he had angrily lashed out consumed her—of the many times she had been left to comfort her terrified little sister. *You've destroyed our family with your temper.*

Each time she tried to remind herself that he was all she had left now, the thought returned. *You've brought this upon us. You've destroyed our family.*

At the northern edge of the cemetery, four big rocks marked the corners of a large square grave. "The Wagon Box Grave," Tessa read at the top of a small headstone that identified a mother, father, and five children.

"Tess," her father said softly from behind her. "What we talked about the other day—God willing, I hope someday you'll forgive me. Until that day comes, I'll do my best to do right by you."

Tessa heard him sniff but didn't speak or look at him.

"You're all I have left," he whispered.

The vise around her heart clenched and she feared she would choke on the lump in her throat—but her pride won out. He had caused too much harm to be forgiven.

Mrs. Holt gently cupped Tessa's elbow with her steadying hand while the young woman made her way across the meadow on her crutches.

"What is the large grave back there?" Tessa asked. "The one called the Wagon Box Grave?"

"That was there when we first arrived," Mrs. Holt said. "Trappers told us about a family of immigrants separated from the company they traveled with. They were slaughtered in an Indian attack, God rest 'em. Trappers found 'em, and were able to find their wagon company a few miles on. With no time to make proper coffins, the family was laid out in their wagon box and the whole box buried."

"That's horrid," Tessa replied.

"Indeed." Mrs. Holt stopped Tessa and walked around to face her squarely. "Tessa, I don't know what, but I know something happened between you and your da at the picnic. This is a harsh land. People go through a lot of heartache out here. You've already gone through your share. Whatever was said, you need to forgive him. There's too much hurt to heap it on each other."

"This is too big," Tessa said. "He can't be forgiven this time."

"Oh, my lass," Mrs. Holt sighed. "Nothin' is as big as that. My sainted mother used to tell me, 'He that cannot forgive others breaks the bridge over which he himself must pass.' You need to forgive him." She turned and led Tessa back toward the assembled group.

"Come, come, ye saints, no toil nor labor fear;
But with joy, wend your way.
Though hard to you this journey may appear,
Grace shall be as your day."

As the service began, Tessa listened intently to the words of the song she had heard Mrs. Holt so often hum. The words seemed at odds with each other from stanza to stanza, one phrase talking of hardships followed by a phrase of joy; one of mourning followed by one of hope. Interspersed were challenges to remain faithful and praise God. At the end of each refrain, "All is well! All is well!"

Your people die all around you, yet you sing all is well? She shook her head. *Such an odd song to sing at the grave site of a young man who was snatched away from his wife and children.* The music also seemed incongruous—a mournful tune sung with enthusiasm.

"And should we die before our journey's through,
Happy day! All is Well!
We then are free from toil and sorrow, too;
With the just we shall dwell."

This is what Pastor Tranter was talking about in Sunday School. She recalled how he had drawn a house with a big porch on a chalkboard. The porch represented the love that God has for each of his children from before they are born. As they try to live good lives and grow to love God, they step through the door until at last they are taken into His house to live in His grace. As she pondered the words of the song and equated them with the church lessons she had learned back home, she came to understand the encouragement and hope that this song represented. Love God, do your best, and all will be well. *It sounds so simple.* She looked around at this gathering of people who had been through so many trials. How could it sound so simple and feel so hard?

As a gentleman who Tessa didn't know began to speak, little Gracie began to fidget. When she saw Tessa sitting under a cedar, Gracie broke away and ran to sit next to her new friend. Tessa was only too happy to keep her busy by braiding long grasses and fashioning the woven strands into a bracelet and a ring to adorn Gracie's chubby hand.

Tessa couldn't help but smile inwardly when she realized William was watching her play with Gracie. She was a bit surprised—and a lot embarrassed—to feel her cheeks erupt with a hot blush. When the short service came to an end, Mr. Pixton said a prayer to dedicate the grave.

The mourners trickled away, and Tessa looked around to find her father. He stood at the edge of the grave helping several men lower the cedar coffin, suspended on ropes, into the pit. As the ropes were removed, Henry Darrow held his hat to his chest and began to sing in his rich baritone voice.

"God be with you till we meet again;
By his counsels' guide, uphold you,
With his grace securely fold you;
God be with you till we meet again."

How many times had she and her mother sang that song at home, during funeral services for neighbor soldiers who returned from war in a box? The now-familiar lump in her throat returned as she listened to her father pay homage to this young man. One by one, voices joined with her father's until, by the last refrain, the air was filled with strains of a song familiar to all.

"God be with you till we meet again;
Keep love's banner floating o'er you,
Smite death's threatening wave before you;
God be with you till we meet again.
Till we meet, till we meet,
Till we meet at Jesus' feet'
Till we meet, till we meet,
God be with you till we meet again."

CHAPTER 8

Tessa maneuvered a five-foot-long log so she could sit on it with her back against the poles of the abandoned Connor Fort. From her perch overlooking the Morristown settlement, she gazed out over the cabins scattered about Soda Creek. Foothills, dotted with golden aspen, rose on all sides of the valley. The changing colors portended the approaching fall. She arranged two pieces of dark blue calico on her lap, then she unwound an arm's length of thread from the wooden spool and snapped it off with her teeth. Retrieving a needle from the pin poppet in Mrs. Holt's sewing basket, she pounced it in and out of a little cotton sack filled with sand before carefully aiming the thread through the eye of the needle.

Tessa reflected on the collection of pincushions her mother and grandmother had kept on the mantle in the parlor back home in North Carolina. The tomato-shaped cushion held the fine needles for sewing delicate fabrics for lingerie and blouses. The cushion shaped like a nest, topped with a ceramic bluebird, held the embroidery needles. Quilting needles pierced a tuffet-shaped cushion, while one made of canvas, shaped and embroidered like a bee skep, secured the blunt needles used for needlepoint.

Tessa remembered well her first needlework project—an alphabet sampler worked on canvas as she learned to recognize and sound out each letter. Though her technique had improved greatly over the years, Tessa had kept her first sampler hanging above her bed. With a pang, she realized her sampler had likely burned up in the house with the rest of their belongings.

Sighing, she picked up the cotton fabric Mrs. Holt had given her. She folded it lengthwise so that the patterned sides faced together. Starting at one corner, she stitched the tiniest backstitches she could manage so her seams would be nice and tight. She looked forward to having a blouse and skirt of her own, fitted to her measurements, instead of Mrs. Holt's hand-me-downs, sashed at the waist to disguise how large they were on her. Though appreciative to have clothes to wear since hers were destroyed when they arrived here, she was eager to wear something more suited to a young woman.

She remembered the many nights she had sat on a footstool in front of the fire at home, embroidering hankies or darning socks. Her father sat at the table near the lamplight or lay on his belly beside her, crafting tiny pieces of furniture. Enchanted by the tiny creations, she couldn't have been happier than coming downstairs the Christmas morning when she was eight to find a dollhouse under the tree. It looked just like their home, filled with the miniature furniture he had been working on.

After working all day in the fields, he seemed so happy to fuss with the doll furniture every night. For months after that Christmas, he continued making accessories or new furniture for the dollhouse.

Oh, how her grandmother would scold him for working until his eyes hurt. *That's when he seemed to get the most angry. When his eyes hurt.* So often he would take to his bed for days, lying in the dark with a vinegar-soaked rag covering his forehead. "Shhh, Tessa, Father's eyes hurt," her mother would say. "Tessa, take Bethany to play in the orchard. Your father has a headache." After his pain eased, his mood would turn dark and his temper flared easily.

Could it be his headaches that make him so quick to anger? Tessa inspected her progress on the seam she sewed. *I wonder if he'd tell me if I asked?* She shook her head. *Unlikely.* He wasn't one for explaining much. And if she asked him about his headaches, he'd like as not just blow up again.

Setting the needlework aside, she leaned back and rested her head against the posts of the fence surrounding the fort. She massaged her brows and temples, yawning in the sunshine of late summer, enjoying the solitude. She stretched her legs out in front of her, grimacing as the gauze bandaging her left leg pulled against the tender skin forming where the lightning had scorched her shin and ankle. Thanks to Mrs. Holt's salve that Tessa applied each night and morning, she was walking without her crutch now, but it would likely take several weeks before her leg would look normal again.

For the two weeks since the picnic at Hooper Springs, Anna Larsen and her two children had lived in the trading post with Mrs. Holt. Anna said she couldn't bear to live in their home without Jens, so she had been sharing Mrs. Holt's bed. Gracie slept on a quilt at the foot of the bed, and baby Christian slept in a drawer placed on the floor. Hooper Springs was an hour north of Morristown, and the Larsen home was at least two hours north of there. *It's no wonder she doesn't want to go home alone.*

It made sense for her to stay with Mrs. Holt, but since they had come, this was the first quiet moment Tessa had had to herself. Gracie followed Tessa everywhere, and if she tried to do something without the toddler, Gracie would erupt in tears. When Gracie wasn't crying, Christian was—or Anna. Tessa couldn't blame the woman—she had just lost her husband. Tessa wondered if one of the men in Morristown would have to take Anna as his second or third wife, as Mr. Holt had taken William's mother. *I couldn't do it*, she thought. *I couldn't share my husband and my home with another woman.* And while Anna and her children stayed in the trading post, and Tessa and her dad stayed in the hay shed, William slept outside under a tarp slung from two cedars.

Tessa felt guilty for occupying the shed, leaving Mrs. Holt's son to sleep outside. *Why wouldn't Mr. Holt have built a room for William to stay in when he came back from the army? Unless he didn't plan on William coming back.* Tessa quickly pushed that possibility out of her mind, supposing instead that William had friends or other family to stay with in Great Salt Lake City.

Regardless of the whys or what-ifs, Tessa knew one thing for certain—there was no longer room for her and her father here. They needed to continue their trek to Oregon. As if in response to her thoughts, a chill wind whistled out of the east, licking at Tessa as it curled around the fence. *It might already be too late this year.*

Tessa was nearly finished with the last satin stitches outlining a buttonhole in the waistband of her new skirt when she heard shouts coming from the valley. Squinting at where the creek cut left toward the southern hills, she saw a man tussling with two women on the bank of the creek. She stood up and cupped her hands around her eyes to shield them from the sun's morning glare. *William!* He was scrabbling with two Indian women by the clothesline.

Dropping her fabric and sewing supplies in a heap, she hurried downhill toward the fracas. Before she reached them, however, the Indian women fled, leaving their booty of the settler's clothing discarded on the water's edge.

William was gathering up the dirty, wet clothing when Tessa slid to a stop in the mud. "What were they doing?" Tessa gasped.

"Winter's coming on," William said. "I guess they're just trying to prepare."

"So they steal clothes from us?" Tessa couldn't understand why William was so calm about the attempted theft.

"They don't consider it stealing. The Indians don't believe that anyone owns anything. Everything is part of the land."

"Well, clothes aren't part of the land," Tessa retorted.

"Everything on this earth is part of the land," he replied. "Everything comes from the land. In the Indian way, everyone contributes to the tribe. You give, you take, you survive together."

Tessa raised her eyebrows at him. "How do you know so much about the Indian ways?"

"How 'bout giving me a hand with this?" he asked, squatting next to the creek and plunging a shirt in the water to rinse off the mud. He tossed her a few articles and swished his garments in the shallow water. "Growing up in Great Salt Lake City, we'd have Indians wandering into town every once in a while. President Young counseled us not to fight with them, but to give them whatever food we could spare. It wasn't long before the Indians would bring woven rugs and baskets, reed dolls for the kids, or other trinkets to trade with us. My favorite was the bags of pine nuts they'd bring us every fall. Mother Holt used to scold me for eating them right out of the shell before she could use them in her Thanksgiving stuffing."

"Well, that certainly is not my experience with Indians," Tessa declared. She recounted how Indians had terrorized so many wagon companies on the plains, including her father's wagon in Wyoming.

"I'm not making excuses for them," William said. "I know there are a good many who have murdered innocent people making the crossing. I'm just telling you how we learned to live with them in Salt Lake City. We can fight with them here in Morristown or we can try to get along with them."

Tessa shook her head, doubting that building a relationship with the Indians could be as easy as William made it sound. "I certainly hope you're right, but I think you're being more than a little naïve."

William chuckled softly but just smiled rather than responding.

Keenly aware that she was scarce more than a little girl, trying to discuss Indian relations with this grown man, Tessa focused her attention on the shirt she was rinsing instead of returning his gaze.

"So," William said at length. "Your father seems to be getting stronger. Has he told you what his plans are?"

"What do you mean, his plans?"

"Well, is he anxious to get back on the trail? Or is he fixing on settling in here for a while?"

Bristling at the thought of "settling in" here, several smart retorts jumped through Tessa's mind, but she was too conflicted to give them utterance. Her father did seem to be making himself comfortable here, but she recalled how passionately he had extolled the Willamette Valley. They'd need to get moving quickly if they were going to continue the journey this year, but they had no money for supplies, and her father still tired easily.

"What about you?" William interrupted her reverie. "What do you want to do?"

"I don't know," Tessa admitted. Aside from just wanting this journey to be over, to get settled in a house so they could send for her grandmother as they'd promised, Tessa had truly not allowed herself to consider what she wanted for her future. She looked up at the man beside her and saw only kind concern—no mocking, no judgment—just a gentle smile. "My dream has just been for my father to realize his dream and to have somewhere to call home."

"You're a good soul, Tessa." His hand brushed hers as he took the wet shirt from her and flipped it up to hang on the clothesline. "Brother Darrow is blessed to have you."

Tessa felt the color rushing to her cheeks again and struggled fruitlessly to contain her smile. She ducked her head, willing her pounding heart to still.

"I'm sorry," William said. "I've embarrassed you."

Well, that didn't help, she silently chided, feeling her flush grow even hotter. She turned away and took a deep breath. Her head wanted her to dash away from him, but her heart kept her feet firmly rooted. She exhaled the deep breath slowly, trying to regain her composure.

She forced herself to continue the conversation. "What about you, William Bates?" She hoped her voice sounded light. "What are your plans?"

Smiling, William chuckled softly. "A fellow in my battalion used to say, 'when man plans, God laughs.' I should have listened to him."

"What do you mean?"

"I planned to stop in Great Salt Lake City just long enough to say hello to my ma on my way to California. I planned to strike gold. I planned to build a ranch and start a family." Taking Tessa's elbow, he guided her across the log spanning the creek. "My ma's gone, and Mother's up here alone. I reckon I'll be settin' up a place here to help her out. So much for plans."

"Oh, but that's not fair," Tessa exclaimed.

"Life isn't fair, Tessa. Life moves on, and we can move on with it or wallow in our misery. Mother's the nearest thing I have left to kin. What kind of man would I be to leave her out here alone?"

"You're a good man," she said emphatically. Tessa's breathing ceased when she realized what she had just uttered. How could she speak on such familiar terms with this man she barely knew?

If William was offended by her freshness, he didn't let on. But Tessa did notice a bit of pink tingeing his cheeks and his smile as he stooped to pick a pillowcase out of the mud.

CHAPTER 9

Snuggling deeper into her hay bedding, Tessa stretched her legs to relieve the ache in her back. For most of the night, she had rolled from her left side to her right, and back again, curled into a ball, trying to stay warm. If she straightened out, her legs hit the cold spots in the hay that her body heat hadn't permeated. If she pulled her knees to her chest, her back was exposed. For over a month, she had lain awake much of each night trying to find a position in the hay that didn't bother her scorched leg. Now that her leg was mostly healed, the chilly nights of fall invaded the hay shed, robbing Tessa of her sleep once more. Her mind and body battled—too cold to sleep, but too exhausted to fully awaken.

She heard her father stirring and felt the weight of the blanket he placed over her. Its warmth reminded her of the many times when she was younger that he'd tiptoed into her room when she had cried out from nightmares or growing pains in her legs. He'd pull the covers up over her securely, kiss his finger, and then touch her forehead and nose. There was magic in that touch to chase away any fear or pain and lull her back to sleep. And just as he used to, she felt the familiar tap of his finger on each of her brows and the tip of her nose. She wanted to respond but comfort won out and she slept.

"TESSABEAR."

She heard her father whispering her name. In the back of her mind, she rebelled that she had only just fallen asleep. It couldn't be morning already. As she slowly awakened, she knew it must be late, but after a sleepless night, she wasn't ready to face the day.

"Tessa."

She cracked her eyes open, hoping she was only dreaming.

"Time to wake up, sleepyhead."

"Mmmm," she murmured. "What time is it?"

"Nearly five o'clock."

"Five o'clock? Can I sleep just another hour?"

"I thought we could take a turn fixing breakfast today."

She rolled over and sat up, preparing to stand. The second her stockinged feet touched the icy floor, however, she recoiled and pulled the blankets more tightly around her. "Glory, it's cold!"

"Indeed."

Her dad wore two shirts and his hat and stood near the door with his hands tucked in his armpits.

"How long have you been up?" Tessa asked

"Couple of hours." His breath came out in little white puffs as it hit the chill air.

She gasped as she realized that she was clutching her father's blanket around her in addition to her own. Jumping up, she thrust his blanket out to him. "When did you give me this?"

"A bit ago. I'm glad it helped you get some sleep."

"You shouldn't have given me your blanket, Da," she chided. "You must be freezing!"

"It's my job to take care of you." He shrugged, then smiled. "And since when do you call me 'Da'?"

Tessa sat down and began lacing her shoes. "I like how Mrs. Holt says it. Do you mind?"

"Nope. I like how she says it too."

Outside, as they rounded the corner of the hay shed, Tessa tripped over William's feet. William, curled up and huddled against the shed, barely moved in the dark.

"William," Tessa cried, "what are you doing?"

"William?" Her father bent down and shook William's shoulder. "William."

The young man lifted his head; then he curled his body tighter and nestled closer to the building.

Henry Darrow wedged himself under William's arm and lifted him to his feet. "Let's get him inside and warmed up," he said to Tessa.

"Is it morning?" William stumbled against Henry. "Where are we assembled?"

"You're in Soda Springs, William," Henry said softly. "You're home with your ma. It's just before dawn."

"What's wrong with him?" Tessa whispered.

"Just cold and a bit confused. You run and put the kettle on."

Slipping on the frozen sod, Tessa hurried to the trading post and lit the lamp hanging inside the door. She plunged the kettle into the water barrel, set it on the cast iron stove, and fumbled to light the kindling under the burner.

Her father had deposited William on a chair and draped a wool blanket around his shoulders. "Help me warm his feet, Tess. He'll be lucky if he doesn't have frostbite."

She helped her father strip the boots from William's feet. He wore no socks, and the tips of his toes were tinged purple.

"Who's got frostbite?" Mrs. Holt rushed in from the adjoining room, still tying her wrapper at her waist. "What's happened?"

"We found William outside near frozen," Henry answered. "We've got to get him warmed up."

"Losh!" Mrs. Holt grabbed a quilt from behind the counter and added it with the blanket around William's shoulders. "Willy! Why dinnae you come in here last night?"

William cracked his eyes open and shook his head weakly. "I didn't think it was that cold. I didn't want to disturb anyone."

"Land sakes, you're lucky you didn't freeze to death!"

Tessa wasn't sure what frostbite was, but the word and the worried look on her father's and Mrs. Holt's faces sounded pretty serious. She knelt and placed one of William's feet in her lap and began rubbing it vigorously.

"No!" William exclaimed, pulling his feet away.

"Here now," Henry said. "We need to get you warmed up. Tess, like this. Just warm them; don't rub them." He wrapped one of William's feet in a towel and cradled it gently next to his body.

Without another towel, Tessa wrapped William's other foot in the folds of her skirt and cradled it close to her body.

"William Bates," Mrs. Holt chided. "Where are your stockings?"

"I wore them ragged," William admitted. "When they weren't any use as socks no more, I used them as gloves."

"Oh, my boy!"

"Mrs. Holt," Tessa's father interrupted. "Perhaps you could fix some coffee for him."

Mrs. Holt's eyes went wide and she looked somewhat stricken. She rushed behind the counter, rummaging through various crocks, bags, and cans.

Seeing Mrs. Holt so flustered made Tessa wonder if William was in graver danger than she had supposed. The woman took charge and knew just what to do when Tessa brought her dying father into town. But now, tending to her son, she seemed to be at her wit's end.

Mrs. Holt returned a moment later with empty hands. "I can't find any." With eyebrows knit together, she looked on the verge of tears. "We don't drink it, so I only stock enough for the travelers passing through. I haven't sent for supplies in a while."

Tessa realized that since they had arrived, Mrs. Holt had never offered them a single cup of coffee. Tessa didn't care for the taste, so she didn't missed it, but her father had never asked for it either.

"I have some reeds and mint," Mrs. Holt offered. "I can brew some tea."

Tessa tried to imagine what reed tea might taste like. Certainly nothing like the Darjeeling, oolong, or orange blossom tea they had back home. Mint tea was her favorite for upset stomachs.

"Anything hot will do," Tessa's father answered.

As if on cue, the kettle on the stove started to jiggle, signaling that the water had come to a boil.

William straightened in his chair and began massaging his foot. "If you have any venison, perhaps I could just have some broth?"

"Yes, of course," Mrs. Holt said, scurrying to take the kettle off the burner.

William began to shiver violently. He dropped his foot and pulled the quilt and blanket tighter around himself. Not knowing what else to do, Tessa pulled his bare foot into the folds of her skirt where she still sheltered his other foot. She repositioned herself against his legs so she could shelter his feet without hunching over.

For several minutes, she warmed his feet in her skirt, massaging them gently to stimulate the circulation. She was amazed at how natural it felt to sit next to him, her shoulder resting against his knee.

At length, his shivering subsided. She was debating whether it was appropriate to keep his feet wrapped in her skirt, now that the warmth was returning to them, when he brushed a tendril of hair behind her ear. Startled, she jumped and self-consciously looked about the room. Her dad sat in a chair next to the table, and Mrs. Holt stood with her back to the stove, holding the mug of broth. Both were watching Tessa warming William's feet. Mrs. Holt was smiling; Tessa's father was not.

"What are you doing?" Tessa gasped, pushing William's feet away from her skirt.

"I just—I only—" William looked as though he had been caught with his hand in the cookie jar. "I apologize, Miss Darrow."

Tessa's voice caught in her throat. Before she could respond, her father let out a loud guffaw, followed in short order by Mrs. Holt.

William grabbed Tessa's hand. "No. Please. Tessa, I'm sorry. I didn't mean to embarrass you."

Seeing the chagrin on his face, Tessa couldn't help but chuckle. As she felt her face flush, the only thing she could think to do was to punch him in the arm. Hard. Prompting another wave of laughter.

"What's all the ruckus?" Anna Larsen stepped out of the bedroom, rubbing her eyes and holding both of her children.

"Oh dear. I'm sorry we woke you." Mrs. Holt lifted Gracie from Anna's grip. "Guess we'd best get breakfast on."

WITH A BREAKFAST of hotcakes, scrambled eggs, and fried salt pork cleanly devoured, Anna put her children down for a nap. By the time she returned, the others had cleared away the dishes and started beans simmering for lunch. Mrs. Holt cut apart a woolen scarf, and she and Tessa were stitching together pieces to form socks for William to wear until they could knit proper stockings for him.

"Don't recall ever seeing a hard frost this early in the season," Mrs. Holt mused.

Henry Darrow stood at the open door, whittling a stick of wood. "Reckon it'll be an early winter?"

"Likely so," she said.

"Mother, I've been thinking," William said. "If Sister Larsen is going to stay with you, we should build a couple more rooms on in back."

"I've been a-thinking too." Mrs. Holt put her sewing down on the table and started counting on her fingers as she continued. "We'll be needing a bedroom for you, one for Anna and her bairns, one for Henry—Mr. Darrow—and one for Tessa. And 'twould be wise to add a couple more for travelers coming through." She leaned forward, her elbows on the table, and held up four fingers and both thumbs. "How long d'ya reckon it would take to add on six rooms?"

William shook his head glumly. "Longer'n the three or four weeks till the snow falls."

"Tess and I won't be staying on here that long," Henry said.

Tessa felt her heart twist in her chest. It was too late to leave. They'd get snowbound before they got out of Idaho territory. What could he be thinking?

Still leaning with his back against the doorframe, Henry stopped whittling and rested his blade on the curved block of wood. "We'll be moving on come spring. If we can cover the shed with grass or thatch or something to keep out the wind, we should be fine for the winter. Mrs. Larsen, what would you think about moving into that empty cabin up the way?"

"The Piersson place?" Mrs. Holt sounded almost giddy.

Tessa felt almost giddy herself, hearing that her father planned on spending the winter here after all. She didn't care how cold it got in the hay shed as long as they didn't have to trek through the snow.

Anna looked rather frightened but managed a wan smile. "I, I suppose that would be all right."

"It would be perfect!" Mrs. Holt exclaimed. "You'll have some privacy, but be right here in town. Place just needs some patching up."

Anna shrugged with resignation. "As long as you do not think the Pierssons will mind."

"Mind!" William almost shouted with glee. "They won't mind a bit. They're building a real nice place near Nashville."

"Nashville?" Mrs. Holt's eyes were wide, and she smiled from ear to ear. "Get on wid ya! They're back in Tennessee?"

William looked like he had eaten the proverbial canary. He was about to say something but then stopped himself. "That's a tale for another day. Today, what say we go look at the Piersson place?"

CHAPTER 10

For two weeks, Tessa and Henry Darrow, Maureen Holt, and William Bates worked on the Pierssons' abandoned cabin, preparing it for Anna Larsen and her children. Little Grace clung to Tessa's side, helping her scoop shovelfuls of clay and fistfuls of dried grass into a wooden trough, soaking it with water from the creek, and then mixing it all together to make chinking mud. Grace particularly loved helping to roll the thick mud into long ropes about three inches in diameter.

The men cut and fit logs to use where the walls had fallen in. They'd scrape the top and bottom edges off with a planer and set the first log in place. Then Tessa and Grace would lay a length of rolled mud on top. The weight from the next log placed atop the mud rope held the logs securely and caused the doughy mud to ooze out and fill the voids. Where the existing walls still stood, the girls rolled the mud into various sized balls and wedged them into gaps to seal out drafts.

Gracie busied herself making mud cakes while Tessa carefully smoothed the chinking mud with a trowel into every crevice. Even Mrs. Holt had become adept at clambering up the ladder, holding her skirt in one hand while carrying sheets of sod for the roof draped over the same arm. As Tessa smoothed one section of mudding, Grace would stand right behind her drawing shapes in the freshly completed section with a stick.

"Gracie, no!" Tessa had scolded when she first discovered the childish scratches in her perfectly smooth chinking.

Seeing the little girl's eyes fill with tears, William knelt down beside her and complimented her artwork. Resigned, Tessa continued smoothing each section as well as she could, knowing that it would shortly be inscribed with Grace's handiwork.

While Gracie napped, Tessa worked up on the roof, helping fit sticks and small branches into place for the mudcat chimney. She helped place fieldstones and smooth mud in the firebox for a while. Kneeling in the small dark space made her feel claustrophobic, so her father traded tasks, and she spent the rest of Gracie's naptime chinking the sticks on the chimney with William. The sun beat mercilessly on them, and William worked with his shirtsleeves rolled up past his elbows. Tessa couldn't help but stare at his biceps pulling taut against his sleeves each time he hoisted a bucket of mud up to where they were working.

Her hair, curling in the late summer humidity, refused to stay anchored in place, and tendrils dangled in her face. With her arms piled with bundles of sticks, she tried blowing the hair out of her face to no avail until William came to the rescue, lifting the offending strand from her forehead and smoothing it back. His hand lingered, resting the back of his fingers against her face, and Tessa felt a shiver slip up her spine at his touch. Tessa's heartbeat quickened, and she allowed herself to meet his eyes and smile before dropping her head. She heard William chuckle softly before turning back to his work.

After the initial hard frost that had prompted this flurry of activity, summer returned to Morristown and the soda springs. Though the days were hot and sticky, nights were turning increasingly nippy. To Tessa's unspoken relief, William finally bowed to Mrs. Holt's insistence that he sleep inside the trading post on a bedroll laid out on the wooden floor. Mrs. Holt relinquished her share of the prized sage hen feathers collected on the day of the picnic so Tessa could stuff a pillow she made for William.

"Hmmph," her father huffed. "Our pillows are stuffed with straw and you give the feathers to him?"

"I'm working on one for you. I just need to find more feathers."

Tessa's father was thoroughly enjoying the role of a laborer. It seemed to be a competition between William and him to see who could carry the most logs or chop them to length the fastest. "Isn't it amazing, the recovery he's made?" Mrs. Holt remarked on more than one occasion. Tessa couldn't help but notice the way the woman's gaze lingered on her father. While it pleased her to see her father's vigor return so quickly, it pained her to think that another woman fancied him less than four months after her mother's death. *Mother would be pleased to see him happy, but still . . .*

When Anna Larsen ventured out of the trading post to check on the progress of her new home, it was only to fret about one thing or another. Were the bark shakes spaced close enough to keep the snow from leaking through the roof? Would the square cuts of deerskin be heavy enough to keep the wind from whistling through the windows? Was the chimney high enough to keep smoke from drawing back into the cabin?

"Help me, Boab, but she's a wee scunner," Mrs. Holt exclaimed one day when Anna had been particularly simpering.

Tessa stepped closer, swiping mud from her brow with the back of her hand. "Pardon me? Boab? Scunner?"

"Oh dear, I'm sorry. That wasn't very Christian." Mrs. Holt guided a tendril of Tessa's hair back into place, tucking it firmly into her topknot. "My mum used to say 'Help me, Boab' when she was upset. And a 'wee scunner' is someone who complains all the time. I shouldnae said it. I know Sister Larsen can't do much to help while she's carrying that baby around, and I know she's missing her husband, but complaining and whining never made anything better."

Silently, Tessa agreed. She had come to dread even seeing Anna. The woman had nothing good to say in return for all of the work everyone was doing on her behalf. And yet, at the end of the day, when they all assembled around the small table in the trading post each evening, Anna would go on and on about what a rough day she'd had caring for the baby. If she bothered to help with meals, she did only the bare minimum, leaving most of the preparations and cooking for the others.

"Maybe Mrs. Larsen will be happier once she gets settled in her house," Tessa offered.

"Och, from your lips." Mrs. Holt touched her lips with her fingertips and then held them heavenward as if sending a prayer.

Tessa was keenly aware that, with all of the work to get the Pierssons' place ready for Anna, they hadn't even begun mudding the hay shed for Tessa and her father. And there still was nowhere for William to stay, unless he spent the winter sleeping on the trading post floor.

As Tessa and Mrs. Holt chatted, Tessa's father and William put the final notches in the log that would serve as the mantle over the fireplace. The two women joined them inside and placed dollops of mud on the supporting brackets and cheered as the men fit the mantle into place. Tessa's father scooted the three-legged iron pot, which Mrs. Holt had scrubbed and polished, into place in the firebox.

"I believe that's that, then," Mrs. Holt declared.

"That's that!" Grace mimicked from the doorway.

Tessa scooped the barefooted girl into her arms. "Where's your mama, Gracie?"

"Hmmmm." Gracie furrowed her brow for a moment as she pondered. "Yup, she's napping."

"Poor dear must be exhausted," Mrs. Holt muttered under her breath as she strode out of the cabin. "Guess it's time to get supper started."

THE NEXT DAY, they hitched up Anna's and Mrs. Holt's wagons to make the trip north to fetch Anna's belongings from the home she had shared with her late husband. Anna shuffled about aimlessly while Mrs. Holt and Tessa assembled food for the all-day journey. When the women went inside to fetch warm blankets in case the weather turned chilly, they found Gracie sitting on the floor rocking the baby. Anna lay on the bed in the adjacent room, partially obscured by the blanket draped in the doorway, with her back to them.

"Anna? We're ready to go." Tessa took the baby from Grace and laid him down to check his nappy.

"Anna." Mrs. Holt pulled Anna's feet off the bed to sit her up. "We need to get moving."

In response, Anna curled her knees back into a fetal position. "I cannot," she whimpered.

"What do you mean you cannae? Are you sick?"

"No," she said, sniffling. "I just cannot."

"Oh, for heaven's sake," Mrs. Holt huffed. "Get up this minute."

Obediently, Anna sat up, brushing tears from her lashes with the heel of her hand. Her eyes and nose were red and puffy from crying. "Sister Holt, please do not make me go up there."

"There now. What's got you broodin' so?"

The anguish in Anna Larsen's face made Tessa want to cry herself. Her heart hurt as she realized how much pain this young widow was living through.

"I cannot bear to go home without him," Anna whispered coarsely.

Tessa remembered watching Jens and Anna walk across the meadow the first time she met them. *That fateful day.* They were so much in love. The way Anna looked up at him with Grace riding on his shoulders, the way he so proudly introduced her as his wife. Of the few young married couples Tessa knew, she couldn't remember having ever seen such tender adoration.

Her mind flitted briefly to William before she quickly shooed that thought away. Though he was pleasant enough, and she certainly enjoyed his company, she was a child and he a man. He'd be settled down with a family long before she was old enough to consider marriage. *But what if*— She chided herself. *There is no what if. Don't be daft.*

Following a tight bear hug while Anna struggled to control her sobs,

Mrs. Holt led the grieving woman to the table. "We'll get you packed up. You stay here with your babies, and we'll bring your things down for you."

"Oh, but I could not ask you—"

"You dinnae ask. It's what friends do. You get your new home swept out and we'll bring your furnishings."

Though her first thought was to protest that it wasn't fair that they had to travel half the day to pack Anna's things while she stayed here, Tessa quickly realized this meant they wouldn't have to listen to Anna complaining or her children fussing. A full day spent in a wagon with William . . .

"Tessa!" Mrs. Holt barked. "Did you hear me?"

With a start, she realized Mrs. Holt had been speaking to her. "Beg pardon?"

"I asked you to go fetch Sister Pixton to sit with Anna while we're gone."

"Yes, ma'am, of course," Tessa answered, before realizing that meant having to ask a favor of Mr. Pixton as well as his wife. Since their encounter on the day Tessa and her father first came to town, when Mr. Pixton had all but refused to help her dying father, Tessa had avoided him at all costs. His wife seemed eager enough to be friendly, but Tessa couldn't get past the fact that she was married to that irksome man. With resolve, she walked quickly up the street to the Pixtons to impose on their good graces.

FOR ABOUT THREE hours, the wagons climbed northward, winding past Chester's Hill, Hooper Springs, meadows of dried grasses, and vast groves of aspen just beginning to tinge with rust and gold. The white bark of the aspens fairly glowed, lit by the mid-morning light filtering through the trees. Several clusters of honking geese flew overhead in regimented formation.

Lulled by the rhythmic swaying and steady creak of the wagon bed, and the comforting warmth of the early September sun, Tessa's eyes grew heavy and she rested against her father's shoulder as they bumped along. The musky sweet smell of sagebrush in bloom wafted upward as the wagon wheels crushed errant branches that overgrew the trail.

"Tess," her father whispered, nudging her with his elbow. "Look over there." He drew the wagon to a halt right behind Mrs. Holt and William's wagon. An azure creek meandered through the valley to the left of the trail and passed groves of aspen that bordered a field of cut grass. A herd of about thirty buffalo grazed at the edge of the field, and two cows watched warily from a safe distance. Large gray birds, wings tipped with russet and wearing brilliant crimson caps, waded in the edges of the creek with long, graceful legs. When a couple of buffalo wandered too close, they flew up en masse, spiraling skyward, only to settle back down in the same spot. The air filled with their chortling bugle calls, sounding like a flock of wild turkeys, only softer and more melodic.

Tessa sighed. "Wouldn't Grandmother love a painting of this?"

"She certainly would. When we get settled, we'll buy you some oils and you can paint it for her."

"Oh, I could never do it justice, Da." Tilting her head, Tessa used her sweetest voice. "But I wouldn't turn down a nice set of oils and a few canvases."

Her father laughed. "I'll just bet you wouldn't."

"The Larsen place is up ahead," William called, pointing off to the right.

Tessa could see the top of a sharply pitched roof on the other side of the rise. The hills to the east shone with bright yellow sagebrush dotted by a few junipers. Mounds of lava littered the slopes here and there, reminding Tessa of the chunks of licorice the farmhands shared with her in North Carolina.

"Looks like we're here," her father said, clicking his tongue at the horse and giving the reins a flip.

Much nicer than the full-log cabins in Morristown, Jens and Anna Larsen's house was built with split lumber that fit tightly together. A porch overhang sheltered the front door, flanked by glass windows on either side. Two pine rocking chairs sat side by side on the gravel stoop.

"Oh," Tessa exclaimed, jumping down from her wagon. "This is lovely!"

William gave a long whistle as he walked around the home's exterior.

"We held a house raising when Jens came up from Great Salt Lake City just after little Grace was born and announced that Anna had agreed to move up here." Mrs. Holt swung the door open wide and slid both windows fully open.

Henry examined the split marks of the lumber, patting them firmly with his hand. "What a lot of work you went to."

"Och, no. That was Jens." Mrs. Holt used her apron to swipe a web from the bottom corner of a window. "He scouted this area by himself, and when we arrived a couple of weeks later, he already had the logs peeled, split, and stacked, and the land cleared. All we had to do was frame it and put up the siding and roof. Dinnae take us more'n three or four days."

"Why would he bring Anna and a tiny baby all the way up here? Why wouldn't he settle in the valley with the rest of you?"

William held his arm out, motioning to the expanse of the field of barley in front of them. "Well, Mr. Darrow, I can't speak for Jens, of course, but if I had a family to care for, I'd be looking for a piece of land to make my own. Somewhere to farm, maybe raise some stock. Somewhere my children and grandchildren could roam without tumbling over neighbors. Somewhere to build a legacy."

"Every man needs a legacy."

Hearing the melancholy in her father's voice, Tessa wondered if he was thinking of their home in North Carolina that had been in their family for several generations. Or was he imagining the land he had hoped to settle in Oregon—before his wife and youngest child died?

Tessa stepped gingerly inside, feeling a bit as though she were trespassing. A table, which looked like it had been assembled from the same lumber used to side the house, occupied the center of the room. Benches fashioned from a log split in half down its length sat on the long sides of the table, and chairs made from stripped branches stood at either end. A white crock painted with blue and yellow flowers held a tangle of long-wilted wildflowers in the center of the table.

A cast iron, three-legged stove filled one corner of the room with a few pots hung from the ceiling on leather tethers. Shelves next to the stove held a collection of plates and mugs as well as an assortment of jars and crocks of beans, grains, seeds, and cooking supplies.

Mrs. Holt picked up a white cotton apron from the back of the chair nearest the stove. She held it open, revealing the blue and yellow flowers embroidered around its edge. William held up a dish towel decorated with the same embroidery. "Do you think Anna made these?"

"Or her mother." Mrs. Holt carefully folded the apron and set it on the table. "Anna and her folks came from Denmark not long before she and Jens were married."

"Were her folks Morrisites too?" Tessa's father asked, joining them.

"No. In fact, Brother Christensen—Anna's father—was quite vocal about calling Joseph Morris a false prophet. Jens's family didn't believe in him either—except for Jens, that is. We were all pretty shocked when Anna agreed to make her home up here with him."

Tessa gently ran her fingers over the table runner embroidered in the center with "Larsen" in block letters, and the date of their marriage—April 14, 1861—just below it. Anna and Jens's names were embroidered in scripted letters on either side. "They were in love," Tessa murmured.

"Aye, that they were. Most deeply in love."

CHAPTER II

As the sun approached its zenith, Tessa and Mrs. Holt dragged Anna's wedding trunk into the middle of the room. The oak chest, painted with wreaths of green leaves, pink roses, and sprays of white blossoms, was about three feet long and nearly as high at the top of the rounded lid. Painted inside the wreath on the left side, Jens and Anna Larsen's initials—J-L-A; inside the other wreath, their wedding year—1861. They packed the couple's few books in the bottom of the trunk. Then Tessa handed pots, pans, and a teakettle to Mrs. Holt to pack next, followed by a handful of cooking utensils. They carefully wrapped Anna's delicate china in linens and nestled each snuggly in place.

Reflecting on all of the beautiful china and figurines destroyed when their home was burned, Tessa sighed. "I feel as though I'm packing away Anna's broken dreams." She looked up to see Mrs. Holt wiping tears away with her apron. "Mrs. Holt, you're crying."

"Och, it's for naught." She waved her hand in the air as though swishing away bad memories.

"Clearly it's not for naught." Tessa put down the creamer she'd been wrapping as she saw fresh tears brimming in Mrs. Holt's eyes and waited for her to speak.

"It's silly, really." She whisked a tear from her cheek and fanned herself with the edge of her apron. "I was recollecting when I became a widow. I was just about Anna's age when my first husband, Stephan, was killed in a mining accident."

"Oh, I didn't realize. I'm so sorry."

"My boy, Hyrum, was just a baby, but he saved me from going mad. Then when Hyrum died . . ." She paused and blinked back more tears.

"What a blessing to have the gospel and know that we will all be together again as a family."

"As a family? Do you think we will be?"

Mrs. Holt came around to Tessa's side of the trunk and wrapped her arms around her.

"Aye, lassie. We surely will be. God would not be so cruel as to give us families here on earth if we could not be with them in heaven."

BY EARLY AFTERNOON, all of the Larsens' household belongings were carefully packed in the wedding trunk, and Jens's assortment of tools packed in a separate crate, ready to be loaded in the wagons. A half dozen chickens squawked in a separate crate. William and Henry went to the meadow to retrieve the two cows while Tessa and Mrs. Holt unlashed the ropes that supported the mattress on the log pole bed. Too large to remove from the home intact, they numbered each log with a piece of charcoal before dismantling it so they could reassemble the bed correctly in Anna's new home.

As the women carried the last of the logs out to the wagon, William and Henry came running up the hill. "The cattle have bolted!" they called.

"What do you mean bolted?" Mrs. Holt dropped her end of the log, rushing across the yard to meet the men.

"They've wandered off! We can't find them!"

"Gone? Well, that's a fine thing. We've got to take after 'em then. Daisy's nearly dry and Anna's got to have milk for those babies."

"They haven't been milked in a month, Mother," William said. "They'll be dry by now."

"It doesn't matter. They're Anna's cows. We'll naw go back withoot 'em."

"Humph," Tessa's father interjected. "And just where do you suppose we start looking?"

Realizing she should have said something earlier, Tessa stepped forward. "I might know."

"What?"

"I saw them up at the end of the meadow earlier." She pointed northward.

"Why didn't you tell us?" Mrs. Holt demanded.

"I don't know." Tessa felt her chest tighten. "I didn't realize they were Anna's. I'm sorry." Embarrassed that she had been so thoughtless, however unintentional, she keenly felt the sting of Mrs. Holt's sharp words.

William stepped to Tessa's side and held his hand up, stopping the recriminations. "She couldn't have known. Let's just get after them."

"You're right, William. I'm sorry, Tessa. There's no use fretting."

"We'd best get after them quickly, then." Tessa's father lifted the rocking chairs out of the bed of the wagon, and sent William with the crate of chickens to secure in the coop. "We can all fit in here and tie the cows to the back."

"There's no sense all of us going. You and William go; Tessa and I will stay behind and finish packing and have supper ready when you get back."

"No—please, let me go," Tessa pleaded. "It's my fault they've gone missing. I want to help find them."

"You go ahead then. I'll finish up here."

"No, ma'am." Tessa's father wrapped his hand around Mrs. Holt's arm, drawing her to the wagon. "I'll not leave a lady out here alone. We'll all go together."

"I hardly think that's necessary."

"We'll all go or we'll all stay. Those are your options."

"Well, the cheek of some men."

The four piled into one wagon and started after the wayward cattle. Despite telling herself to let it go, Tessa's feelings remained on edge. While mentally berating herself for her carelessness in one thought, Mrs. Holt's mild rebuff in front of William rankled her tender feelings in the next. *You're being silly; she didn't mean anything by it.* Nonetheless, Tessa was grateful for the bit of distance separating her from Mrs. Holt.

Mrs. Holt and Tessa's father sat up front, and Tessa and William sat in the wagon bed, one on either side, facing each other. Though fascinated by the scenery they were traveling through, Tessa often snuck a peek at William and was delighted see that he was often watching her.

As they descended into the valley below, following the narrow winding trail, the aspen grew denser, and sparse cedars gave way to spruce trees. Tessa breathed deeply the crisp air, letting the freshness fill her lungs.

"It's the sap."

"What?"

William leaned forward and also took in a deep breath. "It's the sap flowing that makes the air smell like this."

As soon as William mentioned it, Tessa recognized the pungent, fresh smell. It reminded her of the woods up Grandfather Mountain back home.

"It flows best between the trunk and the roots in spring and autumn when the nights are cool and the days are warm."

Tessa cocked her head quizzically. "How on earth would you know that?"

Shrugging, he smiled that I-know-something-you-don't smile she found so charming. "We sometimes got pretty low on supplies during the war. We'd mash up pinesap with lard and ash to make soap. Smells to high heaven, but it makes a real nice lather. And it's just the thing to soothe poison ivy rash."

"William Bates, you are a fount of knowledge." A little embarrassed that she had been so flirtatious, Tessa nonetheless felt rewarded by the grin she received in return. Dropping her gaze to study her hands folded in her lap, she couldn't quite manage to hide her own smile.

"Hey, listen," Tessa's father said.

Ahead of them, they heard the faint lowing of a cow. Hastening their pace, he guided the horses over the meager path that skirted the mountains on their right. The trail made a sharp turn to the east before descending gently through the trees.

A few miles farther, where the trees started thinning out, Mrs. Holt spotted the errant cattle. "There, up ahead, off to the left."

Henry pulled the horses to a stop, and then he and William crept toward the cows with ropes poised in loops, ready to snare the animals.

Kneeling at the edge of the wagon to watch, Tessa whispered, "Please, please, please don't bolt."

"Dunnae think there's a worry there." Mrs. Holt chuckled softly. "Lookit that."

The cows walked toward the men, as though trained to do so, and patiently waited while Henry and William slipped the ropes over their heads.

"Oh, well done!" Tessa clapped her hands with delight. She reached out to pet the animals as they were led past her and tied to the back of the wagon.

Smiling so big his eyes twinkled, William held his hand out to Tessa, guiding her down from the wagon. "I found another scene for you to paint."

Tessa's father helped Mrs. Holt climb from her perch, and then the foursome walked the short distance to the top of the knoll where the cattle had grazed.

Tessa's breath caught in her chest, and she fairly tingled with excitement. "Oh, my. Have you ever—" The valley spread before them in a haze of green, gold, and purple, set against a majestic blue mountain rising in the distance. A crystalline lake stretching northward glittered in the afternoon sun. Great flocks of cranes, geese, swans, and smaller birds rose in swells—circling, dipping, and darting in an avian ballet. A dozen deer grazed fifty yards downhill to their right; two, with their ears keen, kept watch on the intruders while the rest munched on chokecherries and wheatgrass.

"This must be the valley that the Pierssons told me about," William whispered.

"Grays Hole," Mrs. Holt said, her voice filled with reverence. "Jens spoke of it often. He used to trap beaver, muskrat, fox—you name it—up here." As if on cue, a red fox popped its head up from behind a boulder, cocked it quizzically at the group, and then scampered off into the brush.

"Grays Hole? Well, that's a perfectly hideous name. That's a lake in the distance, not a hole." Straightening her back, Tessa folded her arms and assumed her most officious demeanor. "We shall rename it Grays Lake."

William folded his arms as well and, smiling, gave a curt nod. "Thus it shall be."

"Shhh." Tessa's father put his finger to his lips. "Listen."

The aspen soughing in the breeze sounded like gentle rain splashing, and then rising in torrential waves as gusts scurried through, sending slender branches swaying. Tessa strained to discern what had caught her father's attention. Seconds later, the hoarse screech of a hawk pierced through the rustling leaves, its high-pitched, descending call answered by a more furtive, ascending call. Tessa watched, fascinated and horrified, as the hawk darted down and snatched a skunk from the thatch not thirty feet in front of them.

Transfixed by the scene, common sense didn't quite register when Mrs. Holt gasped, and William yelled, "Run!" Until . . .

Tessa clasped her sleeve over her nose and mouth as the stench of the skunk filtered earthward. Mercifully, the hawk had whisked the frightened animal well away from the group before it released its defensive mist, but not far enough away to save them from the nauseating odor permeating the hillside.

Climbing back into the wagon, Tessa held a hanky over her mouth and nose as she waited for the skunk smell to dissipate.

"That was a close call!" William laughed.

"Indeed!" Tessa's father helped Mrs. Holt up into the wagon seat. "It would have taken us weeks to get the stink out if we'd taken a direct hit."

Tessa looked back toward the valley wistfully. "I don't suppose there's time to drive down into the valley, is there?" Though she didn't have much experience painting, she loved to draw. With her father's offer to buy her oils and canvas fresh in her mind, she determined that she would do her best to depict this landscape so she would never forget it.

"Afraid not today, Tess." Her father had already begun turning the wagon around to begin the return trip. "It'll be dark before we get back to Morristown as it is."

"Maybe we could all come back before it turns too cold," William offered, "and even spend a day or two. We should bale Jens's barley and take it into town. And I'd like to take some time to explore the area."

"Well, I don't—"

"Oh, Da, please, could we? Then I could bring my journal and make some sketches."

Mrs. Holt laughed and nudged Tessa's father with her elbow. "I don't think she'll take no for an answer."

He rolled his eyes. "I'm not promising anything."

Satisfied to receive any answer other than a flat no, Tessa knelt over the back of the bench and wrapped her arms around her father's shoulders, giving him a tight squeeze. Then she settled back into her seat to resume memorizing the glory of Grays Lake.

WITHOUT THE ANXIETY of searching for the lost cattle, the trip back to the Larsens' place seemed to take twice as long. Despite the haste with which Tessa's father urged the horse pulling the wagon, the plodding weight of the two cows tied to the back slowed their progress. And while the sun had been to their back on their way northward, it now flickered through the trees to the west, casting its sharp glare square in their faces. Tessa could sense her father becoming more and more tense. From time to time, he'd hold his arm crooked at an angle in front of his face to shield his eyes from the shards of light.

At last they arrived back at the cabin. As Tessa climbed down from the wagon, she recognized the hard set to her father's jaw and his puckered brows that always filled her with dread. "Father, are you coming?"

"In a minute."

Please, not now, she silently pled. He hadn't shown one of his dark moods since the morning of the town's picnic in Hooper Springs. Tired and hungry, she didn't have the energy to navigate out of the line of fire this afternoon.

"Tessa," Mrs. Holt said, "help me get some supper put together before we load up these wagons. Mr. Darrow—" She paused when confronted with his glare. After a moment, she continued in a gentle voice, "Why don't you go down to the creek and freshen up?"

Rubbing the back of his neck, he nodded slowly. "I think I will."

Relieved that she wouldn't have to tiptoe around him for at least a little while, Tessa watched him ease down from the wagon and saunter across the meadow toward the stream. Without benefit of their own cooking utensils, she busied herself sorting through the packed trunk and crate until she located a bowl, a pan, tins of flour and baking soda, and a jar of lard.

Looking toward the stream, she saw William, silhouetted in the afternoon sun, casting a pole and line back and forth in gentle arcs. From this distance, the sun glittering on water droplets looked like stars dancing on the fishing line. Mesmerized, she stared for several moments, trying to sear the image in her memory, until Mrs. Holt called her from her reverie to help carry the table back into the cabin.

Together, they measured and mixed the ingredients for biscuits. No sooner had they kneaded the dough and stretched it into flattened rolls to fry than William marched through the door carrying two large fish.

"William! What have you caught?" Mrs. Holt exclaimed.

"Rainbow trout." He raised the trophies aloft proudly, holding them with his index fingers hooked through their gills, and turned them so the sinking sun glinted off their scales in multicolored prisms. "I found a fishing rod out back. Still had the fly tied on."

"Well, we're blessed indeed. Let's get these biscuits baked up, then we'll fry the trout." Mrs. Holt started a fire in the belly of the stove, and she and Tessa worked together to fry the flatbread to a golden brown.

When they handed the frying pan over to William to cook the trout, Tessa, afraid of repercussions, asked Mrs. Holt to walk to the creek with her to fetch her father. They found him by the water—kneeling—his head resting on his arms that were folded on top of a short log. His hair and collar were wet, as though he had plunged his whole head in the stream. He appeared to be asleep.

"Father?" Tessa didn't know whether to wake him for dinner or let him sleep. She looked to Mrs. Holt for guidance.

The woman squatted down beside him. "Henry? Are you all right?"

"Yeah."

"Are you having a headache?"

He kept his head cradled in his arms. "It's a dandy. You eat. I'll just rest here a while."

"I think it would do you good to eat something. William caught some fish."

"I know." He lifted his head and slowly stood up. A smile pulled at the corner of his mouth. "He cleaned them right over there on the other side of those bushes. I don't think he saw me."

Tessa looked at the gruesome fish guts piled at the water's edge a few yards upstream, and quickly turned away.

Mrs. Holt grimaced and held her fingers beneath her nose. "I don't wonder you're sick. I'll fix you some biscuits and tea. Let's get you feeling better and you can repay William's 'kindness.'"

NOT WANTING TO carry benches back into the house, the four friends sat in the rocking chairs and on the porch steps while eating their dinner. Tessa's father sat in one of the rockers with its back turned to the sinking sun. The ladies washed and wrapped the dishes they'd used while William began hoisting the trunks, furniture, and chickens into the wagons.

Purple shadows slid across the meadow and enveloped the Larsen's home while William lit the lanterns on the wagons. They tied a cow to the back of each wagon, and tugged on the rope, securing the crate of chickens. Despite the blinding pain in his head, Henry adamantly refused to let either of the ladies drive a wagon in the dark. As the first stars glittered on the horizon, the foursome and their menagerie began the three-hour journey home.

CHAPTER 12

"Ugh," Tessa sighed. "It feels like we've been driving forever." After a morning spent in the mountains on the north side of the valley, Tessa and Mrs. Holt made their way homeward with a scant bushel basket each of huckleberries and chokecherries resting in the buckboard, and several empty baskets beside them.

"I think we have been driving forever," Mrs. Holt agreed. Despite their promises to Tessa's father and William to not venture farther than the foothills, they had to travel much higher into the mountains to find berries still on the bush. It was the second week of September, and the berries were just about spent, but they were still able to gather enough to make jam and syrup. "You'll be glad we made the effort, though."

Tessa cast her a dubious look. "That's a lot of effort for a few preserves."

"Huckleberry syrup is just the thing on buckwheat hotcakes," Mrs. Holt said. "And just wait until you taste a venison sandwich spread with chokecherry jam. It cuts through the gamey taste and gives it just a bit of pucker."

After eating venison prepared just about any way she could imagine, and then some, Tessa hadn't yet taken a liking to its sharp flavor. No matter what herbs it was seasoned with, it always ended up tasting like beef "gone off" to her. "Perhaps a bit of tartness would help the flavor."

"Well, we've naught but a half dozen head of cattle up here. Until someone builds a herd, you're not likely to be enjoying a fat beefsteak anytime soon."

"I know." Tessa sat straighter on the bench and put one hand on her hip, wagging the index finger of her other hand at Mrs. Holt's nose, and did her best imitation of a Scottish brogue. "Deer are God's gift an' we're grateful to hae them, we are."

Mrs. Holt pushed Tessa's shoulder in mock affront. "Och, but you're the wee imp."

"Och, och, och," Tessa mimicked, hugging the woman's arm. "Mrs. Holt," Tessa said a moment later. "I'm truly grateful for the care you've taken of my da and I."

"Your 'da'? Do I hear a bit of the Scot rubbin' off on you?"

"Aye, perhaps a tay bit," Tessa said with a smile. "Did you know that some of my father's kin came from Scotland generations ago?"

"Did they now? I wondered. Darrow is a strong Scottish name."

"When my granddad was alive, he'd get rather stubborn on occasion. My grandmother would say that was his Scots coming out."

Mrs. Holt held her hand to her chest, feigning indignation, and exaggerated Tessa's bit of drawl. "Why, Tessa Darrow, whatever do you mean? I don't have a stubborn bone in my body!"

After the waves of giggles passed, Mrs. Holt quietly told Tessa, "I'm glad you and your da are spending the winter here, lass. The few folks left in Morristown are getting pretty worn down. You're like a breath of fresh air. And I know William will be glad for the company as well."

While Tessa's reasonable mind constantly reminded her that an attractive man of William's age wouldn't want to wait for her to become of marriageable age, she found herself more and more taken with him. Hearing Mrs. Holt put voice to their growing friendship made Tessa's heart quicken, and she struggled mightily to refrain from throwing her arms around the woman.

TESSA AND MRS. Holt laughed and chatted like two schoolgirls off on a lark as they pulled the buckboard in front of the trading post. So absorbed were they in their discussion of the merits of the traditional hoop skirt versus the slimmer crinoline, that they didn't even notice the wagon and team behind the building. As they carried their two baskets of berries up the steps, the five men sitting around Mrs. Holt's table rose to their feet.

Tessa's father and William were there, along with one of the Morrisites—Grieg Sundstrom, and two more men whom she didn't recognize.

"Sister Holt," Mr. Sundstrom said, wiping gravy from his chin with the back of his hand. "You remember my son."

"Why of course I do!" She hastily set down her basket and rushed forward to embrace the young man, ignoring his outstretched hand. "It's so good to see you again, Peter."

"And you, Sister Holt."

"My, but you're all grown up."

"I'm sixteen, ma'am."

She smiled, a sad smile. "William's age when he left for the army."

"And have you ever seen a boy so tall," his father interjected.

"Indeed," Mrs. Holt agreed. "I'll bet you have to duck just to get through doorways!" Without waiting for an answer, she turned to the fifth man at the table—a fellow looking roughly the same age as Tessa's father. She held out her hand. "I don't believe we've met. I'm Maureen Holt."

"Well, sure we have, Sister Holt." The man stepped forward and shook her hand. "Kurt Sundstrom. Grieg's brother. We met when I came down from the range year before last."

"Oh, of course! But you had a full beard back then."

"No point shaving when there's no one around but a couple of cow-pokes and a herd."

"True enough. Well," Mrs. Holt said, looking at the laden table. "It looks like you've met Mr. Darrow, and of course you know William. And you've had lunch."

Tessa's faint shuffle as she sat her basket down drew Mrs. Holt's attention. "Goodness! Tessa! Where are my manners?"

Tessa's father stepped forward, wrapping his arm around her. "Gentlemen, this is my daughter, Tessa."

Kurt Sundstrom stepped forward first, taking Tessa's hand and nodded once. "Pleased to meet you."

The gentleness with which he bowed over her hand was in stark contrast to his broad stature and rough clothing. Tessa curtsied in return. "Charmed."

Then Peter stepped up, shaking her hand awkwardly. "How'do."

Tessa stole a glance at her father and William and stifled a giggle. "Very well, thank you." The young man's hair dark hair was so dusty it looked nearly gray. Dressed in canvas pants that were much too short and held up by a drawstring rather than by a belt or suspenders, he looked like a very tall ragamuffin from the back woods of Appalachia. His green eyes, by contrast, sparkled—as though he had just thought of something very clever—and the freckles sprinkled across his nose and cheeks gave his face a rosy glow.

"What brings you to Morristown?" Mrs. Holt placed biscuits on two plates, scooped up the abandoned bowl of gravy, and then whisked it briskly with the serving spoon.

"We're on our way up to the range in Wyoming," Kurt answered. "It's time to drive the cattle down to market."

Mrs. Holt ladled the gravy over the biscuits and motioned for Tessa to come sit down at the table. "That's a big job for two men."

"We've got a couple of hands up there now." Kurt held the chair out for Mrs. Holt. "We were hoping to pick up a few more men on our way through."

Mrs. Holt took a large pinch of pepper and sprinkled it over her lunch. "Well, you'll find slim pickings here, I'm afraid. Most of our young men have moved back to Great Salt Lake City."

Occupied with eating the biscuits and gravy, Mrs. Holt didn't notice the look the men exchanged. But Tessa did. *What are they planning?* Before she could say anything, however, Tessa's father piped up.

"What say you fellas give William and I a hand mudding that hay shed?" He took Kurt and Peter Sundstrom each by the arm and steered them toward the door. "We only got about halfway done this morning. And the ladies don't need you underfoot while they make their jam."

"I'll be right along," William said.

As he passed by William, Kurt's voice was quiet but firm. "You're doing the right thing."

With that, the men were gone, leaving Mrs. Holt to devour her lunch, Tessa to wonder what they were scheming, and William standing there with his hat in his hands, looking like a worried schoolboy.

After gulping down four or five mouthfuls of biscuits and gravy, Mrs. Holt acknowledged William still standing in the doorway. "What's your unfinished business, son?"

Judging from the way he looked back and forth between her and Mrs. Holt, Tessa realized he wanted to have a private conversation with his mother. "I think I'll enjoy the fresh air and get to work on these berries." Without waiting for an answer, Tessa balanced her tin plate on the bushel of huckleberries and carried the basket outside to the stoop.

"There now. What is it, lad?"

I'm not really eavesdropping, Tessa told herself, even while scooting a little closer to the doorway. With William and Mrs. Holt at the table just inside, it wasn't difficult to overhear.

"Mother, I'm so happy I found you up here, and know you're safe."

"Well, of course I'm safe, dear. And now that you're here—"

"Mother, I've come to a decision." William rushed through his declaration without giving Mrs. Holt a chance to break into the one-sided conversation. "I appreciate the kindness you've shown since I've been back. I haven't had much chance to consider what to do next with my life. I've just been settling in. But it's plain to see a fella can't really build much of a life up here without a leg up of some sort. Brother Sundstrom offered me a job to help bring his cattle down to market in Great Salt Lake City."

"Is that all?" The relief in Mrs. Holt's voice was almost palpable.

He's leaving? A knot formed in the base of Tessa's stomach at the thought.

"Well, I think that's a fine idea."

What?!

"You go on that cattle drive with Brother Sundstrom. It'll be good for you."

"Really?" Now it was William's turn to sound relieved. "I'll earn enough money to buy some livestock of my own, or maybe do some gold mining in California, or buy a spread to farm, or I don't know what."

"Well, sure you will. Maybe when you get back, we can even work on cleaning up another of the abandoned cabins for you to live in. I bet we could have you all settled in before the snow falls in earnest."

That's not so long. Tessa sat her half-eaten lunch on the step beside her and idly picked a twig with withered leaves out of the huckleberries.

Several moments passed before William spoke again. "Mother, I don't know when I'll be coming back. Or if I will be."

"William!"

Tessa's own sharp intake of breath created an audible gasp, and she clamped her hand over her mouth. She heard the legs of a chair scrape inside, and then William spoke so softly that Tessa had to strain to hear.

"I'm not saying I'll never be back, Mother. I just don't know. I don't know what my future holds. But I'm a man now, and I've got to make my own way in the world."

Another several moments passed, punctuated by Mrs. Holt's sniffles. "I know you do, son." Mrs. Holt's voice was choked with tears. "But that don't mean it won't break my heart to see you go."

Tessa's heart twisted at the sound of Mrs. Holt's anguish, and she kept her hand pressed tightly over her mouth, fighting back her own tears.

WHAT HAD STARTED out to be a relaxing day picking berries and making jam with Mrs. Holt turned into a whirlwind of activity. Mrs. Holt raced about gathering blankets, woolen socks, jerked venison, flour, beans, and other sundries to add to the provisions the Sundstroms had brought with them. Tessa felt at a loss over what to do to help. Each time she wandered into the trading post to ask what she could do, Mrs. Holt would dash past her with hardly a glance.

The Sundstrom men joined with William and Tessa's father to work like fury on mudding the hay shed and fitting split wood shakes to fashion a floor over the bare dirt. When Tessa ventured to help them, she'd stumble over materials, drop tools, or bump into one of the men as they raced about with their buckets of mud.

Feeling like an unwelcome child who was underfoot, Tessa stayed ensconced on the porch, picking through the huckleberries and chokecherries, preparing them for preserves. *He cares more about that stupid cattle drive than he cares about me.* She realized how churlish her thoughts were, but that didn't deter them. It was going to be so lonely without William here to go hiking or play dominoes with in the evenings. *Who cares. He won't miss me anyway.* It was no use—she felt bereft already and he hadn't even left yet. Mrs. Pixton dropped by to say she'd bring by a nice stew for supper later that evening, and Tessa just glowered at her. It seemed as if everyone but her had some way to help the men get ready to go.

"Aaaaaaaaaaaaaaaaaaaa!" A scream pierced the quiet.

Tessa leapt from her seat on the porch of the trading post, scattering huckleberries in her wake, and raced up the street in response.

"What in tarnation!" Mrs. Holt shouted as she ran up the street on Tessa's heels.

Little Gracie sprinted toward them, her blonde locks billowing behind her, sporting a look of sheer terror.

Her mother, Anna, holding a wooden spoon in the air, flew after the child. "Get back here! Get back here now!"

Wailing like a banshee, Grace ducked behind Mrs. Holt, wrapped her arms around the woman's knees, and buried her head in the folds of her skirt.

"What's happened?" Tessa's father, William, and the Sundstroms—panic-stricken—dashed to the scene from where they'd been working on the hay shed.

"That little—she ruined my—" Tears overwhelmed Anna and she covered her face with her hands, sobbing. "She cut open my mattress."

Tessa gasped, picturing the plump feather mattress that they'd so carefully wrapped in sheets and transported from Anna's former home.

"She was rolling around on it . . ."

"No!"

"There are feathers everywhere!"

True enough, telltale feathers clinging to Grace and Anna's hair and clothing evidenced the misdeed.

Tessa felt rather ill herself to think of the loss of that heavenly mattress. She knew it had been a wedding present from Anna's parents, and Tessa had spent many a night tossing and turning on her crude straw-stuffed mattress dreaming of Anna's plump, feathery cloud.

"Oh, Gracie." Mrs. Holt pulled the frightened girl off of her legs and stood her before the group. "What would possess you?"

With quivering chin, she stammered, "I was making a pillow for Tessa."

"What?" Anna's hand with the mixing spoon shot out, ready to strike. "You little—"

William, however, was faster, catching her wrist in mid swing. "No, you don't."

Anna twisted to free herself.

"You're not hitting her, Anna." Although he spoke evenly, there was no mistaking the firmness in William's tone.

"She's my child, and she needs to be taught."

"Not with a beating, she doesn't." He picked the trembling child up in his arms and turned to face the others. "I'll help Grace clean up the mess."

"No!" Anna stomped her foot, sending a puff of dust billowing out beneath her skirt. "She can't just get away with it. She's got to learn there are consequences."

Mrs. Holt stepped forward, taking the spoon from Anna's grip. "I'd say spending the day picking up feathers is a pretty hefty consequence for a three-year-old." Before Anna could object further, Mrs. Holt started marching toward Anna's house. "I hear Christian crying. We'll gather him up, and you can spend the afternoon with me making huckleberry jam. Tessa, you go fetch my sewing basket. You can help William mend the mattress."

"But, Sister Holt," Anna whined.

Mrs. Holt held up one finger sternly. "I'll hear no more about it. Your baby's crying."

CHAPTER 13

"Duck, duck, goose!" Three-year old Grace danced between William and Tessa, tapping them on the heads before racing around the cabin, squealing with laughter.

"No duck, duck, goose till these feathers are picked up." William reached out, snagging the child in the crook of his arm and sitting her back down next to the ripped mattress.

Tessa leaned her head back in exasperation, shoulders slumping. "How can you be so patient with her?"

"How can I not? She's three."

For the first fifteen or twenty minutes of the great feather cleanup, Grace had steadfastly knelt next to William, shoving fistfuls of downy feathers back into the mattress she'd cut open. Her interest, however quickly shifted to trying to entice her friends into games of tag, ducks fly, hide-and-seek, or seeing how long she could keep a feather afloat by blowing puffs of air at it.

"We could be done already if we'd sent Grace with her mother."

"True, but then she wouldn't have learned not to cut open mattresses."

Tessa looked at William, who, instead of packing for his cattle drive, sat on the floor with a little girl in his lap, helping her repair the damage she'd done. She marveled that he hadn't raised his voice even once and that he had treated Grace with more kindness than the child's own mother had. "You don't have time for this. You should be packing."

He shrugged. "Only have to pack my knapsack. And I'd rather spend my time with you."

Tessa picked up a handful of feathers and threw them at him playfully before realizing that her tease would trigger reciprocation from William—and set Grace into another romp.

After a brief feather fight, he gathered Grace into his arms, whispered something in her ear, and then planted her on her feet.

The little girl placed her hands firmly on her hips, and in a stern voice said, "Tessa, mind your manners."

All three dissolved into peals of laughter until Grace collapsed on the mattress, sending clouds of feathers in her wake.

"Oh, no!" William grabbed the child off the mattress and shook his index finger at Tessa in mock sternness. "You set a fine example, Miss Darrow."

Tessa had to hold her hand over her mouth to stifle her giggles when Grace also shook her finger at Tessa.

"How did you come to be so good with children, William? You didn't have brothers and sisters growing up, did you?"

"No, not directly." He sat Grace down at his side and scooped a pile of feathers into a mound before using a dustpan to transfer them into one of the many slashes in the fabric. "My ma and Mother Holt had a sister-wife named Sarah. She was the oldest of eleven children. I used to call on—spend quite a lot of time at her house before she married Brother Holt. Guess I've just always had a knack with kids."

The piles of feathers were nearly all picked up, leaving single feathers to be retrieved from seemingly every surface, nook, and cranny. Tessa threaded a needle and began stitching the gashes in the fabric. "That's another thing I've been wondering. You call Mrs. Holt 'mother'; why do you not call her husband 'father'?"

"Oh, I don't know. I guess I just considered him to be my mother's husband rather than as my father." William gently slid a feather from one of Grace's curls and smoothed the tendril into place. "He never really treated me as a father would. I always felt like a bother to him—one more mouth to feed—never really welcome. That's why I left the first chance I got."

"Is that why you're leaving again? So you're not a burden to Mrs. Holt?"

"Not in the least. I love her. She's always treated me as good as she would her real son."

Tessa felt the familiar knot constricting her throat at the thought of him leaving. "Then why?" she whispered.

He ran his hand through his sandy hair and looked at her so intently that she felt transfixed by his blue eyes.

"I turn twenty-one at the end of the year, Tess." His voice deepened with earnestness. "I've traveled across the country—three times now. I've fought in a war. And what do I have to show for it?" He held out his empty hands. "I need to move on with my life. I'll send money to help Mother when I find a job, but shoot, Tessa, I don't even have a bed to sleep in. I don't want to spend the rest of my life sleeping on the trading post floor. I want a place of my own. I want a family to take care of."

And there it was again. Despite her girlish dream that he had taken a fancy to her, Tessa knew she was too young for him to seriously consider taking her as his wife. She willed the tears not to fill her stinging her eyes and braved a smile. "Yes, of course."

He placed his hand on hers. "It doesn't mean I'm never coming back."

If we leave for Oregon in the spring, we won't be here if you do come back. She studied the outline of the knuckles on his hand and how evenly his nails were trimmed. A memory flashed in her mind of him leaning against the porch rail at the trading post, his hat tilted low—casting a shadow over his face, trimming his nails with his pocketknife. With tears swimming in her eyes, she couldn't bear to look at him.

"Let's get this finished up." He squeezed her hands. "Gracie and I are hungry for some of that huckleberry jam."

That was all Grace needed to hear to send her into another tizzy of dancing and jumping. "Jam, jam, jam! I neeeeeed jam!"

"THE WHOLE TIME you and William were repairing her mattress," Mrs. Holt grumbled, "Anna was off feeding Christian. I don't mean to complain, but she wasn't in here ten minutes before she disappeared."

Just in the tone of Mrs. Holt's voice, Tessa could here how tired the woman was, so she set to stirring the kettle while Mrs. Holt filled glass jars.

"Michty me!" Mrs. Holt exclaimed, quickly setting the scalding jar on the table and thrusting her burnt hand in the bucket of wash water. "By jing, that's hot!" In her haste to pour sealing wax on the jars of jam, bits of wax had splashed on the back of her hand.

Tessa grabbed the pot of melted wax off the flame and set it to the side before turning to check on her friend's injuries.

"It's just a wee burn." Mrs. Holt dried her hands and rubbed a speck of butter on the reddened mark. "I'm just in too big a rush."

Tessa surveyed the dozen pint jars of purple jam. "Surely this is enough to send with the men."

"I suppose it will have to be."

"That will be plenty," Kurt said as he hefted a bag of pinto beans over his shoulder and carried it out to the waiting wagon.

While the jam cooled on the table inside, Mrs. Holt and Tessa joined the others outside to survey their preparations. True to her word, Mrs. Pixton had fixed a big Dutch oven of stew and biscuits, and the men had enjoyed her hospitality while the women finished the pot of jam. But now it was after three o'clock, and the men were anxious to leave.

"You can wait another fifteen minutes for the jars to cool," Mrs. Holt scolded. "If those jars get jostled, the wax won't seal."

"We'll be lucky to make it to the Tincup 'fore dark as it is," Peter Sundstrom said, cinching the rope that secured his bedroll behind his saddle.

"What tin cup?" Tessa wondered aloud.

"Tincup Creek," Kurt answered. "It's about midway to our grazing range, on t'other side of Grays Hole."

"Grays Lake," Tessa and William corrected in unison.

"That so?" Kurt looked from William to Tessa and back again and then shrugged. "I stand corrected."

Tessa's father emerged from the trading post carrying a small wooden crate fitted with the twelve jars of jam nestled in straw. "This should keep the jars snug in the wagon." He settled the box between the sack of beans and a similar-sized sack of flour.

Seeing the distressed look on Mrs. Holt's face, Tessa realized that her father had just eliminated the woman's last chance of stalling the men from leaving. Furtively, she cast about looking for something to delay their departure. *Food?* No, Mrs. Holt had given them enough to feed a small army for a month. *Axle grease?* No, two full buckets swung beneath the wagon seat. Kurt Sundstrom climbed up onto the bench of the wagon. Crestfallen, she watched Peter swing himself up into his saddle.

William wrapped his arms around his mother, holding her tightly. "We'll come back through in about a week, on our way to Great Salt Lake City."

"Aye. And we'll have more jams waitin' for you when you do." Mrs. Holt placed both of her hands on his cheeks. "*Na h-uile la gu math duit.* May all your days be good."

Clasping her two hands in his, William stooped slightly and kissed her forehead. "God be with you, Mother."

With William and Peter astride their horses, Kurt turned the wagon northward. As the horses moved forward, William looked over his shoulder at Tessa and touched his forefinger to the brim of his hat. Peter also turned and boldly winked at her. Shocked, she turned away until the sound of the horses' hooves and the wagon began to fade.

Tessa surveyed the smattering of people who had come out to say good-bye: Anna, Grace, and Christian; Tessa's father and Mrs. Holt; Peter's parents and their other nine younger children; and the Forsgrens and Andersons—whom Tessa had met at the picnic.

Mary Anderson nodded at Tessa when their eyes met. With her handkerchief covering the lower portion of Mrs. Anderson's face, as it always did, only her eyes were revealed. Such expressive eyes—filled with sadness. Recalling the story Mrs. Holt had told about how Mary's jaw was blown away by a cannon ball in the Morrisite battle at Kingston Fort, Tessa chided herself for wallowing in self-pity just because William left. *How much loss this woman has endured, and now she watches more friends leave. Tessa Darrow, don't be a dolt.*

Feelings of emptiness, however, would not be put off. She realized that, aside from a dozen more families spread throughout the countryside, these were all the people left in the valley. She'd been so busy all summer, first tending her father back to health and then spending every available moment with William, she hadn't had time to feel lonely. Seeing him ride away, however, melancholy swept over her. She missed her friends, her home, her mother, her sister. *Everyone leaves. I hate this.*

"It will get better." The thought came as clearly as if spoken aloud. Her mother's voice. Tessa glanced around, confirming that no one stood near. *I know it will,* Tessa replied silently.

Mrs. Holt came and stood beside Tessa, resting her arm around her shoulders.

"I was just thinking of something my mother used to say," Tessa said. "'Were it not for hope—'"

Mrs. Holt joined with her to finish the quote. "'The heart would break.'"

TESSA'S FATHER SPENT the next week with the other men of Morristown to lay up meat for the winter. Watching them clean deer, elk, and the other game they took made Tessa queasy, so she spent the week taking Grace with her to call on the few families left in town. In the space of a few days, the air had again turned chill and the wind, whistling from the northeast, carried a bitter bite with it. Tessa always made certain Grace was well wrapped before they dashed from the trading post to one of the neighbors, but Tessa hadn't taken the time yet to make a warm covering for herself, so she carried Mrs. Holt's knitting basket with her, hoping to finish a shawl before snow fell.

At the Sundstrom home, Grace romped with the children closest to her age—two sets of twins: two girls who were not yet four, and a little

boy and girl who were barely two. Four more children, ranging in age
from five to eight ran in and out with abandon—laughing, teasing, fighting—while Eliza Sundstrom suckled a newborn. Mrs. Sundstrom went
on and on about Peter—what a dutiful son he was, how so many of the
local girls were sweet on him, how his uncle would be lost on the cattle
drive without Peter's help. *I'm certain the sun rises and sets at your son's bid-
ding, as well.* Was this woman trying to make a match between Peter and
Tessa? Wouldn't William get a chuckle out of that!

Though Grace had fun playing with the Sundstrom children, Tessa
found Mary Anderson's conversation much more engaging, so she made
certain to call on her each day. After a few visits, Tessa no longer had
to remind herself not to stare at the handkerchief covering the woman's
disfigured jaw line, but Tessa frequently caught Grace craning her neck,
trying to see underneath the veil. Mrs. Anderson made light of it but
took to holding her kerchief against her chest when Gracie ventured
too near.

Tessa wished Anna would bring Christian over to visit—since he and
Mrs. Anderson's little Abraham were so close in age—but Anna scarcely
ventured outside of her house unless it was to fetch supplies from the
trading post.

Tessa and Grace were on their way back to the trading post after a
morning of visits when they heard a distant rumbling. It grew louder
and louder, to a thunderous roar as hundreds of cattle came into view
and made their way from the northeast toward Soda Creek. Grace broke
loose and dashed toward them and Tessa grabbed the little girl just
before she reached the creek as the lead steer approached the other bank.
Mrs. Holt joined the two girls to watch the drove of cattle that took several minutes to amble past.

"Don't stand too close to the water," a familiar voice cautioned.

"Willy!" Gracie shrieked, springing into his arms.

Those eyes. Tessa's heart quickened as she stared up into those crystal-blue eyes. The contrast of his slightly sunburned skin made his eyes
twinkle even more brightly, and she had to check herself from reaching
up to stroke the sandy stubble on his cheek.

"You're back!" Tessa fought the urge to throw her arms around him as
well. "We didn't expect you until day after tomorrow."

"William!" Mrs. Holt flung her arms around him, nearly knocking
him off his feet.

"We ran into some weather on the range, so we made short work of
breaking camp and pushed the cattle hard to get them down this far."

Peter Sundstrom whistled loudly and waved from across the creek as he kept the cattle moving forward, and moments later his uncle Kurt and two other men came into view, urging the last straggling cattle to keep up. Several dogs trotted alongside the cattle at the fringes, disappearing in and out of the dust clouds swirling around the crush of cattle, avoiding thousands of stamping hooves and the occasional attempted head butt.

As the herd approached the banks of Soda Creek, it fanned out into the meadow to graze and drink from the shallow stream. One of the men with the Sundstroms gave two short whistles, and the hounds immediately began patrolling the outer edges of the cattle. Tessa watched, fascinated, as the dogs herded the cattle by weaving among them, with nary a growl and scarcely a yip. Not one steer or cow wandered away from the perimeter the dogs established.

THAT AFTERNOON, WHEN Tessa's father and the other men of the town returned from their day of hunting, the trading post filled with neighbors come to visit before the cattlemen rode off in the morning. Elk roasts, potatoes, boiled nettle with fresh mushroom salad, loaves of fresh baked bread, and huckleberry pies disappeared as quickly as the women could lay them out on the counter.

As twilight fell, Mrs. Holt stoked a fire in the fireplace, and Tessa's father brought a fiddle out from behind the counter. "Mind if I play a tune or two?"

"Not in the least." Mrs. Holt beamed at him.

"Tessa, give me an 'A.'"

Without hesitation, Tessa sang "Ahh," then dropped the pitch by a third and sustained that tone while her father tuned the second string from the right to match her pitch. When he moved on to tune the other strings, Tessa stopped singing.

"That's some party trick." Peter stood just behind her, his breath tickling her ear as he spoke.

"It's not a trick," she snapped, stepping away from him. "I have nearly perfect pitch." As soon as the words left her mouth, she realized how uppity they sounded and steeled herself for a deservedly sharp comeback.

Rather than giving tit for tat, however, Peter looked as though he had been duly scolded. He took a step back and thrust his hands deep in his pockets. "Sorry."

Feeling the eyes of those closest upon her, a wave of remorse and embarrassment washed over her. "No, I'm—I'm sorry." She placed her hand on his. "Truly." Urgently, she turned to her father. "Da, what can you play that we can all sing?"

"Well, let's see here. How about this one?" With sure strokes, he bowed an introduction and Tessa and Mrs. Holt led off singing, "Buffalo gals, won't you come out tonight, come out tonight, come out tonight." The others in the room quickly joined in, clapping and stomping their feet in time.

Peter's father left for a short time, reappearing with a guitar that only had four strings remaining and tossed a harmonica to Peter. The three men struck up with "Yankee Doodle," followed by "The Old Oaken Bucket," and song after song till well after dark. As children curled up in the corners and fell asleep, the rousing music turned to hymns. Many times, Tessa would begin singing with a familiar tune only to realize that the folks around her were singing entirely different words.

At the end of the evening, after the visitors had all drifted to their homes, Tessa, her father, Mrs. Holt, and William sat next to the fire, reticent to part for the night. After recounting several adventures of the summer, laughing, and sitting in silence just staring at the dying embers, Mrs. Holt turned to Tessa. "My, but you have a lovely voice, lass."

"It's nothing much." Tessa dropped her head shyly and then smiled. "I haven't enjoyed myself that much since before . . ." Her voice trailed off. *Since before we left home and mother died.*

"Thank you for playing the fiddle tonight, Henry." Mrs. Holt reached over and patted his hand.

Tessa's head shot up. In the midst of thinking of her mother, Mrs. Holt had just called her father Henry—and caressed his hand! *How dare she be so familiar!* Tessa's eyes darted to her father, fully expecting him to reproach the woman. Instead, he was beaming at her!

"My pleasure."

What?!

"What's your favorite song, Tessa?" William asked.

So many emotions waged inside her, Tessa couldn't think what to say. She didn't dare say anything about Mrs. Holt's boldness, and she was appalled that her father was grinning from ear to ear. She knew they were friendly toward each other, but—

"Tessa?" William urged again.

"I, I don't know—" She stopped. She stared at William for a moment. Then she said in the calmest voice she could muster, "I think my favorite"—she turned deliberately to her father—"is one my mother loved."

With her heart pounding, she sang with a soft, crystalline voice the song her mother had sung so often as man after man, fathers and sons, and eventually her own husband left to fight in the war.

"Here I sit on Buttermilk Hill
Who can blame me, cryin' my fill
And ev'ry tear would turn a mill,
Johnny has gone for a soldier."

Her father looked as though he had been slapped. *Do you remember, Father?*

"Me, oh my, I loved him so,
Broke my heart to see him go,
And only time will heal my woe,
Johnny has gone for a soldier."

He dropped his head and stared at his hands clasped between his knees. Despite the pain on his face, she continued.

"I'll sell my rod, I'll sell my reel,
Likewise I'll sell my spinning wheel,
And buy my love a sword of steel,
Johnny has gone for a soldier."

Hearing a soft sniff beside her, she realized Mrs. Holt must be crying, but when she looked up, she glimpsed William wipe his eye with the edge of his fist. She had only meant to remind her father—remind Mrs. Holt—she hadn't meant to upset anyone. As her own throat seized, she struggled through the end of the song.

"I'll dye my dress, I'll dye it red,
And through the streets I'll beg for bread,
For the lad that I love from me has fled,
Johnny has gone for a soldier."

As she ended the song, the others in the room fought to stifle their tears. Her sob wrenched free and Tessa escaped into the darkness, blindly stumbling to the refuge of the hay shed.

CHAPTER 14

"**F**ather?" *From the portico of their family home, Tessa stares in horror as her father, silhouetted by leaping flames, hurls his uniform, then books, toys, and chairs into the bonfire. "Please stop!" Her feet refuse to move, and he utterly ignores her pleas. In the distance, the pounding of hooves—soldiers are coming—several sharp raps—gunshots?*

"Father!" Her scream in her sleep startled her awake and in the same instance, her feet found life. She bolted from the hay shed, flinging the door wide.

"Whoa there! What's wrong?" Peter Sundstrom caught her with an arm around her waist, lifting her off the ground.

As awareness dawned, Tessa realized she'd had another nightmare. She also realized she was dangling in Peter's arms. Thankfully, she had fallen asleep in her clothes, or he might be holding her in her . . .

She pushed away from him, dropping from his grasp, and yelped when her bare feet slapped the frozen ground. "What are you doing here?" she snapped over her shoulder, dashing inside to her straw mattress. She grabbed her socks from under her blankets where she'd kicked them off during the night and thrust her icy feet into them. "Well?"

He stood outside the door, one hand covering the side of his face. "I just—your dad and Sister Holt are making breakfast. I thought you'd be up. I came to fetch you. I knocked."

The gunshots in my dream. It was Peter knocking. She pulled her boots on, tightening the laces around her ankles. "Well, you startled me."

"Didn't mean to."

"I'll bet you didn't," she huffed as she strode passed him, pulling her shawl tightly about her shoulders. She could hear him shuffling along behind her, but she held her head high, marching to the trading post.

Grateful he had awakened her from her horrible dream, she was miffed that it was he who had done so.

"Just in time, Tessabear." Her father turned from the stove and placed a platter of hotcakes on the table.

Mortified that he would call her that in front of others, Tessa darted a look to make sure Peter hadn't overheard. The last thing she needed was for him to tease her over the pet name. "Peter!" she gasped. A vicious red goose egg swelled over his brow and a trickle of blood seeped from a scrape on the side of his nose.

Mrs. Holt spun around and she and Tessa's father converged on the boy.

"Your eye!" Mrs. Holt grabbed his face in both her hands, turning him into the light. "What's happened?"

"You've been in a fight," Tessa's father accused, fixing a pointed stare at his daughter before looking toward the door as if expecting someone to walk in.

"No, he hasn't," Tessa retorted.

"I met with the shed door." Peter pulled the tin mirror off the wall and examined his injury. "I didn't realize the door was open, and I walked right into it. Clumsy of me."

Tessa gasped. *I must have hit him with the door when I ran out!*

Mrs. Holt snatched a dish towel off the peg. "I'll make you a cold compress."

"Here, let me." Tessa took the towel and headed toward the door to fetch ice from the rain barrel, grateful for an excuse to leave the room for a moment, grateful he hadn't blamed her for the mishap, and grateful he hadn't let slip that he had held her in his arms mere moments before.

"I'm sorry," she mouthed silently as she brushed by him.

"SOMETHING SURE SMELLS good in here," Kurt Sundstrom bellowed as he came through the door a few minutes later. Peter's parents followed on his heels, their nine younger children trailing behind, rubbing sleep out of their eyes. The small army filled the trading post, converging on the platters of food on the table.

"Peter!" Mrs. Sundstrom gasped. "What happened to you?"

Her son held the compress to his eye in one hand while he gobbled hotcakes with his other. "It's nothing," he mumbled from a full mouth.

"Did William do this?" his father demanded.

"No," Peter mumbled.

"No!" Tessa was more emphatic. "He walked into a door."

"Not likely," Mr. Sundstrom murmured as he examined his son's eye.

"It's the truth." Peter sighed. " I tripped and met with the door."

Again, he had protected Tessa from the truth.

"Where's William, then?" his father asked, suspicion coloring his tone.

Where is William? Tessa realized that, in all of the confusion, she hadn't yet seen him this morning. She cast a glance at Mrs. Holt, just in time to see her exchanging glances with Tessa's father. "Well?" Tessa demanded, much more sharply than she intended.

"He's up at Sister Larsen's house," Mrs. Holt said.

What? Anna's house?

"Helping her pack." Mrs. Holt pinched her lips tightly together.

"Why?" Peter's mother sounded as shocked as Tessa felt.

"She's coming to Great Salt Lake City with us." Kurt poured purple huckleberry syrup over the plate of hotcakes he held. He sat down, straddling the back of a chair, and began methodically cutting the steaming cakes with the side of his fork.

"Why?" The word escaped before Tessa realized it was she who spoke. Angry thoughts leapt to her mind, imagining all sorts of motives. *Did Anna have feelings for William? Did he encourage her?* She knew she had no claim on him, but they were friends. *More than friends.* Surely she hadn't imagined he was sweet on her. *But he can't be.* For the umpteenth time she reminded herself that this was her infatuation—not his. Anna was closer to his age, and William wanted to start his own family, and . . .

"I found her huddled here on the stoop when I was going down to check on the cattle before dawn." Kurt stared at his plate as he talked, holding his fork in his fist. "I nearly passed right by her in the dark until I heard her crying. She begged me to let her come with us. I woke up Mrs. Holt, hoping she could talk the girl out of it."

Mrs. Holt held the bowl of brown batter in the crook of her arm, whisking it briskly. "She said she was leaving, cattle drive or no. Couldnae stand it here another day. She was even set on leaving her bairns till William talked some sense into her."

"But Gracie," Tessa whispered.

"Not to worry," Mrs. Holt reassured her. "She'll take Grace and Christian with her."

She can't take my Gracie. The all-too-familiar knot twisted in Tessa's throat as she realized she was about to lose the sweet little girl. And to a woman who did nothing but scold or swat when she wasn't ignoring her daughter. "We could keep Gracie here," she offered.

"Not to worry, dear. We helped Anna see how her children need their mother, and how Anna needs her children."

She doesn't deserve her children. Nonetheless, Tessa held her tongue, knowing she was the last one to have any claim on the children—or on anyone else.

TESSA AND CATHERINE, Peter's eight-year-old sister, were drying the last of the breakfast dishes when they heard a wagon rumble down the hard-packed street. The others were already assembled outside restocking Kurt's prairie schooner. "That must be William." Tessa grabbed Catherine's hand and dashed for the door.

"And Anna." With two words, the child brought Tessa to a halt.

Dropping the girl's hand, Tessa straightened her shoulders and smoothed her skirt. "Yes, and Mrs. Larsen."

William guided Anna's wagon to a stop behind the covered wagon, jumped down, and helped Grace, then Anna—holding her baby—down from the seat. Anna, looking sullen, stood resolutely beside the wagon wheel.

Gracie, however, hurled herself at Tessa and wrapped her arms around Tessa's legs. "We're going to Lake City!"

"Yes, I know." Tessa squatted down beside the child and tucked the little girl's blonde curls into her bonnet before tying it securely under her chin. *How could Anna even think of leaving her behind?*

"I'm going to see my *mormor* and *morfar*. We're going to live in their big house on Quince Street."

"Your grandparents?"

"Yes!" Grace jumped up and down, squeezing Tessa's hands in excitement. "And I'm going to sleep in a real feather bed with Bethany!"

"Beth—" Tessa's gasp caught in her throat at the mention of her late sister's name. Her emotions bubbled to the surface before she had the chance to force them down.

"She's my aunt." The little girl chattered on, oblivious to the tears spilling down Tessa's cheeks, or how the young woman's hands shook as she clasped Grace to her breast. "Bethany's five. Mama said we'll be like sisters . . ."

My Bethany was nearly five. Tessa looked toward her father, silently imploring him to do something to prevent her from losing this little girl as well. Her father stood a few feet away, with one hand gripping the cinch strap of the horse he was saddling. She saw his white knuckles, the clench of his jaw, the pain in his eyes, but he did or said nothing.

"... That's it! You can come with us and be my sister too," Grace squealed.

"No—I can't." Tessa deposited the little girl on the step and scrambled into the trading post, flinging the door shut behind her. Collapsing into a heap beside the door, she held a wad of her skirt between her teeth, trying to muffle her sobs.

She heard the door softly open and close. Heavy footsteps stepped past her. Chair legs brushed the floor; the chair creaked as someone sat down. She opened her eyes just a slit—just wide enough to confirm they were his shoes before squeezing them shut again.

"I hate you for bringing me here."

He said nothing.

"I said I hate you."

"I heard you."

His quiet voice made her blood boil. "It's your fault Bethany is dead."

Silence.

"And my mother."

She heard him draw a breath, but still he said nothing.

She lifted her head.

He sat in the chair, head bowed, his hands clasped tightly between his knees.

"I'll hate you till I die."

He lifted his head, tears pooling in his eyes. He looked at her squarely. "And I will love you forever."

The pain in his face was too much to endure. She threw herself into his lap, curling her knees up and laying her head on his shoulder, just as she had done as a child. He wrapped his arms around her, his cheek resting on her hair, and rocked her—just as he had when she was a child.

"I MISS HOT baths. I'm tired of wiping the dirt off with a scratchy washcloth and cold water from the creek. I want to lay in a tub and soak." With tears spent, Tessa stayed on her father's lap, enjoying the comfort of his arms around her, soothed by the rhythmic rise and fall of his shoulder under her head with each breath. For as long as she could remember, sitting on his lap was her place of haven. Not during one of his moods, of course, but if she got scolded by her grandmother or got hurt, curling up on his lap was her comfort. She kept her eyes closed, remembering their life in North Carolina, including the big claw foot bathtub filled with kettles of hot water on Saturday nights.

"I miss watching your mother curling your hair around her fingers."

Tessa smiled at the memory. "And then tie rags through the curls to hold them in place overnight."

Her father combed his fingers through her hair as he spoke. "She used to tell you if you didn't keep your nightcap on in the winter, the fairies would spin your hair into gold."

"Oh, I remember that!" Tessa shivered a bit, enjoying the familiar feel of her father stroking her head. She slid off his lap and sat on the floor at his feet, keeping her head on his knee. "I wish I had mother's dark hair. It was so striking with her complexion. I never thought it fair that Bethany got her lovely hair and I didn't."

"Indeed, she was a beauty." His hand paused on Tessa's head for a moment. "She loved that you got my coloring, though. She used to call you Honeylocks. I'm glad you got her fiery green eyes. I often see her when I look at you."

Reaching up, Tessa intertwined her fingers with his still resting on her head. "How did this happen, Father? We were so happy at home, and now it's all gone wrong."

He was quiet for several moments. He sighed a few times and drew a deep breath. "It's complicated, Tessa. I'm not sure I can explain it all."

Standing up, Tessa pulled out the chair next to his at the table and sat down facing him. "You could try."

He smiled. "You're persistent like your mother; that's certain."

Returning his small smile, she waited for him to continue.

"My battalion made it into Tennessee. We heard there were Union troops just east of us, so I took a few men to scout the area. We were discovered and set upon." His countenance grew distant and he pursed his lips as though carefully choosing his words. "Long story short, the other five men with me were mortally wounded." Again he paused, staring at his hands, then at Tessa, then at some distant spot.

Even while she and her mother stood outside the newspaper office back home, listening to the names of men killed in the war, she hadn't associated the names with real blood spilt. Picturing her father standing over the bodies of his dead friends, however, made the carnage personal. "Go on," she urged gently.

"I was tired of fighting. I was worried about my family. I made my way back to the rest of the battalion and saw that they were in the midst of another battle." He sighed again and shook his head. "I just couldn't do it anymore. I couldn't lift my rifle to kill another man. I turned my horse and rode away."

You just left? You're a deserter? Tessa had heard enough talk in Charlotte to know the ramifications of desertion. "That's why we had to leave in such a hurry. You knew you'd face court martial."

"No. So many Southern men were leaving their posts, I knew very few ever got court-martialed." He sighed again, choosing his words carefully. "It took me three days to get home. As I rode, I realized it wouldn't take long for my battalion to find my scouts. They'd find them dead and me missing. Either they'd think I'd killed my men or that I was a spy and fled with the Union soldiers."

"And that's why—" Tessa felt numb remembering the ashes still smoldering. "That's why they burnt our home."

Henry nodded. "Your mother and I had talked about going west before all this happened. There was an article about Oregon's Willamette Valley in the newspaper. We never discussed it with real intent, but riding home, I became consumed with the idea. By the time I got back to Charlotte, I could think of nothing else."

Tessa said nothing. She just watched as the torment screwed his face. She was proud of his decision to not lift his rifle against another man, but that decision had destroyed their family. *What else could he have done?* He could have talked to his commanding officer, told him what happened. *But they were in the midst of battle. He would have had to fight.* Solutions were beyond her.

He dragged his hand through his short-cropped hair and then covered his face with his hands, massaging his brows and temples.

"You're right, Tessa. It has all gone wrong. And it's all my fault." His voice soft and thick, he studied the floor. "I don't expect that you'll ever forgive me."

I don't know that I ever can. Flecks of silver dotted his hair, and his short sideburns were nearly pure white. The worry lines in his forehead had become permanently etched. Forgiving him wouldn't bring her mother and sister back, but neither would hating him. *You're all I have left. And I promised Mama I'd take care of you.*

She stood, walked behind his chair, and placed her hands on his shoulders. "What's done is done. We can only make the best of it now."

Standing, he wrapped his arms around her, resting his head on top of hers as they embraced. His breath brushed her hair as he whispered, emphasizing every word. "I will love you forever."

⁓✦⁓

TESSA SAT ON the steps of the trading post with Grace balanced on her lap while she braided the little girl's feathery curls. *Will your mama think to tend your hair, my little Gracie?*

The child held a cloth doll with a porcelain head on her lap, stroking the molded hair painted bright yellow. "Rose used to have a bonnet that matched her dress."

"What?" Tessa paused in her braiding to looking at the now-naked doll. "What happened to her dress?"

"I dunno. She lost it."

Tessa stifled a chuckle at the little girl's matter of fact tone. "Oh, *she* lost it, did she?"

Grace nodded her head once, firmly. "Yes. Sometimes she's very careless."

"I see."

"Sometimes she makes Mother powerful angry," the little girl whispered with a conspiratorial air, casting a glance toward Anna.

Yes, I'll bet she does. Tessa turned her gaze to Grace's mother, struggling with a crate in the back of the wagon. Tessa didn't understand Anna Larsen. She could be so sweet one moment and then turn wickedly hateful the next. Happy and lively or melancholy and simpering—changing moods as easily as some women changed frocks. *What kind of life awaits you in Great Salt Lake City, my little Grace? And mischievous Rose?*

"Do you think she'll get cold on the trip?" Grace wrapped a length of Tessa's voluminous skirt around the doll's little cloth body.

Tessa set the girl on the step next to her. "Wait right here," she instructed, dashing into the trading post. When she emerged a moment later, she held a swatch cut from her skirt and wrapped it carefully around the doll, securing it with a length of matching ribbon. "There. Now she'll stay nice and toasty."

"Oh Tessa!" Grace exclaimed, her bright blue eyes round and shining with delight. "She's beautiful! She looks just like you!"

A brood of squawking hens interrupted the two friends' embrace as William and Anna hoisted a wooden pen filled with chickens off the wagon.

"What in the world?" Tessa blinked her eyes hard to be sure she wasn't hallucinating. Her mouth dropped open. In front of them, a dozen or so chickens in the crate—all sporting brightly colored sweaters.

Gasps and guffaws filled the street as the folks loading the other wagon turned toward the ruckus. William held both arms raised to the square, palms out, and slowly backed away from the cage as though disavowing any knowledge of the contents. His lips were pressed tightly, fighting against the grin trying to escape.

"Sister Larsen." Mrs. Holt stepped forward, her hands cupping the sides of her face, eyes wide, shaking her head slowly. "What in heaven's name?"

Tessa couldn't tell if Anna was about to laugh or cry—the young mother's brows pulled up in the center, causing deep furrows in her forehead, and she bit her lower lip nervously.

Mrs. Holt knelt down next to the crate and looked up at Anna. "What would possess you?"

"I—well—" Anna looked at William, who simply grinned. "When you sent me to toss out the mash left from the huckleberries last week . . . well, I got distracted and set it out beside the trading post and forgot about it. When I remembered and went back to take care of it, I guess it had gone off because it smelled something terrible."

Mrs. Holt gave her a sidelong glance. "Go on."

"I did not want to dump it where you would have to smell it, so I dumped it behind my place."

"And what does this have to do with the chickens?"

William folded one arm over his chest, covering his face with his opposite hand, blue eyes twinkling as he peeked out between his fingers, watching the exchange between Anna and his mother. Peter, his family, and the few others gathered in the street waited expectantly.

"The chickens must have gotten into the mash. When I looked out back, they were all laying lifeless on the ground." She looked around at the crowd listening to her tale before rushing on. "I thought I had killed them. Well, I did not want to be wasteful, so I thought to bone them and ask Brother Anderson to smoke them like he does venison."

"But . . ." Mrs. Holt held her hand out toward the poultry, clucking and pecking at the knitted tubes encasing their bodies. Their heads poked out the top of each sweater and their wings were pushed through slits in the sides.

"I got them all plucked and stacked in a pile, but Christian started fussing, then Grace was acting up, and then it was time to fix supper. I cooked one of the hens that night but by the time dinner was finished and cleaned up . . . well, I was just too tired to do anymore, so we went to bed."

"And in the morning . . . ," William prompted.

"When I went out in the morning, ready to haul them down to Brother Anderson, the chickens were all up and running around, plucky as you please."

The townsfolk erupted in laughter and Anna's faced flamed bright red. Tessa fully expected the woman to burst into tears or maybe dash away humiliated. But Anna stood her ground, sheepishly continuing her tale.

"I suppose the mash had begun to ferment, and—"

"And the chickens were falling down drunk!" Kurt Sundstrom shouted, prompting another wave of laughter.

Anna nodded, a smile playing at the corners of her mouth.

"Liquor's a fowl business," Mary Anderson added, and the laughter began anew. Even Anna couldn't help sharing in the giggles.

"With winter just around the corner," Anna continued, "I was afraid they would all freeze without their feathers, so I have spent days knitting little sweaters."

That's why she left me to take care of Gracie all week! While finding the situation rather ridiculous, Tessa couldn't help but sympathize with all of the work Anna had gone through to protect the chickens during the winter.

"In the end," William said, "there's not enough room in the wagon for the chickens and Christian's cradle."

Anna sighed and turned to Mrs. Holt. "I have no choice but to leave the chickens here with you."

"Oh, dear lass." Mrs. Holt draped an arm around Anna's shoulders, giving her a squeeze. "All that work!"

"The upshot is—" Tessa's father spoke up, drawing the crowd's attention. "If we get hungry, the birds are already dressed!"

AS THE TRAVELERS made their final preparations, Anna asked to speak with Tessa and her father in private. "You have been so kind to me," Anna said.

We have? Tessa thought back on all of the unkind thoughts she'd entertained about this woman, her complaining, her moodiness, and her ill temper with Grace.

"I do not plan on ever coming back here," Anna continued. She peered around at the scattered houses before her gaze returned to Tessa and her father. "I know it is really not mine to give, but I am going to mention it anyway. My house—the Pierssons' house—is very comfortable now that it has been fixed up, thanks in large part to your hard work. I thought the two of you could live in it, at least until you are ready to move on."

Tessa pictured the three-room cabin—she could have her very own bedroom again, in a real house, and learn to cook in the big, rock fireplace that she'd helped build . . .

"Well," Tessa's father cleared his throat before continuing. "That's very generous, but—"

"We'd love to!" Tessa threw her arms around Anna, not giving her father a chance to spoil the offer.

"We don't want to be beholden," he said.

"But you would not be!" Anna laughed as she returned Tessa's hug, shifting her sleeping baby to her other arm. "There is no one to be beholden to. I am leaving; the Pierssons already left. It would just sit empty and fall to ruin again."

"Think of it, Da! We'd each have our own room and we wouldn't have to shake the frost off our blankets each morning like we do in the shed."

"Surely you don't!" Mrs. Holt exclaimed as she and William joined the trio.

"It's not so bad." Tessa's stomach sank as she realized how ungracious her words sounded. "Just a bit on these cold mornings." With pleading eyes, she turned to her father. "Think how cozy we'd be—just till the spring."

"But we don't have any furniture to put in it. What would we sleep on?"

Tessa could tell by the tone in his voice that she'd won this round, but he was right—they would have nothing to sleep on, no table at which to eat . . .

"Pish. You can take your cot and Tessa's mattress from the hay shed, and any other bits you please." Mrs. Holt took Christian from Anna's hold. "It's not swish like Sister Larsen's feather bed, but we can keep fresh straw in the mattresses and you'll be warm for the winter."

"Oh!" Anna grasped Tessa's arm. "That is the best part! Well, not for me, but . . . We didn't have room in the wagon for my bed or my table and benches or my cooking pots . . . just what I could fit in my wedding chest, and a few odds and ends for the children . . . and the rocking chairs Jens built . . ." Her voice trailed off for a moment before she continued. "Most everything is still in the house just waiting for you."

As much as she wanted to enjoy even one night in that big feather bed, Tessa innately understood what a sacrifice this was. "Anna, this is too much—too generous. Your husband made that bed, the table. You can't leave them behind." Tessa looked at William, but he just stared at his shoes, his hands thrust in his pockets.

Anna shrugged and smiled a sad smile. "I have no choice. There's nowhere to put them in my parents' home, and I'd have no way to get them to Great Salt Lake City even if there was room."

Tessa looked over at Anna's wagon, where Grace sat on the back edge swinging her feet back and forth as she fussed with the makeshift dress on her doll. Anna was right. The wedding trunk and Christian's cradle took up most of the room with Grace's little bed standing on end at the head of the wagon and the rocking chairs wedged in between the other furniture. There simply wasn't room to take the larger pieces.

"They're only things," Anna said. "Pieces of wood and a pile of feathers. But you know how dear they are to me. I know I can trust you to take good care of them."

A shrill whistle sounded from the lead wagon. "Time to move out!" Kurt Sundstrom bellowed.

"We'll take the best care of them," Tessa whispered as she hugged Anna good-bye. "I promise."

"And when you're ready to have them back, you just let us know," Tessa's father added, holding Anna's hand between his. "We'll figure a way to get them to you."

"I hope we'll someday meet again." Anna's voice was thick as she took her baby from Mrs. Holt and hurried toward her wagon.

Tessa was about to follow when she heard her father's voice.

"William, would you post a letter for me when you get to Great Salt Lake City?"

She turned in time to see her father hand a thick envelope to William. In her father's strong script, "Mrs. J. W. Darrow" was written on the envelope. She wished she had known he was sending a letter to her grandmother and she would have written one as well. *I hardly got to say good-bye.* With a pang, she realized she would have to say good-bye to William in a short moment as well.

"Of course, Mr. Darrow," William answered. "I wanted to ask you something also." He looked from Henry to Tessa and waited for Tessa to join them. "I know things are done differently in North Carolina than here, and I don't want to be presumptuous."

"What is it?"

Tessa saw the flicker of a scowl pass over her father's face and held her breath.

"I'd like to think Tessa and I have become friends."

"And?" her father said darkly.

"I'd like your permission to write to her."

"She's too young to court," he said flatly.

"Father!" She shot him a warning look before coyly wrapping her hands in the crook of William's arm and steering him toward the waiting wagons. "I'd be pleased to accept your letters."

With just a twinge of guilt, Tessa steeled herself for a tongue-lashing. *If Grandmother had heard that, she'd have flicked my mouth and said, "That's enough sass."* But all Tessa heard was the scuff of footsteps behind them and Mrs. Holt's terse whisper: "Oh, let her be." *Thank you, Mrs. Holt.* Tessa and William exchanged a surreptitious glance and the flicker of a smile as they joined the rest of the travelers.

Tessa dropped her hands from William's arm as too many heads turned their way at their approach.

Peter stood up from the wheel where he'd been smearing axle grease and fixed an icy glare on them. "Well, you're cozy."

Oh, go away, Tessa silently commanded.

A smile curled William's lips as he met Peter's stare before brushing passed him. "And you're tiresome."

Tessa diligently schooled her grin, but she couldn't help the tilt of her chin as she too stepped by.

With Anna and her children safely seated on her wagon and all of the good-byes said, Kurt Sundstrom climbed up to the seat of his wagon. He gave a long shrill whistle followed by two short ones. Tessa heard the drovers answer, "Hep! Hep!" from their place among the cattle by Soda Creek, and the dogs took up yipping to get the cattle moving.

William gave Mrs. Holt a last hug before climbing up to sit beside Anna in her wagon. Though she knew Anna couldn't manage the wagon and her children alone, it still rankled Tessa to see William sitting beside the woman.

"I look forward to your letters," Tessa called, instantly embarrassed at sounding so forward—so clingy.

William touched his finger to the brim of his hat and flashed the wide smile that caused his dimples to crease all the way down to his chin.

"Bye, Tessa!" Grace waved her arm wildly. "Come see us in Lake City!"

Tears swam in Tessa's eyes as the wagon moved past.

Peter reeled his horse around in front of her and leaned down from his saddle. "I'll write too," he declared before riding off.

Mrs. Holt gasped. "The cheek!"

"Humph." Tessa didn't try to hide the disdain in her voice, even though Peter's family stood only a stone's throw away. "I doubt he can write his own name."

September 16, 1865

With her journal open on her lap and pencil poised, Tessa stared out the window of her new bedroom. Despite the cold, she'd tied the deer-skin back so she could write by the light of the late afternoon sun rather than lighting a candle. As she contemplated how to record her myriad emotions, she hummed the song she had sung only the night before. *"I'll sell my rod, I'll sell my reel . . ."*

She set her pencil to the paper and wrote, *What would I sell to ensure my love's safe return?* Embarrassed at the boldness of the word, she scribbled out *love's* and wrote *friend's* above it. But he was so much more than a friend. His face, his voice, his smile, his laugh were embedded in her soul. Even thinking of him filled her with comfort. She drew a line through *friend's* and wrote *love's*. She contemplated a moment, then wrote, *I have nothing to sell. Nothing to offer.*

Sighing, she closed the book and set it on the little round table next to her bed. Outside, a few fluffy snowflakes swirled in the waning sun. *It's cotton season back home. Da should be in the fields with his men.* She closed her eyes and could almost see Mama and Eula, their hair tied up off their necks, frying stuffed pork chops, stirring a pot of acorn squash soup, pecan pies resting on the sill, all ready for the harvest feast celebrating the day the sacks of cotton went to market. *This time last year, I was teaching Bethany how to break broccoli "trees" into bite-sized chunks.*

Oh, Mama. Why did you have to leave? I need you. I'm supposed to be telling you that I think I'm in love. You're supposed to scold me and tell me I'm just spoony—and that I'm too young. I think you'd like him, though. She paused, recalling the look on her father's face when William had asked permission to write, and the flit of anger when Tessa agreed, cutting off her father's response. She'd waited all day for the fallout over that move—sidestepping her father as often as she could while they settled their few things into their new home. Though he'd said nothing yet, the tension prevailed throughout the day.

What if William does write to me, Mama? Will Father pitch a fit? And what's proper to write back? Stroking the cover of her journal, she traced with her finger the pressed flowers her mother had glued in place. The ribbon extending from its place between pages evidenced how few precious pages there were left to write on. *What if he doesn't write? What if he doesn't come back?*

Tears trickled down, moistening her pillow. She grimaced as the now-familiar, acrid smell of wet straw wafted up. *I want my fat cotton pillow!* Flinging her stiff straw pillow at the far wall, she cringed with bated breath, hoping the mat wouldn't hit the window and knock the deerskin from its nails.

A lady schools her temper. Tessa almost laughed, hearing the echoes of her mother's voice. "Oh, Mama," she sighed, flopping back into the embrace of the feather bed, "that's one lesson I'll never learn."

"Cooey! Hello, neighbors," Mrs. Holt called. "Anybody home?"

Tessa rubbed her eyes, realizing she had drifted asleep. She heard the latch lift on the front door and its soft sough as her father opened it.

"Well, if it's not our neighbor, Mrs. Holt, come to call!" Tessa's father exclaimed.

Tessa smiled at the sound of his mock surprise, imagining him doffing his hat and bowing deeply.

"Tessa, we have company," he called. "Put on your party dress."

Reluctantly, she rolled out of her feathered cocoon and slipped her feet into her shoes, not bothering to tie them. She smoothed her dress and hair and flung open her bedroom door. "Why, Mrs. Holt, as I live and breathe!"

The three burst into laughter, and Tessa's father hurried to light the lantern on the table.

"I brought dinner to celebrate your new home." Mrs. Holt hoisted a black kettle in the air, nearly upsetting the pie balanced on top. The aroma of freshly baked rolls wafted from the cotton bag swinging from her elbow.

"I appreciate your kindness, but we've imposed too much as it is."

What? Tessa stared at her father, trying to discern any indication that he was joking. Her stomach lurched with hunger. Fully mindful she was speaking out of school, Tessa feigned her most inviting Southern drawl. "Father, you're a dreadful tease to our new neighbor." She took the pot from the beleaguered woman and set it in the center of the table. "We'd be charmed if you'd sit with us for supper."

Thankfully, her father played along without missing a beat. He pulled a chair out for Mrs. Holt. "As the lady of the house said, we'd be perfectly charmed."

CHAPTER 15

"Brigham. Pay attention." Grieg Sundstrom gave one loud clap of his hands, startling his seven-year-old son from his daydream. "Miss Darrow didn't come to watch you draw."

Tessa also jumped at Mr. Sundstrom's clap, realizing she'd been paying more attention to the smell of the Christmas gingerbread baking and studying the cedar boughs draped over the door, festooned with garlands of juniper berries, than with watching the children trace their spelling words.

For the three months since William and Peter left, Tessa had visited with Peter's family daily and helped the two older children with their reading and math. With no school established in the area, the children's only education came from what their mother had time to teach them. And with nine young children still at home, the oldest of who was only eight, Eliza Sundstrom didn't have time to teach them very much.

With little paper available for their lessons, Tessa had brought a pail of sand from the bank of Soda Creek that she spread on a tarp on the table each day. The children practiced spelling and arithmetic by writing in the sand. Mistakes were easily wiped away to make room for another try.

While Brigham and eight-year-old Catherine attended to their studies, seven more children, including the two sets of twins, vied for attention. Since the weather had turned cold and the snow long since blanketed the fields, Grieg Sundstrom, Peter's father, stayed home most days, watching the older children huddled around Tessa. Eliza was left to corral the younger children and nurse the baby.

"Brigham," Tessa said, sighing. "You'll not learn to differentiate similar words by drawing pictures instead of writing the words."

"Huh?" The little copper-haired boy squinched up one freckled cheek.

"You can't learn grammar by drawing animals."

"Can too," he shot back. "See? It's a bare bear."

"All right, smarty. Then write 'bare bear' in its correct form."

"Whad'ya mean"?

"I mean, write 'bare bear' here in the sand, spelling them in the correct way for each meaning."

While his father, Tessa, and Catherine watched, Brigham smoothed a swath of sand and carefully traced the letter B in the sand. He sat for a long moment with his finger poised to draw the next letter before wiping out the B and retracing it. He wrote A next, wiped it out, wrote E in its place, and then wiped that out as well. At last he looked up at Tessa with his brow furrowed. "I don't know which way to spell them."

Tessa fully expected his father to cuff him on the back of his head for drawing pictures instead of paying attention, but when she looked at the man, he stared at the sandy table with a puzzled expression on his face as well.

"How do you spell 'bear' "? she asked the boy.

"B-e-r-e," he answered.

"B-e-a-r," his father corrected.

Tessa smiled.

"Or b-a-r-e," Catherine chimed in, bobbing her head as she spoke each letter.

"Very good. Now, how do you know when to use which spelling?"

The children looked at her and shrugged.

"Ahh." Tessa smiled even bigger and tapped the side of her nose. "This is where language gets fun. Look at the bear Brigham drew. What does he have on his head?"

"Ears," Catherine and Brigham shouted in unison.

"And how do you spell ear?"

Again in unison, the students said, "E-a-r."

"Very good." Tessa stood up and moved to the other side of the table to stand behind Catherine and Brigham's shoulders. Their father moved to her side, craning to watch Tessa's hand.

"So . . ." She wrote e-a-r in the sand and then traced a B in front of it. ". . . we can remember how to spell the animal 'bear' because a bear has ears." She underlined the e-a-r in the word. "But," she said, pausing as she drew e-a-r in the sand again next to the first. She then drew W in front of it. "If a bear has nothing to wear on his ear—" She underlined the word *ear*; then as she spoke, she wrote *b-a-r-e*. "—he must be bare."

"If a bear has nothing to wear on his ear, he must be bare." Mr. Sundstrom studied the table, arms folded across his chest, repeating the phrase. "Well, isn't that clever?"

Tessa looked up at him and realized every member of the Sundstrom household, even Mrs. Sundstrom holding the baby, was gathered around the table watching Tessa's demonstration.

Six-year-old Joseph hastily swished a clear patch of sand at the end of the table, and precisely wrote the words the older children had been studying. "But, if a bear did have something to wear on his ear, where would he wear it?" He placed his hands on his head. "Right here!"

"Joseph!" the children exclaimed.

Amazed, Tessa looked back and forth from the table to Joseph. "You spelled every word correctly!"

The little boy stood next to his father, chin tilted proudly in the air, his arms also folded across his chest. "Now who's the smarty?"

Surrounded by laughter, his father caught Joseph under the arms and swung the boy high in the air. "You certainly are, son! Joseph the smarty."

"Oh my goodness!" Mary Anderson laughed as Tessa recounted the story that afternoon. "What a precocious little boy!"

"He must have been listening and watching while I gave Catherine and Brigham their lessons." Tessa held the Anderson's ten-month old son, Abe, on her knees, bouncing him up and down.

"I think you're making quite the impression on the whole family."

Tessa smiled politely but, remembering Peter's awkward flirtations, took no pleasure in Mrs. Anderson's observation.

She sat Abe on the quilt spread on the floor and picked up the knitting she had secreted at the Anderson's house. With satisfaction, she examined the scarf she was making for her father. Every time she worked on it, she chuckled anew at the uneven stripes of bright colors. As Anna's chickens tried to peck free of their sweaters, Tessa had removed and unraveled the garments. After carefully cleaning the yarn, she knitted it into a scarf for her father's Christmas present.

Now, on the afternoon of Christmas Eve, Tessa finished the last few rows of knitting, cast off her stitches, and tied clusters of yarn fringe on each end of the scarf. Her father had made a new pack mule sawbuck for a trapper and received a warm buckskin hunting coat as payment, but the coat was rather large on him and hung loosely open at the neck. *If only you hadn't burned your officer's coat.* Tessa looked at her handiwork with satisfaction, draping it around her own neck three times to be sure it was long enough for her father.

"He'll love it," Mary reassured her. "Even more when you tell him where the yarn came from."

Beaming, Tessa could scarcely wait to give it to him in the morning. "He will, won't he? I wish I knew how to knit him some mittens to go with it."

Neils Anderson, Mary's husband, burst through the door and thrust it shut behind him. "Brrrr! The snow's really picking up out there." As if to punctuate his point, the door blew open on its leather hinges, letting in a blast of arctic chill. Neils quickly swung the door closed again and dropped the wooden pin into its tether to hold it shut.

"Oh, hello there, Tessa."

"Good afternoon, Mr. Anderson." She stuffed her bits of yarn and knitting needles into the flour sack she used for a tote and then carefully folded her father's scarf and nestled it in the bag. She nodded toward the oiled-paper window. "It's getting pretty dark out there. I think I'd better be heading for home."

"We could get two feet of snow or more out of this one," he replied, shaking the wetness off his coat. "Make sure your pa brings in plenty of firewood tonight or he'll be chopping off soggy bark in the morning."

"I'll be sure to tell him."

"If the snow's not too deep, we'll come wish you a Merry Christmas tomorrow," Mrs. Anderson said as she unlatched the door.

"Oh, I hope you can." Tessa gave Mary a parting hug before pulling the hood of her knitted cape up over her hair. "I'll bake some extra corn pone." With that she set off through the thickening snow, clutching the flour sack concealing her Christmas treasure tightly to her chest.

Between the overcast gloom of the afternoon and the icy flakes falling in sheets in front of her, the Sundstrom home on her right looked like a ghostly silhouette. Shards of light flickered through the cracks of the boards used to close the windows off from the storm. She thought to stop in at the trading post on her left to wish Mrs. Holt a happy Christmas Eve, but the store was dark and the wind was picking up.

A hundred yards farther up the street, Mr. Pixton, looking like a bear dressed in his big fur coat, carried an armload of wood into his house and slammed the door behind him. If he had seen her, he gave no indication. *No matter.* Despite reminding herself to forgive and forget, Tessa couldn't get over their first meeting when Mr. Pixton would have happily left her father to die.

In the few minutes since leaving the Andersons' house, the snow had changed from thick, fluffy flakes to stinging ice crystals driven sideways by the angry gale. She could normally walk the half-mile in a few minutes, but it seemed like she had been walking at least a half hour today. The snow was falling so thickly now that she could no longer see the trading post behind her or her house in front of her. Looking back over her right shoulder, she could just barely make out the Pixtons' house. A nervous knot twisted in her stomach as she realized how easy it would be to get lost in this blizzard. Tessa ducked her head against the wind, holding her bag in one hand and clutching her shawl covering her head and shoulders with the other, trudging her way through the deepening snow.

At last, the outline of her house took shape ahead and to the left. Drawing closer, she realized her father and Mrs. Holt were standing outside her bedroom window on the east side of the building, fitting the last of the storm boards into place.

As she approached, she tripped on something covered by the snow and tumbled to her hands and knees, losing her grasp on her shawl and her bag. "No!" she gasped, her only thought to save her father's gift. Scrambling for the bag, her skirt tangled under her knees, and she skid face-first into the icy drift. "Och, Tessa!" she heard Mrs. Holt exclaim, but before she even had time to lift her head, Tessa's father scooped her into his arms and carried her and her precious bag into the house.

Mrs. Holt brought the lantern over to inspect Tessa's cheek while her father stripped her wet boots and socks off her icy feet. "Och, that'll be nippin' in the morning."

Tessa winced as Mrs. Holt dabbed at the scrape on her cheek. Her father wrapped her feet in a dish towel and then replaced her shawl with the blanket from his bed.

As she started to warm in front of the fire, Tessa leaned her head back in the rocking chair she sat in. *A rocking chair!* She jumped up and spun around to look at it, nearly tripping on the cloth wrapped around her feet. "Da! Rocking chairs!"

"Merry Christmas!" He beamed at her, proudly adjusting the two rocking chairs in front of the fire.

"He worked on them every day while you were off schoolin' the Sundstrom kids." Mrs. Holt looked nearly as proud as Tessa's father did.

Tessa caressed the peeled branches sanded smooth and fitted together to form arms, seat, back, and legs of two chairs. The rockers were crafted from—she stooped down to get a better look. "Are these wagon wheels?"

"Sure are," her father said. "I found a broken wagon out past the Soda Creek."

He had sawn the wheels apart and used portions to create the chairs' rockers.

"Oh, Da." She wrapped her arms around his chest, hugging him tightly. "They're beautiful. I love them."

"Well, I had thought to surprise you with them in the morning, but with this storm, I didn't want them to get all wet."

"The storm!" Almost in unison, Tessa, her father, and Mrs. Holt realized how bad the storm was becoming and that Mrs. Holt still had to get home.

"It's getting Baltic out there," Mrs. Holt said, drawing her fur-lined, canvas cloak up over her head and cinching the leather straps tight under her chin. "I'll be snowed in here if I don't get moving."

Tessa's father pulled on his coat as well and grabbed the lantern off the table. He lit a candle in the lantern's flame, planted it firmly in a candleholder, and thrust it toward Tessa. "You'd best get out of those wet clothes and into your nightgown. There's some chowder simmering on the fire for supper—"

"And some fry cakes," Mrs. Holt interrupted.

"And some fry cakes. You get warmed up while I see Maureen home."

"Wait! I have something for you too, Da!" She grabbed the scarf out of her bag, praying it hadn't gotten wet, and wrapped it snuggly around her father's neck.

"Well, this is just the ticket," he exclaimed, giving her a peck on the cheek. "Now we've got to hurry. I'll be right back."

"Good night, luv," Mrs. Holt called over her shoulder. "Happy Christmas to you!"

Despite the bitter cold on her bare feet, Tessa watched her father and Mrs. Holt from the open door as they hurried toward the trading post. Watched him wrap his arm around her waist to steady her through the blizzard. Watched until the driving snow obscured her view of his lantern.

"I'll see Maureen home," he said. *So you've become just as familiar with her as she has with you.* While the newness of the relationship still rankled her so soon after her mother's death, Tessa was glad her father had a companion to spend his days with. He had changed since they came west. He seemed so much happier now . . . less gruff . . . less worried. *You deserve another chance at happiness, Da.*

She walked out of her bedroom, dressed in the flannel nightgown Mrs. Holt had helped her make. She sat in her new rocker to pull on dry stockings and then cuddled in her da's woolen blanket. She reflected on the different trials she, her father, Mrs. Holt, and William had faced in just the last few years. *After everything we've been through, we all deserve some happiness.*

Mesmerized by the flames dancing in the hearth, she dared to dream what it might be like to sit in front of a fire with William, all cozy, just like this. *Three months, and he hasn't yet written.* Was he still in Great Salt Lake City? Had he traveled west? Was he all alone for Christmas? As she had heard Mrs. Holt do so many times, she prayed, "Dear God, please keep our William safe." She closed her eyes for just a moment and woke up the next morning snug in her feather bed.

CHAPTER 16

Awakening to a silence so thick it felt suffocating, Tessa blinked several times in the darkness to ascertain whether she truly was awake. She looked across the room to the window, but the darkness surrounding her was so complete, she couldn't even make out the outline of the deerskin flap. Enveloped in the quiet, her breaths quickened and she listened to the swish, swish, swish of her pulse reverberating in her ears. *Everything's fine. It's not yet morning. Father's asleep in the next room. It's Christmas.* She smiled at the thought and her breathing eased. *It's Christmas. I'll sleep just a bit longer and then start a lovely breakfast.*

As she contemplated sprinkling dried currants in the flapjack batter, her eyelids slid closed.

Whump.

What was that? Tessa bolted out of bed at the noise and groped her way past the end of the bed, to the wall, to the window. She untied the bottom corners of the deerskin and lifted the flap. A thick crust of frost covered the oiled paper sealing out the cold. Slits of gray showed between the boards her father had put up on the outside of the window. *The storm boards. That's why the room is so dark. The sun must already be up.*

She felt her way back to her bed, fished her stockings out from under her quilt, and pulled them on.

"Merry Christmas, Tessabear." Her bedroom door swung open and her father stepped into the room, holding two steaming mugs in one hand and the lantern in the other.

"Merry Christmas, Da." She took one of the mugs and wrapped her hands around the hot vessel. "Hot chocolate?" With her eyes closed, she held it under her nose while inhaling the fragrant sweetness. "Mmmmm. Where did you get the chocolate?"

"A gift from Mrs. Holt. I had to melt it in hot water instead of milk. What do you think of it? Oh, wait! I almost forgot." He dashed from the room, reappearing a moment later with two peppermint candy sticks. "She left these as well. You stir the hot chocolate with it."

Tessa swished the red-and-white-striped stick in her chocolate, then lifted the candy, and sucked the dripping liquid from it. Her eyes flew open wide. "Oh, that's good!"

Tessa and her father spent several minutes perched on her bed, sipping their cocoa and slurping their peppermint sticks. As Tessa licked the last of the chocolaty peppermint from her fingers, her father said, "How about flapjacks for breakfast? I'll get them started."

In the time it took Tessa to dress and unsuccessfully search her room for her shoes, her father had a fire leaping in the hearth. "Da, I can't find my—oh, there they are." Her shoes hung on the ends of sticks wedged in the seats of the rocking chairs a few feet from the fire.

"They were soaking wet last night. It would have taken them from here to Sunday to dry."

"I barely remember taking them off."

"I don't wonder. That was some storm you walked home in. You didn't even stir when I carried you to bed."

Slowly, Tessa began to recollect the events of the previous afternoon. Walking through the snow . . . watching her father disappear into the blizzard with his arm around Mrs. Holt . . . daydreaming about William while she waited for her father to come home. . . . Rather than chance an argument by mentioning his growing relationship with Mrs. Holt, Tessa pulled on her toasty shoes and changed the subject. "I'll collect the eggs for breakfast."

"I don't believe we'll be having eggs for a while."

"Why?"

He scowled for a moment, pursing his lips. "I heard a ruckus last night. I think coyotes or maybe wolves got into the chicken coop."

"No!" The image of her scrawny, naked hens being ravaged by wolves brought bile to her throat. "Why didn't you stop them?" she accused.

"Because it was the middle of the night. And I wasn't about to charge into a pack of wild animals in the dark, in a blizzard, to battle for some chickens."

Of course he couldn't have gone out last night, but why didn't he check on them instead of wasting precious time fixing hot chocolate? Tessa fixed him with her most withering stare, grabbed her cloak, and bounded for the door. Without breaking stride, she shoved the door to open it, but the door didn't yield. So great was the force of her momentum, her arm crumpled underneath her and she slammed into the door with her shoulder. She clutched her arm and curled forward, gasping to catch her breath.

Her father guided her to one of the rocking chairs and knelt beside her to examine her arm and shoulder. "And that's the other reason I couldn't save them. We're snowed in."

"What do you mean, 'snowed in'?"

"It looks like the snow's piled higher'n the windowsill. We must have four feet or so. The door won't open."

Tessa stared at the door, trying to picture the snow mounded three-fourths of its height.

"That's certainly something we'd never see back home, is it?" he said, chuckling.

"This is no laughing matter," Tessa scolded. "How are we supposed to get out? We're trapped in here!"

"We're not trapped, Tessa. We'll have some breakfast, then I'll pull the paper off a window, climb out, and clear us a path."

"With what?" She struggled not to give way to panic as feelings of claustrophobia clutched tighter.

He held up the fireplace's ash shovel triumphantly. "With this!"

"Father. Be serious," she reproached.

He took his daughter by the shoulders, looking at her squarely. "I am serious, Tessa. I will take care of you. You'll be fine. Now let's have breakfast so I can get started."

AFTER A BREAKFAST of flapjacks dripping with chokecherry syrup, Tessa's father removed the deerskin flap and the wood frame wrapped with oiled paper from Tessa's bedroom window. Standing on a stool, he used the fireplace poker to push the lengths of wood up and off their brackets, letting the late-morning sun—and painfully frigid air—stream in.

He had only removed two of the four-inch wide boards when Tessa heard caroling voices coming their way.

"Hark the herald angels sing,
Glory to the newborn King . . ."

Tessa fetched a chair from the other room and scooted it next to her father's stool so she could see outside. She squinted against the glare of the sun on the snow, trying to see to whom the singing voices belonged. Two tall silhouettes, walking on top of the snow, came into view pulling a wooden sled. As the two drew close enough to block the glare, she recognized Mr. Sundstrom and Mr. Anderson.

"Merry Christmas!" they called.

"Merry Christmas," Tessa returned. Normally, the bottom edge of the window would be at least chest high on the men, but today Tessa stared at their shins as they stood on top of the deep snow outside.

"You can't come inside," her father said, "we're snowed in."

"We know." Mr. Anderson bent down and peered through the narrow opening at them. "We came to shovel you out."

"Give me a hand with these boards," Tessa's father said, "and I'll come out and help."

"What are those paddles on your feet?" Tessa asked.

Mr. Sundstrom lifted the oval frame strapped to his foot off the ground so it was in front of Tessa's face. "Snowshoes," he said. "They keep us from sinking in the snow."

"Well, isn't that something." Tessa's father stuck his arm through the window opening, pinching the roped webbing on the snowshoe. Leather straps woven through the webbing crisscrossed up the men's shins, securing the contraptions to their feet.

"Henry, you stay inside and put the paper back on the window," Mr. Anderson directed. "We'll get your doorway cleared in no time. And we brought a sled to take you to the trading post to have Christmas with us."

Sadness swept over Tessa as she thought about Christmases past. Laughing with her family as they exchanged handmade trinkets, cousins spilling out of every room as her Darrow and Price relations gathered for Christmas dinner—a feast lasting most of the day, the house festooned with garlands of fruits and flowers. *Christmas*, Tessa thought bitterly, knowing the Christmases of her youth were forever gone.

"Neils," Mr. Sundstrom said, "let's get these boards back up."

Just that quick, the window was boarded over again and Tessa and her father were left in the relative gloom of the lamp-lit room. They made short work of fitting the papered frame back in the window opening and then nailed the frame securely in place.

Well, this is a fine Christmas. Tessa watched her father smooth her quilt and fluff the straw in her pillow before gently setting it in place. He whistled cheerfully, as though all was right with the world.

Put the pouting away and make it a better day. Tessa reminded herself of her mother's familiar admonition. *I promised Mrs. Anderson corn pone for Christmas, so I guess I'll make enough for the whole town.* As the rescuers worked outside, Tessa busied herself mixing the batter for dinner's corn pone while her father stoked the flames in the fireplace and kept the kettle hot. Every now and then, she heard the men's shovels scrape against the door, but with no window on that side of the house, there was no way to gauge their progress.

About an hour later, as Tessa was pulling the covered skillet of pone from the fire, the door swung open, letting in a blast of cold and filling the cabin with sunlight. The two rescuers stomped the snow from their boots before stepping into the warmth. They carried half dozen dead, bloodied chickens.

"My chicks!" Tessa gasped at the sight of the birds she had come to regard as her pets.

"Your coop's collapsed," Mr. Anderson said. "We found these in the rubble."

"I heard wolves or something out there last night. I wonder if the coop came down on them." Tessa's father took the tattered hens and laid them in the sink.

"May have," Mr. Sundstrom agreed. "That would explain why they left these behind."

Tessa felt sick to think of what had happened in the night. Nearly two dozen hens lost. Valuable meat and eggs, gone. *I hate this place.* She looked around the room, at the sympathetic faces watching her. *Don't spoil Christmas, Tess.* There it was again, her mother's voice schooling her in the etiquette of the day. She forced a small smile and said, "How does Southern fried chicken for dinner sound?"

WHILE THE MEN warmed themselves drinking huckleberry tea in front of the fire, Tessa and her father plucked the thin new feathers from the chickens. "I can fry them up at Mrs. Holt's so they're piping hot for dinner." After cutting the chickens into pieces, she packed them in a large stockpot and tied the lid on.

With the stockpot and basket on their laps, Tessa nestled next to her father on the bench on the wooden sled, covered by a buffalo rug, while the two men on their snowshoes pulled the sled over the icy snow. At the trading post, the snow cleared from the steps and porch left drifts well over Tessa's head on either side of the path. A larger sleigh was parked outside. It sat upon a steel frame suspended above the metal runners, with two rows of leather-upholstered seats, and enough room for at least eight people to ride in. Two of the little Sundstrom boys laughed on the porch, sword fighting with icicles. Tessa smiled as she imagined what fun the Sundstroms must have whisking across the snow in such a grand sleigh.

Handing the big pot of chicken to her father, Tessa slipped the basket of corn pone over one elbow, and then clung to her father's arm to keep from slipping as they gingerly made their way into the trading post.

"Merry Christmas!" Mrs. Holt called, wading through the crowd of neighbors packed into the room. Her dining table was pushed against one wall and her mercantile counter pushed against the other to make as large an open space as possible.

"Merry Christmas!" The other folks gathered in the room greeted Tessa and her father as they entered. Mary Anderson sat in a chair rocking Abe, and Mrs. Sundstrom stood next to her rocking Patience. The Pixtons took up two of the chairs, and a ragged-looking man reclined in another, stretching his fur-chaps-clad legs out in front of the fire.

As the stranger heaved himself to his feet, a familiar voice cut through the clamor from behind Tessa.

"Merry Christmas, Tessa. Mr. Darrow."

William? Tessa whirled around in time to see Peter Sundstrom duck through the door, his arms piled with freshly cut logs.

"Peter." Disguising her disappointment, she forced herself to be gracious. "Welcome home. And merry Christmas to you." He looked older than he had just three months before. Was he even taller? "When did you get home?"

"Just past midnight, I think," he said, stooping down to place the logs next to the fireplace. "We got slowed down by the blizzard, but we made it in time for Christmas."

Tessa studied how his suede shirt pulled across his shoulders as he stacked the firewood. His hair seemed darker than she'd remembered it, and the fire picked up its coppery highlights.

He smiled as he stood up and caught her watching him. "I hope you've been well."

"Yes," she stammered, "yes, quite well, thank you."

Peter stood next to the stranger and introduced him to Tessa and her father. "Have you met Parley Ellis?"

Tessa tilted her head politely, and her father extended his hand. "Henry Darrow."

"Glad to know you," Mr. Ellis replied, shaking hands.

"That was quite the storm you came through," Tessa's father said.

"Not so unusual for this time of year. Would have been nice if it had held off a day, though."

"Parley's a trapper in the northwest territories," Peter explained. "When I heard he was coming through here, I decided to travel with him."

Peter's mother threaded her free arm through her son's and laid her head on his arm. "What a lovely Christmas present you've brought us, Mr. Ellis."

FOR THE REST of the day, the community enjoyed Christmas together. Mrs. Holt kept busy supplying everyone with sticky pull-apart buns and spiced cider. As the friends ate one batch, another one baked in the cast-iron oven, and another bowl of yeasty dough sat atop the hot oven rising while Mrs. Holt stirred together and kneaded yet another batch.

When the last batch of pull-apart buns came out of the oven, Mrs. Holt placed the large ham roast that Peter brought from Great Salt Lake City in the oven. Tessa stirred together a paste of brown mustard, apple preserves, and brown sugar to warm on top of the oven at Mrs. Holt's direction. She fanned the fumes toward her face, breathing in the spicy sweet aroma. "My mother used to glaze ham with brown sugar, molasses, and a dash of bourbon," Tessa told Mrs. Holt.

"Bourbon!"

Tessa laughed. "She said it was her mother's secret ingredient."

"Miss Tessa," whispered five-year-old Elizabeth Sundstrom. "Can we show them our play now?"

Butterflies tickled in Tessa's stomach. She and the children had been rehearsing secretly, but now that the time was at hand, she worried if the children could remember what they'd planned.

"What's this?" Mr. Sundstrom asked.

"The children have planned a Christmas surprise," Tessa announced, pulling folded lengths of fabric and gunny sacks out of her basket. "We'll be with you in one moment."

She and all of the Sundstrom children except Peter ducked behind the curtain separating Mrs. Holt's bedchamber from the rest of the room.

In a moment, eight-year-old Catherine came forward holding a leather-bound book. In a soft, halting voice, coached only on the more difficult words, she read: "And it came to pass in those days that there went out a decree from Caesar Augustus . . ."

On cue, as each passage was read, the rest of the Sundstrom children emerged draped in bits of fabric or wearing a gunny sack tunic. First, six-year-old Joseph appeared with Elizabeth who sat astride seven-year-old Brigham crawling on his hands and knees. When they reached Catherine, Elizabeth sat on the ground and Joseph stood next to her with his hand on her shoulder. Next came Parley and Jacob, holding tall sticks like shepherds' staffs, and then Priscilla and Jenny wearing braided wreaths of yellow twine on their heads like halos. As Catherine read of the birth of Christ, Tessa placed a squirming baby Patience in Elizabeth's arms.

Catherine closed the book and recited, "And suddenly there was with the angel a multitude of the heavenly host praising God, and saying—"

The rest of the children joined her in proud voices, "Glory to God in the highest, and on earth peace, good will toward men."

The adults in the room applauded and cheered while the children took their bows. As Tessa stood back, watching the children receive their praise, Mr. Sundstrom draped his arm around Tessa. "Well done, Tessa. Very well done."

Back home, a gentleman—especially a married gentleman—never would have touched a young woman in such a familiar manner. She quickly sidestepped from his arm and took one step farther for good measure. "Thank you, Mr. Sundstrom." Then seeing Mrs. Sundstrom watching with tight lips, she added, "But your wife deserves most of the credit."

WHILE THE CHILDREN napped, the adults played card games, using different types of dried beans instead of poker chips. Mr. Ellis and Peter taught the group a new card game, pinochle, played with a special deck that Mr. Ellis retrieved from his pack. Try as she might, Tessa—who barely understood how to play poker—couldn't quite grasp the rules of this new game.

"Not to worry, lass," Mrs. Holt said, heading toward the kitchen area once more. "You come help us women fix supper."

While Peter, Mr. Ellis, Mr. Sundstrom, and Tessa's father continued their game, Mr. Pixton slept next to the fire. Mr. Anderson strapped on his snowshoes to check on the horses in his livery and feed and milk his cows.

"Neils," Mary Anderson called after him, "if you'll bring a bottle of cream when you come back, I'll make a custard tart."

Mrs. Pixton carved open a pumpkin and set the chunks to simmer, and Tessa and Mary peeled and sliced apples retrieved from the barrel out back. Mrs. Holt scooped a cup of dried huckleberries into a bowl of cold water to reconstitute for pie, and then opened a bottle of lemon syrup that Peter had brought from Great Salt Lake City to flavor a meringue.

The women shooed the men off the table so they could roll out piecrusts. Undaunted, the men arranged two chairs face-to-face to suffice as a table so they could continue their card game sitting on the floor. Mrs. Sundstrom sat in the only free chair, nursing the baby while she peeled potatoes.

When the apple pies were assembled, Mrs. Holt withdrew the ham from the oven to make room for the pies. Tessa plastered the sugary paste over the ham. When the pies were done baking, she helped Mrs. Holt guide the fragrant roast back into the oven to finish.

While Tessa's father sliced the baked ham onto a serving platter, Tessa made quick work of dredging the chicken pieces with flour and frying them in bacon grease.

"That sure does smell good," Peter called from his card game on the floor.

Tessa smiled at Peter's praise but thought how much better it would smell if she could remember what spices Eula used on fried chicken back home. *Wouldn't Mama and Eula be surprised to see me cooking supper!* She looked up and caught Peter watching her. She smiled again, not bothering to demure, and wasn't offended in the least when he winked.

Mrs. Holt lifted two mason jars of green beans from the shelf. Instantly, the women in the room swarmed around the six-inch bottles, cooing and admiring the preserved beans.

"That's a lot of falderal over green beans," Tessa whispered to her father.

He shot her a sharp glance. "Well deserved, I'd say, considering out here they can't just send a girl to the market to fetch them."

AFTER DINNER, TESSA'S father brought the fiddle out from behind the counter once more and accompanied the party singing carols. Without the addition of Mr. Sundstrom's guitar or Peter's mouth organ, the clear strains of the violin set the timbre of the carols from reverence to jubilation.

Throughout the afternoon, Tessa listened intently to Peter's resonant baritone as he harmonized with his father's bass. Funny how, in just three months, he had changed from an irritating, gawky teenager into a young man whose attempts at flirtation were rather flattering. *Has he changed so much? Or is it just because William isn't here to compare him to?* As father and son sang "The First Noel," Tessa softly sang a light descant with them, being careful not to overpower the men's voices. At the end of the carol, the others in the room broke into applause and the trio made a dramatic display of bows.

"Well," Mrs. Sundstrom said, handing the baby to Tessa and taking the two-year-old twins, Jenny and Jacob, by the hands. "I think we'd best get these littles settled at home before it gets too dark. Papa, will you bring the sleigh up?"

Peter picked up the three-year-old twins, Parley and Priscilla, swinging each under his long arms like a gorilla would carry her young. "Say good night, monkeys."

"Good night, monkeys." They laughed, clinging to his forearms.

The rest of the Sundstrom family and Mr. Ellis filed out to climb in the big sleigh.

Mr. Anderson balanced himself in the doorway while he strapped on his snowshoes to help haul the loaded sleigh. "Brother and Sister Pixton, I'll be back directly to take you home." When he returned a short while later, Peter came with him.

"I thought I'd give Brother Anderson a hand taking folks home," Peter said. "Mrs. Holt, I hope you don't mind if I visit a while longer."

"'Course not, dear, you know you're always welcome." Mrs. Holt helped Mrs. Pixton on with her coat.

Mr. Pixton gave an exaggerated harrumph when he stepped out on the porch to discover only the little two-person sled waiting to ferry them up the street rather than the Sundstroms' large sleigh. He settled himself and two leftover pies in the center of the bench, leaving his wife to perch on the inadequate corner of the seat.

As she closed the door on the departing neighbors, Mrs. Holt sighed. "Would've been lovely to have our William home for Christmas."

Tessa instantly felt guilty. She'd been so busy helping with the cooking all day that she had scarcely thought of William. *It's not like he's your beau*, she told herself, but renewed guilt surfaced as she remembered the fun she'd had singing with Peter. She wrapped her hand around Mrs. Holt's. "I'm sorry, Mrs. Holt. Maybe another family gave him Christmas dinner like you did for us."

Mrs. Holt paused for a moment before squeezing Tessa's hand. "Maybe so."

When Peter and Mr. Anderson returned from delivering the Pixtons, Mary Anderson lifted two packages from behind the counter. She gave the larger one to Tessa. "Neils and I have been working on something for you."

Everyone in the room watched as Tessa fumbled with the knotted string, then gave up and wedged the package out from under the string's grip and pulled the paper off. With a gasp, she held up a hooded, chestnut-brown fur cloak. She stood and wrapped it around her shoulders, swinging her hips to watch how the fur swirled around her calves. Tears leapt to her eyes as she reveled in the warm softness. "It's so beautiful. But it's too much. I can't accept it." Even as she spoke, she stroked the ring of especially soft fur outlining the hood.

"It's not too much," Mr. Anderson said. "We've seen you traipsing about with just your little knitted shawl. You need something warm."

"We won't take it back," Mrs. Anderson added. "You've become my dear friend." Her eyes misted over and she touched a handkerchief to her nose. "What kind of friends would we be if you got sick in this cold?"

"What kind of fur is this?" Tessa's father fingered the fur at Tessa's shoulder and that on the hood.

"The cloak is coyote," Mr. Anderson answered. "I got lucky and snared a couple of beauts. And the hood is rimmed with mink."

"Mink!" Tessa gasped. Only the most affluent women in North Carolina owned a piece of mink.

"Remarkable." Her father wrapped his hand around the silky fur. "I didn't know mink roamed this far south."

"There aren't a lot, but every now and then I'll find one in a trap."

"Oh, and they're nasty beasts," Mrs. Holt added. "They'll take your finger off as soon as look at ya."

"And there's a muff too," Mary said, pulling another tuft of fur out of the brown paper wrapping.

Tessa caught her breath as slipped her hands into either end of the soft tube. "I'll be toasty for certain! I can't thank you enough."

"You just did." Mr. Anderson laughed and handed the smaller package to Tessa's father. "I made a little something for you, also."

"You really shouldn't have, Neils. I have nothing to give you."

"You got well, Henry. You've given us plenty. And just look at all the help you were rebuilding our smokehouse. And all the fine meat you've helped us store up. Yes, sir, you've earned that and more."

Henry tore open his package and held up two large mittens of darker fur than Tessa's cloak. "My, but these are grand." He pushed his hand into one, holding it up to admire.

"They're muskrat. Keep your hands nice and dry."

"Muskrat! These are just the ticket. Thank you, Neils, Mary."

"You're so very welcome," Mrs. Anderson said.

"Well, I've got a little something for Tessa too," Mrs. Holt said, disappearing behind her bedroom curtain. She reappeared holding something behind her back. "It's not nearly so grand, but . . ." With a flourish, she pulled a carved wooden horse from behind her back.

Tessa and her father both gasped at the same time.

"That looks just like—" Tessa reached out her hand, tentatively touching the bare-wood carving. "Is it—?"

"Aye, child. One of your grandfather's horses."

"I thought you burned everything." Tessa gently took the horse, not bothering to brush the tears from her cheeks.

"I did burn it all. I saw some Indians picking through the ashes in the pit. One of the children was holding this. I traded him some horehound candy for it."

"But you said everything was infected with smallpox."

"Indeed. The fire scorched it pretty good, so I hoped any infection had been burnt off. Just to be sure, I've soaked it in lye several times since then and rinsed it with vinegar each time. I'm sorry, but between the fire and the lye, it lost all of your grandfather's beautiful paint."

Tessa's father stroked the chiseled mane. "It's beautiful just the way it is."

Tessa hugged Mrs. Holt tightly and then her father, unable to speak.

"Well," Mr. Anderson declared, "time to get you folks home. Mary, we'll take the Darrows first, then swing back to collect you and Abe." Mr. Anderson and Peter strapped on their snowshoes to pull the sled through the dusk.

Tessa wrapped herself in her new fur cloak and pulled the hood up over her hair. She bid Mrs. Anderson a merry Christmas and hugged Mrs. Holt once more. "Thank you for a wonderful Christmas." Mrs. Holt smiled but said nothing and Tessa noticed the tears swimming in her eyes. Tessa stood on tiptoe to kiss the woman's cheek before she and her father settled themselves on the waiting sled.

Peter and Mr. Anderson made short work of pulling the sled the quarter-mile up the street to the Darrows' home. Peter ushered them inside holding his lantern high so Tessa's father could light the lantern waiting on their table. Turning to leave, Peter pressed a piece of paper in Tessa's hand.

"What's this?" she asked.

"Merry Christmas," he replied and then ducked out her door.

CHAPTER 17

Dressed in her flannel nightgown, Tessa sat cross-legged in bed with her quilt drawn up over her knees and pulled the candlestick to the edge of her nightstand. She turned the letter over in her hand, noting how it was folded to create its own envelope. *Miss Tessa Darrow, Morristown, Idaho.* No return address.

Though William had promised to write, this was the first letter Tessa had received and she wanted to enjoy it herself before sharing it with her father. Presuming it was from William. *It must be. Peter wouldn't write a letter when he knew he was coming home and would see me.* But how did Peter get the letter? Unless William knew Peter was coming and gave the letter to him to deliver. *Then William must still be in Great Salt Lake City. But if he is, why did he wait so long to write?*

Rolling her eyes at her ability to talk in circles even in her own mind, Tessa pulled the letter open and smiled at the painstakingly crafted script. Here and there, the ink puddled at the bottom of where two letters joined. Though legible, the penmanship looked like that of a child.

Hello, Miss Darrow. She smiled at his formal greeting. *I hope this letter finds you well.*

Line by line she read of his safe arrival in Great Salt Lake City with the cattle, news of Kurt Sundstrom's family, exploring the Great Salt Lake, hiking Ensign Peak—a small mountain that overlooked the city—and plans to pass through Morristown on his way to the range in the spring.

In the spring? When in the spring? Tessa felt the familiar giddiness when she thought of William returning. Eagerly she read on for specifics of his return, but nothing except more mundane details of his time in Salt Lake came.

She scanned down to the letter's end. *Yours with regards, Peter Sundstrom.*

"Peter?" she whispered. *Not William?* Of course it was from Peter. Why else would he have delivered it himself? For several minutes, Tessa contemplated various reasons why William had not yet written, even after going out of his way to secure her father's permission to do so. Was he hurt? Had he traveled beyond Great Salt Lake City? Did he no longer want to continue their friendship? Had her father dissuaded William without her knowledge?

For each possibility, Tessa mentally developed a counter reason of why he hadn't written. In the end, there was no cause she could think of that would keep William from writing to her—except that he just didn't want to. *Well, maybe I do not care to hear from you, William Bates. Getting a girl's hopes up, then ignoring her. Not a proper gentleman at all, if you ask me.*

She looked at Peter's carefully written signature. It was obvious he had spent a great deal of time writing as neatly as he knew how. She wished she hadn't been so mean when he left in the fall with his own promise to write. *Who would have imagined you'd be the one to keep your promise?* Vowing to reward his thoughtfulness with greater kindness, she folded the letter back into its envelope shape and tucked it under her pillow. With her thoughts jumbled between longing and anger at William on the one hand, and gratitude for Peter's diligence on the other, she blew out the candle on her first Christmas in this new land.

THROUGHOUT THE SNOWY days of winter in Morristown, Tessa divided her time between tutoring the Sundstrom children in the mornings, calling on Mrs. Anderson, and spending many afternoons with Peter exploring the area, trudging in snowshoes.

Thankfully, the heavy snows of Christmas Eve did not return, but smaller storms blew through every couple of weeks to leave a fresh layer of powder atop the frozen base. Comings and goings on horseback or on foot had trampled paths between each of the homes and outbuildings, and up to the banks of Soda Creek, creating tall snowdrifts in their wake. Tessa navigated the gloomy channels wrapped in her fur cloak and muff, eagerly noting how, little by little, the drifts receded as the weeks passed.

Her birthday, March 5th, dawned with a chill wind that rattled the paper framed inside the window. Creeping out of bed, Tessa padded to her door and opened it quietly to sneak a peek at her presents. She knew it wouldn't be much this year, but still her heart beat quicker as she tip-toed out to the table. *Nothing?* She glanced around the room. Maybe her father put them somewhere else? After a thorough search of the small room, she returned to her bedroom and eased the door closed behind her.

When she heard her father shuffling around, she quickly dressed and greeted him cheerfully. "Good morning, Father."

"Good morning, Tessa. How did you sleep?"

"Just fine, thank you."

"Good, good." He knelt by the fireplace, blowing on the embers to bring up the flame.

Well, if he's not going to mention my birthday, then neither will I.

Just the same as every other day, she roused the fire in the belly of the cast-iron stove and set the griddle on to heat while she stirred together batter for hotcakes. She made the beds, cleaned up breakfast dishes, put beans and salt pork on to soak for supper, swept the floor, and still heard no mention of her birthday.

Continuing on with her day, she gave the Sundstrom children new spelling words to study for the week. The children, unusually fidgety through their lessons, blocked her path to the door when she tried to leave. They jumped up and down giggling while Mrs. Sundstrom fetched a package from her bedroom.

"Happy birthday!" they shouted.

Mrs. Sundstrom held the package out to Tessa. "We ordered a little something from Great Salt Lake City for you."

Tessa accepted the square box, taken aback by their thoughtfulness to order something for her—far enough in advance for it to arrive for her birthday. One of the trappers passing through must have dropped it off when he delivered other supplies. "How did you know it's my birthday?" *Even my own father didn't remember.*

"Peter told us months ago," Mr. Sundstrom said.

Peter stood to one side, a big grin spread across his face, arms folded. "Surprised I remembered?"

"Indeed," Tessa responded. "I can't even think how you knew."

The smile faded from Peter's face and he shrugged. "I might have overheard you telling—someone else."

I don't think I've told any—William. You were eavesdropping on me and William?

"Open it! Open it!" the children shouted.

Tessa shot a scowl at Peter for his eavesdropping, but at least he had remembered her birthday. William hadn't. Not even her father had acknowledged the day. *This will likely be my only gift this year.*

As gently as her excitement would allow, Tessa untied the string securing the wooden box. Nestled inside lay a four-inch silver hand mirror, with a matching comb and brush.

"These are beautiful," Tessa exclaimed, holding the set up for all to see.

"So are you," Peter said, lifting two-year-old Jenny up to get a better look.

"Ha ha," Joseph laughed. "Peter's sweet on Miss Tessa."

"Joseph!" Mr. Sundstrom lightly cuffed the six-year-old on the back of his head. "We're all very fond of you, Sister Darrow."

Tessa smiled, blushing just a bit. "Thank you," she said, turning to hug Mrs. Sundstrom.

DESPITE HER IMPULSE to run home and show her father her birthday gift, Tessa tucked the package into her knitting bag and went to call on Mrs. Anderson as usual. *We'll just see how long it takes Da to remember my birthday.* She rehearsed in her mind how she would set the wooden box on her bedside table without mentioning it to her father. She wondered how long it would take him to notice it there or that she was no longer borrowing the wooden comb he had carved.

After visiting with Mrs. Anderson, Tessa trudged home to cook supper. Opening the door, she gasped at the sight of the table laden with packages wrapped in brown paper. Mrs. Holt turned from stirring the big pot over the fire and Tessa's father jumped up from his rocking chair.

"Happy birthday!" they shouted in unison.

"You remembered?" Tessa threw her arms around first her father's, then Mrs. Holt's neck.

"Of course we remembered, Tessabear."

Tessa dropped her knitting bag next to her rocking chair. "You didn't say anything this morning." She hung her fur cloak and muff on the back of the door. "I thought you'd forgotten."

Her father smiled and kissed the top of her head. "I wanted to be sure you'd leave the house so we could surprise you with dinner."

"It's a lovely surprise, Da—and Mrs. Holt. Thank you."

After their dinner of venison stew with fluffy rolls, Mrs. Holt presented Tessa with a sweetbread cake drizzled with white icing. Tessa blew out the candle and Mrs. Holt sliced into the fragrant mound, revealing a cake with raisins and currants. "It's the closest I could come to a Selkirk bannock," she explained.

"It's lovely," Tessa said, breathing deeply of the sweet aroma.

"I wanted to bake something special for your birthday. I used to help my mother bake bannock in Scotland." Mrs. Holt hovered behind Tessa and her father, waiting for them to take a bite.

"Delicious," her father pronounced.

Mrs. Holt grinned and clasped her hands in front of her chest.

"Mmmm," Tessa agreed with her mouth full. She stood up and hugged Mrs. Holt, surprised at the firmness with which Mrs. Holt hugged her back.

As they licked the last of the crumbs from their fingers, Tessa's father cleared the plates from the table and laid the pile of gifts in front of her.

"Oh my," Tessa said. "I didn't expect much of anything this year."

"Go on then, " Mrs. Holt said, scooting the packages closer to Tessa. "Open them."

"Where should I start?" She eyed the packages and decided to unwrap a larger one first. A light pink satin ribbon was tied in a bow through the twine holding the paper together. She pulled it off gently.

Grinning, Mrs. Holt snatched the ribbon from her and tied it in Tessa's locks. "I thought you might like this in your hair when the weather is fine."

"Indeed!" Tessa touched the silky ribbon. "Won't I just be the talk of the town?" She untied the twine, pulled the paper from her present, and held up a sky-blue cotton dress dotted with pink rosebuds. "Oh!" Tessa and her father exclaimed at the same time. "Did you make this?"

"I wasn't sure of your size," Mrs. Holt said, "but it looks about right, I believe."

Standing, Tessa pressed the neckline of the dress to her own neck with one hand and crossed her other arm around the front of the waist. She turned from side to side making the skirt swing. "It will fit perfectly! Isn't it beautiful?" She hugged Mrs. Holt again, sandwiching the dress between them. Then she carefully folded it and tucked it back in the paper.

Next she unwrapped her father's present. "What—?" She held up a rectangular piece of what looked like carved marble. About eight inches long by an inch wide and no more than a half-inch thick, it looked like a fork with two long, tapering prongs. A red opaque stone, chiseled and polished, was embedded in the grip above the prongs. She turned it over and over in her hands, fascinated at how the piece looked like bark on one side and ivory marble on the other. "What is this?"

"It's a hair fork," Mrs. Holt said.

Tessa was well aware of the devices used to hold a woman's chignon in place. "Yes, but what is it made of? I can't tell if it's wood or stone."

"It's elk antler." Her father's face shone like he had found gold.

Ew! Tessa held it away from her but couldn't resist the beauty of the smooth prongs. "Honest? Elk?" Holding it to her nose, she sniffed gingerly, expecting it to smell like the carcasses hanging in Mr. Anderson's smokehouse, which it didn't.

"The stone in the handle is garnet," Mrs. Holt added. "Your da found it and shaped it himself."

"It really is lovely." Tessa removed the ribbon from her hair, then twisted her thick locks into a knot and wedged the fork into place. She tied the ribbon around her neck like a choker. "What do you think?"

"You're right." With an approving smile, Tessa's father reached across the table and cradled the side of her face. "You will be the talk of the town."

SITTING ALONE WITH her father in front of the fire later that evening, each in their respective rocking chairs, Tessa reflected on family birthdays in the past. Days filled with well wishes from family and friends, an elaborate cake with thick sugar frosting, presents from her parents, grandparents, and even from Bethany. With a sigh, she tucked those memories away.

She picked up her knitting and remembered the box from the Sundstroms still tucked in the bag. "I forgot to show you what the Sundstroms gave me, Da."

Looking up from the flute he was whittling, he raised his eyebrows and drew in a whistling breath when Tessa opened the box to reveal the gleaming dresser set. "Boy, howdy."

"Isn't it beautiful?"

"I'll say." He picked up the mirror and turned it over to examine the carved metal back.

"Do you think it's silver?"

"It's not heavy enough," he said, balancing the mirror on his fingertips as though they were a scale. "It might be silver plate, but I don't think these people could afford that."

"Well, whatever it is, I think it's beautiful, and they were very sweet to give it to me."

Tessa's father looked deeply at his daughter, a worried expression furrowing his brow. "I don't know, Tessa. It's an extravagant gift."

She knew her father well enough to know where his thoughts were leading. "I can't return it, Da. They'd be so offended."

After a pause, he nodded his head. "It's obvious they think a great deal of you."

"And I them," Tessa said, thinking of Peter, but not willing to admit it. "I love those children ever so much."

THOUGH SO DIFFERENT from birthdays in the past, today had still been filled with family and friends. Knowing how much thought had gone into her gifts and even the Scottish cake, the elaborate trappings of previous birthdays seemed excessive—almost gaudy. She pulled the elk-horn fork from her hair and studied how finely her father had polished it before setting it on her bedside table. *Happy fifteenth birthday to me. And many happy returns.*

IN MID-MARCH, TESSA stepped out of Mrs. Anderson's house to find Peter waiting with his horse hitched to the sled. With the collar of his suede hunting shirt turned up and his hat tilted low, he look very much like one of the suave frontiersmen Tessa used to read about in dime novels. He sat atop his chestnut mare grinning at Tessa.

"Peter? What's going on?"

"I've come to take you adventuring." He jumped off his mare, sinking in snow midway up his shins, and helped Tessa climb onto the sled.

"Adventuring?"

"Unless you have other plans, of course," he said, pulling the buffalo rug up over her legs.

Tessa tucked the fur snuggly around her. "Well, this is a little unexpected. I'll have to check my social calendar." She held up her left hand as though it were holding an open book and ran her right index finger back and forth over its imaginary page. "You're in luck. I happen to have a rare, free day."

"Then adventuring we shall go." He bowed formally, with one hand behind his waist and holding his hat in place with the other.

With a smile, Tessa reflected on how much Peter had changed since she first met him six months ago. He'd matured from a gawky boy to a charming young man. *Or maybe it's because you're not constantly comparing him to William?* She studied how the leather fringe on his shirt swayed as he rocked in the saddle in time with the horse's gait. *I'm glad you came back, Peter Sundstrom.*

He turned the rig to the west and headed for Soda Creek, urging the mare forward as she plowed through the snow.

"How far is this adventure?" Tessa called to him.

"Not far," he returned, his breath wafting back in puffs of white frost.

Tessa wished Peter had brought the large sleigh she had seen at Christmas, rather than this little two-person sled. Sitting low to the ground on the wooden sled with its rough wooden bench, Tessa hunched forward trying to keep the rushing wind from whipping the hood of her cloak away from her head.

After about twenty minutes, Peter pulled the horse to a stop next to the stream and helped Tessa alight from the sled. In front of them, ice crusted the edges of the creek bed. A rust-colored formation rose close to the near bank and a plume of steam slithered skyward from its core.

"Peter, it's beautiful. It's so polished—just like it's made out of amber."

"Have you been here before?"

"No." Of all the hikes she and William had taken, they had never made it this far west. She decided against mentioning her time spent with William. "I've been north to Grays Lake with Mrs. Holt and my father, and Mrs. Holt took me into those mountains to pick berries." She pointed to the hills on the south side of the valley. "But I've never been this far west."

"Then it is an adventure," Peter said, beaming at her.

Just then, the volume of steam coming from the formation began to increase.

"What's happening?"

"We'd better stand back a bit." He took her hand and pulled her back to the waiting sled.

First they heard a low, distant rumble; then it picked up intensity—*chugh-chugh-chu-chu-ch-ch-ch-ch*—like a steamboat building up a head of steam, until the pressure erupted at the surface in a churning tower five feet high. Warm air pulsed past Tessa in its fury. Tessa clapped her hands. "Peter! This is Steamboat Spring!"

"How do you know? You said you haven't been here before."

"I read about it in the guidebook we followed when Da and I came to Soda Springs."

"That right? A guidebook, huh?" A look of skepticism replaced his smile.

"Yes. *The Hastings Guide.*" As quickly as Peter's mood changed, so did Tessa's. *Are you doubting me?* "The book called this area an 'oasis on the Oregon Trail.'"

"Sounds like an interesting book. I'd like to read it sometime."

"Well, you can't. It was burned with the rest of our belongings when my father had smallpox." Before he had a chance to answer, she pounced. "Do you think I'm lying to you? About a book?"

"No. Yes." He rolled his eyes, shook his head, and then sighed. "Of course not. I thought maybe you and William had—I'm being stupid."

She glared at him, recognizing the uncouth boy she had first met.

Then, seeing him standing there—head drooped, hands shoved deep in his pockets, his eyebrows puckered up like a hound dog's—she realized he had spoken out of jealousy. Now she glared even harder—to subdue her smile. "Yes, you are being stupid." She flounced back to the sled and didn't wait for him to help her into it. After tucking the fur rug around her legs, she primly placed her hands inside her warm muff and waited for him to take her back to Morristown.

He put his left foot up in the saddle's stirrup but paused in midair as he swung himself up. Suspended halfway up, he looked at Steamboat Spring for several moments before lowering himself back to the ground. He walked back to the sled and put his foot on the tip of the curved wooden runner. "Tessa, I'm sorry. I don't know what came over me. I've been waiting all winter for the snow to melt enough to bring you out here, and then I let jealousy get the better of me. Please come down and let me show you the rest of the formations."

Seeing him standing there, humbled and holding his hand out to her, Tessa stuck her nose in the air and turned her face away from him—just as she'd seen older girls do back home when they were playing coy in front of a suitor. But she didn't want to be like those girls. She considered them to be uppity and often just downright mean. Peter certainly didn't deserve that kind of treatment. If anything, she was flattered that he would be jealous of her relationship with William.

"No, Peter," she said, turning back to him and taking his hand. "It is I who should apologize. I'm flattered that you'd be so eager to bring me here. I'm sorry for acting churlish." As she stepped down from the sled, she draped her arm through his and followed him back to the stream.

For the next little while, Tessa and Peter examined Soda Creek, noting the several springs lining its bank or swirling beneath its frozen edges. Here and there, formations had built up around some of the springs, with crusty cones of brown, yellow, and red rising several inches.

It didn't take long before the damp soaked through Tessa's boots and stockings, and her feet felt like ice. "I suppose we'd better be getting back," she said. "Thank you for a lovely adventure."

He smiled down at her and cupped her icy cheeks in his big, warm paws.

Her stomach tightened and tumbled. She knew it wasn't proper, but neither did she want to turn away. She prepared to receive his kiss.

"You should have told me you were so cold. Your pa will skin me alive if you get sick." He scooped her up in his arms and quickly carried her back to the sled.

Relieved—but disappointed—that he hadn't kissed her, Tessa kept her head lowered as she fumbled to strip off her shoes and socks under the fur rug. She wrapped the luxurious warmth around her feet and tucked the blanket under her legs.

Before climbing up on his horse, Peter leaned into the sled and tucked the edge of the buffalo under her feet to ensure no drafts crept in. "I do have a question for you."

"Yes?" She wondered what the etiquette answer would be if he asked to kiss her now.

"What exactly is churlish?"

A hearty laugh burst from her lips before she clamped them together. She shrugged and admitted, "I'm really not sure. But my grandmother would say that's what I was being whenever I gave her sass."

Peter pulled the hood of Tessa's cloak up over her hair. "I'll deny it if you tell anyone"—he tucked a few wayward tendrils behind her ear— "but I like your sass."

MARCH SLIPPED BY, ending with sunshine and temperatures warm enough to warrant wearing only shirtsleeves or a light shawl most days. On the valley floor, the quickly melting snow gave way to clumps of meadow grasses and left muddy bogs next to the creek. Trappers frequently stopped at the trading post to restock their supplies and barter wares on their way through the valley.

On the last day of the month, Tessa held split logs in place while her father pounded them down through the soft earth to anchor a new chicken coop. While their initial plan had been to leave Morristown in the spring and continue their journey to the Willamette Valley in Oregon, as the months progressed, and her father made improvements on their home, these plans seemed to diminish. In fact, since last fall, they hadn't even discussed resuming their trip.

"May I ask you something?" Tentatively, Tessa broached the subject as her father used a plumb bob to check the last anchor post for level.

"What's on your mind?"

Tessa tilted the log slightly to bring it into alignment with the level. "Well, actually, I was going to ask you the same thing."

Straightening, her father slowly wrapped the long string around the bob's bronze weight. "Hmmm?"

"Well—" Her stomach twisted in knots as she searched for words to open the conversation without rankling her father. "When we first laid up here, our plan was to continue to Oregon in the spring. It's spring now, and you're building a chicken coop and planning hay crops."

"I thought you were happy here."

His tone was even, but Tessa noted how he folded his arms tightly against his chest, as he did when he got tense. "I am happy," she reassured him. "Well, maybe not happy, but not unhappy. I'm not sure what I am."

He just nodded, his gaze not belying his thoughts.

"I just feel kind of suspended. Like in a dream. Halfway between what was and what will be, and not quite sure of what is." She tried to bore her eyes into his thoughts. "Does that make sense?"

"It makes complete sense."

Well then? Knowing impatience or impertinence would get his hackles up, she pressed forward carefully. "So what will tomorrow bring? Are we still going to Oregon?"

Sighing, he placed the bob in his pocket, hoisted the mallet over his shoulder, and then walked the ten yards back to their house. Retrieving a pocketknife from his other pocket, he sat on the stoop and picked up the stick he'd been whittling.

Tessa sat beside him, waiting for him to take up the conversation.

He sighed again, with his knife poised over his carving. He rested his forearms on his knees and looked off into the distance. "Well, dear, Oregon seemed like a good idea at the time." He looked down at the carving he held. "But that time has past."

What does that mean? As much as she wanted—needed—more, she held her tongue.

"We had such big plans, your mother and I. But things didn't go the way we'd planned."

"So what are we going to do?" Tessa purposefully whispered to keep her frustration from screaming out.

"I'm not sure yet. We don't have supplies to start out this spring. And we don't have the money to buy supplies. We do have a warm place to stay with neighbors who don't mind us staying here."

So we're staying?

"I might be able to make a few bits of furniture or toys to sell to travelers passing through. I'm pretty handy at repairing rigs. Maybe in a year or two, if you want to move on, we'll have the funds to do so."

"So we're staying."

He shrugged. "I don't see another option right now, unless you've got a secret dowry stashed away."

Tessa smiled at the irony. "At least I won't be expected to provide a dowry if I ever marry."

Returning her smile, he said, "Ahh, there's another worry I'll have in the not-too-distant future."

She raised her eyebrows.

"Your mother and I promised your grandmother we'd take you to San Francisco for your coming out."

"I suppose some promises, like plans, change." She remembered the heated exchange she'd overheard as they packed to leave North Carolina. A lifetime ago.

Smiling, her father took her hand in his. "It's hard to imagine that you're nearly old enough to marry."

She thought back to a couple of weeks ago, when she narrowly missed receiving her first kiss. He would not look kindly on that. "Well, there's no need to worry about that just yet. I don't believe Morristown will have much of a season this year."

With a laugh, he patted her hand and then used his whittling stick to scrape the mud off his shoes. "Not the grand launch we planned when you were born, but I'll figure something out." Cupping her chin between his thumb and forefinger, he tilted her face up to meet his soft gaze. "You'll be a Society Bride yet, Tessabear—we just need to find a society."

CHAPTER 18

The next morning, Tessa awoke early, eager to get a start on the Easter festivities. The evening before, Tessa and her father, Peter, and Mrs. Holt had dyed three dozen eggs in a bath of purple onionskins. Today, she and Peter were charged with hiding the eggs around the trading post for Peter's siblings and Abe Anderson to find.

Tessa thought of the stories Mrs. Holt told of when there were many more families in the area and it had taken several hours into the night for the mothers to gather and dye enough eggs for all of the children. Now, with only five families left in Morristown, it took barely an hour to dye enough eggs for the Sundstrom children and little Abe.

She thought back to the years in North Carolina when her parents took her and Bethany to roll their eggs down the lawn at the Charlotte town hall. While there were no lawns here on which to roll eggs, Tessa smiled as she thought of all of the places where she could hide them.

Yawning, she rolled onto her back and stretched her arms overhead but then jerked them back when something brushed her bare wrist. At her movement, a furry black creature the size of her fist dropped from the rafters and dangled mere inches from her face. With a blood-curdling screech, she bounded from her bed, nearly tripping on her quilt puddled on the floor.

Throwing open her door, she slammed into her father standing just outside with a huge grin on his face.

"April Fool's!" he said, laughing.

Gasping to catch her breath, she smacked his arm with the back of her fist as hard as she could and willed herself not to cry from the fright. "That was not funny!"

"Not even a little bit?" he teased, holding his thumb and forefinger an inch apart.

She punched him again, not as hard. "That was horrid." While he had pulled some pretty elaborate tricks over the years, they had never caught her so off guard as this one. "Shame on you." A dratted smile forced its way on her lips despite her best attempt to sound firm.

Together, they stepped back into her bedroom to examine his handiwork. A tangle of black thread swayed from the rafter above her bed.

"I take it Mrs. Holt was an accomplice."

"Not really. I didn't tell her why I wanted the thread."

Tessa stepped forward, examining the creepy object that seemed to dangle in mid-air. "How is it hanging there?"

"Horse hair." Her father pulled on the nearly invisible line that ran from the spider over the rafter and a short way down the wall. "See?" Pulling the thread down, the spider rose into the rafter. "I anchored it in this split." He pointed to a crack in the wood just above her pillow.

"So when I moved, it dropped." Impressed with his engineering, she nonetheless turned her stern face toward him. "There better not be any more surprises today."

A sly smile spread across his face, and he shrugged. "I can neither confirm nor deny."

She narrowed her eyes to mere slits and wagged a finger in his face. "Any more and you'll stand in the corner."

As quickly as possible, she refreshed the fire in the cast iron stove they'd salvaged from another abandoned cabin, put the griddle on to heat, and then stirred ingredients together for hotcake batter. Out of the corner of her eye, she watched her father setting cups on the table. Turning slightly so her body shielded his view from the stove, she set two hotcakes to the side then plucked a big handful of salt from the cellar and threw it on the cakes sizzling on the griddle.

When those hotcakes were sufficiently toasted, she balanced them on a spatula in one hand and grabbed hers in the other.

"Aren't you going to sit down and eat?" Her father pointed to the cup and plate he had set out for her.

"I'm going to be late hiding eggs if I don't get a move on." She cheerfully slipped the salty hotcakes from the spatula onto her father's plate, and stuffed hers into her mouth as she headed for the door.

"I only get two hotcakes?"

"There's fresh batter if you're still hungry," she muffled over her shoulder.

Just as the door was nearly shut, Tessa heard her father spewing his pancakes from his mouth. "Tessa!"

Opening the door just a crack, she called, "April Fool's!" Laughing she dashed down the street to meet Peter at the trading post.

THROUGHOUT THE MORNING, she guided Abe, just past his first birthday, as he toddled around after the rest of the children searching for the eggs hidden in trees and grasses. When all of the eggs had been discovered, the children sat on the porch peeling their eggs while the adults enjoyed brunch inside the trading post.

Before the families moved off to their own homes for a well-needed nap, Mr. Pixton stood up and cleared his throat. "Brothers and sisters, we've grown somewhat lax in our observation of the Sabbath, but on this Easter morning, I feel it fitting to hold a proper service."

While these people did say grace before every meal, Tessa had never seen them hold a formal church meeting. "I didn't know they held services," she whispered to her father.

"Nor did I." He stopped Mrs. Holt as she passed by carrying her chair. He spoke quietly so only she and Tessa could hear. "Should we leave? We're not Morrisites."

"Of course not," she answered. "We're all God's children, giving thanks for the gift of the Resurrection. You are Christian, aren't you?"

"Well, yes, of course."

"Then you're as welcome as any."

Tessa helped round the children up and sat them on the floor in front of the fireplace before sitting on a chair between Peter and her father. Mr. Pixton conducted the service, opening with a hymn that Tessa didn't know, and stories of the Resurrection, which she did. They even partook of the sacrament—a plate of torn bread and mug of water passed from person to person—so different from the wafers and wine doled out by the minister in Charlotte. After Mr. Pixton finished speaking, Mrs. Anderson led the room singing "Christ the Lord Is Risen Today." Tessa and her father joined in the joyous anthem at full voice.

"I didn't know *you'd* know any of *our* hymns," Peter said afterward as they rearranged the chairs around the table.

Tessa's father straightened and raised his eyebrow. "Actually, that hymn was written by one of the founding Methodist ministers, Charles Wesley."

Recognizing the stern tone in her father's voice, Tessa jumped in to assuage the tension. Smiling, she tilted her head and put a lilt in her voice. "I didn't know you'd know any of our hymns, Peter."

One corner of Peter's mouth curled up in a smile. "I suppose there's much you and I can learn about each other."

Hearing his sharp intake of breath, Tessa grabbed her father's arm and steered him toward the door, leaving Peter standing behind with a puzzled look on his face. *Shut up, Peter. If you know what's good for you, just shut up.*

AFTER THE LATE night of dying eggs and the early awakening to hide them, Tessa was more than ready to enjoy a rare noontime nap. Snug in her nightgown, she nestled into her feather mattress and was on the edge of sleep when she heard a knock on the outside door. *Just the house settling*, she convinced herself, unwilling to shake off her peaceful slumber.

The knock sounded again, followed by the unmistakable groan of the door swinging open. With eyes still closed, she listened carefully to muffled voices to hear if the visitor was just passing by or intent on coming in. A soft knock on her bedroom door jarred Tessa into full consciousness.

As she sat up and swung her feet from underneath the covers, her father opened the door just wide enough to stick his head in. "The Sundstroms are here, Tessa," he said. "Get dressed." With that, he closed the door, leaving Tessa alone.

Yawning, she reluctantly slipped from the cocoon of her bed and shed her soft nightgown. *Why would they come calling now?* she wondered while pulling on her dress. *The children will be cross without a nap.* But she didn't hear the expected tumult from nine children—ten, if you counted Peter—crammed in this little cabin.

Hopping to the door as she pulled on her shoes, she leaned against the wall to quickly tie the laces around her ankles. She listened for a moment and heard two men's voices but couldn't make out what they were saying. She patted her hair into place, smoothed her dress, and then pulled the door open.

Mr. Sundstrom, holding his hat to his chest, jumped to his feet when Tessa entered the room. Mrs. Sundstrom, sitting in Tessa's rocking chair and smiling rigidly, eased herself to a standing position. As the woman straightened the apron of her dress, Tessa noticed for the first time Mrs. Sundstrom's slightly swollen abdomen. *You're indisposed? Patience isn't even a year old yet.* A proper upbringing, however, kept Tessa's words unspoken.

"Mr. Sundstrom, Mrs. Sundstrom," Tessa said, standing by the dining chair her father placed near the fire for her, "how nice of you to call." She indicated to the rocking chairs. "Please, sit."

After a few minutes of chitchat, with Mr. Sundstrom extolling Tessa's virtues as a teacher, he stood once more and addressed the purpose of his visit. "Henry . . . Mr. Darrow, Miss Darrow, Mrs. Sundstrom and I have come to discuss a matter of some importance."

"Oh?" Tessa's father sat taller in his chair, a furrow worrying his brow.

"As you know," Mr. Sundstrom continued, "our family has become quite fond of Tessa. The children have grown to love her, and we"—he gestured to Mrs. Sundstrom—"regard her with most favor."

What an odd turn of phrase, Tessa thought. Trepidation built in the pit of her stomach as she watched Mrs. Sundstrom biting her lower lip and twisting her apron in her hands.

Mr. Sundstrom cleared his throat and continued. "The Lord has seen fit to instruct me to take another wife."

Tessa looked at her father in time to see his eyes go wide, and then he folded his arms across his chest and raised one eyebrow.

"Mr. Darrow, I'd like your blessing to marry your daughter."

"Beg pardon?" Slipped from Tessa's lips. Had she heard correctly? She reminded herself to close her gaping mouth.

Mr. Sundstrom took a step toward her. "I'd like you to be my wife," he stated with as much emotion as one would allot to buy a cow.

April Fool's? Was this another of her father's elaborate hoaxes? A smile played at the corners of Tessa's mouth until she saw the tears swimming in Mrs. Sundstrom's eyes.

Wrapping her fingers around the edges of her chair to keep from bolting from the room, Tessa looked to her father for some clue as to the proper response to this man. *You can't be serious? Do I laugh? Do I slap him? He's being disgusting. But I mustn't be rude.* Her father didn't look at his daughter. She stared at his fingertips, white where they pressed against his arm. She feared her father would attack the man. *Da, no. Not in front of his wife.*

When he spoke at last, Tessa's father's voice was steady and measured. "Mr. Sundstrom, I'd like to know what makes you think God wants you to take Tessa as your wife."

"It's an answer to prayer, Henry. As Mrs. Sundstrom and I knelt for our evening prayers, my thoughts were taken with Miss Darrow, and the Lord's Spirit swelled in my bosom."

The edges of her father's jaw tightened, and he fixed Mr. Sundstrom with a steely stare. "We both know that wasn't the Holy Spirit swelling in your bosom."

The look in her father's eyes terrified Tessa. The same look he'd had the night he burned his uniform. Tessa and her father both jumped to their feet at the same time—he with his arms taut, hands curled not quite in fists; she to take shelter behind her chair.

"I'll thank you to leave my home, Mr. Sundstrom." Tessa's father spoke between gritted teeth. "My daughter will not marry you. And you will have no further contact with her."

"Henry—"

Tessa's father took a step toward the man. "Am I understood?"

After a moment of the two men locked in an angry stare, Mr. Sundstrom replaced his hat on his head and scowled at his wife. "Eliza." He cast a look at Tessa but said nothing to her. Tessa's father held the door open for them to leave.

With his wife safely outside, Mr. Sundstrom turned back to Tessa's father. "Pray about it, Henry."

"You pray, Sundstrom. Pray I don't kill you if you ever speak to my daughter again." He pointed out the door, his other fist clenched. "Get out."

Tessa's father closed the door firmly and stood with his hands planted on the back of the door at shoulder height while he took several deep breaths. *Atlas*, Tessa thought, remembering the painting of the mythical Titan carrying the world on his shoulders. *But Atlas didn't carry the weight of the world; he carried the weight of the heavens.* A surge of warmth filled Tessa as she contemplated her father's role as her protector.

He turned around slowly, rubbing the back of his head with one hand. "So . . . that was . . . something."

She turned her head sideways, looking at him out of the corner of narrowed eyes. "No April Fool's?"

He flickered one brow, but his frown remained grim. "Yes, he is a fool. But, no, this was none of my doing."

For several minutes, father and daughter sat in their rockers, contemplating what had just transpired.

"Who would have thought," Henry said at length, "that the first heart you'd break would belong to your beau's father?"

"Da!" Tessa started to protest that this was no time for humor and that Peter wasn't her beau, but a sick feeling wrapping around her esophagus choked off her words.

"Do you think Peter knows?" Tessa whispered.

"I wouldn't reckon."

"Da, this will kill him. Or he'll kill his father."

Tessa's father was silent for several moments, his brow furrowed, mouth pulled down in a frown, and arms folded. He stared at the hearth for the longest time. When at last he spoke, he didn't look at his daughter. "These people are polygamists, Tessa. Maybe this is just what they do."

"What do you mean?" Tessa remembered how vehemently he spoke when he first learned that Mrs. Holt had been a plural wife.

"See a pretty girl and take her to wife—even if you already have another. See how many women you can collect."

"Father!" Just listening to his words made her feel sullied. Did men out here think women were just like cattle? To be collected? *Not Peter. Not William.* Or were they both just too young to have started collecting brides yet? With tears brimming on her lashes, she felt the peace she had known for the last few months crumbling.

"Cooey!" Mrs. Holt called, rapping on their door.

She can't know! But before she could caution her father, the door swung open and Mrs. Holt marched in.

"Wakey, wakey," she called. "Oh good, you're up!"

Tessa turned her back and brushed the tears from her eyes, but too late.

"Tessa? Are you crying?" Mrs. Holt turned Tessa around to face her. "What's happened?"

The protective tone in her voice was too much, and Tessa's emotions spilled out in more tears.

"Henry," Mrs. Holt demanded. "What's happened?"

With Tessa sitting in the same chair in which she'd received the proposal, but now with her face buried in her hands, her father recounted the details of Mr. Sundstrom's declaration.

Pacing from fireplace to table and back again, Mrs. Holt interrupted the tale several times with Gaelic expressions that Tessa didn't recognize, but which definitely didn't sound proper coming from a lady.

"Gingin wallaper. Help me, boab, I'll take a yopper to 'im." Mrs. Holt vowed, showing her fist.

Hearing the woman's outrage, Tessa didn't even have to ask if Mr. Sundstrom's behavior was acceptable here.

"But how could he think I'd be interested?" For the life of her, Tessa couldn't recall what she possibly could have done to give Mr. Sundstrom the idea she was interested in him.

"Because he's daft." Mrs. Holt snatched Tessa's father's whittling stick off the mantle and sat in Tessa's rocker, twisting the smooth wood between her fingers. "Maybe he thought he was doing you a kindness."

"A kindness?" Tessa's father blurted.

"Well, Tessa's getting near about marrying age. You're just getting back on your feet. Maybe he thought it would ease your burden if you didn't have to worry about getting Tessa . . . situated."

Now Tessa bristled. "You make it sound like I'm a piece of furniture."

"My daughter's not property to be pawned."

"I'm not suggesting that she is," Mrs. Holt defended, before Henry cut her off.

"More likely, he wanted someone to mind all those children," he growled.

"And help Mrs. Sundstrom with the new one," Tessa murmured.

"The new one!" Her father gasped. "You mean she's—?"

"I wondered," Mrs. Holt said, nodding.

"Dirty beggar," Tessa's father muttered, "if you'll pardon me saying."

Tessa smiled at her father's observation of propriety despite his anger. "Well," she said, walking to the sink and looking out the window. "That doesn't solve the problem of telling Peter."

"Blimey!" Mrs. Holt jumped up and joined Tessa at the window. "That's why I came over here. Peter's uncle, Kurt, is back to collect Peter for the spring drive. He and his drovers just rode in."

The drovers—did William return with them? Surely Mrs. Holt would have told her already, but Tessa couldn't help asking. "But no William?"

Mrs. Holt shook her head, eyes filled with sadness. "'Fraid not, lass."

"I'm sorry, Mrs. Holt." Though disappointed, Tessa nonetheless felt relieved that she wouldn't have to sort out her feelings for the two young men just yet.

"I wish he'd write to say he's safe," Mrs. Holt said.

"Maybe Kurt brought news," Tessa offered.

"Maybe." Mrs. Holt placed her hands on her hips and stared out the window toward the trading post. "I'd best be getting back. Sabbath or no, they'll want to get stocked so they can head out at first light." As she opened the door to leave, a faint scent of onion wafted into the cabin. "Oh, and Brother Anderson bagged a brace of ducks earlier. Tildy's got them roasting in her iron kitchen if you'd like to come around for supper."

"I don't know." Tessa's father joined them at the door. "What with all that's happened today."

Tessa nodded. "I can't face Mr. Sundstrom."

"I suppose not," Mrs. Holt agreed, brushing Tessa's hair with the back of her hand. "You get a good night's sleep. Things'll look better in the mornin'."

⁓⚜⁓

AFTER A SIMPLE supper of hasty pudding sprinkled with cinnamon and raisins, Tessa retired to her bedroom early, leaving her father to clean up dishes. As she was unbuttoning her bodice, she heard a soft knock on the outer door. She began refastening her dress, then decided against it. *It's just Mrs. Holt.* If her father wanted to invite her in, they didn't need Tessa to keep them company.

Rather than a woman's voice, however, Tessa overheard two men talking. Had Mr. Sundstrom come back? Tessa buttoned her bodice and stood by the door straining to hear. After several minutes, she heard footsteps approach, and she leaped to her bed to avoid being discovered eavesdropping.

"Tessa," her father called while knocking on her door. "You have company."

Tessa pictured Mr. Sundstrom, grinning expectantly. *I can't face him.*

"Tessa," her father said again, opening the door a crack.

She jumped off her bed and met him before he could enter. "I can't, Da. Nothing's changed. I don't want to talk to him."

"It's Peter," her father whispered. "Come out and talk to him."

And tell him what? How could she tell this young man, whom she had grown so fond of, that his father had professed his love for her? That while his mother watched, his father proposed marrying another wife? That—

"Tessa."

"I can't."

Her father stepped into the room and closed the door behind him. "You need to come talk to him. Peter's hurting, too."

Tessa held her lower lip between her teeth and slowly shook her head.

Her father's voice took on a determined edge. "You can't let him leave like this."

Leave? She fought to still her quivering lip as she realized that, of course, Peter would be leaving with his uncle for the summer pasture.

Placing his hand around Tessa's upper arm, her father guided her to the door, stopping before he opened it. He kissed his finger and touched it to her nose, then wiped a tear from her cheek with his thumb. "You can do this."

CHAPTER 19

You can do this. Tessa silently repeated her father's words as she took the few steps to where Peter stood facing the fire with his back to her. He clasped one hand in the other behind him, holding his head high and standing with his back ramrod straight. "Peter?" she whispered.

Further words choked in her throat as he turned toward her. Though his eyes were dry, the flesh of his brows was blotchy and red. *He's been crying.* Then as he turned fully toward her, she saw the raw welt swelling on his cheekbone. *You've been in a fight!* Without asking, she knew with whom. Though she had come to regard Peter as a man of seventeen, before her stood a vulnerable boy doing his best to remain stoic.

"I'm sorry," they both said at the same time. She stepped toward him and Peter pulled her into an embrace, wrapping one arm around her shoulders and cradling her head against his chest with his other hand.

"Ahem." Tessa's father gently cleared his throat.

As Peter loosened his grip, Tessa stepped away reluctantly.

"Beg your pardon," Peter said, still holding Tessa's hands between his.

Tessa led him to her father's rocking chair and then pulled hers so close their knees nearly touched. "I'm so sorry, Peter."

"No," he replied. "This is my doing."

"What? How?"

"I've done nothing but sing your praises since I met you, Tessa. How could my father not fall in love with you? My whole family has."

"And you?" Tessa felt her heart exploding in her chest.

"From the first time I saw you."

Rather than the heady joy she'd always imagined she'd feel when a young man professed his love for her, the twisting sensation in her chest felt like fire. Dark. Fearful. Suffocating. *Is this what love feels like?* Frantically, she sorted through her emotions, desperately seeking the giddy flutter she'd felt when he'd nearly kissed her a couple of weeks ago, but to no avail. She realized he was waiting for her response, but no words would spill from her lips.

He sat silently looking at the floor for the space of several breaths before finally standing. "I'll be leaving with Uncle Kurt in the morning."

"Peter." She clutched at his hand. She couldn't let him leave like this, with so much unspoken.

At last her father stepped forward into their reverie. "Perhaps Tessa just needs time to sort out her feelings."

"Yes. That's all it is. So much has happened. When you come back in the fall . . ."

Peter stared deep in her eyes, searching back and forth from one to the other, his eyebrows crumpled upward where they met the bridge of his nose. "I won't be coming back, Tessa."

"Of course you will. In the fall. After you take the cattle to market."

"I can't come back. Not after he . . ." He shrugged and shook his head slightly. "I can't live near him."

"But, Peter . . . What if I decide I do love you after all?"

Peter's lips lifted in a smile, but his teal eyes drooped with sadness. He lifted her hand to his lips.

"I'm very fond of you, Peter. Perhaps in time—"

"You can't change your heart as easily as you change your mind, Tessa."

"But in time—" Even she could hear the futility of her words. "Will you write to me?"

There was that sad smile again. "Perhaps . . . in time."

That's all we need, Tessa tried to convince herself. *Just give it more time.*

"Godspeed, son." Her father's voice was thick as he shook the young man's hand. Then he pushed the door open for him.

"Godspeed, Peter," Tessa whispered through her tears.

"It just doesn't make sense." Tessa sat on the floor the next morning at Mrs. Holt's feet, her arms hugging her bent legs to her chest, with her chin resting atop her knees. Her tears of the previous night gave way to alternating waves of anger and dejection tumbling over themselves. "You said polygamy was to help the widows and fatherless children. I'm neither."

"I said that's why our merciful God reinstituted the practice in the latter days. But some men have twisted the practice to suit their own lustful hearts." While Mrs. Holt's voice was matter-of-fact, the bitterness of her words was not lost on Tessa.

"Mrs. Holt, if it's not too personal—" Interrupting herself, Tessa stood up and turned her attention to her father sitting at the table. "Da, would you mind terribly giving us a few moments for some words between ladies?" Growing up, that was the phrase Tessa's mother used when she wanted privacy for a bit of gossip or other important conspiring.

"Of course. I've work to do outside. I'll leave you women to it." He lifted his coat and hat from the peg beside the door, and vacated the cozy cabin.

Mrs. Holt occupied Tessa's rocker, so she turned her father's rocker to face Mrs. Holt and lowered herself into the chair primly, spreading her skirt and crossing her ankles. Gathering as much courage and dignity as she could, she took a deep breath and returned to questioning Mrs. Holt. "I hope you'll pardon me for being direct, ma'am, but I have so many burning questions begging to be asked."

A wisp of a smile crossed Mrs. Holt's lips. "I'll do my best to answer."

Before her courage could fail, Tessa launched the first query. "Why did you let Mr. Holt take another wife?"

"Well, I can't say that was an easy decision, because the decision wasn't mine. When President Young called on us and told Mr. Holt that William and his mother needed a home, we both agreed that they did. But when President Young said my husband was to take Elsa as his wife, Isak agreed without so much as a nod from me." Mrs. Holt closed her eyes and pressed her lips together. "The ceremony was performed that very day, and I found another woman married to my husband before I had time to catch my breath."

Tessa dropped her chin, afraid to ask more—afraid to intrude further into Mrs. Holt's private pain.

Mrs. Holt inhaled deeply. "In for a penny . . ." Sighing, she clasped her hands in her lap and continued. "No, I wasn't happy about it, at first. The idea of sharing my husband with another woman—that's not something any woman should be asked to do. But Mr. Holt and I weren't young and infatuated with each other, either. Isak could be an ornery old goat when he wanted to be. Elsa and I were friends on the trek to the valley, and comforting each other when Isak was in a mood brought us as close as could be. I loved her ever bit as much as I'd love a sister. And I loved William as much as a son of my own flesh."

"But there were no more children?" Tessa bit her lip, not quite sure how to broach the next piece of information. "Did you not . . ."

"Live as man and wife—wives?" Mrs. Holt tilted her head and raised her brows. "Yes, of course we did. Elsa and I would take turns . . . doing our duty. Whoever was not sleeping in the big bed slept on the spare bed in William's room. For whatever reason, or perhaps for God's mercy, no children were born of our union."

Tessa pictured the Sundstrom's little cabin, one large room in front—with a fireplace against the north wall, a table flanked by benches in the center, and two wide beds against the south wall—and a small bedroom in back with one bed and no door. The children must already be sleeping five abreast with Peter home. *Where on earth would they stash a spare bed for the spare wife?*

At last, Tessa felt the opportunity at hand to ask the question she'd been burning to ask since the day she'd first learned of their plural marriage at Hooper Spring last summer. "If I'm not overstepping, Mrs. Holt, may I ask why William left home and joined the aggressors?"

"The aggressors?"

"The Yankees? The War of Northern Aggression?"

Mrs. Holt chuckled. "Well, that's a term I've never heard. Out here, we just call it the Great Rebellion."

Unwilling to lose her chance for an answer, Tessa returned to her question. "William?"

"William." Mrs. Holt pressed her lips into a frown. "I was hoping William would be the one to tell that tale."

A quiet knock sounded, and Tessa's father opened the door just wide enough to stick his head through. "You ladies finished sharing secrets? Kurt left a saddle to repair and the rain's starting to drizzle." He held up the saddle, already spattered with dark water spots.

"Do you mind if Da hears this?" Tessa asked.

Mrs. Holt shook her head lightly.

"Come on in," she instructed her father.

"I'll work over here," he said, dropping the saddle on the table. "Quiet as a mouse."

Tessa and Mrs. Holt shared a smile and a wink as he scraped his chair against the floor pulling it out. He shuffled the saddle into position on the table, unsheathed his knife, clomped to the shelf in the kitchen, and came back with a hank of waxed string and a long needle. Then he scraped his chair legs again and sat down.

Tessa settled herself at Mrs. Holt's feet again, resting her folded arms on the woman's lap in hopes proximity would encourage Mrs. Holt to use a more discreet volume. "William?" Tessa urged.

Mrs. Holt rested one hand atop Tessa's head. "William was always a bonny lad. Hair the color of sunshine, and eyes like flax afield. And perhaps you've noticed his dimples."

"I do admire his dimples," Tessa admitted, smiling as she pictured the impish divots.

"As did just about every lass in the Great Salt Lake Valley. But for as long as I can remember, he only set his cap by Sarah Reynolds. He'd walk her to the schoolhouse and to church, and spend every minute he could sneak away over'ta her house. Many a little scamp shoulda got a bloody nose for teasing William about having a lassy, but William never paid them no mind. And Sarah was just as smitten with him."

Tessa sat very still, trying not to give away her misery at the thought of William having a flame that wasn't her.

"From the time that boy was old enough to earn a nickel, he did odd jobs about town and saved every farthing so he could buy some land and build a home with Sarah. He's the most industrious lad you're like to meet."

"He's a good boy, that William," Tessa's father said from his place at the table.

Tessa rolled her eyes and set her jaw, wishing this conversation with Mrs. Holt could have continued between just the ladies. But it wasn't fair to make her father work in the cold.

"Aye. He's a good boy." Mrs. Holt patted Tessa's head and continued. "A few months after William turned sixteen, he sat down with his mum, Isak, and me, and told us his plans to buy a place on the south end of the valley and ask for Sarah's hand as soon as she turned sixteen. Isak told William he was too young, she was too young, he wasn't ready for the responsibility . . . any excuse you could name. It almost seemed like Isak was angry that William would think to marry Sarah. I should have known something was afoot." She shifted in her rocking chair and was silent for several moments.

"What happened?" Tessa asked at last.

"On the eve of her sixteenth birthday—" All of a sudden, Mrs. Holt stood up, nearly knocking Tessa over. "Oh, that dear Sarah. It's just too shameful." She pressed her fingers to her eyes, shaking her head.

Tessa scrambled to her feet and stood beside Mrs. Holt, unsure how to comfort her. Tessa looked over her shoulder at her father, who was watching with a perplexed look.

"Mrs. Holt? What happened?" Tessa touched her friend's shoulder.

Mrs. Holt slowly turned and removed her hands from her face with a sigh. "I'm sorry. Just remembering those days makes me daft. Elsa was so beside herself, I honestly wondered if she would lose her mind."

Out of the corner of her eye, Tessa saw her father turn quietly back to his work, but he held the needle and thread resting on the saddle's cantle, unmoving.

"Sit." Mrs. Holt instructed gently, gesturing to the rocking chair as she returned to her seat in the other. "On the eve of Sarah's sixteenth birthday, William showed his mum and me the gold band he'd bought her. He'd picked a big bouquet of purple lupine—they were Sarah's favorite—in Emigration Canyon, and he came home to shave before going to speak with her father. Isak had been gone the whole day, and we were rather relieved that he wasn't there to spoil the day for William."

Despite the disappointment of knowing that William had been in love with another girl, Tessa couldn't help feeling a bit fluttery at the thought of the young man's proposal.

"William was just about to mount his horse when himself came up the drive with his bride in the buggy."

"Himself?" Tessa's father asked breathlessly.

"Isak. While William was gathering a ring and flowers, Isak snuck off with William's savings and offered it to Brother Reynolds—in exchange for Sarah."

"No!" Tessa gasped.

Her father blurted something not quite as genteel.

Mrs. Holt nodded. "Sarah comes from a large family, and Isak knew they were in a bad way financially. He took the money and the bishop to the Reynolds', and the deed was done lickety-split. Isak married Sarah without any of us having a say in the matter."

Tessa sat in stunned silence, imagining the horror of watching your intended living as another man's wife—your stepfather's wife. No wonder William left home and didn't write. And now Mr. Sundstrom had tried the same thing? Knowing she, though blameless, had been the instrument of Peter's pain made her sick to her stomach. *How could men purposefully inflict such pain on their sons?* This practice—polygamy—saved families and destroyed them, often within the same house. *I'll not be part of it.* She shook her head firmly.

"Tessa?" Mrs. Holt asked.

"I'll not be part of it. No, ma'am. I will not be responsible for destroying Peter's family."

"This is not upon you, Tessa." Mrs. Holt stroked the girl's hair, threading her fingers through the tangles wrought from not braiding her locks the night before.

The legs of her father's chair scraped on the floor, but he remained seated and unmoving at the table.

Tessa blew out one of the hundreds of sighs she had sighed throughout the previous sleepless night. "I know. You've told me. Father told me. Peter told me. But that doesn't change anything. Peter will never come back to his family because of me."

"No," Mrs. Holt insisted, "because of his father."

"Because his father fell in love with me."

Her father slammed his fist on the gullet of the saddle. "Tarnation, Tessa! This has nothing to do with you! Sundstrom's a lustful—" He clamped his lips closed before the next word slipped out.

Startled, Tessa leapt to her feet, instinctively moving to the other side of Mrs. Holt's chair.

"Henry," Mrs. Holt chided. "There's no need for shouting."

"He's thirty-eight years old!" His volume did not decrease. "He's a year older than me! Did he think you'd throw your life away on an old man? What was the man thinking?"

"What do you mean?" Tessa's emotions flipped from despair to indignation. *Is it so hard to believe a man could love me?* "Am I so hideous?"

"Of course not, but you're a child!" he bellowed, standing up so quickly his chair tipped over backward.

"So is that why Peter walked away too? Because I'm a child? Well, I'm not a child!" she shouted at her father. "I'm only a year younger than Mother was when she married you."

With a huff, he folded his arms across his chest. "Yes, but I was twenty-one, not seventeen."

"What does age have to do with it?"

"It has everything to— Peter's a child too! How would he even support you? Gah!" He clutched at his short-cropped hair as though he were going to pull it out.

Exasperated, Tessa repeated his motion, pulling her own hair. "Gah? That's your answer?"

"Blimey, would you listen to the two of you?" Mrs. Holt stood between father and daughter. "Is this how you settle your differences? Shouting and pulling your hair out?"

Tessa glowered at her father, folding her own arms and pinning them firmly to her chest.

He stepped past Mrs. Holt and held Tessa's shoulders in a gentle grip. "It's my job to take care of you. To protect you."

"I'm not a child. I saved your life. I nursed you back to health. I helped rebuild this house. I . . . I . . ." Gritting her teeth to staunch her quivering chin, she mentally recounted the trials she'd withstood since leaving North Carolina. "I. Am. Not. A. Child."

"Sweetheart, you are a remarkable young woman. Strong. Intelligent. Growing more beautiful before my very eyes. I don't doubt that every man in the territory would give his right hand to spend his life with you."

Tessa exhaled a humorless laugh. "That's great, Da. Let's see, what men are left in the territory to pick from? Mr. Pixton?" Tessa pictured the piggish man whose chins bypassed his neck to lay in jiggling folds on his chest. "Mr. Anderson? I wonder if Mary would mind sharing her home with another wife?"

"Tessa—"

She cut him off, intent on driving home her point. "Or maybe you'd rather I marry one of the trappers or peddlers who roam through? I'm sure I could get used to tramping through blizzards and skinning pelts." Her voice rose in volume and pitch, along with her frustration. "Do you see my dilemma, Father? There are no other men in the territory."

Her father sat down in his rocker by the fire and stretched his legs out in front of him. "Are you saying you'd rather marry Sundstrom than wait for love?"

"What?" Tessa clapped her hands to the sides of her face and worked tiny circles on her temples with her middle fingers. "No, of course not. I'm saying—" She felt the blanket of her bleak future settle around her. "I'm saying my only hope of getting married just walked out that door. I sent Peter away. He won't come back. Of course I won't marry Mr. Sundstrom, but there are no other prospects. I'll be a spinster."

"What about William?" Mrs. Holt asked quietly. "You didn't mention him as a possibility."

Are you joking? Or just being cruel? He left me. Tessa glowered at Mrs. Holt, biting her tongue to keep from saying something truly unladylike.

Mrs. Holt pulled a letter from her apron pocket. Grinning, she waved it in front of her face like a fan before holding it out to Tessa.

CHAPTER 20

"This is from William?" Tessa held the thick paper envelope gingerly in front of her, as if it might crumble into dust.

"Indeed, so it is. You dinnae give me a chance to give it to you sooner, did you?"

So relieved was she to see Mrs. Holt this morning, so urgently did she need her advice, Tessa had fairly thrown herself sobbing into the woman's arms when she knocked at the door more than an hour earlier.

Tessa studied the fine penmanship crafting her name on the envelope. Deliver to: Miss Tessa Darrow, Morristown by the Soda Springs, Idaho Territory. She felt a flitter in her chest as she stared at her name—how beautifully William had written her name. Turning the envelope over, she fingered the wax seal securing the flap. *Why did you wait so long, William?*

"Go on then. Open it," her father urged.

As long as she had waited for a letter from William, she now found her nerves a jumble. Why had he waited so long to write? Had he fallen in love with someone else? What would keep him away for so many months? After last night's turmoil with Peter and her tumultuous emotions this morning, Tessa didn't know if she could stand another disappointment just yet. She slid her finger under the flap, pausing before breaking the seal. Her father was watching the envelope expectantly. *I want to read it myself before I share it.* Would it be too rude to excuse herself to read the letter in her room? As she caught Mrs. Holt's eye and darted a look toward her father, Mrs. Holt nodded.

"Kurt brought in another surprise for you, Henry." Mrs. Holt put her hand through Tessa's father's arm and gently steered him toward the door. "Why don't we fetch it and give Tessa some privacy?"

"Well, I want to hear what William has to say," he objected.

"The trunk's too heavy for me to carry by myself. Tessa can tell you about the letter when we return."

With the cabin to herself, Tessa sat in her rocker and slid her finger under the seal on the envelope again, carefully pulling the wax away from the paper. A flutter of excitement tempered by fear snaked through her stomach. *"He who lives upon hope will die fasting."* Tessa pictured her grandmother looking up from her needlepoint just long enough to deliver her favorite quote and squelch whatever girlish excitement had captivated young Tessa so long ago. *But without hope, Grandmother, there is no purpose in life.* She pulled the crisp paper from the envelope and turned it to catch the light.

December 12, 1865

December? Nearly four months to deliver a letter?

> *Dear Tessa,*
>
> *I hope this letter finds you well. How are you enjoying winter in the Rocky Mountains? Quite different from winter in North Carolina, isn't it? I imagine you are busy preparing for Christmas. I wish I could be there to celebrate with you and Mother.*

"I wish you had been here, too, William," she whispered.

> *I am sorry it has taken me so long to write. I wanted to be settled before I wrote so you could write me back. This took much longer than planned.*

In the next paragraphs, he described his journey after delivering the cattle to Great Salt Lake City: traveling across the Sierra Mountains to Sacramento, California, and then up to Oregon City.

> *You and your father described the Willamette Valley with such beauty, I wanted to see it for myself. The forest grows so thick here, you couldn't see a cow if it wandered more than twenty feet. I signed on with a logging company and started learning the lumber business.*
>
> *Please don't be alarmed, but I had an accident and broke my wrist quite severely. My arm was in a splint until just recently.*

Tessa had no experience with broken wrists but recalled a soldier coming home from battle with an arm strapped across his chest in a dirty cloth slung from his neck. She bit her lip, imagining the pain William must have been in. She read on.

> *I hope you will excuse my poor penmanship. I scarce can hold a pen for long even still.*

Poor penmanship? Tessa wondered. His script was every bit as steady and fluid as hers. A far cry from Peter's crude hand. She continued to scan the letter, searching in vain for an indication of when he was coming home. After a few more lines, and far too soon, the letter closed.

> *Please extend my regards to your father. I pray you are both well.*
> *With warmest regards,*
> *William Bates*
> *Cavanaugh Lumber, Oregon City*

That's all he wrote? He's been gone so long and he only wrote one page? Well, I've plenty more than that to write to you. She narrowed her eyes and pursed her lips. *If I write to you. Have you missed me at all? You said nothing of when you're coming home.* She reminded herself that one letter was better than no letters; then, she could hear, in just that way her grandmother used to say, *"Don't pout, dear. It will give you wrinkles."*

After reading the letter again, she studied the elegant way he signed his name with rounded swoops beginning the letters W and B. *A right proper script, I'd say.* Tessa smiled her most approving "teacher" smile. *You've practiced your letters well. I'll show your penmanship to my pupils as an example.*

With a pang, she thought of her students, the Sundstrom children. How could she possibly continue as their teacher after refusing their father—and their brother? She shivered with the knot creeping through her gut. Knowing his intentions toward her, she could never go back into their house. *But the children—how much do they know?* Her father had forbidden Mr. Sundstrom from having any contact with Tessa. Did that include the children? How could she possibly continue as their teacher? *Why should they be punished for their father's ill manners?*

Folding William's letter carefully and putting it back in its envelope, she nestled the letter behind her grandfather's carved horse on the fireplace mantel. A bit of cobweb clung to the inner corner of the mantle so she retrieved a dusting rag from the shelf under the kitchen sink and swiped at the trailing web.

She allowed herself to imagine she was cleaning her own house with her own children playing underfoot, William sitting by the fire after coming in at the end of the day. She shook her head. *Don't be silly, Tessa.* But still, it would be lovely to keep house for someone other than her father. As she worked her way around the room, aimlessly flicking the rag at the split-log walls, she realized that she was mimicking the way Mrs. Sundstrom cleaned while the children were bent over their studies.

Wouldn't William be surprised to see I've become a schoolmistress. But just as quickly, she pictured Peter and his father standing at the head of the table watching her. She had supposed Mr. Sundstrom was just pleased with his children's progress. How long had he been considering her as something other than a teacher?

She thought back to her birthday—to the extravagant vanity set. Was that an expression of his intentions? Her father was right—she shouldn't have accepted it. Then she recollected at Christmas, after the children's pageant, how Mr. Sundstrom had tried to put his arm around her. Why hadn't she heeded her feelings of disquiet that night? *"Trust your instincts, Tessa."* Her mother's admonition—from a time Tessa confessed a misdeed, having known better but doing it anyway—played through her mind. *"That feeling inside is the Holy Spirit guiding you to do what's right."*

"Father in Heaven," she whispered, "what am I supposed to do now?" After Christmas, she should have insisted the children come to her home for their lessons instead of continuing at the Sundstroms'. Then all of this unpleasantness could have been avoided. *I should have had the children come here.* "But that's the answer," Tessa gasped, smacking her dust rag on the table. "I'll have the children come here for their lessons." With a smile, she recognized the warmth in her chest—filling her with light, not darkness. "Thank you, God."

Satisfied that no stray cobwebs had escaped the swish of her dust rag, Tessa sliced and buttered the last of the bread, placed slices of cheese on top, and then set it to warm on the griddle. Just as she was arranging clusters of watercress atop the melted cheese, the door swung open and her father, followed by Mrs. Holt, heaved a chest through the door with a grunt.

"What . . . ?" Tessa stared at the roughly three-foot trunk with its rounded top and ornate latch. She shook her head and blinked. "What in the world?"

Her father stood erect, stretching backward with his hands supporting the small of his back. "It would seem my mother has delivered Christmas."

Tessa's eyes opened wide and a smile lit her face. "Christmas? Grandmother sent presents?"

"Aye," Mrs. Holt teased, "and a sturdy wedding trunk."

"It's not a wedding trunk," Tessa and her father both protested at the same time.

Mrs. Holt smiled and winked, touching her index finger to the side of her nose. "Call it what you like."

A wedding trunk. Tessa pressed her lips together, trying to hide her smile. Despite shunning two proposals yesterday, with the arrival of William's letter, she couldn't help thinking that maybe a wedding trunk would be useful in the not-too-distant future.

"Well, let's see what we have here, shall we? If you'll hold this side up . . ." Tessa's father helped Tessa lift the side of the trunk off the ground. As she held it up, he used his pocketknife to ease a key from a narrow slit hidden behind the forward edge.

"Goodness, how clever!" Mrs. Holt exclaimed.

Tessa set the trunk back down. "How did you know to look for it?"

"Old family secret," her father said. "This is my father's trunk. See here?" He pointed to the initials JWD etched in the brass hasp. "John William Darrow. We sent it to Aunt Arla's with your grandmother."

"Well, isn't that a blessing?" Mrs. Holt said while he fitted the key in the lock.

"If we hadn't . . ." *It would have burned with the rest of our home.* Tessa was careful to heed her father's warning not to speak of events in North Carolina, but nonetheless received a warning scowl from him. She quickly changed the subject. "I thought Granddad's name was Jack."

"John, but folks called him Jack."

"And his middle name was William?" Mrs. Holt asked, a very pleased smile curling the corners of her lips.

"As is mine," Henry replied.

"I know." Tessa covered her smile with her hands as nonchalantly as she could.

Her father lifted an amused brow at her. "Now let's see what we have here." He lifted the lid of the trunk and handed Tessa a small, flat package wrapped in paper. "Would you like to open the first one?"

Tessa squelched her desire to rip through the paper, carefully removing the string instead so she could draw or write on the paper later. Unfolding the paper, she lifted two crisp, white pillow shams from the wrapping and caught her breath.

The open end of each fabric case was embellished with a four-inch swath of embroidery, the scene of a red-brick plantation home with tall white pillars in front of the crimson doors, set on undulating verdant hills. White tatted blossoms graced leafy trees arching over the drive and rising from behind the house. A hedge of deep green bougainvilleas, sprinkled with fuscia-colored French knots, wound between the trees. A vine of leaves topped with puffy white knots like fluffs of cotton secured the double row of bobbin lace dripping from the edges.

Tears swam in Tessa's eyes as she held the sham up for her father and Mrs. Holt to see. "It looks just like Deerfield."

"Your grandmother has outdone herself." Tears glistened in her father's eyes as well. He picked up the matching sham, smoothing it on his lap. "This is—was—our cotton plantation outside of Charlotte."

Mrs. Holt held her hand at the base of her throat, her voice husky. "Bless me, that's lovely." She turned her eyes from the embroidered scene and looked around the little log cabin.

Tessa couldn't tell if it was longing or embarrassment in her friend's eyes, but she instantly felt a warmth toward their new home. "Deerfield was lovely. Was," she repeated emphatically. "This is our home now. It's quaint and charming, and gave us haven when we needed it." She reached over and squeezed her father's forearm. "And we're very happy here, aren't we, Da?"

"Well said, Tessabear." Now his voice was husky as he patted his daughter's hand. "We are happy here."

Tessa blew out a breath and leaned closer to the trunk. "What else did Grandmother send?"

Next her father drew out a rolled package about fifteen inches in diameter and about as long. As he took out his pocketknife to snap the string, Tessa gasped and snatched the package from him. "No, Da! You'll tear the paper!" Once again, she untied the string and carefully lifted the paper away from the package. "I want to save the paper for later."

"Beg pardon," her father said with a smile. "Interested in what's inside? Or just the paper?" He tilted his head at the bundle Tessa had dropped as she smoothed the wrinkles out of the paper.

Tessa rolled her eyes at her father as she pulled the ribbon off the rolled bundle, revealing a squashed pillow. "A pillow!" Tessa squealed, giving it a hard shake to plump it before hugging it to her chest.

Mrs. Holt laughed. "It's a good thing your Grandmother sent two of them, isn't it?" She handed a similar package to Tessa's dad.

"Mmmm," he sighed, snuggling his face in the fabric casing. "No finer scent than fresh cotton." He shook his pillow and plumped it between his fists. "Look here, Tess." He pointed to two initials embroidered in the corner with a simple chain stitch. "ED."

"Eula!" Tessa cried. "They're from Eula! Do you think the cotton's from Deerfield?"

"Couldn't say, but it's had a good season to recover. Might just be."

"Who's Eula?" Mrs. Holt asked.

"Our housekeeper back home." Tessa's eyes lit up. "I think the cotton must be from the plantation. Just think, Da, tonight we'll sleep on pillows from Deerfield! I'll wash our pillow slips right after lunch so they're nice and fresh for our new pillows." She picture how pretty her bed would look with a plump pillow instead of the straw-filled mat she'd been sleeping on. Mrs. Holt had given them linen pillowslips that they'd continue to use at night, but now Tessa could slip their fat pillows inside the embroidered shams when she made their beds each morning. *We'll make this a lovely home yet.*

After a bit of shuffling in the trunk, her father held up a smaller package wrapped in brown paper and a rectangular wooden box secured with a leather strap. "Oh, I think I know what this is." A boyish grin spread across his face as he handed the wrapped parcel to Tessa and proceeded to unbuckle the strap on the box. "Would you look at these," he exclaimed, holding up three steel chisels with turned-wood handles.

Tessa well recalled watching her father hunch over bits of wood late at night gouging details in or carefully shaping chair legs and newel posts of the dollhouse furniture he had made for her many years ago. His old set had been burned with the rest of their belongings when they first arrived here, and though the steel tips survived, he had never been able to fit handles to them securely enough to be of any use. *Of everything she could have sent, Grandmother picked the perfect gift for her son.*

With her father occupied with testing the heft and balance of his new chisels, Tessa removed the paper from her gift. "A book!" Her very own book. *The first book for my very own library.*

"Oh, you'll enjoy that," Mrs. Holt said.

Her father finished buckling the strap on his chisel box. "What book is it?"

"*Aurora Leigh* by Elizabeth Barrett Browning," Tessa read.

"Is it a good book?" Mrs. Holt asked.

"I don't know. I believe it must be. I'll let you read it when I've finished." She passed the book to Mrs. Holt, who began thumbing through the pages.

"Looks like there's something just for you in here." Her father held up two large bundles tied together with string from the trunk, identified by a tag bearing her name only.

Tessa let the paper drop away unheeded this time as she lifted up folds of buttery taffeta that shimmered with flashes of gold when the sun streaming in the kitchen window kissed it. "Oh my," she whispered.

"Tessa," her father whispered as well.

"Have you ever seen anythin' so grand?" Mrs. Holt sighed.

Tessa unfolded the note pinned to the corner of the fabric. "Grandmother says it's for my presentation gown when I have my season." Tessa smiled at the memory of her mother and grandmother arguing on the portico about Tessa's coming-out season. "She's not going to let you forget your promise to present me properly, is she?"

"I'd expect nothing else." Her father chuckled. "But how did you . . . ?"

Tessa returned to the gifts and pulled the paper off the second bundle. Yards of white tulle netting billowed out in a cloud.

"Goodness but this will be a fine frock!" Mrs. Holt marveled.

"I'm afraid Grandmother has greatly overestimated my abilities as a seamstress." With questioning eyes, she lifted a handful of the fluffy confection toward Mrs. Holt.

Mrs. Holt held her hands up, warding off the tumble of netting. "Glory no! I'd be afraid to set scissors to it."

Tessa's father laughed. He rose on his knees, leaning closer to his daughter and draped a length of the taffeta silk over her head. "We'll take you to a proper dressmaker when the time comes." He rearranged the fabric, wrapping it around her shoulders, and lifted her golden tresses to cascade over the silken shawl. "I hope you don't mind waiting a year or two, though. I'm not ready to lose my little girl quite yet."

Tessa leaned into him, wrapping her arms around his chest, and rested her head on his shoulder. "I can wait, Da. But you'll never lose me. I'll always be your Tessabear."

"Well, that's lovely then," Mrs. Holt declared, standing up. "But just look at what you're doing to this fabric." She unwound the silk from Tessa's shoulders and shook it out in front of her. "It'll take a month of Sundays to press these wrinkles out."

Laughing, Tessa stood up to disentangle herself from the lengths of taffeta and tulle. She turned back to her father, placed her hand on the side of his cheek, and whispered, "Just don't make me wait too long."

Over a lunch of cheese and watercress sandwiches, Tessa told them of her realization that she could continue teaching the Sundstrom children if she held class here rather than at the Sundstroms. "You wouldn't mind, would you, Father, if I used our house for a couple of hours each day? I hate for the children to miss their lessons just because . . ." Her voice trailed off, but not before the pall of yesterday's affront descended once more.

"I don't know, Tessa. I don't want Sundstrom to think we'll just forgive what he's done."

"Nor do I. But for the children . . ." Tessa refrained from saying more.

He never responded well when he felt badgered. She looked at Mrs. Holt for support, but the woman kept her gaze trained on the cup that she cradled in both hands on the table.

At length, her father pressed his lips together and sighed. "I don't suppose it will hurt. But I'll be in the house with you whenever they are here. I don't want Sundstrom thinking he can come calling just because his children are in the house."

"Agreed," Tessa quickly said before he could change his mind. "They'll take their lessons here at the table and you can supervise from your rocker while you whittle."

"Hmmph. I'm beginning to think I gave in too easily."

Mrs. Holt finally lifted her eyes—and her cup—and gave Tessa a wink.

"I'll write Mrs. Sundstrom a note." Tessa jumped up from the table and snatched one of the saved pieces of paper from their gifts. She folded a horizontal and vertical crease to outline a square, and then carefully tore the paper along the fold marks. After composing the note, discussing the language with her father before committing it to paper, she folded the message and handed it to Mrs. Holt to deliver.

"No, ma'am," her father stated firmly, taking the note from Mrs. Holt. "I'll deliver this myself. Just to be sure there's no misunderstanding the conditions."

"That's fine, Da, but please be polite so the children feel welcome here."

"Aren't I always?"

Tessa and Mrs. Holt exchanged glances.

"Would you like me to go with you, Henry? It's about time for me to be getting home anyway."

"No harm in that, I suppose." He and Mrs. Holt stood up and put on their jackets.

"Thank you, Da. I love you." Tessa stood on tiptoe to give him a peck on the cheek.

He pressed his lips together again and gave her a sidelong glance. "Hmmm." Then with a quick wink that caused Tessa to smile, he pushed the door open wide, nearly hitting Mrs. Sundstrom standing there poised to knock.

"Mercy!" Mrs. Sundstrom exclaimed, jumping out of the way of the door.

Tessa dashed out to steady her. "Mrs. Sundstrom! What are you doing here?"

The woman's face fell and her chin started to quiver. "I've been—" She sniffed and pressed a handkerchief to her nose. "I'm looking for Grieg. Is he here?" She craned her neck to see past them into the cabin.

"Of course he's not here," Tessa's father barked. "Why would he be?"

"Eliza." Mrs. Holt took hold of the beleaguered woman at the elbow and ushered her inside. "What's happened? Where's Grieg?"

"That's just the thing," she sniveled. "I don't know. He got up early and said he was going hunting, but when I got up a while later, I found his rucksack and all of his clothes missing." She looked at Tessa's father, tears spilling down her cheeks. "Why would he take his clothes if he was just going hunting?" Sobs burst from the woman's throat, and she collapsed to her knees, covering her face with her hands.

Tessa's father and Mrs. Holt lifted her by the elbows and guided her to the rocking chair where she'd sat just the day before. She lifted her eyes to them, nearly choking with the tears racking her body. "He's not coming back, is he?"

CHAPTER 21

September 4, 1866
Dear William,

With the day's lessons over, Tessa had just a few minutes to jot a letter to William before her father came in from the fields for supper. After writing a few lines, Tessa put her pen down next to her inkwell and stepped outside to dip a cup of water from the rain barrel. The warm water did little to rinse the memory of the morning's math lesson from her mouth. She peeked around the corner of the house. Nope. The biscuits were still on the ground. Not even the chickens would eat them.

She picked a mint leaf to suck on before returning inside to resume her letter, eager to have it ready for when the next traveler came through to post it in Fort Hall.

Just imagine biting into a biscuit brackish as a salt lick. Poor Catherine worked so hard on those biscuits too. I should have kept a better eye on her math before I set her loose on the recipe.

We've almost collected the last of the barley from the Sundstroms' field. Do you remember me telling you that Mr. Pixton finished sowing the field after Mr. Sundstrom left in the spring? I've been right amazed at how everyone here has taken care of the Sundstrom family these months since. Mrs. Sundstrom has decided to take the children to her parents' home in Minnesota once the new baby is delivered next month. It will be lonely without the children playing about and coming here for lessons. I'll miss them dearly.

She refrained from writing, *But I'll be glad to no longer worry about that awful man coming back.*

Although her logical mind, her father, and Mrs. Holt told her that the proposition from Sundstrom at Easter was no shame on her, she nonetheless felt sullied at the thought of it. And in the five months that followed, she convinced herself that the proposal from Peter was made in an effort to save his family from disgrace. Thus she determined that no one outside the Soda Springs valley would ever learn of her humiliation—not even William.

She was just about to write how she had learned to bale the discarded barley chaff when she heard shouts and wails from outside. Before she could move from her place at the table, the door to her cabin banged open and eight Sundstrom children tumbled through it.

"The baby's comin'!" three-year old Jenny yelled, her eyes wide. She doubled over with her hands on her knees to catch her breath while the chaos of seven other young children spilled in around her.

"The baby's coming," eight-year old Brigham confirmed, carrying the toddler, Patience, on his hip. "Mama sent Catherine to fetch Sister Holt and told us to wait up here till the birthing was done."

"The baby? Already?"

Though alarm and concern chased through Tessa's thoughts, Brigham just shrugged and released his hold on Patience before making a beeline for the whittling knife on the mantel. Tessa snatched it just ahead of his grasp, then dashed back to the table just as little Jacob picked up her forgotten writing pen and prepared to dip it in the ink well. "Don't you dare!" She yanked the pen away with such force that her sleeve caught on the letter and knocked it to the ground. "Now look what you've done!"

Tears filled Jacob's eyes and his twin, Jenny, rushed over to wrap her arms around him, glaring at Tessa. Four-year-old Parley, standing on Tessa's rocking chair, tipped over backward and he and Patience set up to wailing.

"Stop that racket!" Tessa shouted, grabbing the knife, the pen, the inkwell, and the letter and shoving them on the kitchen shelf out of the children's reach. She turned in time to see Elizabeth embrace Parley, Priscilla embrace Patience, Jenny still embracing Jacob, and Joseph trying to feed her father's whittling stick to the fire. Jerking the rod away from him, she thought for the briefest moment about giving Joseph a rap on the knuckles with it.

Closing her eyes, she took a deep breath and blew it out. *They're only children. Don't be so cross.* In the many months she'd been teaching the older children, she'd never been left alone with the entire brood before. How did Mrs. Sundstrom do it? All day, every day? *"You can do all things*

187

through Christ Jesus." Her mother's voice whispered once more—an occurrence Tessa no longer questioned. *You're right, of course*, she mentally replied. And once more, Tessa instinctively obeyed the prompting.

"Brigham, Joseph . . ." She began pulling the children into the middle of the room, on the rug in front of the fire, and lifted Patience into her lap. "Your mother needs our prayers." Every one of the children knelt and when Tessa clasped her hands together, they did as well. "Our Father, which art in Heaven, hallowed be Thy Name . . ." She recited the only prayer she knew by heart, determined to ignore the children's shifting and rustling. Surely they could keep still through one prayer.

As Tessa concluded her prayer, a sweet voice on her left chimed in. "And Heavenly Father, bless our baby so he doesn't die. And bless my mama so she'll be happy again. In the name of Jesus Christ, Amen."

Tessa wrapped her arm around Priscilla's shoulders and whispered "Thank you for helping me." Neither the little girl or her brothers and sisters said anything for several minutes. They simply sat, staring at the fire.

At length, Catherine arrived, grim faced, and reported that Mrs. Holt and Mrs. Pixton were tending to her mother. An hour later, Tessa's father came in for a bowl of milk and toast before returning to the field to harvest.

Another hour passed when Mrs. Anderson and little Abe carried in an armful of blankets they'd toted in a small wagon. "It's going to be a slow birth this time. I think it's best the children bed down here tonight."

Judging from Mrs. Anderson's sad eyes and puckered brow showing above the ever-present handkerchief covering her lower face, Tessa knew things were not proceeding well with the delivery. "Will she . . . be all right?"

"It's in God's hands."

A coil of dread wound from the pit of Tessa's stomach, curling around her windpipe. She looked at the children clustered at her table braiding shreds of corn husk into ropes or folding and twisting the husks into dolls. Priscilla didn't pray for her mother not to die—just to be happy. Did she sense . . . ?

Tessa took a deep breath and closed her eyes, commanding herself to not let the children see her fear. *No time for drivel. You can do this.* She blew out another breath and squared her shoulders. "I'd best get the children fed and put to bed then."

"It will all be over when they wake up."

"Yes, and if Priscilla is correct, they'll have a bouncing baby brother to play with." Tessa decided against telling Mrs. Anderson the rest of Priscilla's addition to the prayer. It was probably nothing—just a little girl's awkward attempt to pray.

Just as the last shard of sunset flickered and bowed beneath the horizon, Tessa's father pulled open the door and swatted the dust from his trousers before stepping inside.

"Any news yet?" Tessa spoke in hushed tones so she didn't waken the younger children, who had fallen asleep right after dinner. She moved to the stove and cracked three eggs into a bowl.

Her father shook his head and bit off half of a fresh, warm biscuit. "Nothing yet."

The concern in his eyes was evident, but Tessa refrained from asking anything more for fear of alarming the children.

Mrs. Anderson, cradling her sleeping toddler in her arms, joined them in the kitchen. "If you're in for the night, Brother Darrow, I'll take Abe home and put him to bed."

"Yes. Thank you for staying with Tessa."

"Nonsense. She did me a kindness by letting me stay here. Neils has been in Chesterfield trading horses all day, but I expect he'll be home soon."

"I'm afraid the children would have overrun me without your help." Tessa whipped a splash of milk in with the eggs and poured the frothy slurry into the sizzling frying pan to feed her father. "Now that Da's here, would you like me to watch Abe while you pay call on Mrs. Sundstrom?"

"Oh, I wouldn't dare until after the baby's born."

Why ever not? Tessa recalled the many times her mother had rushed to a neighbor's house to lend a hand on the day of the birth.

Mrs. Anderson lifted the corner of her handkerchief mask just enough to remind Tessa of the missing portion of her jaw. "Some people believe that if an expectant mother has a fright, the babe will be born with a horrible defect. I know it's just superstition, but I think Eliza would feel better if I didn't come by until after the baby's safely delivered."

"Oh, that's nonsense," Tessa's father huffed.

"Indeed," Tessa agreed. She had spent so much time with Mary Anderson over the last year that she no longer paid any mind to the cloth covering her friend's mouth any more than she would if the kerchief were tied in her hair.

"Nonetheless," Mrs. Anderson demurred. "I'll be happy to pay my respects in the morning."

"All right, then," Tessa's father said, lifting Abe from his mother's arms, then snatching another biscuit. "Tessa, I'll eat after I see Mrs. Anderson home."

Tessa looked from the fluffy scrambled eggs, already beginning to crisp at the edges, to Brigham lying on his stomach, head propped on his folded arms, looking at the eggs longingly. *Heavens. The eggs'll be cold before Da gets back anyway.*

LONG AFTER THEY should have been to bed themselves, Tessa and her father sat out in front of the cabin on a bench he had fashioned out of stumps and bent willow branches. Unlike last year, the evenings were still unusually warm for late September. Father and daughter whispered their few words so as to not awaken the nine children sleeping inside. A lamp shone in the Pixton's window a quarter mile southward, and nearly another quarter mile beyond that, light spilled into the dark every time the Sundstrom's door opened nearly a half mile away.

The breeze kissed just the tops of the cottonwoods and cedars, and Tessa concentrated on breathing evenly, in rhythm with the rustling leaves. Every now and then, a wail wafted through the valley, at times growing quite sharp. Coyotes, her father said. *Doesn't sound like coyotes.* But she'd hug her arms around her chest and mentally chant, *Coyotes, just coyotes*, to quiet the fear prickling the back of her neck until the next cry.

Long past midnight, a stout shadow shuffled up the street. Tessa and her father grabbed the lantern dangling from the knot of a twisted branch and raced toward the stooped figure. Mrs. Pixton paused at her gate until Tessa and her father arrived, leaning heavily on the fence post.

"It's finished." Her words hung in the air like a cloak.

Finished? Is Mrs. Sundstrom— Tessa couldn't bring herself to complete the thought.

Thankfully, her father gave tender voice to the question. "What is the news?"

Mrs. Pixton shook her head slowly, frowning. "She's had a rough go of it."

"But she's alive?" Tessa held her breath, waiting for the answer.

"Yes, child, she's alive." The heaviness in Mrs. Pixton's eyes made it clear that the statement may not still be true by morning. "Maureen will sit with her through the night and we'll see what the morning brings."

Tessa measured her breaths evenly, trying to keep the weight of her breaking heart from choking her. It couldn't be possible that her friend could die, leaving her children without a mother or father. *But people die.* How well she knew. People die. Especially out here.

"And the baby?" Her father's voice startled her from her thoughts.

"A little boy. Small, but he seems healthy enough."

A boy. Priscilla was right.

The door opened, and Mr. Pixton stepped halfway out—dressed in his robe, a sleeping cap pulled over his ears and down to his eyebrows. "Tildy? You coming in?"

No 'evenin' folks'? No 'by your leave'?

"We'll say good night then," Tessa's father offered. "We appreciate the news."

For the first time, tears shimmered in Mrs. Pixton's eyes. "You'll take care of those young'uns?"

"Of course, Mrs. Pixton." He placed a hand on her shoulder. "As long as need be."

FOR THREE WEEKS the Sundstrom children lived in the Darrow home while their mother and new brother convalesced. Mrs. Anderson arranged for a Blackfoot Indian woman to go the Sundstrom cabin several times a day to wet-nurse Benjamin until Mrs. Sundstrom was strong enough to do it herself. Mrs. Sundstrom had been nursing her son for only a few days when Mr. Sundstrom's brother Kurt and his cattle came through town again for the annual migration to market in Great Salt Lake City. Mrs. Sundstrom adamantly argued that Kurt should take her and the children to her parents in Minnesota, but eventually acquiesced to accompanying the cattle drive to Salt Lake until arrangements for their transport eastward could be made.

> *October 2, 1866*
> *Dear William,*

It took Tessa over an hour to recap the events of the past month, struggling to condense the children's antics while staying with her into a few precious paragraphs. Describing the futility of trying to pack the family's furnishings into one wagon given the lack of men to drive more than one extra wagon was just as difficult.

> *My father built narrow trunks to line the edges of the wagon, and we situated her mattress between the trunks. Now the children will have a place to rest if they get tired walking.*

Tessa rested the nib of her pen on the lip of the inkwell as she stared out the window, wondering if her little darlings had made it to the Salt Lake Valley in the four days since their leaving. With her pupils gone,

Tessa had struggled to establish a routine that didn't include spending most mornings teaching math and spelling.

Tessa faithfully wrote to William every month, keeping him apprised of life in their dwindling settlement. Though she had only received one more letter from him, she kept faith that he was receiving her letters in Oregon, and that they were appreciated.

> *What a blessing that Kurt Sundstrom came through with the cattle when he did. A few weeks earlier, and Mrs. Sundstrom wouldn't have been strong enough to travel. A few weeks later and we may well be covered in snow. It's a shame Peter went east instead of coming back with his uncle, but I'm sure he'll return to Great Salt Lake City when he learns that his father abandoned the family. Maybe he'll take his mother and the children to Minnesota as was her wish.*

Still she wondered if she should tell William what precipitated Mr. Sundstrom leaving, but so much time had passed, she didn't see the point. Someday—maybe.

> *Christmas is but two months away. How it would thrill Mrs. Holt if you could pay us a visit. I hope you'll not think me too forward, but Mrs. Holt is not the only girl here who longs for your visit.*

As soon as she wrote the last line, she wished she had not; but there it was, inked on the page. And with paper so precious, she was not about to throw an otherwise perfectly good page away.

> *With kindest regards from Morristown by the Soda Springs,*
> *Tessa Darrow*

CHAPTER 22

"Oh, let her open it, Henry," Mrs. Holt scolded, handing Tessa the arm-length package she received this morning on the wagon traveling through from Fort Hall.

Tessa hugged the canvas-covered package to her chest trying to suppress her squeals. Since she turned sixteen tomorrow, childish giggles would just not do, but waiting another day to open the package marked with her name from her grandmother would also not do.

"Please, Da," Tessa begged. "It's not as though we'll have a big party for my birthday. What will it matter if I open it a day early?"

"March fifth." He took her chin between his thumb and forefinger. "Others may not consider it particularly special, but March fifth is the day my eldest daughter was born. The day I became a father. March fifth. Not March fourth, not March sixth." He shook her head gently. "Tomorrow is the day we celebrate the birth of Tessa."

Rolling her eyes, Tessa removed his hand from her chin and placed the package on Mrs. Holt's table, well away from the clutter of merchandise spilling out of the shipping crate. "Fine, Da. You can have your special day. Maybe I should have made a present for you."

"It's not too late," he teased. "Help us get these supplies on the shelves and then you can get started."

As Tessa unpacked the tins of Pemmican and stacked them on the shelf behind the counter, she tried to imagine what Grandmother could have sent this time. Anything could be in that supple package, but one thing was for certain—she could save the canvas to draw on with charcoal or pen and ink.

IMAGES OF MAMA pulling a skillet of corn pone out of the oven filled Tessa's dream as the morning sun forced her awake. With a sigh, she cuddled down into her quilt, wishing that her mama and sister, Bethany, could be here on her sixteenth birthday. *Two years since you left us, Mama.* While carrying on day to day since her mother's passing had become easier, Tessa knew that she'd never stop missing how her mother made every birthday a grand celebration.

Coming more fully awake, the scents of bacon and corn pone wafted into her room. Corn pone! *It is corn pone!* Had her father . . . ? She jumped out of bed and pulled on her stockings, hopping toward the door. "Do I smell corn pone?"

Her father turned from the griddle on the wood stove. "Hmmm? Bacon—Oh no, the corn pone!" Scooting the skillet off the flame, he dashed to the fireplace on the other side of the room and used the poker to lift a Dutch oven from the embers and set it on the hearth. "If I've ruined your birthday breakfast . . ." Before he could finish his sentence, a spit of bacon grease sparked and a small flame licked up the edge of the skillet. Like a jackrabbit, he leaped for the skillet, swatting at the flame with the dish towel he'd been using as a pot holder.

"Well," he said, laughing, "I nearly burnt the house down doing it, but I made you a southern breakfast for your birthday!"

"And it smells wonderful." She lifted the lid from the corn pone and tested with her finger the spring in the crust. "Perfect. When did you learn how to make corn pone?"

A sly smile spread across his face. "When Maureen mixed up all but the bacon grease last night and told me how long to cook it this morning. Did you see that I crumbled the first batch of bacon in it too, before I set it to bake?"

"Mmmm. That should taste good. You and Mrs. Holt make quite the pair." As glad as she was that her father had found a friend here, he rarely spoke of his late wife or daughter anymore. *How long before I forget about William?*

"Tessa?"

"Hmm?" She realized that while she was in a world of her thoughts, her father was holding her chair out for her. "Oh. Sorry." She took her seat and poured glasses of milk while her father served slices of corn pone alongside the slabs of bacon.

Her father jumped up after breakfast, directing Tessa to get dressed while he cleaned up the dishes. She emerged from her room to find him sitting in his rocker, whittling on the walking stick he'd been working on for weeks. She sat down across from him and waited for him to look up.

"Did you enjoy breakfast?"

"Very much, thank you," she replied, staring at the gifts sitting between his chair and the little log end table.

He pulled out the canvas package from Grandmother and a box that definitely hadn't arrived yesterday. "So I imagine you might like—"

"Oh, yes please!" She snatched the parcels from his grip. Plopping down in her chair, she lifted the box first, wanting to save her grandmother's gift for last. "This is from you?"

"Came in about a month ago. I've been worried you'd discover it under my bed."

"I've been meaning to dust under there." She pried at the box lid with her fingertips before handing it back to her father to wedge open with the tip of his knife. She found two more boxes nestled inside. The first box, about eight inches wide, was stamped with the name Winsor & Newton. Inside, she found an array of oil colors in metal squeeze tubes. Secured in the lid were several brushes of varying sizes and shapes. "Oil paints? Father!"

"Hold on there. There's more."

The next box, made of tin and covered with bright red lacquer with golden scrolls, revealed a wooden block about twelve inches square and two inches thick. Heavy paper with the texture of canvas was affixed to the block. Before Tessa could examine it, her father pointed out that there were thirty-two sheets of paper mounted on the block ready for her to paint on.

"Oh, Da! This is the best gift I've ever had."

"Better than the elk hair fork I made you?"

She laughed, remembering her shock at finding out it was made from an elk's antler. "Well, perhaps almost as nice as the hair fork." She looked at him intently. "I know just what I want to paint first."

Placing his finger under his chin, he turned his face to profile. "My portrait?"

"I'll make that my second project. I'll need to practice a bit to do you justice. First, I want to go back to Grays Lake and paint a landscape for William."

"Well, if you'd rather paint that than me . . . I'll say yes, but only if you'll agree to paint it three times. For William, for me, and for your grandmother. I think she'd be very impressed with Grays Lake."

"She would, wouldn't she?" Tessa's mind flitted through pastoral scenes from the Hudson River School exhibit she'd visited with her grandmother not long before the war—undulating wilderness land-scapes captured in vivid colors. She ran her hand over the course paper on the block. "I'm afraid I'm not very accomplished yet, but I think I can paint a small scene she'd enjoy."

"Well, speaking of your grandmother, are you going to open her present?"

"Of course." She picked up the package, struggling with the twine holding the canvas secure until her father reached over with his knife and snapped the string. Pulling the canvas back, she lifted a cream-col-ored frock to her shoulders. "It's a dress!" She had alternated between wearing the skirt and blouse she'd made shortly after arriving in Mor-ristown and the dress she'd received from Mrs. Holt for her last birthday until each was pretty well threadbare.

"Isn't that beautiful." Her father lifted the edge of the floral-printed skirt. "It feels almost like silk."

"It is fine, isn't it?" Tessa unfolded the letter still lying on the canvas and read portions to her father. "Grandmother says there's a new seam-stress in Charlotte. Came from London. Oh! She says this dress looks just like one Queen Victoria wore in Paris!"

"Is that right?"

"Won't I look fancy, dressed like Queen Victoria?" Tessa turned back to the letter. A brief giggle escaped. "Grandmother sent Bunny Winkle to the dressmaker hoping our measurements would be similar." Of all the girls her age in Charlotte, Grandmother had picked the one girl who would be most envious of the beautiful dress.

"Bunny Winkle? Well, she's just a scrawny little slip."

"Da, it's been more than two years since we've seen her. All us girls were scrawny little slips."

"Two years. Hard to believe." He folded his arms and shook his head before shooing her to her room. "Well, don't just stand there. Go try it on."

Stripping free of her faded cotton dress, Tessa donned a clean che-mise and stepped into a steel-caged crinoline that a passing woman had left last year in exchange for eggs and preserves. Struggling to lace the hoops, she gave thanks that she was too young in North Carolina to have to wear a full-length hoop skirt. She threaded her arms through a fresh petticoat before letting her birthday dress drop over her head. After much twisting and nearly wrenching her arms from their sockets to reach the buttons extending up the back of the dress, she managed to fasten all but the two buttons nearest her shoulder blades. *Grandmother must have forgotten to send a lady's maid with the dress. Like it or not, Father, you're just going to have to close your eyes and help me with these.* She picked up her silver hand mirror to survey herself.

The creamy lace around her décolleté was accented by two bands of floral fabric that created a V-shape falling from her shoulders to join with a medallion just below her waist. A matching medallion at the top of the bodice modestly disguised her cleavage, but did nothing to hide her bosom gently swelling above the lace even without benefit of a corset. *Grandmother, either Bunny Winkle has not yet matured, or you've become much more permissive in your fashion.* Short sleeves were each capped by a wide ruffle, trimmed with the same lace that decorated the bodice. The silky dress fell in generous pleats to a heavy floral border around the bottom that thinned to scattered petals as it rose to her narrow waistline. Tessa smiled at the reflection of the genteel lady smiling back at her. *What a pity that I don't have anywhere to wear such a fancy dress.* At least she'd have a pretty frock to wear when she went calling or on holidays.

Propping her mirror on the bedside table, Tessa fashioned two braids that she twisted with the rest of her hair into a bun, wove her pink ribbon loosely through the chignon, and pinched her cheekbones to pink them. Satisfied, she stood in the center of the room and moved her hips from side to side, enjoying the swish of the crinoline as it swung with her steps.

Picturing William standing before her in evening tails, she held her hand up, wrist bent just so, and gave her deepest curtsy. She placed her right hand in his and her left fingertips on his invisible shoulder and swayed round and round the room before a knock on the door interrupted their imaginary dance.

"One moment," she called, and then gave a quick curtsy to her unseen partner. *You're a lovely dancer, William Bates.*

Feeling just a bit foolish, she opened the door a sliver to reveal half of her face. "Close your eyes," she commanded her father. "I need help fastening the last two buttons."

"All right."

Satisfied that his eyes were shut, she opened the door and turned her back to him. "Between my shoulder blades."

He fumbled with the buttons. "There," he pronounced. "May I open my eyes now?"

"Not yet." She stepped behind her door again and instructed him. "Go stand by the table. I want to make an entrance."

"Good heavens." He sighed under his breath.

She waited a dramatic moment, surprised at the butterflies tickling her stomach. She pinched her cheekbones again and then swung the door open. Emerging from her bedroom in a floral cloud, Tessa felt every bit the Southern belle ready to take tea in the garden.

Her father caught his breath as he saw her, a smile lighting his eyes. He bit his bottom lip and wrapped his hand around the top rail of a dining chair. "Who is this vision?" His husky whisper brought a clutch to Tessa's throat. He held his hand out to her and twirled her gently under his raised arm.

"Do you like it, Da?"

"Tessa Lillian, you're more beautiful than a summer morn."

As MARCH MELTED into April with no indication that her father planned on resuming the journey to Oregon for yet another year, Tessa didn't even bother asking about it. "It was my dream before your mother died," he'd said the last time they'd spoken of the trek. But that was last year. Since then, he'd planted three and harvested two crops of barley, helped Mr. Anderson expand his barn, built a proper bedroom on the back of the trading post for Mrs. Holt, and salvaged several immigrant's wagons and tack with his clever repairs.

Kurt Sundstrom had come through on his annual trek to the Wyoming range, but Peter wasn't with him, choosing to throw in with some trappers headed to Canada before he joined the cattle drive later in the summer. Mrs. Sundstrom and the children were still in Great Salt Lake City, waiting until the Transcontinental Railroad was completed in a few years to travel to her parents' home in Minnesota. Mr. Sundstrom had not returned and not contacted his family. *At least William is meeting with success in Oregon.* Even though she hadn't heard from him in months, she continued to write to him every month and was certain he was making great strides in the lumber business. He was likely a foreman by now—and much too busy to write.

Tessa tossed a pebble into Soda Creek, studying the way the sunlight glinted on the ripples, and then loaded her paintbrush with cerulean blue and a tip of zinc white to touch the peaks of the gentle current she painted. Her thoughts returned to her father. *He seems so content here.* Contentment was not the state of mind she'd attribute to herself, however. It was peaceful here, certainly, and she adored Mrs. Holt and the Andersons, and was learning to tolerate the quirky Pixtons, but since the Sundstrom children left, Tessa was intensely lonely—and bored.

She cleaned their cabin thoroughly every day, taking pleasure in finding small ways to make it charming, but as she did so, she fretted that she would never have opportunity to keep house for her own husband and children. She visited most every day with Mrs. Holt and Mrs. Anderson, and occasionally with Mrs. Pixton, but fretted that this would be the extent of her social circle for the rest of her life. She practiced drawing, painting, and fashioning figurines out of bits of clay, twigs, and cloth, but fretted that this would forever be the extent of her culture. *Oh, good heavens. Now you're fretting about fretting.*

She wondered if there might be a way to visit her grandmother—without having to marshal a wagon across the plains again. *Maybe Da knows where I could buy a seat on a stagecoach to take me to a train that goes to Charlotte.* Sighing, she realized there was no way he would consent to her traveling nearly across a continent by herself. She packed up her paints and headed for home and the pot of chicken and dumplings she'd set on the coals earlier.

"Da," Tessa said one afternoon in late April while she and her father were finishing a twig fence around their kitchen garden to keep the chickens out, "Easter's at the end of the week."

"Is it?"

"Mmm-hmm." She schooled her voice, trying to sound lighthearted and not pestering. "I was thinking that this might be a nice time to go to Grays Lake to paint—the weather's lovely, and the mosquitoes haven't come out yet, and the cranes are returning, and the field's planted, and you're not busy with a harvest, and—"

"And the leaves are bright, and the cattails are sprouting, and the columbine sways in the breeze," he teased.

"Did you read my list of things I want to paint?"

He laughed, his eyes creasing in that way that made them twinkle. "It's hard not to read your list when you leave it on the table."

"You left off that the Brown's peonies are in bud and filling the meadow with gold and violet."

He rolled his eyes and shook his head. "And the Brown's peonies."

"So we can go?"

"I don't imagine you'll stop hounding me until I say yes?"

"I haven't been hounding you. All right, maybe I have been, a little." She pursed her lips and gave an impertinent shrug. "And, yes, I'll likely keep hounding until you agree."

He folded his arms halfway and rested the knuckle of his index finger in the hollow under his bottom lip. "Would you mind if we invite Maureen to come with us?"

"Of course I wouldn't mind."

"Then let's go—before it gets hot and the mosquitoes come out," he teased. "We can pack up tomorrow and spend two or three days up there."

"Really?" She tore off her garden gloves and threw her arms around his neck.

"Really."

"GLORY, I COULD sleep where I stand." Mrs. Holt leaned against the porch post of the Larsens' abandoned home in the canyon north of Morristown.

After a day of riding in the buckboard along rutted trails followed by a couple of hours cleaning the ravages of neglect from the cabin, then helping Tessa's father sling a tarp between trees for his canopy to sleep under, Tessa didn't have the energy left to cover her yawns.

Tessa sat on the top step and rested her chin in her hands, watching her father stir the pot of rabbit stew slung over the fire out front. "I may be too tired to eat."

Mrs. Holt chuckled, patting her stomach. "I'm never that tuckered."

"Supper'll be ready in half an hour or so," Tessa's father announced, slapping the dust from his knees as he joined the ladies on the porch. "Anyone care to take a stroll while we wait?"

"Oh, Da," Tessa talked through her yawn. "I can't move."

Despite her protests of exhaustion just a moment ago, Mrs. Holt straightened and descended the two steps. "I wouldn't mind a short walk to work the kinks out."

"You go without me." Tessa dismissed them with a wave of her hand. "I'll keep an eye the stew."

"All right then, we won't go far." With that, he held out his arm and Mrs. Holt draped her hand through the crook of his elbow. "Madam, may I escort you?"

"Why, kind sir, I'd be delighted."

Tessa pulled a piece of paper and a bit of charcoal from her kit bag and started sketching the meadow as her father and Mrs. Holt crossed it. They made their way diagonally to the north and then walked south along the river's edge. Tessa couldn't hear their conversation, but their movements were animated and snatches of laughter floated back to her.

Will I ever have a beau to court me? Thoughts of William came shrouded in bitterness. Despite her many letters, she hadn't received so much as a note from him in nearly a year. *Surely he's met someone else.* She'd told herself since their first meeting that he was too old to wait for her to grow up, but as time passed with no news of his engagement or marriage, his devotion was still a possibility. However, now that she was of a suitable age, he couldn't be bothered to write. *I should have given Peter more encouragement. At least he was forthright in stating his intentions.*

Her father and Mrs. Holt came into view once more, as they approached the log where he had recuperated from his headache during their first visit up here. As she watched, her father first leap-frogged over it, then sprung atop the two-foot stump and danced a jig. It looked as though Mrs. Holt were dancing as well, lifting her skirts to her shins and kicking at the grass. All at once, Mrs. Holt gave him a playful shove—just enough to send him off balance and toppling into the stream.

With a cry, Tessa grabbed a blanket from her bedroll and raced to the meadow. Before she traversed even a quarter of its length, her father had clambered out of the water, chased the retreating Mrs. Holt a few steps, grabbed her around the waist, and—

Kissed her? *He's kissing her?* Tessa stopped. Her breathing stopped. The pounding in her chest did not. And while the blood in Tessa's face and hands was replaced by numbness, Mrs. Holt wrapped her arms around Tessa's father's neck and kissed him back.

Standing at the edge of the vast meadow, listening to the pulse pounding in her ears, Tessa watched her father, a world away, drop to one knee.

CHAPTER 23

She didn't mean to shout. She didn't mean to berate. She didn't mean to dissolve into tears.

"Tessa," his dark voice warned.

"But you didn't even ask me," she croaked. She didn't mean to spoil this happy time for him and Mrs. Holt. It was he who spoiled it by not even consulting his daughter before proposing marriage to that woman.

"Tessa. Enough." Her father narrowed his eyes, staring intently at her. His jaw tensed, lips almost disappearing in a narrow line. "I'm your father. I don't need to ask your permission."

His steely voice bit into her soul, just as it had when she was a child—the voice that sent her crouching in the corner to escape the piercing reproach. Knowing she was teetering the line between terse words and his booming rant, Tessa stilled her mouth. She kept her eyes trained on his left pupil, knowing that if she looked away, he would unleash his verbal assault.

He broke the impasse first and Tessa followed his gaze to see Mrs. Holt walking up the hill from Grays Lake carrying a bucket of water toward them. Grateful for the opportunity for a moment's reprieve, Tessa quickly set her sketch block and paintbrush atop the red lacquered tin and jumped up from her canvas stool. "I'll help her with the water."

Her father grabbed her gently by the wrist, interrupting her flight. "I'll go."

Knowing she should apologize to Mrs. Holt and do something to repair this gulf between she and her father, Tessa gently extricated her arm from his grasp. "Please. Let me." Avoiding further discussion, she bounded down the hill toward her soon-to-be stepmother.

"Och, Tessa, I can manage this." Mrs. Holt gave no indication that her feelings were hurt by Tessa's petulance last night or this morning.

When the couple returned to the cabin the evening before, Tessa lied saying she had already eaten a bit of the stew, and retreated to her bedroll in the cabin before her father and Mrs. Holt could announce their engagement. This morning, however, there was no escape as they told Tessa their news while she sat on the porch step eating biscuits and gravy.

She forced herself to smile and recite the proper congratulations before dumping the rest of her breakfast in the fire and staying out of conversation's path by rolling up her bedroll, straightening supplies in the buckboard, and taking inventory of her paint supplies in her bag. She could see the hurt in Mrs. Holt's eyes, the anger in her father's, but in her mind, Mrs. Holt acted inappropriately by flirting and showing her ankles the evening before. What man wouldn't feel encouraged by such behavior? And why would her father—a grown, intelligent, refined gentleman of standing—succumb to that woman's wiles?

Tessa had sat in the back of the buckboard for the duration of the drive to Grays Lake, claiming to want to make more space for them up front but in reality, unwilling to sit that close to either one of them or participate in their chatter. Upon arrival at the summit overlooking the Grays Lake Valley, Tessa grabbed her supplies and marched off to her secluded vantage point, leaving her father and Mrs. Holt to set up the day's camp.

When Mrs. Holt called to Tessa, asking if she'd like a lemon soda, made from the soda water at Hooper Spring, Tessa pretended not to hear. *Don't be churlish, girl,* her grandmother's voice scolded. When Mrs. Holt approached to see what Tessa was painting, Tessa shifted on her stool to block Mrs. Holt's view of the canvas. *A woman of breeding always comports herself with grace,* her mother's voice admonished. As the morning wore on and Tessa played through her emotions, she realized how childish she was behaving and was contemplating how to make amends when her father had approached abruptly.

"Tessa," he boomed, startling his daughter, instantly putting her on the defensive.

Rather than the rational conversation Tessa had planned, her hurt that he hadn't told her he was planning to propose, her disappointment that he had abandoned memories of her mother, her homesickness, and her loneliness tumbled out of their own bitter volition.

Now she stood before the kind woman who had saved her father from the ravages of smallpox, who had shared her meals with them, taught Tessa to cook, and supplied Tessa with fabric and yarn to begin rebuilding her wardrobe. This woman laughed with them late into the evenings, cried with them as they healed from their tragic journey. This woman counseled Tessa as a mother would after the shocking affront from Mr. Sundstrom. This woman had become her mother.

Tears welled in Tessa's eyes, spilling down her cheeks, as she fought for the words to apologize to this woman—this woman who meant the world to her—this woman who had already been like a mother for the last two years.

Mrs. Holt set the bucket down and wrapped her arms around Tessa's shoulders, cradling her head as Tessa's tears dampened her own shoulder.

"I've been acting like a spoiled baby."

"No, lass, you've been acting like a young woman who's been saddled with a great many cares."

"How can you be so kind after I treated you so poorly?" Tessa lifted her head, wiping her tears with the back of her hand.

Mrs. Holt looked earnestly in Tessa's eyes, holding her hands on either side of Tessa's face. "Because I love you, child. Don't you know that? As much as I love your father, I love you."

Except for her mother's dying declaration, Tessa didn't recall ever being told she was loved with such conviction. Warmth spilled through her like Mrs. Holt's hot chocolate on her first Christmas in Soda Springs. And Tessa's feelings were confirmed in that moment. So much more than respect, than gratitude, than friendship. A layer of grief lifted, replaced by the peace that devotion to another brings.

Tessa wrapped her arms around Mrs. Holt's shoulders this time, squeezing them as hard as she could. "And I love you. I'm honestly so happy you're marrying my da."

As the two women turned and lifted the bucket between them, Tessa noticed her father watching from the top of the hill. He was too far away for Tessa to see his expression, but she saw him wipe his eyes with his fist. She blew him a kiss.

THE DAY AFTER returning to Morristown, Tessa donned the floral dress Grandmother sent for her birthday, and prepared to accompany her father and Mrs. Holt as they called on the neighbors with their happy news.

Mrs. Pixton bubbled with joy as she moved a half-finished quilt top and handfuls of fabric pieces off her table and distributed plates of lemon custard tart in front of her guests.

"Hmmmph." Mr. Pixton shoveled a forkful of custard in his mouth and didn't bother chewing before he spoke. "I hope we're not going to be kept awake by a bunch of babies crying through the night."

Babies! Tessa hadn't even considered her father and Mrs. Holt would be living as husband and wife. Tessa ducked her head and stared at her dessert, hoping no one noticed the blush searing her cheeks.

Mrs. Holt folded her napkin and placed it next to her uneaten tart. "If we are blessed with children, Brother Pixton, they'll be of no concern to you." She stood and waited for Tessa and her father to join her. "Tildy," she said, giving Mrs. Pixton a brief hug, "thank you for your hospitality."

Tessa walked behind the couple for several yards, holding her skirts inches above the ground so they didn't drag in the dirt. Just past the trading post, Mrs. Holt stopped, placed her hands on her hips, and blew out an audible breath as she let her rigid posture slump.

"Maureen?" Tessa's father placed his hand under her elbow.

"Sometimes that man just makes my blood boil." She took his arm, stood straight once more, and draped her other hand through Tessa's elbow as well, and the three continued their journey down the street to the Andersons'.

WHILE MRS. HOLT and Mrs. Anderson chattered about most of the events leading up to the engagement—Mrs. Holt discreetly avoiding the kissing scene—Tessa contemplated what life would be like after the wedding. Would their home be big enough for three adults to live there? What if children were born? Where would they put them?

Had her father discussed moving to Oregon with Mrs. Holt? Tessa gazed across the room to where he and Mr. Anderson chatted in the opposite corner, each demonstrating with their hands the configuration of a workshop her father wanted to build. *He has no intention to go west now.* Tessa reached down, absently straightening the wood blocks on the pyramid Abe was constructing, her thoughts filled with the grandiose plans her parents had discussed during evenings on the trail. *"It was my dream before your mother died,"* he'd said.

As the adults in the room buzzed with their own conversations and Abe played with his back turned to her, Tessa drifted in a vast, empty cavern. She had spent the last two and a half years anchored to her father's dream, wading through endless days with an eye to his goal. With a vengeance, she cast about for her own dreams, unable to latch onto any thread to her future. She couldn't go on to Oregon without him, and she didn't know how to get back to North Carolina. Her "season" would be spent here feeding chickens. Closing her eyes, she drifted in her bleak void.

"Gingerbread, dear?"

Tessa jumped at the voice, realizing she'd nodded off. "I beg your pardon, ma'am," she murmured, taking the plate of cream-soaked cake from Mrs. Anderson.

"Well, of course you can have a dress made, but"—Tessa's father sat next to Mrs. Holt on the bench at the table, speaking in hushed tones—"I don't see why we can't just get married in Fort Bridger."

Abe slept on the floor, curled up at Tessa's feet, a toy block still resting in his grip. Mr. Anderson sat in a chair across the room, carefully studying each forkful of gingerbread before it went in his mouth. Mrs. Anderson stood near the sink, drizzling cream over the squares of dark cake and ladling dollops of thickened cream on top.

"Because I'd like a nice wedding this time," Mrs. Holt answered.

They're planning the wedding! Determined not to be left out again, Tessa stepped over Abe and sat down on the bench across the table from the couple. Her father gave her a stern glance but didn't voice an objection.

"My mum had just passed the first time I got married, so we just went to the courthouse without any fuss." Mrs. Holt didn't seem to mind that she had an audience as she discussed nuptial arrangements with her intended. "Isak and I married aboard the ship during our crossing with just my son, the captain, and two deckhands as witnesses." She placed one hand on Tessa's hand and one on her father's before continuing. "I want this time to be different. I know I've been away from Great Salt Lake City for several years, but I didn't leave of my own accord. I still consider my friends there to be family. It won't be a big to-do, but I'd like some of my family there when I become part of yours."

But we won't have family there, will we? Her grandmother would never make the trip.

"But we'd be gone for weeks," her father protested. "The crops will dry up, and how can you close the trading post for that long?"

Mrs. Anderson set the remainder of the gingerbread in the center of the table. "We could take care of the trading post and the irrigating for you."

"You wouldn't come with us?" Tessa blurted.

Mrs. Anderson's eyes crinkled in a soft smile above her handkerchief mask. "No, that bridge is burned. We'll not be returning to Salt Lake."

"I'm sure you'd be welcomed," Mrs. Holt offered.

"Nonetheless."

"Well, Henry? What d'you think? I'll not bully you into it, but it'd sure make me a happy bride."

Tessa's father looked with great tenderness from Mrs. Holt to Tessa and back again. "How can I say no to that? When do we leave?"

THE VISITORS SPENT much of the afternoon at the Andersons' discussing preparations for the journey, making lists of what to take and how to tend the trading post, and the best route to travel to the Salt Lake Valley. At her father's direction, Tessa joined the two women in the bedroom to have her measurements taken for a new dress as well.

When they finally returned home, Tessa gratefully retreated to her bedroom to strip out of her lavish dress and heavy crinoline in favor of her simple skirt and blouse. As she and Mrs. Holt sliced mushrooms and onions into a beef bouillon, they chatted about wedding dress etiquette.

"A proper bride should wear white like Queen Victoria did," Tessa stated with great authority.

"Pish. What would I do with a white dress?"

"You would wear it to your wedding, of course."

"Then what? Throw it in the trash bin?" Mrs. Holt tossed a pile of mushrooms into the broth bubbling in the cauldron suspended in the fireplace and rejoined Tessa by the counter. "The dress would be ruined the first time I wore it here."

"But you wouldn't wear it here. Only for the wedding." As soon as she said it, Tessa realized how frivolous her words sounded.

"The deuce you say! That's a waste of a perfectly good dress!"

Tessa sighed and wiped her hands on a length of flour sack. "You're right, Mrs. Holt."

"And that's another thing." Mrs. Holt stood with her hands on her hips squarely before Tessa.

What did I say wrong this time?

From over Mrs. Holt's shoulder, Tessa saw her father sit forward in his chair and look toward the women, a worry creasing his brow.

"I'm tired of you calling me Mrs. Holt."

Pardon?

"I'm about to become Mrs. Darrow." She took Tessa's hands in hers. "I don't imagine you'd call me 'mother,' but would you give 'Maureen' a try?"

Tessa couldn't remember having ever called someone older than herself by his or her Christian name. Even as close as she and Mary Anderson were, Tessa always called her Mrs. Anderson out of respect. As unnatural as it seemed to address Mrs. Holt by her first name, Tessa couldn't very well call her stepmother Mrs. Darrow. "If you'd like, Maureen." The name felt thick on her tongue—like a stammer.

AFTER DINNER, AS Tessa's father prepared to walk his fiancée home, he turned to his daughter and uttered the request she had been dreading all day. "Tessa, I was thinking. With all this talk of dresses and fashions, why don't we send the fabric your grandmother sent you to Salt Lake City to have it made into your dress for the wedding?"

Because Grandmother sent that for my presentation gown, she refrained from yelling. Instead, she bridled her tongue and smiled. "If you wish, Father."

CHAPTER 24

With Mrs. Holt on one side of her, grasping the side of the wagon at every bump and constantly shifting in her seat and smoothing her skirt, and her father on the other, rotating his shoulder like a nervous twitch as he held the reins, Tessa didn't know how much longer she could sit between them. After five days of bumping through sagebrush-filled valleys, the three travelers rounded the southwest slope of Ensign Peak to emerge into the Great Salt Lake Valley. The day before, Mrs. Holt pointed out Farmington Canyon where she had lived with the other Morrisites before fleeing to the Soda Springs in Idaho Territory. Since then, Mrs. Holt had become more and more anxious, worrying her cuticles until one bled. Today, they followed the dusty road southward, sandwiched between the scrub-covered hills on the east and the Great Salt Lake on the west, pausing at the hot springs north of town to freshen up.

Tessa's father pulled the buckboard to a stop before descending the foothills. Rather than the desert valley with a few cabins that Tessa expected, a well-developed city with tree-lined streets, gardens, green pastures, and brick buildings spread out before her. A gray stone building rose in the center of the city, glittering in the midday sun. Its spire-capped towers reminded Tessa of a fairy-tale castle.

Mrs. Holt fumbled in her pocket and pulled out her handkerchief, dabbing at her eyes. She chewed on her lips nervously. "Oh, I do hope I haven't made a mistake coming back."

Tessa's father brushed a damp lock of copper hair from her neck. "Why would it be a mistake?"

"We did not leave on good terms. I'm not sure how we'll be received."

"SISTER HOLT! TESSA!" Anna Larsen shrieked, bounding down the stairs of her parent's home on the northern bench of the Great Salt Lake Valley. "We waited up half the night for you!" The young widow whose husband died in a lightning strike Tessa's first summer in the Soda Springs was swallowed up in Mrs. Holt's embrace.

"Oh, Anna, just look at you." Mrs. Holt held the woman at arm's length, turning her from side to side before hugging her again. "We've missed you so much."

"And I, you." Breaking free from Mrs. Holt's grasp, Anna hugged Tessa and shook Mr. Darrow's hand. "It's so nice to see you again. Welcome to Great Salt Lake City."

"It's nice to see you," Tessa's father said.

Though not on the scale of the plantations in Charlotte, the two-story home with a gabled roof and bay windows looked warm and inviting. "You have a beautiful home," Tessa said, admiring the flowers lining the walk.

Her father pointed to the side of the house where an eight-foot tree spilled around the corner, loaded with two-inch fuzzy, green fruit. "Look over there, Tessa."

"Peaches?" She slapped a hand her chest and gasped. "Peaches grow here?"

Anna laughed and mocked Tessa's touch of drawl. "Why, yes they do!"

Then Tessa spied three children watching them from behind the lace curtains in the tall window. "That can't be Grace and Christian." She waved at the youngsters and they ducked out of sight.

"Indeed it is, and my sister, Bethany." Anna beamed. "Grace just turned six and Christian is two and a half."

"Do you think they remember me?" Tessa wore the same skirt from which she'd cut a strip to dress the little girl's doll.

"I doubt Christian would, but I know Gracie does. She's just being shy."

A man and woman, both blond and willowy like their daughter, walked down the stoop, greeting the travelers with outstretched hands.

"Ingrid. Max." Mrs. Holt fumbled to shake the man's hand before giving up and embracing both of her friends. "It's been so long. Thank you for letting us stay here."

"Nonsense. We would not have it any other way." Anna's mother hugged Mrs. Holt again. "And you are not just staying here. We would love to hold your wedding here, as well."

"Glory, no," Mrs. Holt said, gasping. "We couldn't impose that on you. We'll just have it at the courthouse. But you and Anna and her children will come, yes?"

Mrs. Christensen folded her arms and gave Mrs. Holt a sidelong glance. "Maureen, you should have heard the cheers when I told the sisters at church you were coming back to be married. I hope you will not disappoint them."

Mrs. Holt looked toward Tessa's father, raising her eyebrows. He just smiled and shrugged. "You wanted a wedding."

Mr. Christensen stepped toward Tessa's father with his hand outstretched. "You must be Mr. Darrow."

"Henry, please. And this is my daughter, Tessa."

Tessa curtsied. "I'm pleased to meet you, sir."

"All right, Ingrid," Mrs. Holt said. "We can have a small dinner." Then, when Mrs. Christensen clasped her hands together—just as Anna used to do when she'd gotten her way—Mrs. Holt interrupted, pointing her index finger at the woman. "I said a small dinner. I won't be having a big to-do."

"You leave everything to me. We'll have a lovely day." Mrs. Christensen put her arm around Tessa's shoulders and ushered her and the other women up the steps. "You are just as pretty as Gracie said."

Tessa smiled to think that the little girl she had tended two years ago cared enough to mention Tessa to her grandmother. She looked over her shoulder to see her father and Mr. Christensen ambling down the street leading their rig, already conversing like friends. *It's no wonder Maureen considers these people as family.*

FOR THE NEXT several days, the women of the household bustled about with wedding plans, and the men kept busy fulfilling the women's orders. The simple wedding and dinner Mrs. Holt agreed to let Mrs. Christensen host turned into a gala event involving all of the neighbors in food preparations. Under Mrs. Christensen's direct instruction, Tessa and Mrs. Holt spent their days wandering through the shops of downtown Salt Lake, staying out of the way of Mrs. Christensen's legion of neighbors preparing the home and yard for the weekend.

On Wednesday, while Mrs. Holt attended to her wedding dress fitting at the Eagle Emporium, Tessa wandered alone through the city. After watching men bustling in and out of the temple carrying all manner of construction supplies, she strolled passed the shops on Main Street, stopping in at Allens' Mercantile to check the time. She was meeting Mrs. Holt for lunch before Tessa went for her own dress fitting. Leaving the shop, she nearly bumped into two of the girls she'd met at the picnic her first summer in Soda Springs.

Too late to duck back in the mercantile, Tessa forced a smile, grateful to be wearing her pretty birthday dress. Tessa saw the recognition flash in their eyes as they walked past her, not even bothering to nod.

Insufferable bores.

Tessa had to keep from laughing out loud as her grandmother's voice rang in her thoughts. Holding her head high, Tessa rounded the corner onto First South.

A cluster of people coming out of the drugstore nearly knocked Tessa off her feet as she passed the storefront. Emerging from the sea of "beg pardons," she braced herself against the cool brick façade to catch her breath. A young woman with hair the color of a copper penny strolled across the street midway down the block, her hand coiled around a gentleman's arm as he pushed a perambulator.

He reminds me of William. Tessa smiled, watching the couple walking toward her.

That is William!

Panicked, she ducked into the drugstore, flattening her back against the wall beside the door, and peeked through the lacy curtains as the couple approached. Right in front of her, the couple stopped and William picked up the baby's rattle, jiggling it in front of the baby lying in the pram. William and the woman laughed while the baby waved its tiny arms in the air trying to reach the toy.

He's married? He has a child? No wonder he hadn't returned her letters. *But why wouldn't he tell Mrs. Holt?*

The baby's mother was tall and slender, dressed in a light green dress with emerald brocade that set off her flaming hair and dark brown eyes. She adjusted her gloves and her hat, reminding Tessa that she owned neither. The woman didn't stop talking for all the time Tessa watched— not even when she looked at the window and caught Tessa staring at her. When she motioned toward the window with her head, causing William to look over, Tessa jumped back, crouching beside the wall, praying they wouldn't come in.

"Are you all right, miss?" The shopkeeper, dressed in a white shirt with a red-and-white apron and black sleeve garters, held a chair out for her.

Numb, Tessa stared at him, the image of William and the red-haired woman seared in her mind.

"Miss?"

The light tap of the chair on the back of her knees was enough to cause them to buckle and Tessa collapsed into the chair with a thump.

"You've had a start, miss. Let me fetch you a soda water."

As the numbness settled firmly in the pit of Tessa's belly, she became aware of the man setting a glass of water in front of her. She held up a shaking hand. "Thank you, no, sir. I've left my money at home," she lied, knowing she didn't have a cent to call her own.

"No need, miss." He pushed the water toward her. "Did something frighten you?"

Frighten? No, not frighten. She sipped her soda water, feeling the bubbles snap on her nose. No, frighten wasn't the correct word. What was it then? What one word expressed what a person felt when all hope was dashed? Despair? Resignation? Tessa took another sip. *You're right, Grandmother. He who lives on hope dies fasting.*

CHAPTER 25

"You left her there. To wander the city looking for you. What would possess you?" Her father's pounding voice kept time with the pain thrumming in her head. "Do you never think about anyone but yourself?" Tessa lay curled on her bed, facing the wall. She didn't know how much time had passed since she'd fled to her bedroom at the Christensen's, clutching her pillow over her head so the family wouldn't hear her sobs.

She hadn't meant to abandon Mrs. Holt at the dressmaker's shop or miss her appointment for her own fitting as she rushed up the hill from the shops, trying to breathe, praying she wouldn't stumble into William. Throughout the afternoon she'd heard the comings and goings of the family, watched as the shadows in her room grew longer, smelled the sweet fragrance of frying chicken turning acrid as the dinner burned. But every time she thought about going downstairs to smile and pretend everything was all right, she became physically ill.

"You need a good spanking," he threatened.

Tessa steeled herself for a series of swats, unable to remember the last time she had been spanked.

"Henry, no," Mrs. Holt gasped. "There's no need for that."

Tessa hadn't realized the woman was in the room.

"I won't have her disrespecting you."

"She didn't mean naw disrespect," Mrs. Holt pleaded. "She wasn't feeling well."

Tessa held her breath for several moments until she heard her father move toward the door. "Don't come out of your room tonight if you're so sick," he grumbled.

When she was certain he was gone, Tessa rolled over. Mrs. Holt stood by the bureau looking hurt and tired.

"I'm sorry, Mrs. Holt—Maureen." She swung her feet off the bed and sat up.

Sitting on the bed next to her, the woman removed the pins from Tessa's hair and stroked damp tendrils from her brow. "You've been crying powerful hard. Would you like to tell me what's happened?"

As much as she wanted to sob her heartbreak to her soon-to-be stepmother, Tessa had already determined not to tell her that William was in town. Or that he was married with a family. Mrs. Holt would find out soon enough. If William wanted her to know, he'd tell her himself. Better for Mrs. Holt to think he was still in Oregon, unable to come to the wedding. Tessa would not spoil the day by divulging William's secret.

"I just wasn't feeling well," she lied. Her lips twitched as she struggled to speak without crying. "I didn't want to be sick in public." Not a total lie. "I didn't mean to be inconsiderate."

Mrs. Holt lowered her eyes and clasped her hands in her lap. Her shoulders raised and lowered with her sigh.

She knows I'm lying.

Standing up, Mrs. Holt plucked Tessa's nightgown from the hook on the door and laid it on the bed beside her. "I hope you're feeling better in the morning."

THE NEXT DAY, Tessa dressed in her blue work dress as the eastern horizon began to pink. She crept down to the kitchen and sliced a piece of bread, smearing it with butter from the icebox, and poured a glass of milk. Careful to not let the door creak, she tiptoed outside to eat her breakfast on the back steps where she wouldn't disturb the sleeping family.

The shops wouldn't open for a few hours yet, and she didn't think it safe to wander through deserted streets, so she knelt down and plucked stray blades of grass out of the tomato patch. She was nearly finished when Mrs. Christensen stooped down beside her.

"Tessa? What are you doing out here?" With a sharp intake of her breath, she picked up a handful of the green blades.

"I woke too early to go for my fitting, so I came out here to see if I could be useful. I'm just about finished with this grass. Is there something else I can help with?"

Mrs. Christensen smiled a weak, tight-lipped smile and gathered the greens into her apron. "These are new chives, dear, not grass. But thank you for picking them. They will be nice to use for the dinner Saturday."

Hmmm. The chives in North Carolina grow much larger with flowers on the tops. Tessa lifted Mrs. Christensen's forgotten egg basket and strolled to the chicken coop.

Her father and Mrs. Holt looked up from the table as Tessa walked into the kitchen with the basket of eggs.

"Good morning, Tessa," Mrs. Holt said. Her father glared at her but said nothing.

She set the eggs on the counter and turned to go up the stairs. "Good morning, Maureen."

"We're taking a drive to Lindsey Gardens this morning. Would you like to come?"

Her father looked out the window, still not uttering a word.

"Thank you, no, ma'am. I have to go downtown for my fitting." As nervous as it made her to go to the shops alone, it was her own fault that the fitting hadn't been accomplished yesterday. *I won't be selfish and impose myself on you.* If she got lost, she would deal with it. If she bumped into William, she would deal with it. If she fell in a great crevasse and got eaten by tigers, she would deal with it. No one would miss her, anyway.

Anna looked up from the corner where she was braiding Grace's hair. "If you'd like to wait until the children go down for their naps, I could go with you."

No, she stood a better chance of not seeing William if she went as soon as the Emporium opened. "Thank you, but I'd rather go early and get it taken care of."

Grace watched them with her big cornflower-blue eyes. She hadn't said much of anything since Tessa arrived. So different from the little chatterbox she'd been in Soda Springs. Her fat baby cheeks had hollowed out and her blond hair flowed nearly to her waist. And, rather than flinching when her mother spoke to her, Grace clung to her, always standing just behind her skirt. *Perhaps she's turned a bit shy being around so many people?* Tessa also hadn't seen much of Anna's sister, Bethany. The eight-year old spent most days playing by herself in her room, or in the street playing with her friends, leaving her younger cousins behind.

"Maybe we could take the children for a picnic lunch when I get back," Tessa offered. "Would you like that, Grace?"

The little girl just shrugged.

⚜

WALKING DOWN THE hill toward the temple block, Tessa considered ways she could win Grace over. Maybe the seamstress at the Eagle Emporium would let Tessa take a few scraps of fabric to fashion into a doll. As she crossed Brigham Street on the south side of the temple, she paused to let a horse and rider go by.

"Tessa?" The man pulled the horse to a stop and swung down from the saddle. "It is you!"

She shielded her eyes against the morning sun, craning her neck upwards. There was no mistaking the tall man with the coppery hair glinting in the backlight. "Peter!" Happy memories sprang to mind of the months they'd spent exploring the area around the soda springs until his father—*don't think of that now*. What she couldn't push away, however, was the image of Peter's face, stricken, when she didn't immediately return his affection.

He turned her, stepping to the side so she didn't have to stare into the sun to look at him. "How are you? What are you doing in the valley?" His eyes shone as he looked at her—like they had whenever he showed her an amazing discovery like Steamboat Springs.

"I'm here with my Da and Mrs. Holt. They're being married on Saturday."

"Married! Well, isn't that something."

"I'm sure they'd love to see you." *And I'd like to have someone to dance with.* "Why don't you come to the wedding? Do you know where the Christensens live? Anna Larsen's parents? Just up the hill on Quince Street."

"No, but I'm sure I can find it."

"Is your mother still in town? It would be lovely to see her and the children." The last she'd heard, Mrs. Sundstrom and all of her children were still living with Peter's uncle Kurt, waiting to make the journey back to Minnesota, but Tessa hadn't had time to pay a visit.

Peter dropped his gaze, examining the reins in his hand. "She's here. Well, west of here, in Grantsville. Uncle Kurt says my father came back— with a new wife and kid—built a couple of houses south of the lake."

Why did I bring that up? She didn't want to hear about his father. It was obvious he hadn't seen his family. Judging from the hurt in his eyes, he likely wouldn't. *Talk about something else—anything else.* She reached up and stroked the side of his horse's chestnut neck. "What about you, Peter? What are you doing here?"

"Just passing through to collect my pay from Kurt and buy some supplies. I bought a little place in Wyoming."

You bought a house? Before even realizing what she was doing, she smiled and tilted her head coyly. "Do you have someone special in mind to keep house with in Wyoming?" *Tessa! Hush your mouth!*

"Matter of fact, I do—now that I have something to offer." His voice held that familiar tease he took on whenever she flirted with him. He reached in his pocket and pulled out a fabric pouch. "That's why I'm in Salt Lake. I just came from Mr. Jennings's." He dumped the contents of the pouch into his hand and held up a narrow gold band. "What do you think?"

"Peter!" *Wyoming. Hmmm.* Now that marrying William was no longer an option, perhaps she should reconsider Peter's offer. He'd cut ties with his father, so she wouldn't have to worry about that anymore. *Wyoming wouldn't be that far away from my father*—but far enough from Morristown that she wouldn't be reminded of William. And there wasn't a string of young men in Idaho waiting to fill her dance card. She stared at the golden band before returning her eyes to his. "It's beautiful." She refrained from taking it from him, waiting instead for him to place it on her finger.

"I need to have a conversation with a certain young lady's father first, of course. But maybe he'll have time to see me tomorrow."

Tessa rested her hand on his wrist, just below the fingers that held the gleaming promise. "I'm certain your young lady would be charmed to have you speak with her father."

Grinning, he placed the ring back in its pouch and shoved it deep in his pocket. "I hope her father feels the same way. Maybe we'll have an announcement to make at the wedding."

No, he wasn't as handsome or polished as William, but she loved how Peter seemed so devoted to her. She kissed her fingers and placed them on his cheek.

Taking her hand in his, he looked deep in her eyes. "Miss Darrow, what a pleasure to see you." He lifted the back of her hand to his lips.

Clouds couldn't float as lightly as Tessa did, wafting into the Eagle Emporium. She followed a matronly woman into a back room for the fitting, resisting the urge to squeal she'd just become engaged.

Tessa shed her cotton dress and then patiently waited as the seamstress laced Tessa's corset and tied a hoop skirt around her waist. Tessa donned a petticoat as the woman lifted voluminous layers of taffeta and tulle from the dress form and slid it over Tessa's up-stretched arms.

As the woman turned to fasten a pin cozy on her wrist, Tessa discreetly shifted her bosom into a more comfortable position above the corset—perhaps causing her figure to swell above the rounded neckline of the dress a little more than necessary. She followed the woman out of the dressing room into a larger area lined with a semicircle of mirrors.

Stepping up on the round platform in the center of the room, Tessa tried not to grin at the reflection of the belle looking back at her. The golden taffeta rested at the edge of her shoulders, the fitted bodice dropping to a deep point below her waist, tulle-covered cascades flowing to a generous train. Each swoop of the skirt was caught by a large taffeta bow. Sheer sleeves billowed to her elbows, gathered by smaller bows. Golden ribbons wound through the tulle ruffles outlining her neckline, peplum, and hem.

Mrs. Holt's common sense rang through Tessa's thoughts as she studied her reflection. Where would she wear such a dress again? She could wear it when she wed Peter, but then she'd tuck it away in her wedding trunk and stow it in the corner of a room—in a cabin—somewhere in Wyoming. A cabin in Wyoming—away from her father, away from Mrs. Holt and Mrs. Anderson. She wondered if she'd even have neighbors. But she would have Peter, and Peter loved her.

She turned in a slow circle as the seamstress pinned her hem and adjusted the gathers around her waist. And what about when children are born? Mrs. Sundstrom had nearly died in childbirth, and she had Mrs. Holt and Mrs. Anderson to attend her. Would Tessa have to bear children with no one to guide her through it? And what if there were no children? How would she spend her days in this cabin in Wyoming?

Maybe Peter would reconsider living in Wyoming. Maybe they could live here in Great Salt Lake City. No, she could never live here, knowing that Mr. Sundstrom lived just a few miles away. And as nice as the shops were to visit for a few days, there were too many people. She recalled the tumult of bodies that had nearly knocked her over yesterday. No, she liked the quiet of the country—with just a few families around with whom to visit.

And if they lived here, there were too many chances to run into William. *Too painful. But I'd be married to a husband of my own . . .* No, Great Salt Lake City was out of the question. Morristown? In his parents' old house? "That will never do."

"What will never do?" the seamstress barked. "This is just what you ordered."

"Pardon?" Tessa blinked, returning from her reverie. "I'm sorry, my mind was elsewhere. The gown is lovely."

Tessa felt the black void enclosing her again. *I can't do this. I can't marry Peter just for the sake of being married. What do I even know about him—other than his family? Will he be a farmer? Or gone all the time on cattle drives? What kind of life does he want? What are his dreams?* She mulled over the dilemma she'd been contemplating for weeks. What were her dreams—aside from being a wife and mother? *Until I know what kind of life I want, I'm not ready to share it with another.*

As TESSA RETURNED home just before noon, Anna and her children waited on the stoop with a basket of food. Struggling to hide her gloom, Tessa stumbled through the picnic. They ate in the park at the top of the hill, and she played tag, stickball, skipping rope, and formulated a way to get out of marrying Peter.

When her father and Mrs. Holt returned from Lindsey Gardens, Tessa waited while her father helped Mrs. Holt from the buckboard. Thankful they'd made up this morning, she climbed up to sit beside him while he returned the rig to the livery. "Da, I bumped into Peter today."

"Oh?"

"He's bought a place in Wyoming. He means to come speak to you tomorrow."

"I'll not have it," her father blurted before clamping his mouth shut. The muscles in his jaw hardened. He sighed and frowned, and he sighed again. "Do you love him?"

"I thought I could, but no. Not enough."

"Then why is he coming to see me?"

Feeling terribly foolish, she admitted, "It happened so fast, I wasn't thinking clearly. Before I could sort out my feelings, he was gone, thinking we had an understanding."

He looked off in the distance, a smile playing at the corners of his mouth. "So you want me to set him straight."

"Would you?"

"It's what fathers do."

She hugged his arm and then added, "But be kind about it."

"Aren't I always?"

CHAPTER 26

Yawning, Tessa turned her head away from the sliver of light streaking through the gap where the blind met the window. *Friday. I wonder what time Peter will call?* She'd stayed up much too late last night pressing her freshly laundered skirt and blouse with a hot iron in preparation for his visit. Then, while the household slumbered, she lay in bed unable to sleep while she considered and reconsidered her decision to refuse Peter a second time. If she turned him down this time, he certainly would not ask again. *What if I never have another opportunity?* The questions remained and, even as the sun rose fully, she contemplated telling her father that perhaps she should marry Peter after all.

Sighing, she draped an arm across her eyes and opened them slowly, adjusting to the brightness of the sun-filled room. A pair of bright blue eyes, nearly hidden in a tumble of yellow curls, stared back at her.

"Gracie? What are you doing?" She yawned again and rose up on one elbow to look over the edge of the bed at the child sitting on the floor. "Grace!"

The little girl jumped to her feet, dropping Tessa's calico skirt and a pair of scissors in her wake. She stood with her back to the wall, hiding something behind her as she inched toward the door.

"Oh no!" Tessa cried, scrambling out of bed. "What have you done?" A rectangle of cloth, cut on three sides, dangled from the skirt Tessa had sewn her first summer in Morristown. She held the skirt up in one hand and the nearly severed strip of cloth in the other, trying not to raise her voice. "Why would you do this, Grace? You've ruined my skirt."

The girl said nothing but continued to slide toward the door.

"What's behind your back, Grace?"

The skin around the child's furrowed brow began to pink with impending tears, and she held her trembling bottom lip between her teeth.

"Gracie." Tessa took a step toward her. "I'm not going to yell, and I'm not going to spank you, but you need to show me what you're hiding."

She blinked her long brown lashes, sending the first of her pooled tears slipping down her cheeks. "It's Rose," she whispered. Slowly, she revealed the fabric doll with the porcelain head she'd cradled as she left Morristown two years earlier. "She lost her dress again—the one you made her."

Tessa closed her eyes and drew a deep breath, recalling the day she'd cut a swatch of cloth from the hem of her skirt to dress the doll in—the day Anna had taken Grace and her brother away. *I guess I set the example. What's done is done.* With a sigh, Tessa stooped and picked up the scissors to finish the job the little girl had started.

Throughout the day, Tessa invented ways to keep the three youngsters, Bethany, Grace, and Christian, out from underfoot while neighbors scurried about, preparing the house and yard for the next day's festivities. Though it would have been much easier to take the children to explore City Creek Canyon for the day, Tessa didn't want to travel too far from the house—where Peter would call.

Just past noon, Mr. Christensen drove Tessa and Mrs. Holt in his buggy the few blocks downtown to collect their dresses for the wedding. On orders to not venture even as far as the backyard, Tessa's father stayed behind to wait for Peter. Scarcely an hour later, the ladies returned toting their muslin-covered dresses.

"Did anyone drop by?" Tessa asked lightly as she carried her dress past her father sitting on the porch.

He stood and held the screen door open for the ladies. "Not a soul."

"Expecting someone?" Mrs. Holt asked.

Tessa shrugged. "No, guess not."

In her room, Tessa hung her gown on the door of the armoire and removed the sheeting, fluffing the folds of taffeta and tulle. "On second thought," she said, spying Grace watching from the hallway. She lifted the dress and moved it safely inside the wardrobe and turned the key at the top of the closet door for good measure.

I don't know what's taking you so long, Peter Sundstrom. She'd already changed her mind about marrying Peter two or three times this morning. *If I have to tell Da I've changed my mind again, he's like to make the decision for me.*

Just before supper, three men in black suits strode up the walk.

One—clean-shaven and balding with curly brown hair around the back of his head—plucked Christian off a low branch of the sycamore out front. "Brother Larsen? Aren't you a little high up there for your own good?" He set the little boy safely on the ground and smiled at Tessa before rejoining the other men.

Before they reached the porch, Bethany raced past them and bounded up the steps. "Ma! Pa! The bishop's here!"

Just as quickly, Mrs. Christensen appeared in the doorway, drying her hands on her apron, and stepped onto the porch. "Bishop. Elders. Thank you for coming."

Before the men were finished with their greetings, Mrs. Holt hesitantly stepped through the door, nervously tucking stray tendrils into her topknot and smoothing her apron.

"Sister Holt." The gentleman with the larger belly, silver hair, and a short-cropped beard held his hand out to her. Then he pulled her into a full embrace just as Tessa's father walked around the corner of the house. "Welcome home, sister. Welcome home."

Mrs. Holt's eyes flew wide when she saw her fiancé observing. Tessa's fingertips covered her mouth. Her father folded his arms, looking none too pleased.

"Henry." Mrs. Holt moved to stand beside him and motioned for Tessa to join them. "I'd like to introduce you to three dear friends: Elder Cannon, Elder Benson, and Bishop Grow."

The three men, imposing in their black suits, smiled warmly and shook hands with Tessa's father, then Tessa. With the "pleased-to-meet-yous" out of the way, the tall, slender man with a long reddish beard—Bishop Grow—turned to Tessa. "I've seen you downtown watching the construction of the temple and tabernacle, haven't I?"

Tessa darted a look at Mrs. Holt and her father, hoping for some clue as to how to respond. "Yes—yes, sir. I didn't mean any harm."

The Bishop laughed. "No harm done, sister. I'm flattered you're interested in our work there."

"Tessa," Mrs. Christensen said, "Bishop Grow is the architect in charge of building the temple."

Her father's eyes lit up. "Is that right?"

"Not in charge." The bishop held up his hand, waggling it back and forth. "I oversee some of the work on the temple and on the tabernacle."

"He's being modest," Elder Benson said. "Bishop Grow is the architect of the Tabernacle dome. They just completed construction on it a couple of weeks ago. It's the largest self-supported roof in the country."

"That's quite the impressive undertaking," Tessa's father said.

"And what of you, Sister Darrow?" The silver-haired gentleman directed the conversation back to Tessa. "How do you find our city?"

"I find it most charming. Your temple reminds me of a castle from my childhood storybooks. And the domed building is most impressive, as my father said."

"I hope you'll be a frequent visitor," Bishop Grow replied. "And if you'll pardon me saying," he added with a nod to Tessa's father before continuing with Tessa, "knowing you're watching has added a certain vim to the work of some of my younger carpenters."

Tessa blushed and dropped her head demurely, not displeased that her presence had not gone unnoticed.

"Well." Elder Cannon clapped his hands together in front of his barrel chest. "I believe we have the matter of a wedding to discuss."

Mrs. Holt beamed as she draped her hand through Tessa's father's elbow. "Would you gentlemen like to come inside?"

AFTER SUPPER AND baths, a line of women and girls sat on stools on the back porch, aligned back to front, rolling rags in each other's hair. Mrs. Christensen curled Mrs. Holt's, who curled Anna's, who curled Tessa's, who curled Bethany's. Grace, with her hair already in rags, danced between the stylists, making sure each had sufficient rags at her disposal.

Tessa's father stopped his daughter at the base of the stairs before she retired to her room, and gave her a hug. "Things happen, Tess."

With eyes downcast, Tessa nodded, knowing precisely to what—to whom—he referred.

"Don't be discouraged. Maybe he'll come tomorrow."

"You're getting married tomorrow. Let's just concentrate on that." She leaned up on her tiptoes and kissed his cheek. "Love you, Da."

"Love you, my Tessabear."

LONG SINCE THE last stirrings of the household quieted, Tessa let her candle burn, lying in bed with her knees up and her hands clasped behind her head, staring at the ceiling. Why hadn't he come? Things happen— what things? Why were men so inconsiderate—not coming when they promise—not writing when they promise? *Am I doomed to spend my life waiting?* She tried to tell herself she was being melodramatic, but the thoughts just kept repeating in her mind.

If I don't get some sleep, I'll have purple rings around my eyes for the wedding. She climbed out of bed and retrieved the Bible from the bureau's top. Maybe reading a few verses would help her feel drowsy.

She opened the New Testament, starting at the beginning. *Matthew, chapter one, verse one . . . Matthew, chapter two, verse one . . . Matthew, chapter three . . . chapter four . . . chapter five . . .* At last she began to yawn a bit, but still felt fully awake. . . . *Chapter six . . .* Her eyes were beginning to get heavy. One more chapter should do it. *Matthew, chapter seven, verse one.* Her eyes skimmed the last of the familiar passages of the Sermon on the Mount until her eyes lit on the passage her mother had embroidered on a sampler:

> *Matthew 7:7 Ask, and it shall be given you; seek, and ye shall find; knock, and it shall be opened unto you:*

She shut the book and slid out of bed to her knees, silently reciting verse eight from memory—*For every one that asketh receiveth; and he that seeketh findeth; and to him that knocketh it shall be opened.*

Whispering her prayer, she wrestled with her decision until her knees ached, still no closer to a decision. She sent up one last plea before climbing back in bed. "Father, I know Thou worketh in mysterious ways, but will You please, just this one time, let me know what to do?"

CHAPTER 27

"Tessa, Mama says she's ready to do your hair now." Grace snatched one of the stuffed eggs off the tray Tessa was carefully arranging and chomped down on the mixture of egg yolk, sour cream, and pickle relish before Tessa could swat the child's hand away.

"One, Gracie Larsen," Tessa scolded. "You only get that one angel egg or we won't have enough for the guests."

"But I'm soooooo hungry," the little girl wailed with a bit of yellow mush squishing out the corners of her mouth.

"How can you be hungry? You've been eating half of everything I've cooked this morning. Not to mention the food your mama and grandma fixed." Tessa turned from the galvanized metal tub half-filled with ice where she'd nestled trays of stuffed eggs. She tickled the little girl's stomach. "How can that little tummy hold anymore?"

Grace shrugged and took another bite of her egg. "Can I take one for Christian?"

"No, he'll make a mess." Tessa reached into a basket and retrieved a crustless quarter of melted cheese sandwich. "Here. Give him this."

"Can I have one too?"

Tessa rolled her eyes and handed another sandwich quarter to Grace. "But this is the last nibble you're getting until after the wedding." She turned to go up the back stairs to have her hair arranged before donning her new gown.

"Yoo-hoo," a neighbor woman called, letting herself in through the front door and emerging into the kitchen. She was lugging a wooden crate covered with a checkered tablecloth. "Anyone about?"

"Good morning, ma'am," Tessa greeted her. "Everyone's upstairs getting ready. I was just on my way up."

"Good, then I'm right on time." She set the crate on the table and began unloading trays, baskets, and bowls of cut fruits, vegetables, and rolls. "You run along and I'll make myself useful down here."

"Thank you, ma'am. Sister Olmstead, is it?"

The woman smiled broadly. "You remembered! You're such a sweet girl."

Hardly a girl, Tessa thought, but refrained from commenting. "Would you kindly keep an eye on Grace? She'll try to convince you she's starving."

Already the little girl was reaching for one of the rolls piled in a cloth-lined basket.

"Well, of course I will," Sister Olmstead chirped, handing Grace a roll. "Grace and I are fast friends. Aren't we, dear?" Grace just looked up from behind the fluffy mound she was biting into and nodded.

"All right, then, I'll leave you to it." Tessa cast a quick look out the kitchen window at the collection of chairs arranged on the back lawn, the ribbons floating gently from the tree branches, and the white arbor festooned with netting and roses. *Lovely day for a wedding.*

"How did our simple wedding with a few of Maureen's friends turn into such a circus?" Tessa's father sighed.

"I think it's wonderful that Mrs. Hol—Maureen has been so warmly welcomed." Tessa tucked the tails of his tie inside the edges of his waistcoat and plumped the tie's bow outside the coat's lapels.

Tessa and her father stood in the north side yard, waiting for their cue to take their places. He had been shooed from the house to prevent any chance of him seeing his bride in her wedding dress, so Tessa waited with him, enjoying the final moments of having him to herself.

He pulled at the high collar of his white linen shirt, barely visible above the gray tweed waistcoat and black morning coat. The suit, borrowed from Mr. Christensen, fit remarkably well aside from the gray tweed trousers that were just a bit loose around the waist. "I'll have heatstroke if we don't get this underway soon," he grumbled, fanning himself with the brim of his top hat.

Bethany skipped up to the pair, waving a square of cloth in the air. "Guess what you forgot," she taunted, dangling the woven plaid in front of Tessa's nose.

"Oh dear." Tessa snatched the fabric from Bethany. "Thank you, Bethany," she said, waving the girl off with the back of her fingers. "I'm sure your help is appreciated inside."

Tessa held the square in front of her, turning it this way and that.

"Mrs. Hol—Maureen wanted you to wear this. It's her family tartan, MacLaren." She traced with her finger the narrow red and yellow stripes that formed the plaid over the blue- and green-checkered field.

"Shouldn't I wear the Darrow tartan?"

"Do you know what the Darrow tartan is?"

"Well, no, not exactly."

"Then you'll wear this," Tessa declared. "If I can remember how to fold it like Mrs. Holt did." She rolled her eyes and corrected herself. "Maureen."

While her father held his hat out to her, Tessa used its flat top as a surface on which to refold the pocket square.

"Tessa, if it's so hard for you to call Maureen by her given name, would you consider calling her Mother? Or Mama?"

Her own mother's image floated through her memory. The porcelain skin, green eyes, and black hair. *I can't.* Tessa had a mother. A sainted mother. And Mrs. Holt could never replace her. "I can't, Da. 'Mother' is, well, my mother. I can't share that name."

With the fabric folded to form three points, Tessa lifted the cloth and folded the last corner around the arrangement, tucking the end in to form a secure packet.

"I'll tell you what, though." She lifted the tartan and turned to tuck it into his breast pocket. "Mrs. Holt refers to her departed mother as 'Mum.' Do you think she would mind if I call her 'Mum'?"

With a smile, her father assumed a bit of Mrs. Holt's brogue. "Mum and Da. I think tha' 'twould be lovely."

Tessa laughed; then, as she looked over her father's shoulder, her smile faded. She stiffened and gripped his arm. Peter emerged into the yard from the opposite side of the house and, spying Tessa and her father, walked across the lawn toward them—with a young woman strutting beside him.

As he turned and saw Peter, Tessa's father wrapped her hand around his left elbow and held it firmly against his waist. Drawing a deep breath, he led Tessa forward and extended his right hand to the young man. "Peter."

Peter pumped the man's hand, beaming. "Mr. Darrow, Tessa, I'd like to introduce my fiancée, Katie Brown. You might remember her from Morristown."

Yes, I remember her. Tessa concentrated on smiling and on pulling breath into her lungs, remembering the girl who had gone out of her way to snub Tessa that first summer—who had snubbed her again just days ago when they'd passed on the street downtown.

Peter prattled on, oblivious to the numbness clawing its way from the pit of Tessa's stomach to suck the life out of her lungs. "Tessa encouraged me to speak to Katie's father, and yesterday he gave his blessing for us to marry."

I encouraged you . . . to speak to Katie's . . . I thought you wanted to ask for my hand. As the realization of her misunderstanding seized her heart, Tessa clamped her knees together to keep them from buckling.

"Well, that's just wonderful," she heard her father say. "We certainly wish you every happiness." Tessa stared at the young man's chest, unable to draw her eyes up to meet his. "Now if you'll excuse us," her father continued, "Tessa's needed inside."

She felt herself being led away as the edges of her peripheral vision faded to white. Heard the back screen door squeak open. Saw a flash of blue tartan dash forward. Felt her knees hit the wooden floor. And from the darkness, heard her father's frantic voice order, "Someone get her out of that corset!"

"No," TESSA INSISTED. "I'm fine now. I've already made the wedding an hour late." Sitting on the edge of her bed, she took a sip of her lemonade, feeling foolish at being the center of so much fuss.

"Well, I'm just going to tell him to leave," Anna declared.

"You'll do no such thing. It was a simple misunderstanding. My misunderstanding." *How could I have misread his intentions so horribly?* Tessa closed her eyes, breathed in, and blew out her deep breath. Then she pressed the cool glass against her forehead. "Can we please just get this over with?" Her eyes flew open and she grabbed Mrs. Holt's hand. "That's not what I meant."

Mrs. Holt laughed. "I know that, dear. No harm done." She recommenced fanning the back of Tessa's neck. "But you're right; we shouldn't keep the guests sitting in this heat much longer. Are you steady enough to walk up front?"

"I'm fine," Tessa insisted again, accepting Anna's hand to pull her to her feet with the awkward crinolette. As she stood there, taking several deep breaths to ensure she wasn't likely to faint again, she thought how grateful she was that the seamstress recommended this trimmer version of the hoop skirt, grateful that her father had insisted she not be strapped into a corset for the rest of the day.

Pausing in front of the armoire's mirror, she discreetly admired her reflection in the creamy yellow gown that shimmered gold where the sun fell on it. Her ringlets flowing past her shoulders were only a shade more golden than the dress. Her green eyes shone nearly as much as the fabric. *This is truly the most beautiful gown I ever could have imagined. Grandmother would be so pleased.* She checked the fall of her taffeta and tulle cascades. With her narrow waist, she doubted anyone would guess she wasn't wearing a corset anyway. Mrs. Holt stepped beside her and nestled a delicate wreath of ivy and yellow rosebuds among her upswept curls.

Tessa took the woman's hands in hers. The bright blue, green, red, and yellow plaid dress brought out the color in Mrs. Holt's cheeks. Long sleeves, high neck, and full skirt made from the wool tartan must have been terribly warm, yet she seemed to take no notice as she fussed over Tessa.

"I've never seen a more beautiful bride," Tessa said.

"Och, go on with ya. Don't you make me cry today."

"Before we go down, I wanted to ask . . . would you mind if I call you 'Mum'?"

Mrs. Holt caught her breath and placed her hand on her chest, her blue eyes sparkling with tears. She pulled the handkerchief Tessa had embroidered from her sleeve and dabbed her eyes. Her voice quivered and then choked. "Nothin' could make me happier."

TESSA'S FATHER WAITED at the bottom of the stairs for Tessa to descend as a violin hummed strains of a Chopin "Nocturne." "You're feeling better, then?"

"Yes, Da, I'm fine." Despite the shock of Peter's engagement, she really was fine. *Rather relieved actually.* Peter had put all of her questions, her wavering, to rest with his announcement. *Nothing left to do but wish him well.*

"You have grown into quite the remarkable woman, daughter. Beautiful and gracious in every way."

Reveling in the pride in his eyes, Tessa hugged him lightly—careful not to muss her dress. "Do you mind if I stay your 'Tessabear' just a while longer?"

He threaded her hand across his arm, preparing to walk up the aisle with his daughter. "You'll always be my Tessabear."

As they reached the head of the aisle and turned to face the neighbors assembled, Tessa's father stepped to stand beside Elder Cannon, officiating, and Tessa stepped to the side, waiting for the bride to emerge. Tessa nodded to Anna, to Peter, and to Bishop Grow seated in the back—next to the woman and baby William had been with in town. *So William did come to the wedding, after all.* Tessa checked her posture and filled her lungs with air. *You can do this,* she reminded herself. *Just smile.*

The "Nocturne" ended and a cello joined the violin playing Mendelssohn's "Wedding March." The fifty friends and neighbors stood and turned toward the house, with oohs and ahhs as Mrs. Holt stepped through the doorway—beaming—on William's arm.

Despite knowing he belonged to another, Tessa's heart swelled when William fixed his gaze on hers. *Were you hiding from your mother too? Or just from me?* Reminding herself to breathe despite the ache in her throat, Tessa stared at the young man walking down the aisle, dashing in his gray frock coat and bowler. *Have you told her you're married?* She stared, transfixed by his sparkling sky-blue eyes, by the golden fringes of hair peeking out beneath his hat, by those dimples that deepened as he stared back at her.

She stared as he reached the top of the aisle and delivered Mrs. Holt to her father's side. And only when Elder Cannon instructed the onlookers to take their seats did Tessa and William break their gaze.

CHAPTER 28

Stop looking at him. But she couldn't help it. Throughout the ceremony, every time she snuck a peek at William, he was looking at her. This man—in his proper coat, holding his proper bowler—this proper gentleman was the kind of man she wanted to spend her life with. A man whose eyes shone when he looked at her. A man who made her feel like a proper lady.

But a proper lady doesn't moon over a married man. She stared at her father's hands as he held those of Mrs. Holt's while they repeated their vows. She recalled William's hands—how he waggled the rattle in front of the baby in the carriage. *He's married. He has a child.* Why would he not have written to tell her he was getting married? Why did he not tell Mrs. Holt? Careful to avoid his eyes, she studied William's hands—his right hand, with four fingers resting lightly in his trousers' pocket, his left hand cradling the crown of his hat, holding it against his chest. Strong hands.

She pulled her gaze back to the ceremony, watching her father twist a golden band on Mrs. Holt's finger. She watched as the couple briefly kissed. She held her hands clasped in front of her chest, feeling the incessant beat of her heart, as the onlookers applauded the newlyweds.

Caught in her father's bear hug, she plastered a smile on her face as he twirled her around in a circle, then she turned and hugged her new mother.

"My daughter," Mrs. Holt said, laughing and kissing Tessa on each cheek.

"My mum," Tessa replied, trying to keep her voice cheerful. *"Be gracious, Tessa,"* that familiar voice whispered. *I'm trying, Mama.* If only William hadn't led her on. If only he weren't married. If only Peter hadn't led her on. If only he weren't engaged. *If only. If only. If only. Stop feeling sorry for yourself.*

As the crowd of well-wishers surged forward, Tessa smiled and nodded and shook hands and repeated names as Mrs. Holt—her mum—introduced them. William dashed back and forth, greeting his old friends, largely ignoring his wife and child. His wife mingled on her own, proudly displaying their daughter.

Tessa nervously watched as the woman made her way toward the receiving line. *What do I say to her? How do you do—I'm so pleased you married the man I'm in love with? Thank you for coming—did you know you married the man I'm in love with? What a lovely child—she looks just like the man I'm in love with?*

"Tessa? Are you all right?" Peter lifted her hand in his, bending down to speak with her.

"What?" She looked from his kind eyes to his fiancée's arm entwined in his.

"You're eyes are all scrunched up," his fiancée said, "like you have a headache."

Like you would care. Tessa straightened her shoulders and put on her most charming tone of voice. "Katie Brown, how kind of you to be concerned. You've always been so dear. But I'm quite well, I assure you."

Tessa saw the flicker of a smile cross Peter's lips. "This is a nice wedding, isn't it?" he said.

Katie looked around and shrugged, hugging Peter's arm. "Ours will be quite a bit larger, of course. My father ran for mayor, you know."

But he's not the mayor, is he? William's wife was approaching Mrs. Holt, and William trotted up and took the baby from her arms. Tessa turned her attention back to Peter and his fiancée, intent on ending the conversation. "I'm certain you'll have a lovely wedding—before you move to Wyoming."

The smile faded from Katie's face and she lifted her nose in the air. "Who knows where we'll end up."

Oh, Peter, what have you gotten yourself into? Tessa placed her hands on each of theirs and said with as much sincerity as she could muster, "I do wish you every happiness."

Turning back to the receiving line, Tessa maintained the smile on her face as her new mum embraced the woman with William as warmly as old friends. *So you've met already.* The muscles just in front of her ears ached with the effort of smiling.

"Henry, Tessa," Mrs. Holt said, "I'd like you to meet my sweet sister, Sarah."

Sarah? The Sarah William courted before Mr. Holt? Somehow, thinking he'd married the girl he'd loved for so long—who'd been stolen from him—took some of the sting away.

The woman, dressed in powder-blue today, clasped Tessa's father's hand and then turned to pull a gentleman—probably in his early thirties—forward.

"May I introduce my husband, Richard Kennedy?"

Her husband! Unlike Mrs. Holt, Tessa politely withheld her gasp and joyful shout. Her grin, however, would not be contained. She dared a glance at William, but he was absorbed in tickling the baby now in Mrs. Holt's arms.

Sarah picked up both of Tessa's hands in hers, squeezing them tightly. "Tessa, I'm so pleased to finally meet you."

Finally? Tessa snapped her mouth shut and tried to tame her desire to hug this woman. "I'm charmed, I'm sure."

Before Tessa could think what else to say, Sarah pressed her cheek to Tessa's and whispered, "William has told me so much about you."

"He has?" Tessa blurted. "I mean," she tried to recover, "has he?"

Sarah laughed, and Tessa—feeling quite foolish for having tried to sound refined—felt her cheeks flame.

Putting her arm around Tessa's shoulder, Sarah turned so both ladies had their backs toward the others. She leaned in, as a conspirator would, and whispered again. "Indeed. He spoke of you in all of his letters. Had I not been married, I would have been quite jealous."

"He's been writing to you?" *And not me?*

"Of course he has." Sarah laughed. "He introduced Richard and me."

"You're not telling Tessa all my secrets, are you?" William spoke from so close behind them Tessa jumped and nearly bumped into him.

"Of course not," Sarah teased. "I'm saving the best to blackmail you with." She retrieved her daughter from Mrs. Holt and then called back over her shoulder. "We'll chat later, Tessa. I've got plenty of tales to tell. Nice to meet you!"

As the next guests came through the line, cutting off any chance to interrogate William, Tessa began compiling a lengthy list of questions for him. At the top of the heap, *You had time to write to her and not to me?*

WITH SEVERAL NEIGHBORS occupying the space under the arbor with their fiddles and horns, Tessa busied herself behind the buffet tables next to the house. She marveled at her father and new mum's prowess at dancing waltzes and jigs and polkas. Her father even sportingly tried a square dance, bumbling through the caller's first few instructions before bowing and do-si-doing with finesse.

Peter and Katie stood off to the side, with Katie leading him in a simple box step and Peter tripping over his gangly legs. *I hope you've not got your heart set on dancing at your wedding, Katie, or your wedding may be a very long time coming.* But at least Peter was trying to learn.

As she arranged dishes at the front of the table to make room for a tray of strawberries, a man's arm reached around in front of her, holding a pink rose in front of her face. "Would you care to dance?" he murmured.

Startled, she spun around, staring into his blue eyes. His arm tightened around her, and for the length of a heartbeat, William held her in his embrace. Looking nearly as startled as she felt, he released her and stepped back a proper distance. One eyebrow darted upward as he flashed his impish grin and held the rose out to her again.

"That gown should be gliding around the dance"—he glanced over his shoulder at the grass beside them—"the dance lawn, not serving cookies. May I escort you?"

Tossing her apron under the table, Tessa accepted the offered rose, sniffing its sweet fragrance and noticing how he had scraped the thorns from the stem. "How kind of you."

"Sister Olmstead won't think so if she realizes it came from her yard."

As she reached to place her hand in his, to be led to the dance floor, she jerked her hand back, her eyes wide. "I haven't any gloves." It simply would not be proper to hold a man's hand dancing without gloves, even though she had been shaking hands all afternoon barehanded.

"Few of the ladies here have gloves." Nonetheless, he pulled his tartan pocket square from his breast pocket and covered his upturned hand. "Will this be acceptable?"

"Extremely. Thank you." Placing her fingertips in his palm, she followed him onto the dance floor and waited as he—unlike most of the other men—placed his folded handkerchief between his hand and her back so as to avoid touching her bodice.

For several moments, William and Tessa floated in gentle circles to the steady, triple beat of a waltz. He was just tall enough that she could rest the edge of her hand on his shoulder—while holding the delicate rose between her thumb and middle fingertips—without craning her neck to look in his eyes. "Where did you learn to dance so beautifully?"

"My ma taught me," he replied. "She and Mrs. Holt made me dance with them for hours before I attended my first dance as a child. They taught me every step they could think of so I'd never be embarrassed to dance with a lady."

"You learned very well," she said. "Did your mother teach you about pressing a hanky to a lady's back?"

He chuckled. "Indeed, seeing's how I'd likely not be called to an affair that required gloves."

"Most of the men here don't heed that standard."

"My ma would have a thing or two to say about that, 'twere she here." He changed the pattern of his movements, leading her in a sideways line to the other side of the lawn closer to the newlyweds. "Besides, most of the men here won't be dancing with you."

"Why, William, you don't mean to hog every dance, do you?"

"Of course not." He pulled her in a bit closer and twirled her under his arm, handing her off to her father. "I'll share you with your da."

THROUGHOUT THE AFTERNOON, when she wasn't dancing with William or her father, Tessa mingled with the neighbors, charming the new Mrs. Darrow's friends. If she happened to speak to a young man, William made any excuse to appear by her side.

As the sun dipped low on the western horizon, leaving the sky awash with magenta, Tessa's father and his bride gave Tessa and William hugs and then disappeared into the house. Mr. Christensen nonchalantly leaned against the fence separating the back and front yards until several minutes later when he gave a shout. "There they are! They're leaving!"

Well-wishers streamed out of the backyard as the buggy pulled away, throwing rice and slippers after the couple until they turned the corner and rode out of view. As the ladies collected their shoes from the lawn and a few of the gentlemen scoured the street for errant slippers, Tessa stood at the edge of the sidewalk with her hands on her hips, peering into the near darkness.

"Tessa? Is something wrong?"

Tessa held her hand out to William, showing him her delicate slipper covered in doeskin the same color as her gown. "I've lost my left shoe," she admitted sheepishly. "I think it landed in the buggy." She stood on tiptoe, feeling the moisture of the grass seeping through her stockings.

William looked around and smiled. "Hold your train," he whispered.

Obediently Tessa wrapped her trailing skirt against her legs. "Why?"

"Because I've been wanting to do this all night." Whisking her off her feet, he strode across the lawn, ignoring the gasps from the few guests who hadn't already departed.

Tessa clapped her hand over her mouth so her grin wouldn't be revealed. "William Bates," she whispered. "I'm a shamed woman!"

"Oh my stars!" Mrs. Christensen rushed to the porch as William stood Tessa upon the top step.

He shrugged innocently. "The lady lost her slipper."

"I'm beholden." Tessa lowered her chin and pressed her lips together to disguise her smile.

He lifted her hand, stopping just short of touching it to his lips. "M'lady, good night." He turned and fairly skipped as he dashed across the lawn and disappeared down the street into the darkness.

CHAPTER 29

"Tessa?" Tap, tap, tap. "Tessa?"

Through the warm haze of her slumber, Tessa heard a little voice calling her name amidst the gentle taps on her door, but she couldn't quite seem to open her eyes to the sunlit room or move her limbs.

"Tessa."

The soft whisper in her ear jolted her awake and Tessa sprang from her bed with a start. Catching her breath, she whirled around to confront the intruder, but saw no one. The voice had sounded so real—in the room with her. "Who's there?" She held her breath, hoping a specter wouldn't answer—or appear.

"It's me. Grace." A tiny, frightened voice wafted from under the bed. A pair of big blue eyes peeked out from the shadows.

Tessa let her breath out. "Grace! You scared me half to death. What are you doing? Get out of there."

The little girl wiggled out from the darkness, clutching her doll, and stood toe-to-toe with Tessa, displaying all the defiance the six-year-old could marshal. "Well, you scair't me half to death first! I just said your name and you flew out of bed like a shot!" She slapped the dust from her dress and hands and perched a balled-up fist on her hip. "You should be 'shamed of yourself."

Tessa fought to not laugh out loud, recognizing Anna's temper spilling out of the child's mouth. "You're right, miss. Please accept my apology."

"Apology accepted," Grace pronounced with her nose in the air, walking toward the door. "Mormor says it's time to get ready for church."

Not wanting to go to a strange church—with people she'd only just met, without her father or a proper pair of shoes since she'd lost a slipper the night before—Tessa began formulating excuses.

Grace stopped and turned back to Tessa "Oh, and William's downstairs waiting to go with us." She pulled the door shut on her way out.

AFTER A DASH down the back stairs and outside to visit the necessary, Tessa slipped back to her room. She traded her nightgown and wrapper for her crinolette and petticoat, and the floral dress she'd received from her grandmother. Thankfully, her updo from the wedding hadn't sustained much damage from being slept on, so it took Tessa only moments to recomb the ringlets cascading down her shoulders.

Rather than weaving her pink satin ribbon through her hair, Tessa tied it around her neck like a choker, fluffing the bow at the hollow of her throat. And, since she was going to church rather than an afternoon affair, she pleated her handkerchief into a fan and tucked it into her chemise so the lacy edges more discreetly shielded her womanhood.

After quickly scrubbing her teeth with her moistened finger dipped in baking soda, she rinsed her mouth with rose water. She poured a bit of the rose water on her washcloth and wiped her underarms. Then, because it would be a warm day, she tucked a petal in her cleavage from the rose William gave her. She pinched her cheeks to pink them and surveyed the results in the armoire mirror. *Grandmother would be pleased—especially with the handkerchief preserving my modesty.*

She tiptoed down the back stairs again so William wouldn't see her heavy black boots under her skirt, as he would if she descended the front staircase, and then quietly stepped through the kitchen to make her entrance.

He jumped to his feet when she entered the parlor, his eyes wide, and his dimples creasing like exclamation points on either side of his smile. "Good morning," he whispered.

"Good morning," she whispered back, flattered at the awe in his voice and gaze.

After a long moment, Mr. Christensen cleared his throat and suggested they leave for church. "Mama," he called to his wife, "Bethany, Anna, time to go."

As much as she wanted him to escort her, Tessa was charmed when William hoisted the toddler, Christian, onto his back, and held hands with Grace to walk the three blocks to church. If she had to share him with another girl, Tessa was grateful it was Grace who held his hand.

THAT EVENING, AFTER a supper of chilled tomato soup and cheese sandwiches, the two families rested in the backyard, enjoying the view of the Great Salt Lake sparkling in the sagging sun. The men had untied the ribbons from the tree branches, and now the children danced and spun, letting the streamers swirl about them.

Tessa and William sat speaking in soft tones in chairs placed side by side under the peach tree. "William," Tessa nervously broached the subject, "Sarah mentioned yesterday that you have written to her several times."

"You're not jealous, are you?" he teased.

A smile played on her lips, and she bumped his shoulder with hers. "Perhaps a bit. But I'm wondering—you asked my father for permission to write to me, but I've only received two letters in all the time you've been gone."

"What?"

"And not a word in over a year."

"Tessa, that can't be," he said with earnest, taking her hand in his. "For every letter I wrote Sarah, I've written you and Mother at least three. I always sent the letters together because I didn't know if your father had money for postage."

"But Mrs. Holt"—Tessa sighed at herself—". . . my mum didn't receive any either."

"I sent letters every month, Tessa. We ship a load of lumber to Fort Hall every month, and I send your letters to be dispatched from there."

"To Fort Hall? William, the army turned Fort Hall into a reservation for the Blackfoot Indians over a year ago. I know there's still a small outpost there, but maybe they no longer dispatch mail?"

William looked dubious. "Surely they still send military reports. I'm beginning to suspect my team that makes the lumber delivery had something to do with it. Tessa, I'm truly sorry. What you and my mother must have thought."

Tessa looked down at her hand, still clasped in his, thinking how perfectly they fit together. "We're both just happy to know you're alive, and that you're here now."

"It puts my mind at rest, as well." His voice took on the lilt of his teasing.

"Oh? How's that?"

"I feared you had become terribly vain—only ever talking about your life and never responding to the deep dark secrets I revealed of my heart."

Deep dark secrets? "William, you didn't."

He shrugged nonchalantly, a twinkle in his eye. "The letters are lost. Now you'll never know."

~❧~

EARLY THE NEXT morning, Tessa packed her crinoline and new crinolette, each collapsed in concentric circles, side-by-side in the traveling case her father made for the trip. Next, she nested her fawn slippers, the left one safely retrieved from the buggy. For a moment she considered leaving behind the skirt that Grace had cut a chunk from, but since that would leave her with only one work dress, she packed the skirt to be repaired at home. Lastly, she carefully folded her golden taffeta gown, wrapped it in the linen the seamstress had supplied, and then laid the bundle in the traveling case, tucking in errant puffs as she squeezed the lid shut and secured the leather straps.

With a sigh, she thought of the long trip ahead of them—five nights of sleeping in the wagon with Mrs. Holt while her father slept underneath. Or, now that they were married, would she be expected to sleep underneath? *That question will need to be settled before I go anywhere. I will not sleep with snakes and vermin.*

As much as she dreaded the long journey, she looked forward to sleeping in her own bed, in her little room, not hearing the clamor of a large family, or the frequent rumbling of buggies and horses in the street. *Yes, I definitely prefer my quiet country life with only a few neighbors. But it's nice to have new friends to stay with if we ever come back.*

Tessa nestled a mason jar of rosewater Mrs. Christensen had given her into the small bag with her nightgown and brush. She followed her father down the stairs. William waited on the porch, rising from a rocking chair as she emerged from the house.

"You're still here," she said, trying to sound cheerful. In reality, as hard as it was to tell him good-bye last night, it would be harder to watch him ride away in the daylight.

"I brought you something." He lifted a small rosebush from the porch, holding it while she sniffed the single pink rose blooming on the three canes growing from the burlap-covered roots.

"William, it's beautiful."

"It's the same as the one growing in Sister Olmstead's garden."

Tessa stood on tiptoe and whispered in his ear, "I pressed that one in my book of poetry."

"Now you'll have plenty to press. And if this one survives, I'll send you more. We'll have a whole garden of roses."

She heard it. She wondered if anyone else had heard it. *He said "we'll" have a garden. He and I. We.* "I'll take the very best care of it."

Tessa's father put a hand on William's shoulder, steering him away from the stairs. "I'd like a word with you before we leave."

Tessa and William exchanged a glance before she stepped down the stairs, and then paused at the bottom to adjust her shoelaces—hidden behind the hedge lining the porch—careful to stay within earshot.

"Young man," her father said, "I'll be straight with my purpose, and I hope you'll be straight with your answer."

"Of course, sir," William answered.

"Tessa's my daughter, and it's my responsibility to take care of her."

"Yes, sir."

Father, what are you doing? Embarrassed her father would choose now to interrogate William, Tessa thought about standing up and putting an end to it but didn't want to admit she'd been eavesdropping.

"I'm sure you know she's already had two proposals of marriage."

Father! No! I didn't tell him!

William hesitated for just a moment before answering. "No, sir, I didn't know, but I'm not surprised. She's a lovely young lady."

A lovely young lady? Is that all I am to you? A young lady?

"So you have no intentions toward her?"

Tessa held her breath.

"That's not what I said." William kept his voice perfectly level, perfectly calm, revealing no emotion.

On the other hand, Tessa heard the tension creeping into her father's tenor. "You said you'd be straight with me, William."

"Mr. Darrow, your daughter is a lovely young lady. Indeed, she has become a most beautiful woman. She is refined, thoughtful, intelligent, and I find her happiness at the center of every decision I make."

"Then you do have intentions toward her."

"Yes, sir, I do."

He does! Tessa bit her lip to keep from shouting and held firmly to her shoelace to keep from racing back up the stairs.

"But," William continued, "I know how much she's lost coming here from North Carolina. She's used to a large home with fine furnishings and beautiful clothing."

"Surely you know those trappings aren't important to her," Tessa's father interjected.

"But they're important to me, Mr. Darrow. Not to have for myself, but it's important to me to be able to give them to her if she ever does want them. I hope you can understand that."

In the same instant as Tessa rejoiced to hear what William desired for her, her heart broke for her father. Of everything she had lost, he had lost so much more. And living on the frontier, he had scarce opportunity to rebuild a fine home or give his new wife a better future.

"I've invested in a lumber mill in Oregon," William continued, "and I'm saving every nickel that comes my way. Another couple of years, and I hope to have a conversation in earnest with you, sir."

"I appreciate the thought you've given this, son," her father said, "and your candor. I'd caution you, though: don't wait too long. The Oregon trail is teeming with young men eager for a wife."

Tessa clapped her hand over her mouth to keep from laughing out loud. *That's right, William. You'd best not keep me waiting too long.* She heard footsteps closer to the edge of the wooden porch and then heard the leaves of the hedge rustle. She looked up, into the faces of her father and William.

"Tessabear," her father said, "does it always take this long to tie your boot?"

CHAPTER 30

Spreading a damp flour sack on the scrubbing board next to her wash-basin, Tessa smeared a paste of sodium bicarbonate on the flattened fabric and scrubbed it with a rock until the printed label nearly disappeared. After rinsing the fabric and dunking it in a bluing rinse, she hung it on the horsehair clothesline her father had suspended from the corner of the house to the sycamore tree. She could get another four dish towels out of that precious sack.

She dumped out the bluing rinse and poured a bucket of fresh water in the basin. As she scrubbed her hands with soda to remove the blue stain, she mentally inventoried the linens she'd sewn and embroidered over the last three years and stored in her wedding trunk. *At least a dozen dish towels, four sets of pillow slips, two sets of sheets, and two bath towels. Surely that's enough to set up house.* She dumped the three basins required for wash day and carried them and the scrubbing board to the shed, stowing them under her father's workbench.

Picking up her gardening supplies and the packet of beans she'd collected from last year's garden, she headed for the patch of ground her father had turned for her a few days earlier. *Maybe I should start laying up nappies. Surely we'll have babies, in time. Best be prepared.*

As she crawled along the furrows of earth, pushing dried beans down with her gloved finger, she mentally listed the chores she hoped to get done in the next week. *Pull up the radishes, wash the feathers in the mattresses, help Da mend the chicken coop.* She peered over at the peas clinging to the teepee-shaped trellises. *Might be ripe by the time William gets here.* A grin spread across her face.

One more week. In his last letter, he said he was coming at the end of May. She thought back over the three years since her father's wedding.

Three years of trying to fill every day so she wouldn't have time to miss him. Three years of evenings spent sewing linens for their home. Three years of nights filled with dreams of him. And now, only one more week and he'd be here. A nervous flutter swirled in the pit of her stomach.

Will he ask for my hand at last? Of course he will. He wouldn't make such a long journey just to visit. But as she allowed herself to believe they would soon be married, her one concern chased itself around her mind like a puppy chasing its tail. *What if he doesn't want us to stay in Morristown? What if he wants me to live in Oregon City by his lumber mill? I can't leave my Da, and Mum would never leave the trading post. But what is here for William, besides me?*

With only three families left in the valley, there was no need for a lumber business. Mr. Anderson had set up a blacksmith shop and livery, her father repaired broken rigs, and the two men grew enough hay to feed whatever livestock came through with travelers. Her mum's trading post did a fine business, but there was no need for another store. How would William make a living if they stayed?

Hearing a wagon approaching in the distance, Tessa cast a glance over her shoulder, but her view of the western valley was blocked by her father's work shed. *Probably Cariboo Jack coming through again. Mum can get him supplied without me this time. If I don't get these beans in today, they'll wither in the heat before I see a harvest.* She laid the edge of a one-by-two in the dirt, wiggling it down in the turned loam to make another furrow. The rumble of wagons increased, and puffs of dust dotted the sky above the shed. *Must be a whole wagon train coming in.*

If she hurried, she could get the last two rows planted before dashing down to the trading post to help restock the travelers.

Just as she poked the last few seeds into the last furrow, a shadow fell across the row in front of her.

"That rosebush sure took a liking to Idaho."

The familiar voice sent her stomach for a tumble. She put her hand up like a visor above her eyes and lifted her face to the afternoon sun. Dressed in tan leather chaps, a black vest over a gray shirt, a blue kerchief around his neck, and a gray hat tilted back to reveal those blue eyes, he stood with his thumbs resting on the edges of his belt, next to the rosebush he'd given her three years before.

She rose slowly, willing herself not to fling herself at him, and dusted the dirt from her skirt and palms. "Hello, Willia—"

Before she could finish his name, he'd closed the ten-foot gap between them, encircled her waist with one arm, swept the hat from his head with the other, and firmly pressed his lips to hers.

And before she had time to think, she discovered her arms looped around his neck, clutching him closer. *Someone will see you.* Reluctantly, she released him, keeping her fingers tangled in his mop of sandy hair. "You weren't supposed to be here until next week."

"Couldn't wait another week."

She settled her shawl around her shoulders and smiled up at him. "I'm glad. Though I wish I'd had a chance to get cleaned up before you saw me." She tucked a few stray tendrils under her bonnet. "I must look a fright."

He took her gardening gloves out of her grip and tossed them on the half-closed lid of the rain barrel. He backed her up against the house where they were mostly shielded from view by the five-foot rosebush. "You get more beautiful every time I see you," he murmured, loosening her bonnet and nuzzling her temple before kissing her again.

Though her heart hammered wildly, and she was quite enjoying this new sensation of kissing him, propriety forced its way like a sail steering a raft. "William, stop. Someone will see us."

He leaned a forearm against the cabin's wall and, finding a loose tendril at her nape of her neck, wound his finger with it until his hand cupped the back of her head. He pulled her face close to his but did not kiss her. Instead, he closed his eyes, drew a deep breath, and held it for the longest time before releasing it—and his hold on her—with a sigh.

She ran her finger along the hollow of one of his dimples, smiling, wishing she dared initiate her own kiss. "We should let your mum know you're here."

The fifth wagon was just pulling up in front of the trading post as William and Tessa sauntered down the street leading William's horses and wagon. They walked shoulder to shoulder, secretly holding hands behind them until just before they reached the store.

"Ted! 'Bout time you caught up!" William shouted greetings to the company, calling the drivers by name.

Surveying the wagons and the half-dozen men marching out of the trading post with supplies, Tessa's stomach twisted. *He's traveling with this outfit. They're delivering this load somewhere.* The wagons were piled with lumber and great bales of wire. *Did he come just to leave again?* Her heart started racing, at odds with the lump settled in the pit of her belly. She pulled William to a stop before they reached the others. "Are you traveling with these men?"

"Yes, I am," he said, his answer as light as if she'd just asked if the sky was blue.

She struggled to not let her face betray her anger. She struggled to not let her voice crack with despair. "And when were you going to tell me?"

"Tell you what?"

"William. Honestly."

Taking her by the arm, he led her to the side of the trading post, farther from view—and earshot. "Honestly what, Tessa? What are you so upset about?"

How can you even ask that? "It's been three years, William. Three years since I last saw you, and two more years since the time before that. And you're getting ready to leave again? You never gave any indication in your letters that you were just passing through. You led me to believe—" Tessa drew a deep breath, through her nose because her teeth were gritted so tight, and willed herself not to cry. *I let you kiss me!* She stared at him, at his calm blue eyes. He betrayed no emotion; just let her sort her thoughts. *I'm done. You go have your adventure, but I'll not spend another minute pining for you.*

She swallowed past the stone choking off her airway and raised her gaze to the sky, blinking back the tears. "I'm tired of waiting for you, William. I just can't do it anymore."

As her tears spilled down her cheeks, William picked her hand up in both of his, staring at it as he caressed her knuckles. "Do you think you could give me three more weeks, Tess? Maybe four?"

"What's the point, William? A month, a year, what will change?"

"These are my men, Tessa," he said with a nod to the street. "My men, my lumber. They've come to help me mark off some rangeland and build a home—for us—by Grays Lake."

The air began to fill her lungs again. Too much air. So rapidly, she made herself woozie.

He put his hand under her elbow to support her but didn't stop talking. "If you could give me just one more month, I'd have a home to offer when I come to speak with your father."

She pressed her lips together, willing the tears to stop.

His eyebrows furrowed together and he wrapped her shoulders with his gentle hands. "Tessa, you have to marry me."

"William Bates." She cast about in her memories of southern ladies flirting with their intendeds, for something witty to say, but her one desire overwhelmed all thoughts. Throwing all propriety aside, she placed her hand against his chest and marched him the few steps backward until his back was against the wall of the trading post. She gave one quick glance around to make sure they were safely out of view before gripping his collar with both hands and pulling his face down to meet hers.

"MUM?" TESSA CALLED as they entered the trading post. "Are you here?"

From the back room, Maureen grunted. "Give me a hand with this, will you, Tess?" She appeared in the doorway with a fifty-pound sack of cornmeal slung over one shoulder.

William bounded across the room before Maureen even had time to look up, and snatched the meal like a bag of feathers.

"Tessa!" Maureen exclaimed and then saw William shouldering the heavy bag. "William! Bless my stars." She flung herself at him so quickly, he nearly dropped the cornmeal.

"Hello, Mother." William set the sack on the floor and kissed his adopted mother on the cheek.

"Well, it never rains but it pours, does it?" Maureen said. "Coming in at the same time as all these wagons. William, would you give me a hand getting this cornmeal out to the wagon train? The men'll be heading up north in the morning."

"Those are William's men, Mum." Tessa glanced over at William, looking for a cue as to how much she should say.

"How's that?" Maureen dropped the corner of the sack and turned to look at them.

William put his arm around Tessa's shoulder. "They're my men. I've come to build a house at Grays Lake."

"You have?" Maureen's eyes flew wide. "You have! Oh my stars and garters," she exclaimed, hugging William and then Tessa. "Well, it's about time."

"Mum, is Da back yet?" Tessa didn't want her mum to let the news slip before she had time to talk to her father. *Now that Mum knows, William really should ask for my hand before he leaves for Grays Lake.*

"No, he's not back yet. He and Brother Anderson went up Chester Hill to chop wood." Maureen squinted at the watch fob pinned to her chest. "Goodness, it's after three already." She wound the watch's knob absently as she peered toward the door. "I expected them back by now."

"It's not like him to keep you waiting," Tessa said, a plot forming as she spoke. "Why don't William and I drive up there to see what's keeping them?" She cast a glance at William, realizing how tired he looked. *He's already driven the wagon all day.* She assuaged her bit of guilt telling herself that her Da would be happy to see him. Then they could have their talk on the way home.

"I'm sure there's no need," Maureen said, even while casting another worried look toward the door.

"I'd be happy to drive up there," William offered without hesitation. "Tessa can show me the way."

"Oh, she can, can she?" Maureen raised her eyebrows. "I see what you two are up to. Still, I suppose it wouldn't hurt to take a drive up while it's still light out. But I'm goin' with ya. I'll not be having Tessa traipsing the countryside without a chaperone."

You never worried about that when I spent all day exploring with Peter. Of course, I suppose I was just a young girl then. But Peter and his father both thought I was old enough to . . . Tessa shook her head, dispelling the memories. "I'll put some sandwiches together, shall I?"

"Yes, you do that," Maureen called as she headed outside with William.

Tessa listened to William issuing orders to his men to unhitch the horses and take them to the Anderson's livery and to make camp over at the Sundstroms' old place. Maureen's voice joined in, telling them to help themselves to the stew in the pot and fresh bread on the counter.

"And I've got some custard tarts cooling." Tessa smiled to hear Mrs. Pixton's voice calling. The men certainly wouldn't starve with Tildy Pixton on hand.

Tessa gasped and spun toward the door. Tildy Pixton! The Pixtons would have had a clear view of William and Tessa kissing at Tessa's house and here at the trading post. *If she tells my Da . . . That's that, then. William's going to have to speak with my father before we get back here. Now, how do I tell William and make him think it's his idea—without Mum overhearing?*

Along with their sandwiches, Tessa packed four jugs of water and a bag of dried apple slices. It took forty minutes to drive to the base of Chester Hill and begin their climb. All the while, Tessa plied her mum with the apples and plenty of water until at last her preparations paid off and Maureen asked William to pull the wagon to a stop.

As Maureen walked a distance into the scrub, Tessa grabbed William's hand. "I think we've been discovered."

"What?"

"I think Mrs. Pixton saw us kissing."

William smiled. "Well, that's just too bad. I'm not going to kiss her too."

"William, be serious. I'll be ruined!"

"You won't be ruined."

"I will," Tessa insisted, trying to take on a bit of panic in her voice. "If my father finds out you kissed me without so much as a promise—"

"He'll challenge me to a duel?"

Tessa gasped. "Oh, do you think he would?" she said, before seeing the glint in William's eye. She slapped his shoulder. "Be serious, William. Kissing before marriage—before we even have an understanding—well, it's just not done."

"Well, clearly," he said, stroking her bottom lip with his thumb and bringing his face closer, "it is done."

She turned her head away from him and folded her arms across her chest. "Not in well-bred society, it's not."

He put his finger under her chin and turned her face back to him, speaking quietly. "Would you like me to speak to your father tonight? Before we get back to town?"

"Oh, William—" She threw her arms around his neck. "Would you?"

"Tessa Darrow!" Maureen's voice from beside them made Tessa nearly leap from her seat.

"I guess I should have told you she was coming," William teased, jumping down to help Maureen into the wagon.

Tessa just glowered at him before covering her face with her hand.

"Tsk, tsk," Maureen said. "Leave you two alone for one minute . . ."

Tessa covered her face with both hands, secretly smiling. *By the end of the evening, we'll be engaged!*

CHAPTER 31

As William steered the wagon higher into Long Ridge canyon, the aspen and cedar trees grew denser. The fresh trail ran parallel to the stream trickling down the canyon, weaving through shadow and sun. William balanced the horses' reins in his left hand while he took the last few bites of a stew-meat sandwich Tessa had packed.

Rounding a corner leading into shadows, the report of a rifle echoed off the canyon walls. The horses startled just enough that William dropped one of the reins and the horse on the right bolted, checked only by his tether to the other horse. Tessa and William lurched toward the loose rein at the same time, crashing into each other and knocking Tessa sideways into Maureen.

"William!" Tessa threw her arms around her mum, trying to keep the two of them from toppling from the reeling wagon. Tessa held her breath as they careened up the trail, trees whipping past and the canyon drop-off close enough that Tessa feared they would slip off the edge.

"Whoa, there!" William shouted at the horses, tugging on the reins. "Whoa!"

At last the horses settled and William slowed them to a stop. "Tessa! Mother! Are you hurt?"

Tessa struggled to catch her breath. "I . . . I don't think so."

"I'm fine. But, William, was that a gunshot?" Maureen peered up the trail. "Can't think why they'd be hunting when they came for wood."

"Nor can I," William admitted. "I think you ladies had best stay here while I take a look."

"Not on your life," Maureen declared, settling her skirts on the seat.

William pressed his lips together and narrowed his eyes at his mother, but he didn't argue. "First sign of trouble, you light out for the trees and find a rock to crouch behind." He reached into the back of the wagon and lifted his rifle from the two hooks mounting it behind the seat. He pulled it from its leather scabbard and leaned the rifle on the seat next to him with the barrel down into the footboard. He then pulled a pistol wrapped in canvas from under the seat. William unwrapped the gun and set it, still in its holster, on Tessa's lap with the grip next to him. "You keep a hold of this and don't let it drop."

Tessa set her hand firmly on the holster, tilting the barrel well away from her and Maureen. "Might it fire if we hit a bump?"

"You don't need to worry. The strap's holding the hammer down and I don't keep a firing cap on the first round."

"Say what you like, William," Maureen said. "I don't like the notion of a gun pointed at me."

Fear mounted with William's preparations. *What if Father's been way-laid? Will two guns be enough?* Tessa closed her eyes, silently uttering a prayer.

Holding onto the pistol with one hand and the edge of the wooden bench with the other, Tessa concentrated on maintaining her seat during the breakneck flight along the narrow, winding trail. She had to stop glancing at her mum's frightened face or the grim set to William's mouth. *Everything will be fine. Mr. Anderson just can't pass up a meaty buck for his smokehouse. That's all it was.* Nonetheless, between the worry and the fear of overturning the wagon in their haste, Tessa felt her stomach churning and she clenched the seat even tighter.

As they descended into a shallow valley and rounded another curve, William slowed the horses and stopped twenty yards uphill from a tangle of logs piled just off the trail. William pointed up at the boulder-strewn hillside. "Been a landslide."

As Maureen, her eyes wide, clutched her skirt to step down, William leaped across Tessa and out of the wagon, spinning to pin his mother in her seat. "Mother, no. You wait here."

"I'll naw wait," she said with a stony voice, her eyes trained on the mass ahead.

William's face was white as a sheet.

"William?" Tessa pulled her eyes from his and looked back at the logs, finally discerning a wagon buried beneath logs and boulders. "Da?" She felt the blood draining from her face as she too scrambled over Maureen to bound from the wagon. "Da!" ripped from her throat.

William caught her with his arm around her waist, trapping her against the side of the box. "Stay here, Tess."

She grappled with his arm, trying to free herself. "No! My da!"

"Tessa, Mother, please," he pleaded. He released his hold on Tessa and began to walk backward down the trail, holding his hands flexed in front of him like a sheriff holding back a crowd. "Please let me take a look first."

Tessa felt her mother climb down beside her. Blindly, she grasped for Maureen's hand, not daring to take her eyes off William's back as he raced toward the landslide. No thoughts formed in her mind, just a numbing emptiness. A steady whisper thrummed in her ears in time with her heartbeat, and she realized her mum was whispering a prayer.

The two women watched, clinging to each other, as William reached the buried wagon and disappeared behind it. Tessa held her breath, waiting for him to emerge. At last, his head popped up over the wreckage, and he waved for them to come over. Tessa sprinted forward, watching first one log then another fly from the heap as though of their own accord.

Gasping for breath, she skidded around the edge of the pile, nearly stepping on her father pinned beneath the wagon. He lay on his back, right arm slung across his eyes, the side of one back wheel of the overturned wagon resting on his chest, its axle pinning his shirt just under his left armpit.

She dropped to her knees beside him, relieved to see his arm flinch and his chest rise and fall. "Da? What happened?"

He slid his arm to uncover one eye. "Well, hello there, Tessa."

"Henry!" Maureen crouched beside him.

"Hello, love. Mighty glad to see you," he said as evenly as if he'd just woken up from a nap.

"How bad are you hurt?"

"Not too bad, I don't expect." He tried to turn his head, grimacing with the effort. "Can you see Neils?"

Tessa and Maureen looked toward the head of the wagon where William was flipping logs from the mound like tinder sticks.

"Mother, can you take care of Henry? I need Tessa's help over here."

Tessa stumbled forward, grasping the edge of the wagon to steady herself. "Mr. Anderson?" She cast her eyes to William. "Is he . . . ?"

"He's alive," William assured her. "But he's pinned under his horse."

The chestnut gelding lay motionless on his side with his back to them, his two back legs crushed and splayed. His head lay in a patch of blackened dirt, bloodied from the shot to the base of his skull.

"Charger," Tessa whispered through quivering lips. "He was Mr. Anderson's favorite."

"Mary? Is that you?" Mr. Anderson lifted his head before letting it sag back to the ground, turned away from them. He lay sprawled on his stomach with his right leg trapped under the horse's midsection, his hand resting on the horse's shoulder—still holding the rifle.

"Mr. Anderson, it's me, Tessa Darrow. I'm here with William and my mum. We're going to help you."

"Tessa. Good. Abe's been waiting for you. Been practicing his letters all morning." He sucked in a deep breath, coughing as he exhaled.

"Brother Anderson." William knelt beside the man, carefully taking the rifle from his grip. "We're up Long Ridge. Do you remember? There was an accident?"

"Oh, that's right," Mr. Anderson said calmly. "I remember." He tried to lift his head again before letting it drop with a moan. "Ida Mary, run and fetch Mama. Tell her Tessa and Peter are here."

Tessa caught her breath and looked at William's puzzled expression.

"Ida Mary's the new baby?" William asked.

"Yes," Tessa whispered, "she's two."

William nodded once. "And Peter?"

"He's delirious. He doesn't know what he's saying."

William nodded once more, but his eyes lingered on Tessa before he turned back to the injured man. "Brother Anderson, I'm William Bates, Maureen Darrow's son. You're pinned under your horse. We've come to get you out. Do you remember now?"

"Yes, yes, I remember. There was a landslide and Charger got hit." Mr. Anderson's voice caught. "I tried to help him, but he was thrashing about. Got my leg wedged under him good." He stopped talking and his head went limp.

"Brother Anderson?" William leapt to the other side of the man to where he could look at his face.

Tessa held her breath, fearing Mr. Anderson had taken his last.

Mr. Anderson finally relaxed, letting his hand rest in the horse's mane. "Had to put him down. Couldn't let him suffer like that."

"It was the merciful thing to do, Neils. Now, how bad are you hurt?"

The injured man sniffed and rubbed the heel of his hand across his face. "I think my leg must be broken. Maybe just my ankle. Can't really feel it anymore."

"Can you move it at all?"

"No. It's pinned too tight."

"All right, Brother Anderson. Let's get you out of there."

Tessa knelt down beside them. "What can I do?"

"You sit with him a moment," William instructed. "We've got to get the horse off him. Mother!" he called, standing up. "I'm going to need you too. We've got to work quickly."

William raced back to his wagon, returning a moment later with a coil of rope. He knotted two loops about two feet apart at the center of the rope, pushing one loop under the breeching and shaft at the horse's hind quarters, and the other loop under the girth just behind the shoulder. He threaded the free ends of the rope through the loops, then tied additional loops at each end, creating a harness for himself.

"Now," he told the women, "each of you take one of Brother Anderson's arms. When I give the word, I'm going to roll the horse off his legs, and you're going to pull him out." With that, he stepped to the opposite side of the horse and stomped on the fresh dirt several times, packing it down. With his back to the horse, he slid his arms through the looped ends of the rope. He clutched the ropes at the front of his shoulders and braced his feet, one in front of the other.

"Ready?" he yelled over his shoulder.

"Ready," Tessa yelled back.

"Now!"

The rope pulled taught, and the horse's rigging groaned under the strain of the rope's pull. Little by little, Tessa watched the weight of the horse shift off Mr. Anderson's leg. With the releasing of pressure, Mr. Anderson cried out.

"Now!" Maureen yelled.

Both women heaved on his arms, dragging him free of the horse, shuddering at his screams. William eased the horse back and released himself from the rope. He fell to his knees and rested his weight on his forearms, clasping his hands on the earth in front of him to cushion his head.

The bottom half of Mr. Anderson's pant leg was bulging where the injured leg swelled. "We can cut his trousers at the knee then use that piece to bandage his leg," Tessa directed.

Covering her mouth with the back of her fist, Maureen peered over Tessa's shoulder. She barely managed to say, "Don't cut the trousers; they'll keep pressure on the break," before dashing into the brush to empty her stomach.

"William! I need your knife," Tessa yelled, not waiting for a blade to start tearing a strip from her skirt—the same skirt Grace had cut up for her doll. *I'm afraid there's not going to be enough left to patch. Well, it's been put to good use—several times.*

William strapped broken branches to either side of Mr. Anderson's leg, securing the splint with the long strip of fabric.

"You saved him," Tessa said, observing William's handiwork.

"Not yet, we haven't." William stood up, rubbing the joints where his shoulders met his chest. Then he and Tessa helped Mr. Anderson to a sitting position, braced against one of the logs. "We've got to free your father and get them off this mountain. Will you bring a couple of your water jugs?"

Running as fast as she could, Tessa returned a moment later with the water. She helped Mr. Anderson sip from one jug while Maureen held the other to Tessa's father's lips as he lay still trapped by the wagon wheel.

William lifted Henry's arm from his forehead. "We could do with another strip of fabric if either of you could spare one."

"No, it's just a scratch," Henry said.

Maureen inspected the gash running diagonally across his brow from just shy of his hairline nearly to his temple. "Good, the bleeding's slowed." She took hold of her skirt with both hands to tear it.

"No, Mum, let me," Tessa said. "My skirt's already in pieces. William, let me have your knife." Deftly, she pierced through the hem of the dark blue calico that had already created two doll dresses for Grace and bandaged a splint for Mr. Anderson. She sliced a two-inch swatch from all the way around the bottom.

With Tessa's father's head tightly bandaged, William and the women worked to clear the fallen aspen and rocky earth covering the wagon. A large boulder lay just behind the wagon, inches from the wheel.

With the side of the wheel resting on Tessa's father's chest, William didn't think it was safe to drag him out as they had done with Mr. Anderson. "Mr. Darrow, can you feel your legs?" William asked. "Are they injured?"

"No, I don't believe so," Tessa's father answered. "I seem to be lying in a depression of some sort. I might have a bruised rib or two, but I don't think anything's broken."

"All right then, here's what we're going to do . . . ."

After William firmly wedged a sturdy log between the boulder and axle of the upper wheel, Maureen and Tessa stood on either side of the log and leaned on it with all of their strength, levering the wagon upward. Reaching under the wagon, William grabbed Tessa's father and pulled him clear.

Tessa watched her father rise up on his knees, and she started to release her weight from the wagon when the log cracked with a clap like thunder.

"Take cover!" Tessa's father yelled, slamming William to the ground, covering the young man's chest with his own.

"Henry!" Maureen screamed, letting go of the lever so abruptly Tessa was thrown to the ground. She jumped toward him. "Henry, what's the matter? It was just the log cracking."

Tessa scrambled around the boulder to find William lying on the ground, pinned beneath her father.

After a moment, he lifted himself off William. Her father knelt, curled in a ball, clasping his hands behind his head, forearms pressed against his ears, rocking and trembling. Maureen knelt beside him, rocking with him and shushing as she cradled his head against her chest.

William rose to his knees, staring at Henry like he saw a ghost. "It was you. You grabbed me out of that ditch in Tennessee."

Tessa crouched on her hands and knees, unsure of what had happened, afraid to approach.

William squatted with one knee on the ground in front of Tessa's father. "It was you, wasn't it? You saved me."

What are you talking about? Her father had only ever told her of one battle in the war—the battle in Tennessee that caused him to desert. "What are you talking about?" she whispered, slowly stepping forward.

William looked up at Tessa and then back at her father. "Was it you?" He emphasized every word.

Her father lifted his head and sucked in a deep breath before nodding.

"Why didn't you tell me?" Now William whispered, his voice thick like the air was being choked from his throat. "You just disappeared. I didn't even have the chance to thank you."

"I didn't want your thanks," her father choked. His hands shook. "At the time I wanted to kill you. I thought that choice cost me everything!"

Maureen gasped; she pushed away from him, kneeling off to the side, halfway between her husband and her son, her hands clasped to her chest.

What? Tessa looked from her father to William. *What are you talking about?* She turned back to her father. "Why didn't you tell me?"

"I wasn't sure it was him."

The stricken look on Maureen's face evidenced in her voice. "You saved my son? You wanted to kill my son? Henry, please."

Step by step, minute by minute, Tessa's father and William told the tale of the battle in Tennessee. Her father's squad of scouts being trapped in a trench . . . shooting at William's forward team . . . William being wounded and falling in their trench . . . Henry being dispatched to make sure he was dead . . . tying a bandage around William's leg . . .

the cannon ball exploding in the trench as Henry pulled William to freedom . . .

Hearing the sum of events laid out, rather than the cryptic pieces her father had told her, Tessa's stomach wrenched and she struggled to drag breath to her lungs.

Her father drew his knees to his chest, resting his brow on his cupped fists. "I thought when they didn't find my body with the rest of the squad, they'd brand me a traitor. I thought they burned our home down. I thought I was saving my family, hauling them across the plains."

You thought? Tessa stared at him, afraid to give voice to her thoughts. But a low, painful plea leaked out of its own accord. "What do you mean 'you thought'?"

"It wasn't them, Tessa." He lifted his face to her, eyes moist and rimmed with red. "The men from my regiment didn't burn the house."

Tessa felt her lungs collapsing, her gut turning in on itself. "We saw them coming."

"They were coming to tell your mother I was missing in action."

"What are you talking about?" Tessa demanded. "Mother was with us. The soldiers came and burned our house. Why are you telling me these things? We returned to find our home in ashes." Tessa kept her fists balled at her sides to keep from beating on him.

"Tessa," he said, rising to his knees and holding her shoulders firmly. "It wasn't them. Eula and Buck, and the other servants saw the soldiers coming and hid in the fields. Maybe Eula left something on the stove, or knocked a candle over, or I don't know what, but the house was already on fire."

"You don't know that!" Tessa flung his hands away from her. "Of course you don't know that!" She rose on her knees to stare him eye to eye. "You weren't there. We came home to ashes. The soldiers weren't there. Eula and Buck were there, trying to save what they could. Why would you blame them?" She shoved his shoulders with the heels of her hands. Standing, she backed away from him, still shouting. "Why are you lying to me?"

Clutching his ribs, he stepped toward her, his voice steady, pleading. "I'm not lying. David wrote to me. Told me."

Uncle David? Why would he— "Uncle David wasn't there. Why would he say such things?"

"He bought the house, Tessa. It was his house that burned." Her father's voice took on the steely edge that signaled he was tired of discussing a subject, but unlike in years past when he'd abruptly end a conversation and stalk off, he set his jaw and continued speaking. "When David came the next day and surveyed the damage, Buck told him what had happened. Buck said the soldiers tried to put the fire out. David found my regiment and they confirmed what Buck had said." His voice softened and he stepped toward his daughter. "It was just an accident. I was never wanted for treason."

"How long have you known, Father? How long have you been lying to me?" The muscles behind her jaw ached with being clenched for so long, and the back of her head felt like it might explode. She kept her eyes trained on his, unflinching.

"I've never lied to you, Tessa."

"How long?" Her head boomed with each word she shouted, and she lowered her voice. "When did Uncle David tell you?"

He released a breath and stood tall and stiff, like a proud man marching to the gallows. "Christmas, three years ago."

Three years. She filtered back through snippets of memories to that Christmas after the Sundstroms left, when she was so lonely without the children to teach. The whole dreary winter she'd had nothing to occupy her time other than watch snow fall and listen to her father and Mrs. Holt enjoying each other's company without a mind to her misery. That winter when she'd so desperately wanted to go home, but couldn't because her father was a wanted man—only he wasn't—and he knew it.

Now the stony voice came from her own aching throat. "Why didn't you tell me?"

He looked past her, and she became aware of Mrs. Holt—Maureen—her mum and William standing on the periphery of her vision.

"Because I was content here," he said simply. "For the first time in I don't know how long, I was content."

"You kept me from our home. From our family," Tessa whispered.

Her father stepped toward her but didn't touch her. He still held one hand wrapped around his left ribs. He spoke slowly, resolutely, quietly. "No, Tess, it wasn't our home. It was the Darrow home, filled with furnishings from generations of Darrows, but we just lived there—caretakers over someone else's memories. This is my home now. Just about everything we have here, we've built with our own hands. Everything we have is filled with our own memories."

Tessa looked from her father to Maureen to William—the man she had waited so long for and, now, was soon to wed. If she had known she could go back to North Carolina three years ago, Maureen wouldn't be her mum and William wouldn't be her beau. This had become her home too.

"You should have told me, Da."

He nodded solemnly. "I know."

IT TOOK ALL of their strength, but William, Tessa, and Maureen were finally able to hoist Mr. Anderson into the wagon with William holding his arms clasped around the man's chest under his armpits, and Tessa and Maureen each lifting a leg. Unable to lift or put any strain on his ribs, Tessa's father held Mr. Anderson's lower leg steady as the others situated him in the wagon.

Maureen and Tessa sat in the wagon bed on either side of Mr. Anderson, trying to keep him from jostling too much. Tessa's father and William sat up in the seat box. With every word they exchanged, Tessa waited to hear if William broached the subject upon which—she was sure—her every happiness relied.

"William," her father said, "I never asked what brought you to town this time. Some business with your lumber mill?"

"Well, sir—"

William's voice was so quiet, Tessa had to strain to hear him. Maureen's eyes flicked toward Tessa before she quickly turned her head the other way, and Tessa knew her mum was eager to hear this conversation as well.

"I did come on lumber business, in a manner of speaking." William cleared his throat. "What I mean to say is, I brought a load of lumber with me, and several men."

"That right?" Tessa recognized the nonchalant tease in her father's voice.

"Yes, sir. I've come to build a home at Grays Lake. Cariboo Jack's struck gold up on the mountain up there and I figure those parts'll be swarmin' with miners looking to strike it rich."

"So you'll be staking a claim early."

Her father's tone took on a note of suspicion and Tessa looked toward her mum, hoping she'd intercede. Maureen just lifted her hand, signaling Tessa to stay still.

"Yes, sir. Well, no, sir—not a mining claim. I'm staking out rangeland. If there's a boom on the mountain, those men'll need beef and lots of it. I've got cattle coming in later this summer."

"Good for you, son. Should be a lucrative business."

"Yes, sir."

William. Get on with it. Ask him. Tessa started worrying her little fingernail with her teeth.

"Now tell me, William," Tessa's father continued. "About this house you're building. Big house?"

"Well, not too big to begin with. I was thinking three bedrooms to start, and a parlor, maybe a separate kitchen big enough to eat in. Later on, we could add a few more rooms, and maybe we'd even build a second story. It'd be nice to build a cabin at the side so we could have visitors stay with us."

"And by 'we' you mean—?" her father prompted.

Tessa and Maureen stared at each other, Tessa's surprise reflected in her mum's eyes. The wagon jerked to a stop and Tessa flung her arm over the side to keep from toppling onto Mr. Anderson.

"Oh, I've made a hash of this," William said.

Maureen put a finger to her lips, reminding Tessa to keep quiet. This was a conversation between a father and suitor that wives and daughters typically weren't privy to. It wouldn't do to have Tessa or her mum sticking their noses in.

"You're doing just fine, William," Tessa's father said with kindness. "Why don't you tell me what's on your mind?"

"Mr. Darrow, I told you what was on my mind three years ago in Great Salt Lake City. Since that time, I've naught thought of much else lest your daughter was a part of it. I've done quite well in the lumber business. I've put together a herd more'n a thousand cattle strong. I've invested in the railroad and even have a few other shares in the stock exchange back in New York City. I've done what I said I was going to do. I've built up enough to make sure your daughter never wants for anything."

Tessa and her mum sat in shocked silence in the back of the wagon. Even Mr. Anderson was staring at Tessa, his mouth agape. *Lumber, cattle, railroads, stocks? All since he left five years ago?* While Tessa's thoughts jumbled over each other, William kept talking.

"I'm in love with your daughter, Mr. Darrow. I'd like your permission to make her my wife."

My wife. It was real. He'd said it. *My wife.* Tessa played the delicious phrase over and over in her mind, waiting for her father's answer.

"Tell me one thing, William."

Father! No! Just say, "Yes, you can marry my daughter."

"You've done so well for yourself, why move back to Idaho? To Grays Lake? Why not build a big house in Oregon by your mill or San Francisco or New York? Why a shack in Grays Lake?"

William didn't answer for several moments. When he did, he spoke with conviction—and tenderness—all rolled together. "Well, sir, first off, our house won't be a shack. It may not be a grand plantation, but if Tessa is there with me, it will be a home—no matter the size. Second, the two of you have been through an awful lot together. You've seen each other through some terrible tragedies. What kind of man would separate a father and daughter after all that? That's why I'd like to build two homes up there, so you and Mother can come visit as often as you please, and it's only a day's ride away. And third—I don't have a great many possessions; I've saved every penny I could toward this day. But my most cherished possession is the painting Tessa made me of Grays Lake. That picture's kept me true to my goal. To me, Grays Lake felt like our home since we first laid eyes on the valley five years ago. And judging by her letters, I think Tessa feels the same way."

Tessa reflected back on the first time she'd seen the Grays Lake valley—with William. Gold and russet grasses swaying in the meadow surrounding the glittering lake, teaming with deer and elk and geese and cranes. The fox peeking out at them, and the hawk that snatched the skunk from right in front of them. He was right. Grays Lake was nestled deep in her heart. Grays Lake is where she pictured when she thought of home.

"Sir?" William asked after a lengthy silence settled over the wagon. "Have I answered your questions sufficiently?"

"I believe so, William." Then, without changing his cadence, Tessa's father asked over his shoulder. "Tessa? Anything else I should ask?"

Tessa raised her head, stunned.

Maureen straightened, turning her face from Tessa to the front of the wagon. "You could ask when the wedding is!"

CHAPTER 32

"You, there! Get away!" Tessa shouted, clapping her hands at the two deer sniffing the edge of the irrigation ditch that ran from Soda Creek to carry water through the Morristown fields. While she knew the deer wouldn't hurt her, she still didn't like the idea of having to walk so near them to lift the irrigation gate. With Mr. Anderson laid up because of his broken leg, Mrs. Anderson in her state of illness, and her father still favoring his ribs, Tessa took responsibility to lift the gate to divert water to the fields every second and third morning except Sundays.

After cranking the horizontal wheel and watching the pole lifting the gate to let the water flow, Tessa pulled her shawl tight around her shoulders. She loved this time of the morning, especially now that the sun lit the fields and burned off the chill earlier each day. She studied the water snaking its way under the buck and pole fences surrounding Mr. Anderson's fields. The blue ribbon wound through Mr. Anderson's barley, toward his wheat, corn, and potatoes, and finally to Mrs. Anderson's kitchen garden before it would rejoin Soda Creek and wind its way westward.

Setting her daily routine according to the watering schedule helped Tessa keep track of the days and weeks creeping by as she waited for William and his men to finish their house at Grays Lake.

On Mondays and Thursdays, Mr. Pixton watered his garden, and while he didn't grow fields of crops like Mr. Anderson and Tessa's father did, Mr. Pixton refused to give up a drop of his water rights. So Tessa spent Mondays doing the wash in a barrel with a washboard, and Thursdays helping her mum take account of supplies coming in and out of the trading post, writing lists to reorder, and parceling out staples to lay aside in preparation for setting up her own larder.

On Tuesdays, she turned the water out to Mr. Anderson's fields, then rushed to get her ironing done before the heat of the day set in. Wednesdays meant watering her father's crops and then seeing to any mending. Fridays were Andersons' days for water again, sandwiched in between a full day of cleaning. Saturdays meant water for her father's crops again, and a day spent baking. It didn't matter how much she and her mum baked, they never seemed to make it past the weekend without running out of something. By noon each day, she could lower the irrigation gate and have the rest of the day to herself.

Tessa leaned against the stone and wood water gate, watching the deer nibble at the lupine and balsamroot sprinkled throughout the meadow surrounding Soda Creek. *One of these mornings I need to find time to bring my paints out here.* Since word leaked out about Cariboo Jack finding gold on the mountain above Grays Lake, Tessa's mum stayed busy in the trading post supplying the miners streaming through at least every other day, so the daily chores were mostly left to Tessa.

I do hope we won't be able to see the mining camps on Cariboo Mountain from our new house. William had certainly been right about the need for cattle up there. They'd likely do a booming business keeping the miners supplied in beef. "Well, my dear, I hope you've planned for a slaughtering shed well away from the house." The deer looked up at her, perking their ears in Tessa's direction. "Don't you worry, my friends," she called to the deer. "Until Mr. Anderson's leg heals, you're safe down here."

As busy as she stayed throughout the week, each passing day served to mark the march toward Sunday—when William and his men would arrive before noon for devotions and Sunday dinner and then head back to Grays Lake by early afternoon. Four weeks had passed since work on the house began, with another two weeks likely needed before William would deem the house ready to move in. With the house, guesthouse, and range taking this long to prepare, Tessa was glad her wish for a smaller house to begin with had prevailed. If William had proceeded to build the house he'd described to Tessa's father, there was no telling how long it would take to finish—and for them to be married.

She picked several stalks of purple lupine and yellow balsamroot and tied a few wisps of grass around the bundle. *This will look pretty on the Sunday table.* Four weeks more and she could carry a bouquet into the general's office at Fort Bridger for her wedding. *It's too bad Grandmother won't be able to see me wed. Or Uncle David, or the Andersons.* Tessa tried to ignore the pangs of envy that sprang up when she compared her upcoming wedding—in a frontier army post, standing in front of the post's commanding officer, with only her father and Maureen there to witness it—instead of her mum and father's beautiful wedding filled with friends and music. *It won't matter.* She sighed. *I'll have everyone I need. Mum, Da, and William.*

Tessa followed the irrigation ditch down toward her father's house, wondering what scripture they'd be discussing this week. "Devotions" were William's idea since there weren't organized church services to attend here. They each took turns reading a favorite scripture, then discussing its meaning before sitting down to dinner.

Tessa smiled, chuckling to herself, thinking of some of the workers' awkward attempts to pronounce unfamiliar words in the unfamiliar books. She was glad she wasn't the only one who let the Holy Bible or Book of Mormon drop open and picked a random verse to read aloud from the page. It never failed but that William or her father would find something interesting about the verse to discuss. *Wouldn't Granddad, the Methodist Sunday School teacher, have something to say if he'd lived to see them reading the Mormon's book alongside the Bible!*

Hearing the rumble of wagons, Tessa shielded her eyes and peered toward the southeast. Several wagons, six open and two covered, made their way past the abandoned Fort Connor post and down the slope toward Morristown. *They're awfully early. Must have gotten on the trail before dawn.* Though most of the miners came through from the west, Morristown still saw at least one wagon, or group of wagons, each week following the Oregon Trail from the east. She quickened her pace to meet them.

To her amazement, Mr. and Mrs. Pixton stood in the middle of the street in front of the trading post, confronting the men driving the lead wagons. "I wouldn't care if God called you himself!" Mr. Pixton shouted, his great jowls jiggling beneath his chin. "This is our valley and we're not turning it over to the likes of you or him."

God wants our valley? Has Mr. Pixton lost his senses? Tessa climbed up the side of the trading post's porch, avoiding the steps, not wanting to cross in the line of the confrontation.

"Pixton," one of the men said, "you don't own the whole valley and we've the right to build a home where we please."

"What's happening?" Tessa whispered to her mum.

"These men are from Paris," Maureen whispered back.

Paris? France? Really?

Tessa's astonishment must have shown on her face, because her mum hurried on. "Paris is a day south of here. It's a Mormon settlement. Brigham Young sent these men to build a home for him here."

Hearing the back door squeak open, both women retreated into the shade of the store to apprise Tessa's father of the development.

"I think this is my fault, Henry." Maureen stood with her back against the trading counter, arms folded across her chest, watching the altercation through the window. "At our wedding, I talked and talked about how beautiful it is up here. I may hae spros't a wee," she said, holding her thumb and forefinger slightly apart and squinting one eye.

"I don't think you 'spros't' at all," Tessa's father assured her. "It's every bit as beautiful as you said, and then some. Besides, even the guidebooks talk about the area."

"Yes," Tessa jumped in. "The book we followed called the soda springs the oasis of the Oregon Trail."

"Well, be that as it may, I sure as michty didn't mean to encourage a flock o' folks to come up here. Once Brother Brigham comes, there's no telling how many will follow." Maureen nodded out the window to where Mr. Anderson hobbled up the street on the crutches Tessa's father had fashioned for him. His wife followed, trailed by their two children.

Maureen pulled her husband's arm. "We'd best get out there."

"Why not just head further west," Mr. Anderson was asking the lead man. "There's plenty of land out by Fort Hall. You leave us alone here, and we'll leave you alone over there."

"Because Brother Brigham directed us up here, and we don't aim to disappoint him," the man said. "Besides, there's only a handful of you left. Wouldn't you like the support of a few neighbors?"

"We're doing just fine without you!" Mr. Pixton yelled again, his face turning a deeper shade of pink with every breath. "We won't do business with you or any of the rest of you Mormons. You'll have to go back to Paris to buy supplies."

Maureen's head shot up and she leaped forward, giving Mr. Pixton a shove backward. "You speak for yourself, Pixton. This is my trading post and I'll do business with whom I please."

"Thank you, ma'am." The primary spokesman nodded to her. "Nice to hear a voice of reason. I'm Elder Merrill."

"I'll thank you to not cast dispersions on my friends, Elder Merrill," Tessa's mum said. "These are men of very sound reason, you can be sure."

Very sound reason? Tessa glanced at Mr. Pixton, his face now beet red and his gullet still waggling. *Perhaps Mum's sprousin' a wee again.*

Maureen continued, her voice measured, firm, but not unkind. "We've endured a lot to make this our home, and we'll not take kindly to being shoved out just because Brother Brigham told you to."

"We meant no disrespect, ma'am . . . gentlemen," the second man said. "Brother Brigham told us we'd find you up here and instructed us to treat you as brethren."

Mr. Pixton bristled. "We're not your brethren. And you can tell Brigham to—"

Maureen interrupted. "What Brother Pixton means to say is we're not all willing to have neighbors just yet."

"Don't put words in my mouth, Maureen."

"I will when your words aren't fit to hear."

Listening to the back and forth, Tessa held the insides of her cheeks between her teeth to keep from smiling. Her mum was handing Mr. Pixton the come-uppance Tessa had wished several times to give him herself, and comporting herself with dignity at the same time.

"Elder Merrill, I'm Maureen Darrow. This is my husband, Henry, and our daughter, Tessa. I still consider myself a Mormon, but my late husband was a Morrisite, as is the rest of this community. We've been through great sorrows, but some of us are keen to let bygones be bygones."

A second man stepped forward. "Sister Darrow, I'm Bishop Horne." He turned so he was addressing the entire group gathered in the street. "We know of your troubles, and we sorrow with you for them. Brother Brigham's desire is to live up here with you in a spirit of friendship. He only wants a place to relax from time to time in the summers or to shelter in when he's visiting the settlements. We'll build a few small homes near his in case family or brethren travel with him."

Mrs. Anderson whispered something to her husband that Tessa couldn't quite hear, and Mr. Anderson shook his head. He turned back to the men. "If you'll not be dissuaded, we'll not stand in your way. We'll be hospitable, but we most certainly won't be friendly. Keep your settlement to the north of the creek and we'll stay to the south."

Mr. Pixton's mouth fell open, and Mrs. Pixton gasped, giving Tessa's mum a look of betrayal.

Mr. Anderson continued his admonitions. "And mark my words, gentlemen, for good or ill, reward for your actions will be meted out without reserve. Am I clearly understood?"

Mr. Pixton held his finger out, shaking it at Mr. Anderson. "You'll rue this day, Anderson. They'll not stop with a few cabins. They'll overrun the whole valley. This is on your head."

Two days later, when William and his men came in for the day, Tessa didn't need to tell him about their new neighbors. William brought some of them with him. Henry and Maureen sat outside in the shade of the sycamore with William's six men and eight Mormon men. Tessa and William stood inside the Darrow house, scooping fluffy mounds of sweetened cream into bowls and sprinkling red raspberries on top.

"How would you feel about not going to Fort Bridger next month?" William asked.

What? Tessa pulled the cream-filled spoon she'd been licking from her mouth. She gently closed her eyes and drew a deep breath, trying to stifle the angry words crawling up from the pit of her stomach. They'd already delayed the wedding day by a month because the house wasn't finished. He'd already said he was putting on the finishing touches. Not that she'd know—he wouldn't let her even see their home until after the wedding—and now another delay? *Do you even want to marry me?*

Wiping the sticky cream from her lips with a dish towel, she forced a cheerful tone. "Beg pardon?"

His blue eyes sparkled as he arranged the last raspberry on top of the last bowl. "Well, I was thinking that, since the house is nearly finished, and we've got two members of the clergy sitting on the blanket out there, maybe we could get married here instead of going all the way to the fort."

"William! Do you mean it?"

"Of course I mean it," he said, cupping her face in his hands. "This way your friends here can come."

She grabbed his hands and, standing on tiptoe, pecked his cheek. "Of course! Yes! Yes! A thousand times, yes!"

He wrapped his arms around her waist, pulling her close, and laid his chin on top of her head. "We're getting married, Tessa Darrow."

She rested her head on his chest, breathing in his scent of musk and cedar smoke. *We're getting married.* "Wait," she said, pulling herself away from him. "You don't mean today, do you?"

He shrugged and grinned. "If you'd like."

"Oh, I would very much like," she said, grinning right back. "But I don't think my mum would be very happy with us. And we haven't so much as a table or"—she whispered the last words—"a bed."

"Ah, but we do have a table. I've built us a table with chairs, and even a hutch in the corner with shelves for books."

"And I suppose I could bring my bed," Tessa offered.

"The only thing we're missing is furniture for the parlor, but we could order that while we're on our wedding tour."

"We're going on a wedding tour?"

He placed her head back on his shoulder and rested his cheek against her hair. "Shhhh. It's a surprise."

Her breathing fell into rhythm with his, and she tried to shoo away thoughts of the raspberries sitting in the melting cream.

"Dessert just about ready?" Maureen called, opening the door.

Tessa jumped away from William and grabbed two of the bowls.

Tessa's mum turned her head and gave the two a sidelong stare. "What's going on in here?"

William kissed Tessa's forehead and grabbed two more bowls. "We're getting married."

CHAPTER 33

With a tickle of giddiness, Tessa turned to the last page of the journal her mother made for her—the page she'd saved for this very day. Sitting on the floor of her bedroom with her back against the wall under her little window, she looked at the room now bereft of everything but a bedroll, her wedding dress, her new traveling dress, her traveling chest and valise, and a candle in its holder. *My wedding dress.* The dress she'd worn to her father and mum's wedding three years ago. Made from the fabric her grandmother had sent for her presentation gown. *Well, Grandmother, the dress did its job. I wore it in society and landed the most wonderful fellow. I wish you could be here today to see us get married.*

She gently touched the faded pressed flowers glued in place along the left margin where her mother had used waxed string to sew the pages of the journal together. *What I wouldn't give to have you here today, Mother.* She closed her eyes, imagining her mother's voice replying that she was always with her. Tessa pressed her journal to her chest, whispering, "I know you are, Mother. Thank you."

Despite the early hour, she heard her father and mum bumping about in the kitchen. She pictured her da lighting the fire in the fireplace once flanked by two rocking chairs, then three, now two once more. He'd made another rocking chair, this one for William, and sent it to Grays Lake last week along with Tessa's.

Her mum would be setting out mixing bowls and laying logs in the cast iron stove, ready to put the finishing touches on food for the wedding. *I'm going to miss seeing them every day.* Even though William talked of all of the people coming through Grays Lake to set up camp on the mountain, Tessa worried she'd be lonely without her mum and da and the Andersons to visit every day. *I'm sure I'll have plenty to do to stay busy keeping house for William.* That one thought, keeping house for William, never failed to make her smile.

Monday. Mr. Pixton's day to water if he were still here. I'm going to miss that old curmudgeon too. I'll miss Mrs. Pixton more. Tessa looked at the quilt she'd been using as her bedroll for the last week. Blue ticking stripes combined with green checks and yellow calico that Tildy Pixton had pieced into a cheerful quilt for Tessa last Christmas. Another quilt, in a double wedding ring pattern, waited for Tessa and William at their new home, along with a full suite of parlor furniture that the Pixtons gave her last week when they left "the Mormon invasion" to go live with their daughter in Montana. *Mrs. Pixton would have been in heaven baking sweets for the wedding.* Too bad they couldn't make peace with the past and try to live with their new neighbors like her mum and the Andersons were trying to do.

Tessa filled her pen with ink and laid a careful hand to the journal page.

July 4, 1870

> *Today I wed William Bates, to whom I feel certain Providence has led me. We will make our home on the southeast bench of Grays Lake, next to Cariboo Mountain. No man and woman were ever more in love. By God's grace we were brought together, and in God's grace we will raise a goodly family.*
>
> *How fitting that my wedding day should fall five years to the day from when I first arrived at Morristown by the Soda Springs. I laid aside my childhood and began a new life that day. Today I cast aside the young woman and become a wife. God has seen fit to give me a new family and a righteous man to wed.*

Saving the last small space to fill in after the wedding, Tessa replaced the stopper in the ink bottle and cleaned the nib on her pen. She packed them snugly in a special compartment in her writing box filled with scraps of paper she'd collected over the years for letter writing. Since she didn't know where William planned to take her for her wedding tour, or how long they'd be gone, she packed the entire writing box so she could record every minute.

"REALLY, MUM, I can help carry water, at least." Despite Tessa's protests, her mum and father carried heated water into a tub in Tessa's room, rebuffing her offers to help.

"I'll no hae my daughter carry bath water on her wedding day," Maureen insisted.

So Tessa sat next to the fireplace, dressed in her wrapper and slippers, rags still firmly tied in her hair, reading poetry until her bath was prepared.

Following her bath, complete with lavender-scented soap, she rubbed her arms and legs with lanolin lotion before dressing.

She had just donned her chemise when her mum knocked gently on the door. "Tessa, are you decent, dear?"

She grabbed her wrapper, tying it snuggly at her waist, and then opened the door a crack, keeping herself hidden behind the door in case her groom had arrived. "I'm decent, Mum. You can come in."

The door swung open and Tessa's mum marched in, wearing the plaid dress she'd worn for her own wedding. Mrs. Anderson came in as well, cradling a length of lace. "I brought something for your wedding, Tessa."

Tessa clasped her hands to her chest as her friend draped the white lace over one shoulder of the wedding dress hanging on the wall. "Mrs. Anderson, is this your wedding veil?"

"It is. My dress was ruined years ago, but I've managed to keep this safe. It will be many years before my own daughter can wear it. I thought you might like to wear it as your 'something borrowed.'"

"Oh, I completely forgot about that!" *Something old, something new, something borrowed, something blue.* Tessa looked around her room, slightly panicked. Not that she was superstitious, but this was tradition. There was certainly nothing else traditional about getting married on the frontier by a preacher she'd only just met. *I'd like to do something in the proper way.*

"Not to worry, dear," her mum reassured her. "I have something old for you." She opened a small black leather case. "These were my mum's pearls. She wore them for her wedding, and I've worn them for each of mine," Maureen said, fastening the strand of pearls around Tessa's neck.

"Your mum's?" Tessa whispered, running her fingers along the row of smooth beads. Words were not sufficient to convey her gratitude for this gesture tying Tessa to her new mother's family. Tears welled in her eyes as she hugged Maureen. "Thank you, Mum."

Mrs. Anderson unfolded a bundle of fabric, revealing long, buttery tanned gloves. "Here is your something new. They're not white, but they'll match your dress beautifully. And now you won't have to hold William's pocket square when you dance."

"You told her?" Tessa asked her mum, feeling the softness of the leather gloves against her cheek.

"No, your da told Brother Anderson."

"So this gift is really from Neils." Mrs. Anderson's eyes crinkled above her lacy mask.

Now Tessa hugged Mrs. Anderson. "Then my thanks to both of you. Thank you," Tessa whispered past the knot in her throat, "for being such a dear, dear friend."

"Well then," Maureen said. She cleared her voice and pointed to the veil. "You have your something borrowed, and I brought you something blue." She reached into her apron pocket and, with a flourish, pulled out a lacy garter woven with a blue ribbon.

"Mum!" Tessa gasped. She spun around, hiding her face from the women, mortified as they giggled hysterically.

"Oh, come now." Maureen laughed, swatting Tessa on the bottom. "No need to tek affront. We're all married women."

Tessa scowled, trying to give them a stern look despite her flaming cheeks. "Really, I don't know what to make of you."

"Now don't get pitten aboot." Her mum struggled to keep a straight face as she danced the garter in Tessa's face. "It's really more for William!"

"Oh, give me that!" Tessa snatched the frilly piece and stuffed it in her pocket, blushing—and trying not to smile—as she thought about her groom discovering it on her leg, well after the wedding.

Her mum and Mrs. Anderson worked for what seemed like hours fixing Tessa's hair. Braiding bits, and rolling bits, and weaving the braided bits through the rolled bits. "Oh good heavens," Tessa said, yawning and stretching her aching neck. "I'm sure it looks lovely. Are you nearly finished?"

Her mum mumbled with hairpins in her mouth. "Just about. Don't move."

Mrs. Anderson rubbed a bit of pomade on the last tendril for the last ringlet, combed it around her finger, and pinned the base securely beneath one of the rolls at Tessa's crown. "There," she pronounced. "I believe that's that."

Picking up her silver hand mirror, Tessa turned her head from side to side, pleased with the way her hair puffed in the front and sides from her hairline, sweeping up to a collection of rolls at her crown, then cascading down her shoulders and back in ringlets. "It's a shame to cover this with a veil," she said, meaning to compliment the stylists.

Mrs. Anderson's eyes lost their usual sparkle. "You don't have to wear the veil if you'd prefer not to."

Realizing her mistake, Tessa spun around, grabbing Mrs. Anderson's hands. "Of course I'm wearing the veil! It's too lovely not to! It's my 'something borrowed.'"

The sparkle returned, and Mrs. Anderson grabbed the veil. "Perhaps if we do this," she said, folding the lace's length by a third, "we could pin it here and here." She secured the folded edge under where the rolls met the ringlets, pinning in gathers here and there.

"How would it look to tuck a few rosebuds here on the side?" Tessa asked. "To match my bouquet?"

"We can do whatever you like," Mrs. Anderson said, moving to the door. "I'll fetch a few. Today's your day to paint the lily."

"Here," Maureen instructed, holding up the full crinoline for Tessa to step into. "Let's get you dressed while Mary's out."

Tessa placed one stockinged foot and then the other through the center of the hoops, balancing with a hand on her mum's shoulder. "I do wish I could just wear the crinolette today. It's so much lighter."

"Bah. You can wear that when you dress for dinners on your tour." Maureen stood up, pulling the laces to cinch the hoops around Tessa's waist. "This is your wedding. You want the full effect today." She reached for the corset tucked in the side of the traveling chest.

"Absolutely not." Tessa snatched the boned wrap from her mum's hands and stuffed it unceremoniously back in the case. "It'll be a hundred degrees out there. You remember what happened last time I wore it. I am not wearing a corset."

"You most certainly will. You're not the child you were three years ago." She looked pointedly at Tessa's chest, covered only by her chemise. "'T'wouldn't be proper for you to go without it now."

Tessa folded her arms and lifted her chin. "I'm telling you now, I will not wear it. I'll not be fainting on my wedding day."

After a moment's staring contest, Maureen folded the corset and tucked it back in the wooden case. "You're as stubborn as your da. Don't be surprised but that he makes you wear a shawl to cover your—your bosoms." She said the last word with such emphasis that she and Tessa both broke out laughing.

As Maureen smoothed Tessa's petticoat over her hoops, Mrs. Anderson knocked and stuck her head in the door. "How are you coming in here? There's a groom outside looking pretty eager to see his bride."

Butterflies swirled from her knees all the way up to Tessa's heart and she had to remind herself to breathe. If she passed out now, she couldn't blame it on her corset.

While Tessa knelt on her folded bedroll, her mum and Mrs. Anderson lifted the golden taffeta gown over Tessa's head, careful not to muss her hair, and settled it on her shoulders. Tessa threaded her arms through the puffs of tulle sleeves, and then stood so her mum could fasten the buttons up the back.

"Oh dear," Mrs. Anderson murmured. She took hold of the fabric at Tessa's décolleté, trying to lift it higher.

Tessa clasped her arms across her shoulders, blocking her friend from grasping at her neckline. "Excuse me."

"It looks just fine, Mary." Maureen moved Tessa's arms and made a few adjustments of her own, forcing Tessa to stand up straighter. "Mary, would you ask Henry to bring in Tessa's bouquet?"

Tessa looked down at the tulle frill peaking out from above the creamy taffeta bodice, pleased with the fit. Womanly but not immodest.

Mrs. Anderson retrieved the rosebuds she'd left by the door. "What about these?"

"Those will be perfect." Tessa broke the stem off one of the pink buds, leaving a small shaft, and tucked it next to her friend's topknot. She wrapped her arms around the woman, laying her cheek against hers. "Thank you, Mrs. Anderson. Thank you for everything."

"Blessings on you, Tessa Darrow," Mary Anderson whispered. "Blessings on you and your posterity."

Alone with her mum, Tessa sat in the dining chair while Maureen tucked the remaining rosebuds into the curls above the wedding veil, arranging them in a loose cluster. Then Tessa lifted her skirt, pointing her toes into the fawn-skin slippers her mum guided onto her feet, grateful they still fit this long since her mum's wedding. She stood and tried to be patient as Maureen fluffed the yards of taffeta billowing around her. All the while, she reflected on her years since coming here, and the woman who now dressed Tessa for her wedding.

This woman stood against a town set to turn Tessa and her dying father out. This woman lodged them, fed them, ministered to them. This woman quite literally saved her father's life. *This woman succored me when my heart was broken and healed my father's soul.*

"Tessa? What is it, dear?" Her mum pulled the hanky from her sleeve and dabbed Tessa's eyes.

Tessa fought in vain to keep her voice in check. Through the tears, she choked. "I'm trying to think how to tell you how grateful I am for you, Mrs. Holt. Mum. You've become my mother in every sense of the word, and my dearest friend." Now Tessa used the hanky to wipe her mother's eyes. "I don't know how to tell you how much I love you."

A soft knock sounded at the door and Tessa's father stuck his head inside. "There's a young man out here waiting for his bride. Tessa?"

He jumped inside, closing the door behind him. "Maureen? What's happened?"

"Nothing's happened, Da." Tessa brushed her lingering tears with the tip of her finger. "Everything's fine."

"Just a mother and daughter gettin' teary eyed." Maureen blew her nose in her handkerchief. "Oh dear, that was my wedding hanky." She and Tessa burst into laughter.

Tessa's father pulled his own handkerchief from his pocket and held it out to his wife. "You women and your sentiments."

"I think you'd best hold onto that, Henry. You're like as not to need it." Maureen took Tessa's hands in hers. "You realize you'll be my daughter twice blessed. I married your father, and you're marrying the boy I love as my son."

"I am blessed, Mum. So very blessed."

Maureen kissed her on each cheek and squeezed her hands. "I'll go tell William you're nearly ready."

As much as Tessa had wished for a full-length mirror to check on her dress, she no longer needed it when she saw the awe reflected in her father's misty eyes as she turned in a circle before him.

"I wish your mother could be here to see you," he murmured in a husky voice.

"My mother is here. Both of my mothers are here today."

"I'm so proud of the woman you've become. You know that, don't you?"

"I know, Da. Thank you. I think we've both changed—for the better."

Tessa pulled on her new gloves and patted her garter to make sure it was firmly in place. Her father held out the bouquet of pink roses she'd snipped the day before from the rosebush William gave her. "Thank you, Da, for saving William's life so he could marry me."

Standing with his hand on the doorknob, her father kissed her cheek. "You'll be a good wife, Tessabear."

This may be the last time he calls me that. She closed her eyes, breathed in a great breath, and then blew it out briskly. She tilted her chin up to him, winked, and smiled. "I know."

As a FIDDLE scratched out a tune Tessa didn't quite recognize, her father pushed open the door of their home and Tessa looked through the sea of men to where William stood under the sycamore, the bishop at his side playing the fiddle. William took a step toward her, and Maureen put out her hand to stay him.

William, in his dashing gray frock coat, black waistcoat, and trousers, stared as she glided toward him, a smile so soft on his lips, his gaze so admiring, that she felt a blush erupting.

As her father delivered the bride to her groom, the bishop set down his fiddle and officiated over the ceremony. In a blink, their vows were exchanged, and William held her in his arms, his lips pressed to hers for all the world to see.

"I NEVER WOULD have imagined every one of the Mormon men would come to see us married." Tessa pulled her mum to the side. "I'd better make more sandwiches."

"You'll do no such thing," her mum scolded. "You're the bride today. You'll do no cooking. There will be plenty. And if there's not, they can just go home." Pulling Tessa by the arm, she handed her over to William. "Take your wife and sit her down. I'll naw hae her in the kitchen today."

William grinned and accepted his charge, threading his hands around her waist. "My wife. I like how that sounds."

She snuggled in against him, enjoying the feel of his arms enveloping her. "Tessa Bates. Tessa Bates. I've not dared say that out loud till now."

Throughout the wedding lunch, Tessa kept her left hand resting in her lap so no one would see her staring at the gold band set with an emerald and pearls on her finger.

"Do you like it?" William whispered in her ear.

"I've never seen anything so beautiful."

He glanced around before lifting one of her ringlets away from her shoulder and kissed her neck. "I have."

CHAPTER 34

After saying good-bye to the Andersons, Tessa and William stood in front of the house with Henry and Maureen. One of William's men had brought his horse and buggy around front, ready for William to take his bride to their new home.

"We'll spend a few days getting settled in Grays Lake," William said, "then circle back this way before heading for Ogden."

Ogden? For our wedding tour?

Maureen clasped her hands exclaiming, "Ogden's lovely. You'll have a lovely time there."

Ogden?

"That's just where we're catching the train."

"The train? You didn't tell me we were going on a train." *Oh, this will be an adventure!*

"I thought for a wedding gift, I'd take you to see your grandmother."

Tessa wasn't sure she had heard him correctly. "You're serious. You're not joking with me?"

"Tessa, what's wrong? I thought you'd be pleased."

"William, I can't think of a more perfect gift."

With a relieved sign, William kissed her on the nose and then turned to her father. "I thought you and Mum might come with us. I can buy four tickets as easily two."

Tessa caught her breath. *Wouldn't that tickle Grandmother!* She wrapped her arms around William's waist, squeezing him as hard as she could.

After a moment's hesitation, her father smiled. "Well, if you don't mind us coming on your wedding tour."

"No, I'm sorry, we can't."

All eyes turned toward Maureen.

Tessa let go of her husband. "Mum, why? You'd love North Carolina."

"I'm sure I would," she stated matter-of-factly, "but I'm—" She looked at Tessa's father. "I'm ill, Henry."

Panic flashed in his eyes as he grabbed her hands. "Ill?"

Her pronouncement made Tessa feel sick herself.

"But we won't be leaving for near a week," William offered.

"Thank you, William, but I expect I'll be ill until sometime in February."

"February?" Tessa's father puzzled.

It took a moment to sink in, but Tessa and her father both realized what Maureen was saying just a heartbeat ahead of William.

"February!" Her father lifted his wife clean off the ground, twirling her around and around.

"Henry, please," she said, laughing. "You'll make me sick!"

"Oh, Maureen, sweetheart, you can't know how happy you've made me."

Maureen dabbed her eyes with her apron. "I wasn't sure how you'd take it," she said, wiping his eyes as well. "This means we'll have to put our plans on hold till the spring."

"Plans?" Tessa looked from her mum to her da and back again. "What plans?"

"We've been debating how to tell you," Tessa's father began. "We've been talking about leaving Morristown."

"What? No!" Tessa cried. "You can't!"

"Henry. That's no way to say it," Maureen scolded. "Brother Pixton was right. With Brigham Young building a home up here, the whole valley will fill with folk before you can bat an eye. We just don't want to be surrounded by that many people."

"But where will you go?" Tessa cast a dark look at her father. *Did you talk her into going to Oregon?*

Henry put his arm tenderly around his wife's shoulder. "We'd like to move into Anna's house up at the pass to Grays Lake. Build a new store where we could be closer to the mining camps and supply wagons coming off the Lander Cutoff."

"Still do business," Maureen added, "but in our peaceful way."

"That means you'll only be an hour away from us." *Could this day get any happier?*

"We'll need to build another room or two on Anna's cabin for the children," William said with authority. "I can keep my men here and set them to work while we're gone. Mr. Darrow, you'll need to keep an eye on them from time to time. Tell them how you want the store laid out."

"Will you listen to that?" Henry laughed, shoving William's shoulder. "My son-in-law for less than half a day and he's bossing me about."

Tessa laughed, hugging her mum and da before returning to the shelter of her husband's arm. "Just think. This time next year, our babies may be playing together."

AFTER A LONG, bumpy ride, William at last steered the buggy around the turn at the top of the hill overlooking Grays Lake. He pulled the horse up next to where Tessa had painted his scene of the valley and lifted his bride from the cart.

As much as she wanted to reach their home and get settled, her heart swelled as they made their way, hand in hand, the few yards to the crest of the hillside where the view of the valley spread before them. Between the borders of pine and aspen, blue larkspur and white asters swept down the hillside, merging with the azure waters of Grays Lake. A single deer sipped at the edge of the water, ignoring the cranes rising and settling in their aerial ballet. The late-afternoon light lent a violet cast to the gentle mountains rising on the far side of the lake, the majestic Cariboo Mountain standing sentinel in the center of the range. *This is home.*

She snuggled into the warmth of William's arm draped around her shoulder, looking across the lake to the southeast to where a swath of green meadow nestled in the foothills. From here, she could just make out three homes at the northern end of the meadow with a few outbuildings. A smattering of white sheep clustered at the southern end. She pressed her hand to her chest, just taking in the scene, searing it into her heart.

William stood behind her, with both arms wrapped around her shoulders. His voice hushed like a breeze stirring through aspen. "Are you ready to go home?"

Home. She hugged his arms more tightly against her. "I'm ready." She took his hand and led him back to the wagon.

A half hour later, William turned the buggy from the well-worn trail and steered the horse between the two pine-pole gates standing open in front of their home.

Tessa clasped her hands over her mouth. "Oh, William, it's beautiful!" The timber-framed house sat upon a stone foundation high enough that four steps led up to the front door with a wide porch spanning the breadth of the house. The door faced west with one mullioned window on the left and two on the right.

"Glass windows," she exclaimed. "We won't have cold drafts seeping through the oiled paper!"

"All the way from Sacramento," he told her. "The smaller cabins have them too."

Despite wanting to see the inside of their home, she patiently strolled with William as he toured her around the exterior. One rosebush, a pink one like William had given her in Great Salt Lake City was planted to the right of the front door, and a yellow rosebush was staked to climb between the two windows. A twiggy bush was planted on the left corner in front of the rock chimney.

"Lilacs," he explained to her questioning glance. "It will have clusters of purple flowers every spring. And see?" He pointed out front to the gate. "I planted a lilac on either side of the gate as well." He led her around back, showing her the apple tree, the low fence he'd built to outline a kitchen garden, a back door leading into the kitchen, a chicken coop, and the "necessary." He showed her the corrals—one for the milk cows they'd keep nearby, and one for horses—and the fenced pasture beyond for the sheep.

As they completed their circle of the house, they paused on the front steps, watching the last rays of the sun set behind the western ridge, sending streaks of crimson and gold dancing above the indigo lake.

A wave of nerves swept over Tessa and she timidly asked, "Shall we go inside?"

William smiled, biting his bottom lip, and flickered his eyebrows. *Are you nervous too?*

"Wait here," he said. He jumped off the steps and fetched her traveling case, carrying it into the house, and then dashed back to the buggy to retrieve her valise, a basket of food, and a handful of other items.

A light illuminated the single window on the left, and then another light, not quite as bright, filtered through the two windows on the right. She peeked through the door at the parlor filled with the Pixton's elegant parlor suite. Her painting of Grays Lake presided proudly above the fireplace mantle. *Our bedroom must be at the back of the house.* At the thought, her heart started hammering and her breath came in short snatches. She closed her eyes and drew in a deep draught, trying to stay her nerves.

At last William came outside again, standing beside Tessa on the steps. He placed his hands on either side of her face and kissed her tenderly. "Thank you for waiting all these years for me."

At a loss for words, Tessa just wrapped her arms under his, feeling the strength of his shoulders under her fingertips. She stared into his bright blue eyes—blue as flax afield. *I wasn't waiting for you, my love. I was growing up.*

Pulling out his pocketknife, he reached over to the rosebush growing beside the steps and cut a single pink rose, presenting it to her before sweeping her into his arms. "Welcome home, Mrs. Bates."

THE NEXT MORNING, as William built a fire in the hearth, Tessa sat cross-legged on their feather bed and opened her journal to the last page. She reread what she wrote the day before:

> *Today I cast aside the young woman and become a wife. God has seen fit to give me a new family and a righteous man to wed—*

Then she recorded her final entry.

> *Our children will grow up surrounded by mountains and trees and a loving family. How blessed I am to have found this oasis on the Oregon Trail.*

ACKNOWLEDGMENTS

With loving thanks to my children. For believing in this journey; for understanding when I say, "Can't talk now, I'll call you later;" for always being there when "later" happens. You inspire me and never cease to make me smile.

To Bill and Julia Rasmussen for exploring Soda Springs with me and patiently answering my endless questions. Your generosity epitomizes the spirit of Grays Lake.

I'm so grateful for my critique friends: Susan Knight, Chris Scott, and Jeanette Anderson. Your encouragement, advice, and POV and "show, don't tell" reminders brought life and depth to this story. Thank you for keeping me on task. You make me a better writer.

My sincere thanks to Dawn Ives, for sharing the true tale of the sweater-wearing chickens from her family lore, and giving permission to use it in Soda Springs.

Thank you to my talented friends at Cedar Fort: to Emma Parker, for seeing through my shortcuts and making me flesh them out; to Melissa Caldwell, for figuring out how to punctuate my brogue and deleting my plethora of commas; to Michelle May, for listening to me whine and producing a stunning cover despite it; and to Kelly Martinez, my marketing guru, who tirelessly coaches and encourages me. I'm so grateful to work with you.

And lastly, to my readers. I appreciate each of you. I love to hear when my stories strike a chord, when you've learned something new, when your heart is touched. Thank you for your kind reviews on Goodreads, Amazon, and other bookstore sites; and thank you for connecting with me through social media. Through friendship, we are all enriched.

SELECTED BIBLIOGRAPHY

Carney, E. *Historic Soda Springs*. Wayan, Idaho: Traildust Publishing, 1998.

Howard, G. M. (2010, June 2). *Men, Motives, and Misunderstandings: A New Look at the Morrisite War of 1862*. Retrieved July, 9, 2014 from http://www.gordonbanks.com/gordon/family/Morrisite.html.

Jenson, A. (1941). *Encyclopedic History of the Church of Jesus Christ of Latter-day Saints*. Retrieved June 6, 2015 from http://contentdm.lib.byu.edu/cdm/compoundobject/collection/BYUIBooks/id/2694.

Nelson-Burns, L. (n.d.) *Johnny's Gone for a Soldier*. Retrieved October 12, 2014 from http://www.contemplator.com/america/johnny.html.

Soda Springs Chamber of Commerce, City of Soda Springs. (n.d.) *Travel the Oregon Trail in Caribou County*. Retrieved January 11, 2014 from http://www.sodachamber.com/resources/pdf/soda_history.pdf.

ABOUT THE AUTHOR

Carolyn Steele enjoys ferreting out obscure history and weaving it through her tales. With a career rooted in business writing, she loves researching details of her novels to ensure their historical accuracy, drawing praise from Pony Express reenactors for her first novel, *Willow Springs*. Carolyn works full-time writing communications for health care providers and then spends evenings indulging her passion for writing historical fiction. When not at the computer, Carolyn loves traveling with her husband and visiting with her four children and thirteen grandchildren. In her spare moments, she traipses about Utah with a camera in hand, and occasionally muddles through a round of golf. She dreams of one day traveling the world, photographing all of those mystical lands that beg to be backdrops for her novels.

To say "hello," visit her on Facebook at facebook.com/AuthorCarolynSteele, Twitter @CarolynSteeleUT, or on her website, Carolyn-Steele.com. Thanks in advance for your kind reviews on Amazon, Goodreads, and anywhere else you care to post—it's what friends do.

SCAN TO VISIT

WWW.CAROLYN-STEELE.COM